UNFORGIVEN

THE FORGOTTEN: BOOK THREE

M.R. FORBES

Published by Quirky Algorithms
Seattle, Washington

This novel is a work of fiction and a product of the author's imagination.
Any resemblance to actual persons or events is purely coincidental.

Cover illustration by Tom Edwards
tomedwardsdesign.com

ACKNOWLEDGMENTS

THANK YOU for joining our heroes for the grand finale. It's going to be awesome!

THANK YOU to my beta readers. 100s of errors corrected and counting.

THANK YOU to my wife. Your support is the best support there is.

Hayden looked down at his wife. He still couldn't believe she was here. He still couldn't believe she was alive. He had hoped beyond reason that Ghost had left her behind. He had risked his life and Casey's to search the place or die trying, even as it was being overrun by trife.

His hope, his desire, his faith had paid off. They were together again, at last. It felt like it had been years, even though it had barely been a week. She was an apparition to him. A different kind of ghost. Now that she was here, he wouldn't let her go again. He wouldn't let anything happen to her, either.

Casey said the trife didn't kill her, either because she was expecting or because she couldn't bear children. But Hallia had proven she wasn't barren, even if their daughter hadn't made it to term. If there was any solace to find in the miscarriage, it had to be that.

Which meant it was more than Natalia's life he had to worry about. At least, that's what he was going to assume until something proved otherwise.

But what about the contagion? What about the trife

disease that threatened to kill one, both, or maybe all three of them?

There was nothing he could do about it, except to wait and see. Some things were beyond his control.

The door behind them shook again, the chains holding it fast rattling loudly. The trife weren't going to give up on this room. Not when the servers lining it were giving off so much energy in the form of heat.

Some things were beyond his control.

Some things weren't.

"You should answer them," Casey said, bringing him back to the present.

He looked at the terminal's display. Someone was communicating with them through it. USSF Western Command Lewis-McChord.

Whoever that was.

"What should I say?" Natalia asked.

"Start with hello?" Casey suggested.

Natalia glanced back at Hayden, and then started typing:

WESTERN COMMAND LEWIS-MCCHORD, THIS IS DATALINK BUNKER PORTLAND. WE ARE OPERA-TIONAL, BUT UNDER HEAVY ATTACK BY THE XENOTRIFE.

All three of them waited, staring at the screen in anticipation of the response.

ROGER, DATALINK BUNKER PORTLAND. I WISH WE COULD SAY WE'RE IN A POSITION TO ASSIST, BUT WE HAVE TRIFE TROUBLE OF OUR OWN. WE THOUGHT EVERYONE ELSE WAS GONE. YOUR NODE IS THE FIRST TO COME ONLINE IN NEARLY ONE HUNDRED YEARS.

Natalia's head snapped around, catching Hayden's eyes. He could tell she was thinking the same thing he was. One hundred years? Who was in Lewis-McChord, and how long had they been there?

She started typing again:

MY NAME IS NATALIA DUKE. I REPAIRED THE DATALINK MAINFRAME.

She sent the message. Hayden reached into his pocket, withdrawing the Butcher's transmitter. It was blinking green.

Casey noticed, glancing at the device.

"Is it coming?" she asked.

"It's not dead," Hayden replied. "I hope so."

"Is what coming?" Natalia asked.

"The cavalry," Casey replied.

"As long as the transmitter managed to send the signal up the shaft and into the open."

Their attention returned to the screen as new text appeared:

YOU AREN'T FROM SPACE FORCE?

Natalia typed back quickly:

NO.

It didn't take long for the response to come.

CAN YOU HELP US?

Natalia started typing again, without hesitation.

WHO ARE YOU?

They waited nearly a minute this time. Was the person on the other end trying to decide what to write?

SPACE FORCE. WE HAVE BEEN LIVING UNDER-GROUND SINCE THE WAR.

"Seriously?" Casey said.

Natalia sent another message:

WHAT IS YOUR SITUATION? WE HAVE GUNS AND VEHICLES.

She looked back at Hayden after she sent it. "Okay, maybe I'm exaggerating a little bit."

The reply came back:

SO DO WE, BUT THE TRIFE HAVE OVERRUN OUR POSITION. THEY CAME IN NUMBERS WE HADN'T SEEN IN YEARS. THEY NESTED NEAR OUR FUSION REACTOR, AND CUT US OFF FROM OUR MAIN FACILITY.

Natalia looked at Hayden.

"We have to stop King from getting into the Pilgrim," he said. "We can't help these people, love. I don't know if we can help ourselves. There are about a thousand trife between us and the perimeter of the city."

She bit her lower lip, the way she always did when she was thinking. He had never stopped believing it was the cutest thing he had ever seen.

Natalia typed:

DO YOU HAVE AIRCRAFT?

The reply came after a few tense moments:

YES.

"What? Is there a whole grepping army waiting out there?" Casey said.

"It almost seems like it," Natalia said. "And they say they have aircraft. If we can reach them, if we can get them out, they may be able to help us deal with King. They may be able to help us stop him from pillaging Metro."

"We have to get out of our own mess, first," Hayden said, checking the transmitter again. As long as it was flashing green, the roid was still alive, and hopefully on its way down.

Natalia returned to the terminal and entered another message:

SEND US YOUR COORDINATES. WE WILL ASSIST IN EXCHANGE FOR USE OF AIRCRAFT AND PERSONNEL.

"Are you sure you aren't making promises we can't keep?" Casey asked. "They didn't say how many trife there are."

"How many trife are there between the Pilgrim and here?"

Natalia replied. "No matter where we go, we need to deal with them. But if we can help these people get out? We don't have to kill the trife; we just need to lead them away. We have to do something, or the people on the Pilgrim, thousands of people, will die."

"The colonists aren't ready for this world," Hayden said. "Hell, I'm still not ready for this world. We opened this can of worms. We need to try to close it." He put his hand on Natalia's shoulder. "I was going to talk to you about this later, but since it came up... Getting King out of power is pretty high up on my list of goals."

She put her hand on his. "Good. It's one of mine, too. I met him, Hayden. He's insane. He thinks he's a god. An actual god. He doesn't care who he crushes to be in control."

"I got that impression from his militia."

"How cute," Casey said. "You both want to overthrow the despot together."

FROM DATALINK PORTLAND, HEAD DUE NORTH UNTIL YOU HIT THE WATER. FOLLOW IT NORTH-EAST. APPROXIMATELY 150 MILES.

"That isn't very far," Casey said. "We can get there in a day."

"A day that King is spending organizing the Scrappers to take the Pilgrim," Hayden said.

"There are only three of us," Natalia said. "We can't stop King with what we have. But maybe Lewis-McChord can give us more, and an aircraft can bring them and us to the Pilgrim ahead of them."

"Are sure you're up for this?" Hayden asked. "I can see on your face, you've been through a lot these last few days. I'm sorry I wasn't here for you. I'm sorry I couldn't catch up until now."

Tears welled in her eyes, and she squeezed his hand.

"You're here now. I can see what you went through to reach me. If it's not my fault, then it isn't yours, either."

"Pozz," he said, leaning over and kissing the top of her head. "It's your call, Nat. You've always been smarter than me."

"Bull," she replied. She paused. "I know it's a risk, but I think we should try. It's our best chance." She turned to Casey. "What do you think?"

Casey was surprised Natalia asked. Hayden wasn't. On the Pilgrim, she got the most out of her team by showing them how valuable they were.

"I think we should go north," Casey said. She pointed at the screen. "Stuff like this, it just doesn't happen out here. We have to try."

"Then it's settled," Hayden said.

Natalia returned to the terminal, typing a response:

LEWIS-MCCHORD, WE WILL ATTEMPT TO ASSIST. WE SHOULD ARRIVE IN ONE TO THREE DAYS. IS THERE ANYTHING ELSE YOU CAN TELL US THAT WILL HELP US REACH YOU?

Casey reached her hands out, placing one on Natalia's shoulder, and one on Hayden's.

"This is going to be awesome," she said.

Hayden hoped she was right.

2

"You do know, once I do this, we can't turn it back on again?" Natalia said.

She was looking up at Hayden from the bowels of the HVAC unit, a hammer in her hand.

"Are you sure you can't break it a little more delicately?" he asked.

She laughed in response. It felt so good to hear her laugh again. It was the best sound in the world.

"If you want to wait an hour or two."

Hayden looked back at the door. The chains were beginning to strain, the door denting inward. They didn't have another hour or two.

The hope was that if they shut off the HVAC, which would force the mainframe to shut down, the loss of heat and energy to the room would convince the trife that getting inside wasn't worth the effort. Since the Butcher had yet to make an appearance despite the connection to the transmitter, it was their best approach to a plan B.

"Be careful," he said.

She looked back at the unit. A protective plate on the side

had already been removed, and now she drew back the hammer and threw it forward into the delicate circuitry there. It cracked and sparked on the first hit. Pieces came off on the second hit. With the third, the HVAC started beeping in a tense warning, and then the servers began to shut down. The unit shut down with them.

Inside of a minute, the only remaining light was coming from dim strips of diodes overhead. Hayden leaned down, offering his hand to Natalia. She took it, and he pulled her out.

"Nothing to do but wait," he said, looking back toward the door. The trife were still there, but the pounding had already diminished somewhat.

"Hayden," she said softly. "I know this isn't the best time, but I don't think there's going to be a good time for a while, and I have something I need to tell you."

He glanced over at Casey. Her attention was fixated on the door, ready to cry out in warning if it gave way.

He turned his attention back to her, looking down into her eyes. They were beginning to tear again, showing him that whatever it was she wanted to say, it was causing her pain.

"What is it, Nat? You can tell me anything."

She nodded, swallowing hard. Her lip started to quiver. "It's. I just. I thought you were dead. I wanted to get closer to Ghost. I thought. I thought maybe I could get him interested in me, and turn him against his father." She paused. "Oh, Hayden. It was so stupid. The idea that I could seduce him was so stupid. I don't know what the hell I was thinking."

"I told you, it's not your fault. If you were under half the stress I've been under the last few days; you can't blame yourself for anything you did. Everything changes when you're fighting to survive."

"I don't even know if I was fighting to survive, or if I

wanted to die. I would have killed myself if he had given me a chance. He took everything out of my room, even the water in the toilet. He stuck me in there naked. No blankets. No anything. And he had someone watching me."

She shook again, and he held her tighter. His eyes started to tear, following the rise in his fury. When they caught up to Ghost, he knew exactly what he was going to do to him.

"That's not what I wanted to tell you, though," she continued. "He let me believe I was getting somewhere. He let me think he was different, and he cared about me. I was so stupid, Hayden. So stupid. I had sex with him. I thought it would help me survive. I thought it would help me get back at King. I'm so sorry. I wish I hadn't done it. I wish-"

He held her tighter. "Nat," he said, cutting her off. "It's okay. It didn't mean anything. I know that. You did what you thought you had to do. We've known one another too long for me ever to think you would try to hurt me. I know you know that."

She was sobbing into his shoulder. She drew back, looking up at him. "I do know that. But I had to tell you. I couldn't hold that in forever. I had to get it out."

He put his hand on her face, cradling it gently. "I won't say I'm not angry because I want to kill that asshole more now than I did before. But I'm not angry at you, and I don't blame you. I love you."

"I love you, too."

"What happened to the greppers who tried to rape you?"

"Ghost killed two of them. I shot the other one. Your lessons came in handy."

"You killed a man?" he asked.

"Yes."

"How did it feel?"

She was silent for a moment while she considered. She knew how hard taking a life could be.

"I'm not sorry I did it. He was a bad man. I won't be sorry to kill any of the Scrappers that cross us. I've seen what they do to people. Ghost told me to survive out here; you have to be the biggest and the baddest."

"Do you believe that?"

"Maybe if your only goal is to survive. If you want to thrive? I still think compassion and unity are the way to do it."

"Pozz that," Casey said. "Otherwise, all you end up with are a bunch of cannibalistic assholes who think they're gods running the show."

"You were listening?" Hayden said. She still had eyes on the door.

"Sorry. You didn't say anything about privacy. It's all square, Sheriff. I've been through plenty of hard times of my own."

"I'm sure you have," Natalia said.

"Huh," Casey said. "The door. It stopped thumping. I got so used to it, I barely noticed."

Hayden looked at the door. It was finally quiet and still. "Or maybe you were too busy eavesdropping?"

"Should I open her up and take a look?" she asked.

Hayden shook his head, letting go of Natalia and walking toward the door, closing his replacement hand into a fist and extending its claws.

"I'll do it," he said.

He was halfway to the door when something hit it again, harder than before. Hard enough that the chains strained to hold it in place.

"Uh-oh," Casey said.

Hayden put out his arm, urging them back. The trife hit the door a second time, the chain snapping with a loud crack, leaving the rifle alone to prop the door closed.

"That's not going to hold," Casey said.

Hayden drew his hand back, ready to fight the demons when they started pouring through the door.

They hit it again, snapping the rifle in half and throwing the door from its hinges, casting it two meters into the room, where it landed near Hayden's feet.

A mass of trife didn't flow through behind it. Instead, a massive humanoid entered through the dust and debris, coming to a stop with its arms at its sides.

"Well, it's about grepping time," Casey said.

3

THEY FOLLOWED THE BUTCHER FROM THE BOTTOM OF THE facility, back up the stairwell and into the garage. The roid was slick with trife blood, covered in scratches and scores from the demons' claws, and made a grinding noise with each movement of its left arm, but it had managed to clear the path for them, leaving behind a trail of dead that numbered in the dozens.

That didn't mean the trife were gone. Far from it. They could hear them every time they reached the next floor, moving in the corridors just outside the stairwell, probably searching for survivors. Their hisses grew louder as Hayden and the others got closer to the garage, the sheer volume of the trife meaning there was no way to maneuver without being seen.

"When we get to the top, we make a hard, fast line for the tank," Hayden said. "Don't slow down, don't look back. The Butcher will cover the rear."

"Pozz that," Casey said.

They made it to where the stairwell met the top level of the garage, stopping there. Hayden directed the Butcher to move in behind them, rewarded immediately when a lone trife entered the stairwell from one floor down and charged them. The Butcher grabbed its neck in its large hand, snapping it easily.

"How did we lose with machines like that?" Natalia said.

"Machines break down," Casey replied. "But you probably know all about that."

"So do people," Natalia replied. "But point taken."

Hayden pushed the door open slightly, just enough so he could see into the garage. The Scrappers had taken almost everything, save for a pile of half-carved trife in one corner, and a pile of garbage in the other. There weren't as many of the creatures loitering there as he had expected. Most were either deeper into the facility or had abandoned it completely to continue ahead.

"If the trife joined together to head south, hopefully that means we'll be pretty clear going north," Casey said.

"Hopefully," Hayden agreed. "There are about a dozen trife in the garage. We run straight for the exit, up the ramp and turn right. The tank is two hundred meters away." He looked at Natalia. "You can do this."

She nodded. "Don't worry about me. I'll be right behind you."

He lifted the transmitter to his mouth. "Take the rear, follow us to the tank. Stop any trife that try to stop us."

The transmitter flashed twice in acknowledgment.

Hayden breathed in, preparing himself. He looked back at the others. He was worried about Natalia, but he couldn't coddle her. They would all die that way.

"Here we go," he said.

He started running, sprinting out into the garage. It was only after he had gone a dozen steps or so he realized how tired he was. How beat up he was. His legs burned with every step. His heart raced. His body hurt. His face was killing him, the gash in his cheek still open and oozing. There was a medical kit on the tank. They just had to reach it.

The trife saw him emerge. They hissed at one another, quickly organizing and breaking apart, moving to attack from every direction.

He kept his eyes on them, watching how they used their powerful limbs to bounce from one place to another, quickly getting ahead of him in a loose wedge formation.

He stopped running.

"Sheriff?" Casey said behind him.

"Keep going," he said. "They want me."

He could tell they only had one target right now. The male in the group. The one with the claws. It was as though they knew who he was from the trife on the Pilgrim. It was as though they knew which one offered the most challenge.

Casey ran past. Natalia slowed, coming up beside him. "Hayden."

"Natalia, go," he said.

"I'm not leaving you."

"I'll catch up. Do you know how many of these things I had to kill to make it here?" He squeezed the replacement hand, the claws extending out. "Go, or I'll order the Butcher to take you."

She looked him in the eye, angry and fearful. If the Butcher was carrying her, it wouldn't be helping him. She started running again without another word.

The trife started closing in around him. He stood at the center of their target, tired and bloody, bruised and battered. He held up the replacement. "Come on," he said. "I don't know how much longer I can stand."

The trife hissed at one another, and then they charged.

Four of them, all at once, a wide assault from the front. It was perfectly synchronized and impossible to defend against.

Hayden only had a few seconds to react, and he did the only thing he could think to do.

He threw himself forward, rolling on his shoulder. He felt the trife claws reach for him, cutting through his coat and scraping along his armor. He came to his feet, the long jacket peeled away, left in the creature's grip. He turned back toward them as they adjusted for his escape, throwing up his hands as one of the trife jumped on him, knocking him back down. Its head pushed toward his face, trying to reach him, large teeth looming. He pushed back, the added strength of his prosthetic able to throw the lighter demon aside.

Another one took its place, joining the sudden frenzy as the creatures sensed the kill. Its claws slashed across his chest, nearly cutting through the armor before scraping along one of the hardened plates. A third creature came at him with its teeth, and he barely got his hand up to block it.

Then the Butcher arrived behind him, hard metal hands snapping out, slapping the creatures away. They hissed and danced away from the machine, two of them falling to its overpowering strength in the few seconds it took to reorganize.

It stood over Hayden, waiting patiently for him to get up. He winced as he fought his way back to his feet, turning and continuing ahead. The trife were watching them, wary of the machine, likely waiting to see if it stopped functioning altogether.

It stayed back while Hayden rushed forward, making it to the ramp. As he started climbing, he saw Casey and Natalia remained inside, staring out toward the street.

Natalia heard him coming, and he could see the relief on her face and the concern at the new damage to his armor.

"Why are you still here?" he asked.

Casey pointed. "They shredded the treads. I didn't know they had it in them."

Hayden looked out, finding the tank in the street. It was surrounded by corpses, both Scrappers and trife. The area was otherwise clear. He could see immediately that the tread on the left side was broken, slashed apart by who knew how many trife claws. It must have taken a lot of work to make it happen, but with the numbers the trife possessed, it probably wasn't all that difficult.

The Butcher pounded up the ramp behind them, suggesting they were clear of the creatures.

"We need the weapons and ammo on the tank," Hayden said. "And I could use some bandages."

"And some stitches," Casey said.

He led them out of the garage, toward the vehicle, scanning the area for signs of more trife. The street was deserted, but the smell of blood and gunpowder lingered. All of this was such a small scale compared to the initial war against the alien invaders. He could only imagine what that had looked like.

They were halfway to the tank when he heard the movement. It started with a single bit of mortar that fell from an already crumbling building twenty meters away, crashing into the street and drawing his attention. He looked up, finding the trife perched there, wings spread in preparation to launch.

A dozen more appeared around it. A second group moved into view on the next building. A third group materialized behind that one.

"Shit," Casey said.

"Run!" Hayden shouted. "Get in the tank."

They made a beeline for the vehicle. Maybe it couldn't move, but the tank could protect them indefinitely, and they needed the guns and ammo on board.

They crossed the street, reaching the tank as the trife swooped down. Hayden turned toward them, claws raised to defend his wife. Only the demons weren't targeting them.

They wanted to take down the Butcher.

They swooped in on it, the claws on their feet dragging over its head as it swung its arms to hit them. More of the creatures dove into it, landing and pouncing on it, kicked away, smashed down, or crushed beneath its feet.

Hayden climbed onto the tank, helping Natalia up. Casey hopped up on her own, climbing to the hatch.

She shouted, falling back as a trife reached out for her from within. Hayden barely caught her before she tumbled off, grabbing her with his human hand. The trife dove after her, rewarded with a set of claws that sank into the side of its head. Hayden used the momentum to carry it up, over, and off the vehicle, sending its corpse to the ground.

"Grepping hell, that was close," Casey said, recovering her balance on the tank.

"I'll go first," Hayden said, moving past her.

He looked into the tank. A Scrapper was there, dead on the floor. The smell was horrible.

He climbed into the machine, claws raised and ready to defend. There was only one trife inside, waiting to ambush whoever came back. There were two more dead Scrappers. One of them was sitting in the driver's position, apparently trying to steal the vehicle.

"Clear!" he shouted.

Natalia joined him a moment later, followed by Casey.

"Grab the rifles and magazines. I want a full inventory," he said.

"Pozz," Casey replied.

Hayden climbed back to the top of the hatch, looking out at the Butcher. It was on its back, only one arm still operational, throwing punches at the trife that tried to get near it. He was sure it wouldn't survive much longer.

He grabbed the heavy lid of the hatch and pulled it down, locking it in place. He didn't want to stay in here with the dead, or with the smell, but they needed to rest, regroup, and reload.

At least they had made it outside.

4

"HOW DOES IT FEEL?" NATALIA ASKED, HER FINGERS LIGHTLY brushing the side of his face, just above where Casey had stitched the deep wound.

"I'm numb to the pain at this point," Hayden replied. "If we survive long enough for it to heal, I'm going to be too ugly to kiss."

"You were already too ugly to kiss," she said, smiling.

He smiled back at her, grateful she was there once more.

"Where did you learn to treat wounds?" Hayden asked, looking over at Casey.

She was organizing their remaining weaponry, dividing it for the three of them.

Three hours had passed. At first, they could hear the trife hissing and moving around outside. Now, it was silent. The roid's transmitter had gone dark, confirming the Butcher was destroyed. The trife hadn't returned to the tank after that. Maybe they didn't see the three humans as enough of a threat? Or maybe they had enough of the city covered; there was no way they expected them to get out alive?

"It's pretty much on the job training for a Driver," Casey

replied. "I'll tell you, Sheriff, it's a hell of a lot easier to stitch someone else up."

"You've done your own stitches?" Natalia asked.

Casey stopped what she was doing, turning and pulling down the back of her pants, exposing the top of her rear. There was a relatively smooth scar there, about ten centimeters long.

"Closest I ever came to being killed by a trife," she said. "Well, before I met your husband. Now it's an hourly occurrence."

"You did that yourself?" Natalia said, impressed. The location was tough to reach.

"Propped up a mirror. I just had to keep reminding myself that everything was reversed." She covered herself again, turning back around. "So, Sheriff, we need to cover one hundred fifty miles through trife-infested landscape, and we lost our ride. Any ideas?"

Hayden had been thinking about it since they had sealed themselves into the tank. "We have to head north on foot," he said. "At least until we get past the river. Then we can try to find an old vehicle. I'm sure between the two of you we can get something functional."

"If we can find something to repair," Casey said. "I don't know if the Scrappers ever crossed the bridge, so it could be there's a whole lot filled with old cars. But, I can guarantee they'll have dead batteries."

"How do we fix that?"

"We might be able to salvage the power supply from the Butcher," Natalia said.

"If we can get it out before the trife come back," Casey said. "Have you opened up a roid before?"

"Not yet, but it shouldn't be too hard."

"Speaking of the river," Natalia said. "Do we know which direction it flows?"

"I'm not sure," Casey said. "Why?"

"Maybe instead of crossing over it, we can travel on it? If it goes north, it would seem a lot safer than passing through the rest of the city."

"Not from those flying greppers."

"From the rest of them. That would at least eliminate one threat."

"It's worth considering," Hayden said. "Maybe we can find a boat?"

"You never know what you might find out here," Casey said. "Especially this far north. We'll need to grab the battery either way. Anything that used power once is going to be drained."

"Do we have tools?" Natalia asked.

Casey moved to another part of the tank. She had to push the dead Scrapper out of the way to reach the small compartment where the tools were kept.

"Will these do?" she asked, dragging the box out.

Natalia opened it, looking through them. "It should."

"I'll keep watch over you while you work," Hayden said.

Casey picked up one of the rifles, holding it out to him. "It's a good thing we took extras. We've got three rifles left, twelve magazines, fifty shots each. One secondary with three explosives in it." She smiled, tapping the magazine. "I'm giving that one to you, Sheriff."

Hayden took the rifle, placing it at his side.

"We've also got four Marine Corps sidearms, and three revolvers I pulled off the corpses. Six magazines, and twenty-eight bullets."

"I hope it's enough to make it to Lewis-McChord," Natalia said.

"And to get the people there out," Casey said. "Me, too. I would have felt much better about this whole thing if we still had the tank and the Butcher."

"We have to try," Hayden said. "The colonists on the Pilgrim are depending on us."

"And we told the people at Lewis-McChord we would try to help them," Natalia said. "We're committed."

"If we pull this off, we can change the entire complexion of this part of the world," Hayden added. "We can start fighting back. Really fighting back."

"It's been four hundred years, Sheriff," Casey said. "Do you think you're the first person to come along saying that we can fight back? Do you think you're the first person who thought they could make a difference? It's happened before. Somebody tries to do good. They organize an army. They go out to fight the trife. Then they die. They always die. Every time you fire that rifle, you're using a bullet that can't be replaced. I don't know what kind of stuff Lewis-McChord has, but it better be something special if we're going to stand a chance."

"I'm not trying to save the whole world, Casey," Hayden replied. "Just the people on the Pilgrim. Just the people under King's control. It's clear humankind has learned how to survive with the trife threat. We need to make a difference one small group at a time if we can."

"I agree with the sentiment, Hayden," Natalia said. "I'm not as confident that we can continue to survive out here. Maybe in the past, but these trife are working together. Ghost said he's never seen that before."

"On the Pilgrim, the two groups I ran into killed one another. It is a new development."

"Which could mean the end of all of us," Casey said. "Of everything."

"I'm still alive," Hayden said. "I'm still fighting. I'm not giving up on the future." He looked at Natalia. "Our future. And our baby's, if you are pregnant. That's the way this thing has to work. No quit. No surrender."

Even if they could be dead in three months, regardless. He couldn't live with himself any other way. He knew Natalia understood.

Casey smiled. "At least if we die, we'll die with a purpose."

"Exactly," Hayden replied. He pushed himself to his feet, ignoring the growing soreness in his body. "How long until nightfall?"

"About three hours," Casey said.

"Then we have three hours to try to pull the battery."

Natalia stood. Hayden could tell she was afraid, but she wasn't going to let that stop her. It never did. "Let's do it."

5

THEY SUCCEEDED IN REMOVING THE BATTERY FROM THE
Butcher, needing a little over an hour to remove the armored
plating covering the rear of the machine and detach the
connections holding the power source to it.

The battery was small and dense. Hayden could hold it in
the palm of his replacement hand, and at the same time, the
mechanical appendage was the only reason he was strong
enough to lift it to place it into a pack he could put on his
back instead. Not that it would be fun to carry a twenty-
seven-kilogram block anywhere on his body.

After that, they had retreated to the tank, taking the time
to remove the corpses from inside of it rather than having to
spend the night with the dead. The trife were scarce during
their activity, having moved on from their location or
possibly satisfied with having removed the Butcher from
service. It was nice to be outside and not be under attack by
someone, even if they were still surrounded by the vestiges
of war.

Night had come, leaving them all tucked into the tank
together. They had spoken at length together. About the

24

Pilgrim. About the world both Inside and Outside. Hayden could tell Natalia was forming a quick attachment to Casey, and vice versa. In some ways, the girl was like the daughter they never had. At least, he had that thought while he was watching the two women talk and laugh together. He buried it as deep as he could, unable to deal with the idea. It was too easy to die out here, and if it came down to a choice, he was going to take Nat every time.

It was a truth he didn't want to deal with.

They had settled in together then, all three of them, huddling close for warmth as they slept. The rest came easy for him, and he managed to avoid the nightmares for the first time since leaving the Pilgrim. He held Natalia close, while Natalia kept her arms around Casey, forming a bond that, when he woke up the next morning, he decided he would do everything in his power to keep from breaking.

Not that it would be easy. They had a long way to go, and they already knew the trife were out there and the goliaths weren't. He had hope that maybe the people in Lewis-McChord could tell them why. The giants didn't differentiate between human and trife, but they were still better for the humans.

They cleared the southern part of the city without incident. There were trife around, but in small numbers and easy to avoid. They slipped past them, taking longer routes around, moving carefully north toward the river. When they couldn't get past, Hayden did his best to confront them unaware, to take them by surprise, and on the occasions when he couldn't, to prioritize his claws or Ghost's knife to deal with them, and to avoid a gunshot that could bring an entire army their way.

There was nothing comfortable about any of it. Hayden's entire body was sore, especially his face. Casey had cleaned and stitched the wound, but it still hurt every time he breathed. So did his sides, where other lacerations pulled every time he swung his claws or stabbed with the knife. Each confrontation was an exercise not only in physical strength but overall constitution. He wasn't only fighting trife; he was fighting himself.

And yet, having Natalia there with him made it all worthwhile. Whenever he felt like his muscles were going to give, he remembered why he was fighting and who he was fighting for. Casey, too. Jake had died trying to help him. He didn't want the same thing to happen to her.

He didn't succeed because he was a superman. He succeeded because he gave himself up to the cause, heart and soul. Mind over matter. He was the Sheriff, and it was his job to serve and protect.

"Well, we made it to the river," Casey said.

They were standing at the edge of a massive slab of concrete, looking at the water running beneath it. The slab had been part of a bridge once. Not the same one the Scrappers had blown, but another further to the west, that looked as though it had collapsed or been destroyed many years earlier. The concrete was cracked and pitted, and overgrown with vines and other vegetation, but it offered a pretty good view of the river in each direction.

Hayden turned to the south. He could see a line of crumbling, abandoned buildings on their side of the river, spaced less densely than the blocks around it, but still covered in ancient cement. Further down, he could see trees in the middle of the river. An island of some kind, green and lush and likely home to plenty of animals.

He shifted to the North, in the direction Natalia and Casey were already facing. There was another bridge there, or at least what was left of it. The center was sticking up out of the middle of the water, a grave marker of old cement and bent steel.

Beyond that, he could see boats.

They were hard to distinguish from the distance, but they were definitely there. Dirty and stained, rusted and likely in terrible shape, but present, and maybe still afloat.

"That's our target," he said.

"Pozz that," Casey replied.

The three of them backed off the bridge, still keeping a sharp eye out for trife. They cut to the north as soon as possible, following the bank of the river until they reached the start of the next collapsed bridge and a thick growth of greenery beyond it.

"Should we go around?" Natalia asked.

She was worried about the tall grass and trees. Hayden didn't blame her. The trife could disappear into the brush, and they were smart enough to organize an ambush if they entered.

Still, they had already lost a night against Ghost and the Scrappers. They were betting on the soldiers at Lewis-McChord to provide an aircraft to help them catch up, but if they lingered too long, it wouldn't matter how fast they moved. King would beat them back to the Pilgrim, and then?

He didn't want to consider what would happen then.

"We have to go through," he said. "We can't waste more hours circling."

Natalia didn't argue. She shifted her rifle in her arms, more prepared to use it on short notice. Casey did the same.

They entered the foliage. There was an old path cutting through it closer to the water. It was split by tree roots and weeds, but it left them a narrow gap to move through. They stayed close to one another, Natalia and Casey facing forward, Hayden bringing up the rear. They moved quickly, not trying to be quiet as they made their passage, keeping their eyes fixed on the surrounding grass for signs of motion.

They were nearly through when that motion occurred, a

sharp crackling of the brush to their left, and the sudden rise of a filthy smell. All three of them pivoted to face it, rifles up and ready to fire.

A trio of dogs broke through the greenery, freezing when they saw the armed humans. They bared their teeth, growling for a moment before turning and scampering off.

"Geez," Casey whispered. "I almost shot them."

"That's the first time I've seen a live dog," Natalia said.

"Me, too," Hayden said. "Man's best friend?"

"There aren't many domesticated dogs around anymore," Casey said. "And definitely not out here."

They left the brush behind, passing the rubble of a few taller buildings, getting closer to where the boats were resting. They could see the craft more clearly now. More of them were hanging from the ties that moored them than Hayden realized, no longer floating on the surface but dangling from the dock. Judging by the condition of the dock, he was surprised the whole thing hadn't already collapsed.

"It doesn't look good," Casey said, eyeing the boats. "I don't know if any of the floating ones will stay that way with our weight in them."

"How many years has it been since any of them were used?" Natalia said. "Three hundred?"

"Probably. But even if we can't get the engine going, if we can find some paddles or something we can drift downriver. That has to be faster than walking."

They moved closer to the docks, timid about walking out onto them. The whole thing looked like it would sink with the slightest nudge.

"I'll go out there," Casey said. "I'm the smallest and lightest."

"Not with those chains over your arms," Natalia said.

"I'll have to take them off."

She reached to her left arm to start unclasping them.

Hayden scanned the area around them, keeping an eye out for trife. He was surprised by how quiet it was over here. Then again, Jake had said the creatures didn't like water. Why would they linger closer to it than they had to?

Casey had taken all of the chains off her left arm when Hayden spotted a boat further downriver, resting directly against the shore. It was as old and dirty as the rest, but it appeared to be afloat.

"Casey, wait," he said, pointing. "Look there."

She followed his finger, smiling when she saw it. "Good eye, Sheriff."

She didn't re-clasp her chains, gathering them quickly and wrapping them around her arm. They moved as a group, running toward the boat.

It was tied off to the shore, the rope holding it almost clean compared to everything around it. That fact gave Hayden pause.

"I think this belongs to somebody," he said.

"Belongs?" Casey said. "It's finders-keepers out here, Sheriff. One hundred percent of the time. Now isn't the time to bring your sense of justice into the equation."

Hayden glanced at her and then sighed. "Just this once, I'll agree with you," he said.

Casey climbed onto the stern. The boat was at least fifteen meters long, composed of a lower deck and a secondary, exposed deck with a cockpit. It wasn't made of wood, but rather some kind of composite material Hayden didn't recognize.

Casey grabbed the handle of the door into the lower deck, pulling it open.

She barely had time to react as something sprang forward toward her. She raised her arm, the chains the only thing saving her as large, sharp teeth clamped down on it.

"Shit," she said, falling backward.

Hayden raised his rifle to shoot the dog that had emerged from the cabin, but then Casey started to laugh.

The dog had removed its jaws from her arm and was furiously licking her face.

"Okay, okay," she said. "Stop it. Stop it."

Hayden looked at Natalia, who was already looking back at him. They shared an amused smile.

His grin faded a moment later when a sharp red dot appeared on Natalia's forehead.

"Hayden?" she said. "What is it?"

"Whoever the hell you are," a voice shouted from somewhere nearby. "Get the grepping hell away from my boat."

6

"CASEY," HAYDEN SHOUTED, GETTING THE GIRL'S ATTENTION.

She pushed the dog away from her, getting back up and looking over at him, still petting the animal, who was shoving his head against her leg. The dog was large, with wiry hair and big eyes. Its tail was low but wagging gently, swishing back and forth.

They were both unaware of the threat on Natalia. The red spot marking where a bullet would sprout if the man, wherever he was, decided they were too much of a threat.

"We're going," Hayden shouted. He swiveled his head, leading with his eyes, trying to track the source of the laser.

It wasn't hard. The man wasn't trying to hide. He was walking toward them. Average height, a stocky build, covered in thick robes, like the Scrappers but much darker. He had a mask hanging from the side of his face, a line leading toward his back. Small eyes, a larger nose, not much hair. What he had was wispy and wild.

"Who are you?" he demanded, keeping the weapon aimed at Natalia but looking at Hayden.

"Travelers," Hayden said.

The man laughed, a high-pitched wheeze. "Travelers? There aren't any travelers out here."

"Then what are you?" Natalia asked.

He stopped laughing. "A traveler," he replied seriously. He waited a couple of seconds and then started laughing again.

He was high.

"We don't want any trouble," Hayden said. "We thought this boat was abandoned."

The man kept laughing. "Yeah, right. I believe that, Mister. This boat is the only boat on the damn river what floats, but you expected it to be abandoned. Do you think I'm an idiot? You were gonna steal her."

"Just lower the gun, and maybe we can talk," Hayden said. "Honestly, we don't mean you any harm. We're just trying to go north."

"What the hell for? There's nothing to the north. Nothing but trife. Nothing but death. I should know, that's where I live. All alone."

"What about him?" Casey asked, still patting the dog.

"That mongrel? He barely counts. He eats more than his share, and his farts stink up the whole damn cabin. Hoo-boy."

"Can we talk?" Hayden repeated. "Without you pointing that thing at my wife?"

The word seemed to have an effect on him. "Wife?" he said, looking at her with fresh eyes. "You have a wife?"

"She's pregnant," Hayden said.

The man looked stricken. He lowered the gun and his head.

"My apologies, ma'am," he said. "I didn't. I wouldn't. I didn't know." He grabbed the mask and put it over his mouth, breathing in before letting it go. Then he put his hand up in greeting. "I'm Duncan. That hairy crap machine over there is Gus."

"Hayden," Hayden said. "Natalia. And Chains."

Duncan looked back at Casey. "Chains? That's an odd name."

"I had odd parents," she replied.

"Well, if you aren't planning to kill me, then it's good to meet you. But I'm still going to have to ask you not to steal my boat."

"We're trying to go north," Hayden said again. "We're looking for a place called Lewis-McChord."

The man started a fresh round of laughter. "Lewis-McChord? The Lewis-McChord? You might as well be telling me you're looking for the lost city of Z."

"I don't know what that is," Hayden said.

"Haven't you ever seen a movie, Hayden?" Duncan replied. "I've got thousands of them back at my place. Probably the biggest collection in the world. That's why I came down this way. I'm a scavenger at heart. A film buff. A bit of a tinkerer. I look for old data medium. Solid state, blu-ray, you name it. Every week I tell myself, this week I'm going to give it up because one day I'm going to get myself killed, but I can't. I can't give it up. It's an addiction."

"Like the happy gas?" Casey said.

"Okay, you've got me. I come down here every few months. I used to trade with the squatters here, dupes for refills."

"Dupes?" Natalia said.

"Duplicates. Extra copies of films. They didn't kill me because they always wanted fresh material. I've got a few on the boat. Anyway, I got here at the wrong time. I saw the trife preparing to attack. That was some big ass group, wasn't it, Hay? Do you mind if I call you Hay? Like what horsies eat?" He laughed again, talking through the chuckles. "You survived it?"

"Barely," Hayden said. "And now we're trying to go north."

"You live alone?" Natalia asked.

"Yup. Like I said, just me and the four-legged area rug. There's nobody up to the north. Nobody. Not anymore. Not for a long time."

"You survived," Hayden said.

"I'm smarter than the rest of them," Duncan said. "Oh, I wasn't born up north. I came from Angelico originally. It's a small settlement near Haven. I left when King started taking over. I'm a Collector. I was a Collector. Then I decided to be a hermit. I like movies more than people. Movies aren't out to take advantage of you, or kill you."

"Yet you're trusting us right now," Hayden said.

"I dropped my guard five minutes ago. If you were going to kill me, you would have. If you could. I live in the north, Hay. I live surrounded by trife. You think I'm an easy mark?"

He whistled, short and quick. Gus was docile and friendly one moment. The next, he had Casey on the floor of the boat, snarling over her face.

Hayden extended the claws of the replacement, getting them up against Duncan's neck before he could react.

Duncan's face paled. He whistled again. Immediately, Gus was calm once more and started a fresh round of face-licking.

"Just a demonstration," Duncan said. "Shit, Hay. You've got secrets of your own. I like it."

Hayden pulled back the claws.

"Can I see?" the man asked.

Hayden held out the replacement, letting him look at it.

"Accelerated Industries," Duncan said. "They made good stuff. It's a little beat up, but it's boss."

"You know about these things?" Hayden said.

"I saw a documentary about the company. They were into some pretty kooky shit, back in the day. Did you know, they had a model with a thermal blade on it? Got so hell-hot it

34

burned right through trife flesh and bones like they were made of air. Kept shorting out the internals, too. They had to refit the lucky owners. How'd you lose the hand? Trife?"

"Scrappers."

"Not an uncommon answer. Well, anyway, it was nice meeting you folks, but it's about time I headed back to my little shack in the woods." He took another breath of gas, turning his shoulder to show off his sack of stuff he had scavenged. "Good luck finding Lewis-McChord." He laughed again.

"Hold on a second," Hayden said. "Aren't you going north?"

"Yeah. So?" Duncan stared at Hayden a moment. "Oh. You want a ride?"

"If you don't mind."

"This isn't a charity. What do you have to trade?"

"One of our rifles?" Hayden suggested. "They're United States Marine Corps issue. Better quality than anything being produced today."

"Nah. I don't need guns. I've got plenty already. What else?"

Hayden and Natalia looked at one another. They didn't have much.

"Are you lonely, Duncan?" Casey asked.

Duncan looked over at her. "No. I don't like sex. It's too messy. Too, I don't know. Interactive?"

"You like movies," Natalia said. "What about stories?"

"Stories?" Duncan said.

"I can tell you all about where we're from. Does the Pilgrim mean anything to you?"

"No. Should it?"

"I can tell you all about it on the way north. You can decide for yourself."

"You're going that way, anyway," Hayden said.

"I think you may have missed the part where I said I don't like people," Duncan replied. "But hearing about something new is tempting."

"What about the battery?" Casey said.

"Battery?" Duncan replied, growing more interested.

"From a Butcher," Natalia said. "Still half-charged."

"Battery and stories, and we have a deal," Duncan said. "I'll take you three as far north as I'm going. About eighty miles."

"Sounds good to me," Hayden said.

"Me, too," Natalia agreed.

"Fine," Duncan said. "Get in the boat. Stay in the cabin."

He walked past them and climbed into the vessel. Gus shuffled over to him for a moment, before moving back to Casey.

"Damn traitor," Duncan said. He turned back to Hayden and Natalia. "Don't just stand there, lovebirds. Departure is at now o'clock."

7

THE BOAT WAS BATTERY-POWERED, CUSTOM ASSEMBLED BY
Duncan after he had found a few books and video tutorials
out in the wilds of what he said used to be called Seattle. It
wasn't a powerful engine by any means, but it was enough to
push him against the current at a leisurely pace, able to make
it to Ports and back on a charge, and enough to steer when
moving with the current.

The scavenger took to the cockpit on the top of the craft,
settling his larger frame into the smaller chair there, after
removing the moorings from land. Hayden, Casey, and
Natalia headed into the cabin as Duncan had suggested,
stowing their weapons and taking seats on the cushioned
benches that lined the sides of the lower deck.

The cabin was anything but tidy. There were items
thrown everywhere, from old magazines to electronics, to
guns and ammunition, to extra canisters of nitrous oxide, to
different, mismatched pieces of clothing in various states of
cleanliness.

There was a bed located in the bow of the craft. A laptop
similar to Jake's was resting there, the USSF logo obvious on

its face. A spread of small, square bits of metal sat beside it, which Natalia identified as data storage devices.

Duncan called it his adult collection, whatever that meant.

They took a slow and easy route away from Ports. Hayden couldn't say he was sad to see the city go, though there was a part of him that still wished they were headed in the opposite direction. He had made peace with their plan. That didn't mean he had to love it.

He sat back against the side of the boat, with Natalia resting against him. Casey was on the other side, with Gus sitting at her feet, satisfied to have someone to reciprocate attention. There was no way the dog could climb the ladder up to the cockpit, so he probably spent a lot of time in the cabin alone.

Duncan had given her another gadget with a small screen that accepted silver discs. He had also offered her a box full of the things, each with an image and title printed on the front. He claimed those were more suitable for someone her age. Hayden didn't know what that meant, either.

She had put one of the discs in and was watching it now, turning it so Hayden and Natalia could see the screen.

"Look at this," she said. "These aren't real people. How do you think they did that?"

"Computers," Natalia replied, watching the screen. "Though why they would use computers to make something like this is beyond my comprehension.

It was something about a woman in a dress with long blonde hair and a white creature with an orange nose that could talk. Hayden was equally confounded by the whole idea. Didn't people have anything better to do with their time back then?

Maybe not. They didn't have to worry about being

attacked by trife or eaten by goliaths, and he had watched plenty of videos on the PASS.

Casey watched it for a few more minutes before ejecting the disc. She looked through the box, pausing at one, her face turning red.

"Uh. I think this should have been in a different box," she said, taking it out. The image on the cover showed a pair of naked women with overly large breasts in a very compromising position together.

"They used to film that?" Natalia said.

"Maybe it was done with computers?" Hayden suggested. "No woman's body looks like that naturally."

"Maybe I should put it in?" Casey said.

"Maybe you shouldn't," Hayden replied. "It's disgusting."

Casey dropped it back into the box, digging for something else.

Hayden glanced outside. The landscape was easing past. They had left the city behind, and were planted firmly between two banks of trees, headed north. The sun had vanished behind gray skies, and a light drizzle was falling. In another place, another time, to be here with Natalia like this, to imagine Casey as their own, that could have been a dream come true.

Not a brief respite in the midst of a nightmare, like he knew it was. Lewis-McChord was overrun. The soldiers inside couldn't get out. And yet they were somehow going to save them? Maybe they could do more with less from the outside, but he had no delusions it was going to be any less challenging than what he had already been through. And the Pilgrim? He couldn't bear to think about the Pilgrim.

Take advantage of what you have, when you have it. That's what he decided to do. He wrapped his arms tighter around Natalia, kissing the top of her head. Whatever happened next, he was glad it would happen with her there. At least something had turned out the way he wanted it.

He drifted off to sleep like that. With Natalia resting in his arms. With Casey watching an old movie nearby. With Gus laying on the floor and Duncan in the cockpit, taking them downriver. It wasn't a long rest, but it was a content one.

8

THEY HAD BEEN ON THE WATER FOR SIX HOURS WHEN HAYDEN decided to leave the cabin, despite Duncan's request they remain there. The river had widened considerably, and the position of the sun suggested they were no longer headed north.

He climbed the ladder up to the cockpit, his body sore and burning with every move from his arms and legs. The cut on his face had settled down some, at least, offering a little bit of relief.

When he crested the top deck, he found Duncan settled back in his chair, face mask on and eyes closed. His hands were off the wheel, but somehow the boat had managed to keep from running aground.

"Duncan," Hayden said.

The man didn't answer.

"Duncan."

He grabbed his shoulder and shook it. Duncan's eyes snapped open, and he reached for the gun on the console before realizing it was Hayden. He ripped the mask off instead.

"Didn't I tell you to stay in the cabin?" the man said.

"You were sleeping," Hayden replied.

"So? This is my boat. I drive it how I like. I've made this trip a thousand times. It's not a problem."

"We could have slammed into the shore."

"Do you think I'm an idiot? I rigged some sensors. They keep us centered in the channel. Go back to the cabin. You're bothering me." He laughed.

"I came up here to ask you where we are. We aren't headed north."

"West," Duncan agreed. "We linked up with a larger river a handful of miles back. It'll bring us out to the sea for an hour, hour and a half, and then we'll go back east and dock at my humble abode." He looked at Hayden. "Do you not trust me, Hay?"

"I've learned you can't trust anybody," Hayden replied.

"Truer words have rarely been spoken," Duncan said. "That's why I live alone, save for that stinky-ass mutt in the cabin. But, your wife still owes me a few stories. And besides, what kind of monster would hurt a pregnant woman? Even the trife won't go that far."

"How far is your home from Lewis-McChord?" Hayden asked.

"What's your deal with Lewis-McChord?" Duncan said. "The place is gone. Wiped out and painted over with enough damned trife you could make a bridge around the whole damned planet if you connected them ass to head."

"We were in contact with someone who claimed to be communicating from there," Hayden said.

"Like radio?" Duncan replied, surprised. "I could tell you I'm in Timbuktu, are you going to believe me?"

"Not radio," Hayden said.

"And you aren't going to tell me the rest?"

"No."

Duncan shrugged and looked back out at the river.

"What else can you tell me about Lewis-McChord?" Hayden asked.

"It's suicide to go there," Duncan said.

"That's what I heard about Ports."

"Ports is south. Everything gets worse the further north you travel. You've made it this far despite the obvious ass-kicking you've taken, so I imagine you're pretty tough. But don't compare where you're headed with where you've been. You'll be making a deadly mistake if you do."

"Pozz that," Hayden said. "Thanks for the advice."

He put his foot on the ladder, ready to return to the cabin. Duncan looked back at him.

"Are you sure you aren't going to tell me the rest?"

"I'm sure."

He took a few steps down. Duncan kept staring at him.

"Ahhh, damn it," Duncan said. "Forget the stories about the Pilgrim, whatever it is. Who did you hear from that said they were at Lewis-McChord, and how?"

"Are you changing the terms of our agreement?" Hayden asked.

"I'm asking to change the terms, yeah. This story is a hell of a lot more personal."

"Why? I thought you were a loner?"

"It just is."

Hayden knew the man was lying. Maybe he hadn't always been alone?

"Did you know there was a Space Force facility in Ports?" Hayden asked.

"No. Was there?"

Hayden nodded. "King sent my wife there to get into a mainframe. A computer."

"I know what a mainframe is."

"She did. Once she got access, we started getting

43

messages on the display from someone saying they were at Lewis-McChord. He said they have trained soldiers there, along with weapons and vehicles, but they can't get out past the trife. We're going to help them."

"Why?"

"Why what?"

"Why are you going to help them? People don't help one another out here. It's stupid, and will only get you killed."

"Maybe you believe that. I believe we're stronger together than we are apart. Natalia and I are a living example of that."

"Come on, Hay. You aren't trying to mow through a mountain of trife out of the goodness of your heart. There's no way in hell I believe that even if you're as much of a white hat as you say."

"White hat?"

"From the old westerns? Have you seen those? Roy Rogers?"

"A few. The only person with a white hat out here is King's Courier, Ghost."

"That's not the kind of white hat I'm talking about. If you know Roy, then you know what I mean. What's in it for you? Honestly?"

"They have aircraft," Hayden admitted. "Between that and the weapons, we're gambling they can get us back to the Pilgrim before King."

"The Pilgrim again. So it's a place?"

"Sort of."

"And what if King gets there first?"

"A lot of people are going to die."

"So you're risking your lives on the slender hope that you can do something about that by going to Lewis-McChord?"

"Pretty much."

Duncan leaned forward in his chair, taking another drag of nitrous. He smiled, shaking his head. "You're crazy. I love that you're crazy, though. It's entertaining as hell. My place is a good five day's walk from the fence at the perimeter of the old base. Thing's rusted to hell but still standing, believe it or not."

"Five days?" Hayden said.

That was far. Too far.

"I know, you don't like that answer. You'll like it less knowing how many damned trife there are between the two points. I made that trip once. I'm never making it again." Duncan stared at him, meeting his eyes. "You took a gamble, Hay. Sorry, but you lost."

"I don't accept that. I can't. I'm going to-"

Hayden was cut off when something on the console made a sharp noise. Duncan's head snapped back to it, looking down at once of the screens there.

"Shit," he said, getting to his feet.

"What is it?" Hayden asked.

"Get below. Get below now. Damn it. Son of a bitch. Of all the damned times to have to deal with this shit."

"What is it?" Hayden asked again.

"You heard of Sanctuary, Hay?" Duncan asked, urging him down the ladder. Hayden dropped to the lower deck, moving aside as Duncan pulled the cover off the motor in the stern.

"No. What are you doing?"

"Powering off," Duncan replied. "Sanctuary is an old oil rig, about fifteen miles out that way. There's a so-called city there."

"The Borger who gave me this hand told me about the place. He said people call it a utopia."

"If the only criteria for being a utopia is that there aren't any trife, then I guess it is." Duncan stood and put the cover back on the motor, and then scanned the horizon, putting his hand over his eyes to cut down the glare. "I don't see them yet. That's good. Hopefully, they won't pull in close."

"You're saying it's not what the stories claim?" Hayden asked.

"I'm saying it's a great deal for the people who founded it and their offspring. It's not a great deal for anyone else. They have limited resources. Do you know what it means to live in a place like that?"

"Better than you might think," Hayden said.

"Yeah, so then you understand equilibrium. Too many mouths, not enough space, it becomes a problem. Word about the place got out a long time ago. I don't even know how. Folks started doing crazy things to get there. I've killed more than one asshole who tried to take my boat."

Duncan moved from port to starboard and back to port, searching. Gus was at the cabin door, pressed against it with his face visible through the glass.

"Why didn't you kill us?" Hayden said. "We were stealing your boat."

"You were nice about it," Duncan said. "Usually, they just shoot first or try to cast off the lines before I shoot them. So anyway, Sanctuary. Bad news. Anyone shows up uninvited, they give them a nice warm welcome, then they make them fight one another. The losers get dangled in the water on hooks. Shark bait."

Hayden winced at the gruesomeness of it. "And you know this how?"

"I met someone from Sanctuary once. They were trying to get away from the place. They said the whole rig was rampant with rape, incest, and any other kind of degrading garbage you can think of. Give a man an island and complete control, and sooner or later it's going to turn into a shitpile. That's my thinking, anyways."

Hayden couldn't disagree, between what Casey had told him about her background, and King's current actions.

Duncan climbed along the port side railing to the bow,

looking out ahead of them. The boat was riding the current, turning slightly as it continued. Natalia and Casey had noticed the commotion and were peering out the cabin's windows.

"Shit," he said again, retreating quickly. "Shit, shit, shit."

"What?" Hayden said.

"Look, those assholes are dumb as hell. I've got enough firepower on this tug to kill all of them in a hurry, but you see, I don't really like killing people."

"Me neither."

"Yeah, well it doesn't look like they're giving us a choice. They're coming this way. Are you any good with that rifle of yours? Hell, you must be if you want to go to Lewis-McChord."

Hayden stared out where Duncan had been looking. He could see a pair of small boats as specks on the horizon.

"Who are they?"

"They're from Sanctuary," Duncan said. "Scavengers, like me. They raid the coastal areas. I get hits on them every once in awhile, but most times they don't get into visual range, and they don't have radar. My luck is shit today, though. First you, and now this. If we lay low, they might think we're a derelict that broke free of our moorings. Maybe we won't have to kill anybody."

"Sounds like a good plan."

Duncan opened the door to the cabin. Gus tried to run out, but he pushed the dog back.

"Get inside, you hairy, flea-infested mongrel. Get inside."

They both entered the cabin. Hayden closed the door behind him.

"What's going on?" Natalia asked.

"Grab your rifle," Hayden said. "We may have trouble."

Natalia slid off the bench, scooping up her rifle. Duncan moved past them into the berth, lifting the mattress and

47

pulling out an unfamiliar weapon. It looked like a rifle, but it didn't have a magazine attached.

Duncan flipped a switch, and it hummed to life.

"What is that?" Hayden asked.

"United States Space Force PL90 Mark Two," Duncan said. "Also known as a plasma rifle. The last weapon out of Space Force labs before the fall." He handed it out toward Hayden. "I'm betting you're a better shot than me."

Hayden took it, surprised by the dense weight of the rifle. It had a knob on the side near the handle, and a display with a targeting reticle and potential networked connection, similar to the Marine Corps rifles.

A small indicator suggested it had thirty-eight shots in its current mode, which was a single line on the display.

"Don't shoot at them unless they start shooting at us," Duncan said. "Stay out of sight."

Hayden took it, ducking low and exiting the cabin, under cover as he emerged onto the rear deck. He rested the barrel of the rifle there, sighting through the display at the incoming boats. They were still a few hundred meters away, slowing as they approached. He spotted six people split between the boats, their genders hard to identify through heavy coats that protected them from the cool air.

They were all armed, carrying what looked like cross-bows and harpoon guns. It was nothing that could stand up for what they had on the boat.

"Turn around," he said softly. He didn't want to shoot them. "Turn around."

The boats kept coming, slowing and angling to intercept them as they floated downriver.

"Turn around, damn it," Hayden said. "There's nothing here for you."

Nothing but death.

They didn't turn around. They drew closer, making it within fifteen meters of the boat.

Hayden heard Gus start barking at the same time the scavengers did. He saw them redirect their attention, following the source of the noise. To them, a dog on a boat meant the boat wasn't abandoned.

The scavenger's boats accelerated, adding speed to get closer to them instead of drawing back. One of them fired their crossbow, the arrow hitting the glass ahead of Gus and causing it to break, but not hitting the dog.

"You tried to shoot my grepping dog?" Hayden heard Duncan roar.

He tracked the closer boat, lining up a shot. Instead of targeting the people, he fired on the rear of the craft, intending to disable it.

He felt a wash of heat as a blue-orange bolt launched from the rifle, slamming into the hull a split second later. The side of the boat exploded outward, and then the motor and battery followed, a violent detonation that took Hayden by surprise, and turned their entire vessel sideways.

Hayden fell onto the deck, the force of the explosion knocking him back. He felt the heat of it pass through the air before rolling back over to return to his feet.

The other boat met them on the starboard side, and both vessels rocked as the two craft slammed into one another. Hayden turned to face the first of the scavengers, who was holding a harpoon aimed at his eyes.

The man hesitated to pull the trigger, and it cost him his life. A red dot appeared on his chest, and a bullet followed after, punching through his coat, the force knocking him back over the side and into the water. Crossbow bolts thunked into the wood near the cabin as Duncan emerged, taking quick aim with his pistol and squeezing the trigger.

It was over that fast. All six of the scavengers from Sanctuary were dead, one of their boats destroyed. The other one remained tethered to the side of their craft with a pair of hooks.

"Damn," Duncan said sadly. "Stupid assholes." He lifted one of the bodies, casting it overboard and moving to the next. He lifted that one, too, dumping it over the side. "It didn't have to be this way."

Hayden found the power switch for the rifle, shutting it down. "They didn't give us a choice."

"No," Duncan agreed. "And they shot at Gus. Are you okay, you ratty old beast?" He faced back toward the cabin, where Gus was standing, tongue hanging out of his mouth. He didn't seem impressed by the violence.

"We need to cast off their boat and get the hell out of here," Duncan said. "I wasn't expecting you to blow up their speeder." He laughed. "If there are any others around, they'll be heading this way as we speak."

"You didn't tell me this thing packed such a punch," Hayden replied.

"That's the lowest setting. Try switching it to the highest. The plasma comes out like a grepping flamethrower." He lowered his voice, speaking in an odd rhythm. "Kills hundreds of trife on contact. Not seen in any stores. Order today, and get a free hunting knife. Only ninety-nine, ninety-nine plus shipping and handling." He laughed at Hayden's confusion, clasping his shoulder and squeezing. "I'm going to power up and get us the hell out of here. Nice shooting, Tex."

9

IT WAS APPROACHING NIGHTFALL BY THE TIME THE BOAT finally came ashore again, brushing gently alongside a freshly constructed dock that poked out into the water from a muddy embankment. Duncan jumped from the boat to the dock, expertly tying the vessel off and pulling it to a total stop.

"All ashore that's going ashore, you landlubbers," he shouted.

Hayden opened the door to the cabin, leading the way out.

"You're in a better mood," he said to the scavenger.

"I'm home. It's a start."

Hayden couldn't see anything past the end of the dock, where a small light was providing guidance. The rain was falling heavier than before, hiding the stars that might have allowed more visibility.

"How do you know there aren't any trife waiting for us out there?" he asked, pointing toward the light.

"If there were, Gus would be barking his doggone head

off," Duncan said. "Doggone. Get it?" He laughed. "Gus. Come here, Gus."

The dog trotted out of the cabin to Duncan's side, waiting there patiently.

"See? No troubles. At least not right now."

Hayden stepped out of the boat, onto the dock. He turned to help Natalia off, taking her hand while she climbed out beside him. He offered his hand to Casey, too, but she jumped out on her own.

"I've got it, Sheriff," she said. "But thanks."

"Sheriff?" Duncan said. "Did she say, Sheriff? Like Wyatt Earp? Tombstone?"

"Yes. I was the Sheriff where I'm from."

"Pilgrim?"

"Yes."

"That used to be John Wayne's catchphrase." He changed his voice to do the impersonation. "Whoa, take 'er easy there, Pilgrim." Hayden had seen Stagecoach on the PASS. It was the only John Wayne movie he was familiar with. Duncan sighed when he didn't react. "That was a good impression, Sheriff. I promise."

"I believe you," Hayden said, forcing a smile.

"Bullshit," Duncan replied, laughing again. "Come on."

Duncan started down the dock, with the others trailing behind him. Gus ran ahead, vanishing into the darkness.

"You don't worry about him?" Casey asked.

"He can take care of himself," Duncan replied.

The stocky man led them from the dock to the shore, through the soft ground, and up a short slope. As they neared the end of the small light's ability to guide them, Duncan produced a flashlight, shining it ahead and revealing dense brush split by a worn path through the center. He kept walking, leading them with the light through a hundred meters or so of foliage and into a clearing.

Duncan's place wasn't some tiny shack in the middle of the wilderness. It was a massive house, larger than anything Hayden had ever seen. It was made of brick, wide and tall, with three levels of broken out windows along the back and a split stairwell branching to either side. A heavy, tiled roof perched on top of it, partially coated with a thick layer of moss, each exposed shingle glistening in the wet.

"It isn't much," Duncan said. "But it's dry and warm, and it keeps my collection safe."

The homes' better days were clearly behind it, but that didn't matter. Hayden wasn't planning on staying long.

Gus was waiting for them at the top of the steps, near a wood door that had rotted a long time ago. It hung slightly open, and the dog made his way inside ahead of them, scouting the path. Duncan pushed the door aside, leading them in. He tapped something on the wall, and strings of lights illuminated, bringing the house to life.

The inside wasn't as bad as the outside. Hayden could tell the scavenger had put a lot of work into the home, both in repairing and decorating the space. The interior was clean and decorated with old rugs, chairs, sofas, tables, and lamps. It reminded Hayden of the Governor's Mansion, only more densely appointed.

"Wow," Casey said. "I thought the inside would be as shitty as the outside."

"You should be honored," Duncan said. "You're the first people I've ever let in here. Don't break anything."

They moved through the first room and into the next. This one was overflowing with Duncan's collection. Hundreds of hundreds of boxes were scattered around the floor, each of them near to overflowing with data storage devices, CDs, and smaller electronics. An entire stack of players for the silver discs rested in the corner, next to a pile of thin, long, rectangular blocks.

"You brought all of this stuff back here?" Casey said, her eyes traveling the room.

"This is just the salvage I picked up the last couple of months. I've got more items in the other rooms. I even have some books. If you head out to the garage, there's a pair of old all-terrainers parked in it. The rust-buckets were there when I came across the place, six, seven years ago. Natalia, you got the battery out of the Butcher, maybe you can get them charged and running again?"

"If she can't, I can," Casey said. "Point the way, and I'll take a look."

"I'll come with you," Natalia said. "I don't think anybody should be wandering off alone."

"It's that way," Duncan said, thrusting his finger down a hallway to the left. "I'll send Gus with you, too. He starts barking, you come on back here and lock the door behind you. The trife can get in through the windows, but usually they hear Gus and think there's only a dog in here with the rats and spiders."

"What about the lights?" Hayden asked.

"I don't know. They don't seem to pay attention to them. Or maybe they know someone is in here, but it's too much trouble? I've been here seven years; I've never gotten attacked inside the house."

"What about outside?" Casey asked.

"A few times," Duncan said without going into detail. "Like I told you - if Gus starts barking, you head on back here right away. Sheriff, I want to talk to you about something, if you don't mind."

"Be careful," Hayden said, bringing Natalia close to him. "Please."

"I will," Natalia replied, kissing him. "Don't worry. We have Gus."

Hayden smiled and let her go. She squeezed his hand once before following Casey down the hallway toward the garage.

"Quite a pair you've got there, Sheriff," Duncan said. "Your wife and your daughter."

Hayden opened his mouth to correct him, then decided against it. Maybe it was better if the man thought they were all related?

"What can I help you with?" Hayden asked.

"Follow me."

Duncan led Hayden to a door, opening it to reveal a set of stone steps leading downward. Hayden paused at the top, eying the scavenger suspiciously.

"Oh, come on," Duncan said. "You still don't trust me?"

"Truer words," Hayden said.

"I'll go first," Duncan replied.

He turned on his flashlight, leading Hayden down into a basement. Everything down here was stone, the air damp and cool. It was well-stocked with food, water, and what appeared to be old bottles of wine.

"I always figured if I needed to, I could hide down here for weeks. But that's not what I wanted to show you."

He walked to the end of the open space, to what appeared to be a solid stone wall.

"I lived here three years before I found this," he said, pushing on one of the stones.

The wall slid aside.

"Right?" he said, seeing Hayden's surprise. "This way."

He brought him into a second room. This one was filled with a whole different kind of collection. Satellite photos. Maps. Drawing and notes. Dark displays that the scavenger went over to and turned on.

"What is this?" Hayden said.

Duncan looked at him, a big smile on his face.

"This, my friend, is United States Space Force Western Command Lewis-McChord."

10

"I don't understand?" Hayden said, looking around the room.

"I would have told you sooner, Sheriff," Duncan said. "One: I didn't trust you enough to tell you. Two: I figured it would be easier to show you. I've been to Lewis-McChord once before. Me and my partner went there looking for answers." He paused, looking at the ground. "He didn't make it back out."

"What kind of answers were you looking for?"

"We've been out here quite a while. We mainly scavenged up north, near what used to be the Seattle-Tacoma area. It got hit hard during the war, but it's also been overrun for a long time, so the looting is minimal. If you can avoid the trife, you can find a lot of good stuff up there, and me and my partner were real good at avoiding the trife."

He approached one of the displays. He pulled out a drawer beneath it, revealing an old-fashioned physical keyboard.

"You're probably wondering where the power comes from. The tiles on the roof are solar. There's a big battery down here, too deep and too cool for the trife to notice it. Anyways, one day we were rooting through this lab in downtown Tacoma, and we came across a laptop. That laptop had a storage drive in it, which contained this video."

Duncan hit a key, playing the video on the display. It was a fixed view from the upper corner of what appeared to be a prison of some kind. It had bars all around it, four inches thick. There was a bed in the corner, and a large humanoid sleeping in it.

"Specimen K42," a voice said over the video. "Sample KA-9. Day thirty-three."

The shot lingered on the sleeping humanoid for another ten seconds. Judging by the scale, Hayden guessed it was around three meters tall.

A sharp tone sounded, seeming to wake the creature. It shifted on the bed, coming up to a sitting position.

Hayden's head snapped toward Duncan. "That-"

"I know. Watch."

Hayden returned his attention to the display. A part of the cell opened, and a trife was thrown inside, the door slamming behind it.

The trife hissed, turning and trying to squeeze itself through the bars. The humanoid charged toward it immediately, growling and reaching for it. The trife turned around, slashing with its claws. It cut the humanoid's arm, but it didn't matter. The humanoid opened its mouth. Rows of teeth came into view, right before they sank into the trife's head, biting through the soft bone and into the skull, killing it in an instant. The humanoid dragged the trife to the ground, sitting with it as it started eating. Two seconds later, a pair of cracks sounded, the humanoid's head snapping to the side and spraying blood. It collapsed, too.

"Specimen K42 was damaged," the voice said. "The Specimen is non-viable."

"That video wasn't made in the lab up north," Duncan said before Hayden could find words to try to express what he had just seen. "That video came from Lewis-McChord. I'm damn sure of it."

Hayden stared at the frozen frame of the creature laying on the ground. It was three meters tall, not one hundred, but it looked just like a goliath.

"The Pilgrim had a research lab," he said. "There were bodies in the cells. One of them was enlarged. The Space Force was working on genetically modifying soldiers, to make them big enough and strong enough to balance out the trife. I saw another video of a soldier who was fast and strong. He was non-viable, too."

"I can't say I'm surprised. People out there, they think the goliaths came from space, like the trife. You and me, we know better. The Space Force scientists, they made them from human beings."

"But how? How do you grow a person to that size? That can't be possible."

"Why not? They were growing meat in a lab and selling it in grocery stores. I know, because I've seen the packaging. How is it different than growing meat? That thing on the video, that's just where they started. Where they ran their tests. A scale model." He laughed. "A grepping scale model."

Hayden was surprised when tears formed in Duncan's eyes. The scavenger rubbed at them as he headed to another display.

"That's part one, Sheriff," he said. "Take a look at part two."

He turned on the display and ran another video. This one was lower quality and appeared to have been taken outside. A man was in it. Middle-aged and lean. He was wearing dark clothes, his face hidden by a mask. He had a familiar looking gun in his hand, with a laser sight mounted to the top.

"The video is infrared," Duncan said. "That's why it looks like that."

Hayden watched as the man moved out into a small clearing, split by a rusted, half collapsed fence. He climbed over the lowest portion, heading from the clearing back into the woods after turning back toward the camera.

"We're in," he said.

Duncan leaned forward, tapping the keyboard. The video sped up, showing the man moving through the woods, stopping and dropping on his stomach a few times, the cameraman following suit. One of the times, Hayden caught a glimpse of a group of trife moving through the area.

Duncan kept advancing for what the timer on the video suggested was nearly an hour. Finally, they broke out of the woods again, reaching the side of a hilltop and looking down.

Organized beneath them were trife. Thousands of trife, in rows and columns, standing silently at attention, two distinct types. The ones in the front were larger, like the trife he had seen on the Pilgrim. The other style was smaller, but he could see the wings folded on their backs.

"What does this mean?" Hayden said.

He recognized the army. It had attacked Ports yesterday.

"Something smells rotten," Duncan said. "And Lewis-McChord is at the center of it." The camera kept panning while he spoke, crossing back and forth over the creatures. "You see, Sheriff, I was happy living here with my partner. His name was Jack. Me and Jack, we were best friends. Not lovers. Neither one of us had any use for sex, but companions. Out here, you need someone to watch your back. Human or canine. Anyways, we did this run to Tacoma, up north. We were looking for new movies, maybe some more equipment, food and other supplies. We found our way into this space. It was nearly buried. Just a grepping hole in the ground, really. I don't know what convinced Jack to go in there, other than he fit. If you couldn't guess, I didn't.

"So he goes down there with Gus, and they're gone nearly two hours. He comes back up with that PL90 I handed you, tells me there's a lot more good haul down there, and that he found an active terminal. The last thing on it was a message from Lewis-McChord, begging for help."

Hayden stared at the display, his mind going. "So you went to help them?"

"We went to see what there was to see, yeah. Being a Collector, it's the thrill of the hunt, you know. The drive to discover new things, to uncover secrets, to dig up the past. I brought that camera along. I wanted to record the moment we uncovered a hidden slice of civilization."

He laughed again, but there was no energy behind it. It was a sad laugh. A pained one.

On the display, someone whispered beside the camera. "Drop it."

The camera fell to the ground, laying sideways. Three pairs of booted feet came into view as Jack spun around, surprised. He barely had a chance to open his mouth when they slammed him in the gut with a rifle, knocking him down.

"Jack," Hayden heard Duncan say. "No. Leave him alone."

"Shut up," the voice said near the camera.

"Who are you? We were told to come here. We were told people were in trouble."

"Yeah," the voice said. "Sorry, pal. We tell that to anyone who'll listen."

Hayden's heart was pounding hard in his chest. He felt cold. Completely cold.

On the video, there a growl and the sound of someone being knocked over. Then the camera was scooped up, facing the wrong way, Duncan's face obvious as it shook back and forth. He was running, out of the clearing and back into the woods.

Duncan stopped the video. His face was serious. He had lifted the mask feeding him the nitrous oxide over his head and dropped it on the table, along with the tank on his back.

"I don't know how I made it out of there alive," he said. "I ran until my legs collapsed. I would probably have been eaten by something if Gus hadn't been with me. The video doesn't show it, but those men in it, they were soldiers. They were wearing full Space Force gear, helmets and all."

"You're telling me Lewis-McChord isn't waiting to be rescued?" Hayden said.

"I'm telling you that and more," Duncan replied. "At first, I thought they were just suckering people in. But the more I thought about it, the less likely that seemed. I mean, how many idiots are going to come running to clear out trife and help someone else? Besides you, I guess."

"They drew you in."

"They got Jack. He was always too damn curious, or he would have never gone in that hole. He wanted to know if what he had seen was real. Then those assholes took him, so I started to dig. What you see in this room? It's three years of research. Three years of sweeping every town I could find within fifty miles of Lewis-McChord, and that place is pretty damn big on its own. There used to be people up here, Sheriff. Smaller communities that managed to hide from the trife. Used to be. Until the USSF came along and took them, and brought them back to their base."

"They were experimenting on them?"

"That's my theory. They grabbed the survivors, brought them in, ran their so-called grepping Samples on them, and repeated the process until they got what they wanted."

"The scale model for a goliath."

"At first, yeah. I think the goliaths came from Lewis-McChord."

"But they don't walk up here."

"Nope. I think they were designed or ordered not to."

"Why?"

"Didn't you just watch my video? How can they screw with the trife if the goliaths are munching them all?"

Hayden stared at Duncan, trying to process what the man was saying. He was a Sheriff. It was part of his job description to get to the root of things. To break them down and understand them. To solve the mystery.

"Those trife have been out there for three years?" he asked.

"At least. I don't know if the scientists are making them, or training them, or what. All I know is the leathery bastards were under some sort of control."

"But now they're heading south. I didn't see any soldiers with them."

"Could be they escaped their handlers? I just don't know."

"We were walking right into a trap."

"You were."

Hayden's face flushed, a sudden anger roaring through him.

"Why the fuck didn't you tell me this before we left Ports?" he shouted in Duncan's face. "King is on his way to the Pilgrim, and when he gets there, my people are going to die in the thousands."

Duncan flinched back, retreating. He put his hands up in defense.

"Sheriff, please," he said. "I-"

Hayden didn't let him speak. Why should he? The man had killed the colonists on the Pilgrim. For what?

"You brought us another fucking day out, and there's nothing waiting at Lewis-McChord that's going to help me.

There's nothing but more lying sacks of shit hurting innocent people for their own gain. I can't believe you could be so
fucking selfish that you would do something like that, you
son of a bitch."

"Sheriff," Duncan said, still backing away. "Wait. Please.
Wait."

"You tricked us. You lied to us. You led us here the same
way the Space Force was trying to lead us here. The way they
led your partner here, and then took him from you. You did
the same damn thing they did."

"Sheriff."

Duncan made it to one of the tables, and he reached
down, shifting some of his notes and papers, and finding a
tablet device underneath. He held it up, facing away from
Hayden, tapping it furiously.

"I need your help, Sheriff. I brought you here because I
can't do this on my own, and you made it through that trife
assault alive. I wasn't out there looking for you. I was doing
what I've done for the last three years. Surviving without my
best friend, knowing that he's out there, in the hands of those
assholes, and probably being exposed to who the hell knows
what. When you said you wanted to go to Lewis-McChord?
That was my chance. My one and only chance. The only
opportunity I'll ever have to maybe see Jack again. To either
bring him home or put him out of his misery. Whichever, but
I can't stand the thought of him trapped there. Do you know
what that's like?"

Hayden froze. All of the anger fled from him in an
instant. His hands fell to his sides. His body relaxed. He kept
his eyes on Duncan, his heart starting to slow.

Natalia.

"I do know what that's like," he said softly. "I know
exactly what that's like."

"Then you understand?" Duncan said.

"I do."

"Then you'll help me?"

Hayden didn't answer right away. He did understand, but what about the people on the Pilgrim? What about King? He couldn't abandon them. But how could he still help them?

"I get it," Duncan said. "You want to get back to the Pilgrim. You're a real white hat. I saw that in you with the scavengers from Sanctuary. Don't give up on me, Sheriff. Maybe we can both get what we want."

"How?" Hayden asked.

Duncan turned the tablet around. There was an image on the display. It was taken from a distance, but its nature was undeniable.

"That's a-"

"Starship," Duncan said. "Our civilization isn't as dead as we thought, and the war with whoever sent the trife? It's not over."

Hayden stared at the ship. It was fifteen meters long, half as wide, angled and mean. There were turrets mounted under the wings and at the nose. Three huge thrusters filled the rear.

"What about Earth?" he asked.

"They've given up on Earth, Sheriff."

Just because it was a starship, that didn't mean it had to go to the stars.

"I haven't."

11

"WE WERE GREPPING DUPED?" CASEY SAID.

"Lied to by the United States Space Force," Hayden replied. "Or whatever they might be calling themselves now."

"They're fighting a war in the stars," Natalia said. "And we're the test subjects for potential solutions to defeating the enemy."

"That was my conclusion, too," Duncan said. "Those assholes. They let us stay on the brink of extinction. They use us as tools. It doesn't matter if it helps them win the war in the end, it's just so grepping wrong."

Hayden and Duncan had left his research behind, making the trip from the basement out to the garage. They had found Casey and Natalia there, the pair of ATVs already half-disassembled, parts scattered on the floor. Gus was spread out on the floor nearby, sleeping.

He had explained the situation to them, reiterating everything Duncan had told him. About Jack. About the messages from Lewis-McChord. About the soldiers. They had brought the tablet along, and he showed them the starship.

"What I don't understand is how we went from being

half-dead, to having the resources to build starships in the first place?" Casey said.

"The Pilgrim is a starship," Natalia said.

"It is?" Duncan said.

She nodded. "A colony ship. And there were more than one. What if one of the ships made it somewhere closer to Earth? What if they built their colony, and in time started sending other ships back here? Four hundred years is a long time. Maybe they could do it?"

"They would have to have discovered Warp Drive technology," Duncan said. "Or Hyperdrives. Or used the Force."

"What?" Hayden said.

"From the movies. Faster than light. They would need to have developed faster than light travel."

"That isn't impossible."

"No. Just improbable."

"Which doesn't affect us at all," Casey said. "Not really. We're here. Now. We've got problems of our own, against our own damn kind, not to mention the aliens that are already here."

"Pozz," Hayden said. "Whatever is happening in the greater universe, we have to worry about the present, the people on Earth and the colonists on the Pilgrim. For us, it means we need that ship."

"And someone who can fly it," Duncan said. "Because as smart as we all are, I don't think any of us are qualified."

"You mean turn the tables?" Casey said. "Take one of them for once?"

"Exactly."

"I'm not in favor of kidnapping anyone," Natalia said.

"What are our options?" Hayden said. "We need that ship, which means we need a pilot."

"I know. That doesn't mean I have to like it."

"None of us like it," Duncan said. "If we did, we'd be just like them."

"What about the ATVs?" Hayden asked. "Can you fix them?"

"I can fix anything," Casey said. "It would be easier if we were in Carcity surrounded by raw materials, but I think I can make it work."

"How long?"

"A day?"

"That long?"

"I'll work as fast as I can. I'm good, Sheriff, but I'm not a magician."

"Sheriff, you and me can prepare the supplies in the meantime," Duncan said. "I've got a good stash of weapons and ammo, and some other equipment that could come in handy. I've been planning for this since I lost Jack. I just didn't think I'd ever have the chance to make good on the idea. It means a lot to me that you're helping out, even if it is because you have your own motives."

"We're in this together," Hayden said. "The reasons don't matter, only the outcome." He put his arm around Natalia's shoulders. "How are you feeling?"

"I'm fine," she said, leaning into him. "A little tired. A little hungry. But otherwise, I'm okay." She looked at him. "You're the one that looks like hell. How are you?"

"Better with you here. Better knowing you're safe."

"I wouldn't go that far," Duncan said. "I don't think any of us are safe."

"Compared to the people on the Pilgrim?" Hayden said. "Compared to the people in Sanisco? That army of trife is headed their way. I don't think we'll ever be truly safe, but we're in a better position than they are right now."

"At least we can fight back," Casey said.

Natalia pulled herself away from him. "We need to get to work. We can rest once the ATVs are running."

"Pozz that," Hayden said, kissing her hand. "Keep them safe, Gus."

Gus lifted his head at the sound of his name, and then put it back on the ground and closed his eyes again.

"Useless old bag of fleas," Duncan said.

Hayden left Natalia and Casey a second time, following Duncan to another part of the house, where he revealed a large collection of guns, ammunition, clothing, MREs, transceivers, and other assorted items. They spent the next two hours sorting through it, deciding what to take to optimize their effectiveness. Once that was done, they moved on to the kitchen, where Duncan revealed a large supply of what he called pemmican. At first, Hayden was hesitant about it, but the fact was it hadn't killed the scavenger yet, and after trying it, he decided it was a hell of a lot better than the nutrition bars in Metro.

Then they waited, sitting in the main living space on a pair of old armchairs. Hayden fulfilled their original deal, telling the scavenger all about the Pilgrim, Metro, and how he and Natalia had wound up on the Outside. Telling the story reminded him of the deal he had made with Wiz. Would she honor it when he returned?

Considering how he was hoping to return, he had a feeling she would.

NATALIA AND CASEY CAME IN FROM THE GARAGE FOUR HOURS later, sometime in the middle of the night. They were both dirty and greasy and smelled like old metal, rust, and dirt. Duncan and Hayden had more of the pemmican on a plate waiting for them. Casey picked it up without hesitation, while Natalia eyed it more suspiciously.

"It's good," Hayden said. "Don't worry."

She took a bite. "Not bad. I like bacon better."

"Bacon?" Hayden asked.

"Where did you get bacon?" Duncan said.

"Ghost gave me some," she replied. "And eggs. I don't like eggs."

"I haven't seen a chicken in a long time," Duncan said. "These are made from deer and different berries nearby. The good thing about pemmican is that it lasts forever."

"It'll do," Casey said. "I was starving." She picked up another piece of it. "The ATVs are both running, but we'll need the Butcher's battery to give them a full charge. They should be good for a hundred miles or so."

"That'll get us there," Duncan said. "If you two want to get cleaned up, there's a working shower upstairs. It pulls the water in from a tank outside and gets heated on the way up. One of my few luxuries."

"It sounds perfect right about now," Natalia said.

"A bed would be good, too," Casey said. "I'm beat."

"It doesn't make sense to leave in the middle of the night," Duncan said. "Chains, you can sleep on Jack's mattress. Sheriff, if you and your wife want a little privacy, there's a larger bedroom upstairs. The mattress isn't great, but I'm sure you can make do."

Hayden and Natalia looked at one another.

"That sounds perfect, too," she said. She took a few more pieces of the pemmican. "Chains, do you mind staying dirty for another thirty minutes or so?"

Hayden smiled. With everything they had learned, and with everything they were planning to try to do, he was still happier now than he had been in his entire life. He didn't care what the universe threw at him, as long as he was taking on the challenge with her.

"I've got to go get the battery and charge up the ATVs anyway," Casey said. "Of course, if I didn't like you both so much I think I would puke from all the love."

"Jealous, kid?" Duncan asked.

"Why would I be jealous? I've got Gus." She laughed, patting the dog on his side.

Hayden stood up, walked over to Natalia, and took her hand.

"Up the stairs, turn right, the last door on your left," Duncan said. "The bedroom is two doors down."

"Thanks, Duncan," Hayden said, letting Natalia lead him away.

They went up the stairs and into the bathroom. The shower was small, but that was fine. Hayden unclasped his armor, Natalia helping him out of it when his sore muscles refused to cooperate fully. She stared at the prosthetic as the suit dropped to his waist, tears welling in her eyes.

"You lost your hand for me," she said.

"I would give up both of them, and both my legs for you," he replied. "But don't feel bad for me, Nat." He shook the replacement. "This thing has saved my life more times than I can count."

He continued stripping until he was naked in front of her. She smiled as she started undressing, and Hayden's heart began to race.

"When you called me from Section C. When you told me you found a body. When I came to help you, and you weren't there? I've never been so afraid in my life. Everything that's happened since I left the Pilgrim, none of it has been as frightening as that moment. To be here, now, looking at you in all your beautiful perfection. It's a dream come true." He paused. "I hope I'm not too ugly, now."

"Hayden, you've always been ugly," she replied, getting her lighter armor off her shoulders. "That's not why I love you." She continued to remove the armor, and he moved forward to help pull it over her calves and ankles.

That was when he saw the blood.

"Nat," he said, suddenly worried, old memories making him panic more than he probably needed to. "You're bleeding."

She looked down at her side, her body going stiff.

"Nat?" Hayden repeated. "What is it?"

The tears flowed more freely from her eyes. She reached down to her shirt, pulling it up and over her head, leaving her upper-half naked. Hayden's eyes landed on the bandage there, the blood leaking out through it.

He pulled at it, gently bringing it away from her skin to see the wound beneath.

"Is that a knife wound?" he asked. "Did Ghost?"

"No," she said, interrupting. "It's from a trife. It got me, right through the suit."

"When?" he asked. "I thought-"

"Hayden, I'm sorry," she said. She was sobbing openly now.

He stood up, taking her in his arms, holding her close. He felt his own eyes watering at her fear and pain.

"Nat, it's okay. I told you before. Whatever comes we'll deal with it. I didn't go through all of this to find you, just to turn around and judge you. Whatever it is, I love you."

"Hayden. Damn it. I don't know how to deal with this. It didn't occur to me. It's wrong. Everything is wrong."

She kept crying on his shoulder. He held her as the minutes passed until she calmed enough to speak again.

"The trife attacked Ghost and me outside Ports. It almost got me. That was the night. That was right before I slept with him. Do. Do you know what that means, Hayden? What that has to mean?"

A sudden chill washed over his body. He fought to keep himself steady against her. To support her despite his own powerful emotional response. He was resolved not to let her feel guilty or blame herself.

"I do," he said.

The trife didn't attack her after, but they did attack her before. That meant she wasn't barren, and if she were pregnant, it wasn't his.

"Don't give up on me, Nat. Don't give up on this. I'm not giving up on you. It doesn't matter. Do you hear me? It doesn't matter."

Inside, he tried to convince himself of the words he was saying. He didn't blame her, but damn it was hard to absorb. At least she had consented to it. At least she was doing it to survive. At least she hadn't been attacked. That would have been worse.

"We wanted another chance," he said. "We got the ticket from the Governor. Who knows, maybe I'm shooting blanks by now? I'm an old man."

"I'm older than you," she reminded him.

"It doesn't matter. I mean that, Nat. I love you, and if we're lucky enough to survive the contagion, if we're lucky enough to have this baby, I'm going to love them, too."

"Contagion?" Natalia said. "What do you mean?"

He backed away from her so he could look her in the eye. Hers were bloodshot. Red from her crying. Wet and tired.

"You don't know?" he said.

She shook her head. "Know what?"

"The trife virus. The one that killed ninety percent of Earth's population? Ghost didn't tell you about that?"

"He mentioned it. That was a long time ago."

"Not for us. Not for the people on the Pilgrim."

Her expression changed as she realized the implications.

"Shit," she said, face turning pale. "That's why you're so worried about King getting Inside?"

"That's part of it. A major part. I'm worried about it for us, too. What if I die, and you don't? What if you die, and I don't?"

"How will it affect our baby?" she said.

Hayden smiled, tears running from his cheeks. "You said 'our,'"

She returned the smile. "Why wouldn't I? That's the way it's going to be, isn't it? If you tell me it doesn't matter, I believe you. You've never lied to me before."

"And I never will," he said, taking her in his arms again.

"Maybe it can be cured?" Natalia said. "If the Space Force made the goliaths, maybe they can fix the virus?"

"Maybe," Hayden said. "We'll find out when we get there."

"I love you," she said.

"I love you, too," he replied.

Their eyes met. Then their lips. They didn't have to rush this time. There were no trife coming after them. No Scrappers on the horizon. They hadn't been apart for that long by days, but to Hayden, it felt like forever.

He washed her off, gently and lovingly, and she did the same for him. They laughed and cried together, and held one another under the warm water, letting it wash away all of the dirt and grime, physical and emotional.

"We should give Casey a turn," Natalia suggested, sometime later.

"We should," Hayden agreed.

They abandoned the shower, not bothering to dress to cross the hallway into the bedroom Duncan had mentioned.

The mattress was lousy. Lumpy and barely softer than the floor.

Neither one of them noticed.

13

"WE'RE READY THEN?" DUNCAN SAID, LEANING OVER THE handlebars of his ATV.

Casey was behind him, an arm across his chest, a rifle in her other hand. A pack was loaded onto the rear of the vehicle, strapped down to keep it from becoming dislodged.

"We're ready," Hayden replied.

He had taken the rear position on the vehicle, preferring to let Natalia drive so he could defend. The PL90 plasma rifle was cradled between them, a similar pack on the back of their machine.

They had both traded in the increased protection of the Marine armor for the dark clothes Duncan offered, more suitable for hiding, creeping, climbing, and any other range of motion maneuvers they might need to make. The scavenger had gathered an entire supply of clothes from somewhere to the north and had a full wardrobe to fit nearly any size. Even Casey had agreed to forego her custom stitched leather for the sake of the cause.

"Are you sure Gus will be okay here by himself?" Casey

asked, looking back at the dog. He was sitting near the doorway into the house, wagging his tail.

"He's a filthy stink, but he's also a good guard dog," Duncan replied. "He'll be fine. There are lots of rabbits and squirrels around if he gets hungry." He looked back at Gus. "You be a good boy, and keep an eye on things for me, you got it?"

Gus didn't move.

"See?" Duncan said. "Let's go."

He turned the throttle, putting the electric vehicle in motion, leading them out of the garage. Hayden and Natalia followed behind, getting their first look at the world outside of the house in the daylight.

A large, overgrown lawn was split by broken cement, which they rattled over to a second column of land covered in gravel. They rode down that as well, following it to a small street that had nearly been hidden by the overgrowth of trees and bushes around it, forcing them to duck as they passed underneath.

That road continued for a few kilometers, bypassing a number of other deserted houses arranged on either side of it before joining with another road that was slightly less overtaken. They rode along it for a few more kilometers, the peacefulness of the landscape, the sunlight, and Natalia's presence allowing the ride to almost feel normal.

Hayden held her close, enjoying the smell of her as the breeze ahead blew it back into his nostrils. He appreciated the crisp air, the wind, the birds that crossed overhead. This is what life should have been, on this planet or any other.

He knew it wasn't meant to last, and it didn't.

Duncan had warned them before they left that the route he was taking would be faster, but also more dangerous. If he were alone, and if he had time, he would have stayed on foot and burned the time to cross through more of the wilderness, rather than travel cleared lanes on the ATVs. But he wasn't alone, and they didn't have time. The ATVs could get them to the edge of Lewis-McChord's perimeter in hours instead of days, as long as they could make it past the trife.

They weren't going to make it, though. Not without a fight. They were passing through a smaller town, between two rows of buildings, when the trife emerged. Scouts, who had likely seen them coming and organized to launch the ambush. They didn't have huge numbers. A few dozen. But every encounter, every shot fired, would leave Hayden and the others weakened for the next one.

"Over there," Hayden shouted, pointing toward a stone building near the edge of town.

Duncan adjusted course immediately, turning the ATV and standing slightly as it hit crooked, cement steps, climbing up toward the entrance to the building. The trife changed course, too, aiming to cut them off.

"Natalia, stop," Hayden said.

She didn't question. Their vehicle came to a halt. He jumped off, flicking the switch to turn the plasma rifle on.

"Go," he said.

She looked back at him.

"You can cover me once you get there," he said. "Go."

She took off, scooting toward the steps. Duncan and Casey were already there, the scavenger off the ATV and pushing in the door to the place while she pulled a second rifle from the pack. She carried it up to Duncan, and they took a position in the doorway.

Hayden kept the rifle on the same setting as before, backing up toward the building, taking his time to aim. The trife had separated some, giving them a wider field to fire into. He got the first in his reticle and pulled the trigger, the orange-blue bolt zipping across the street and through the creature. He quickly targeted the second, starting to move laterally. That one died too, getting the attention of the other demons.

He picked the small black transceiver Duncan had given him from his hip.

"I'm going to lead them east. Pick them off as they follow."

"Pozz," Duncan said.

Hayden stopped shooting, turning and running. The trife hissed and charged behind him, gathering together more in their pursuit. He stopped and fired on them again, killing a third, keeping them tracking what they believed was the biggest threat. He ran again, hopping onto the first step of the building where the others were holed up, racing horizontally across it.

The trife reached the same area. Pop. Pop. Pop. Pop. The bullets hailed down on them, three rifles firing single shots in unison. Trife fell at his back.

He stopped and turned again. There were still some left, and they began to turn, to rush toward the top of the steps and the others. He turned the toggle on the plasma rifle, to a graphic of a wide arc. He pulled the trigger, watching in surprise as a gout of superheated gas poured out from the weapon, the range and angle more than enough to engulf the remaining trife. They hissed and burned, their darkened husks tumbling to the ground.

He let go of the trigger. He checked the display. Instead of a count, it read '4s.' He assumed that meant it could fire that way for another four seconds. He switched it back to the first setting, and the number changed to 15. He had used a lot of the weapon's munitions for that short burst.

He ran up the steps to where the others were already returning to the ATVs.

"Some weapon, eh, Sheriff?" Duncan said. "Careful you don't burn through all the ammo."

"You should have told me that sooner," Hayden said. "I wouldn't have wasted it."

"We made quick work of them," Casey said. "Good shooting, Natalia."

"I'm not sure I hit anything," Natalia said.

"It doesn't matter, we're clear," Hayden replied.

"Good thinking to get them bunched back up like that," Duncan said. "What made you think of that?"

"They like chasing me. I don't know why."

"They must know you're the law." He laughed. "Not a bad first effort all around. I think our odds of pulling this off went up from zero to maybe a third of a percent." He laughed again.

"We're going to do this," Hayden said. "We don't have a choice not to."

He climbed onto the ATV behind Natalia, kissing her on the cheek. "Thanks for trusting me enough to leave me out there on my own."

"I believe in you, Hayden," she replied. "I believe in us, and in this."

Duncan pulled out again, bouncing back down the stairs and into the road. Once more, they followed behind.

A dozen meters away, a small drone lifted from behind cover, rising a hundred meters into the air and trailing behind them unseen.

14

"FASTER, NAT!"

The ATV zipped forward as Natalia gave the machine a little more throttle. Hayden used his free hand to grip her a little tighter, the mechanical strength causing her to gasp as it pressed too hard into her ribs.

"Ease off, Hayden," she said, getting him to loosen up.

He kept his eyes on the road behind them, where a mass of trife were scampering along the broken street at their backs, continuing to give chase.

They had come upon the sunbathing creatures by accident, taking a wide path around a narrow stream whose bridge had collapsed a long time ago. They had to find a spot in the creek that wasn't too deep to cross over, and that search had led them out of a thicket and into a clearing where the demons were soaking up radiation, refueling in preparation for their reproductive cycle.

The trife had spotted them and immediately rose to give chase, a group at least a thousand strong that almost had them completely ensnared. He had already used up the last of the plasma ammunition to keep them honest at their backs, and now he was leaning back, trying to grab something from the back on the rear of the vehicle to defend them with.

Casey still had her rifle, and she continued to fire behind them, in short bursts of two or three rounds at specific targets. Her aim wasn't the best on the back of a moving vehicle, but there were so many of the demons it was hard to miss completely.

"Hayden, hold on!" Natalia shouted in warning.

He turned back forward just in time to balance himself for a sudden turn, the rear end of the ATV sliding out along the dirt as they made a quick change in direction. Another group of trife was charging them from the north, cutting off their escape.

Duncan accelerated ahead, getting in position to lead them. Casey was reaching into their pack, grabbing for a fresh magazine. She removed the empty one and threw it back toward the trife.

Hayden spun back again, managing to push the PL90 into the pack and grab a pistol instead. His arm was flailing all over the place as they bounced over rough terrain, so he saved the ammo and focused on not falling off.

The ATVs roared over the landscape, the trife closing in from the rear and the side. They must have been from the same group because they didn't attack one another as they merged, instead forming a larger, denser mass that nearly had them choked off.

"Follow my lead!" Duncan shouted.

Natalia flashed him a quick thumbs up, and then nearly collided with him as he spun the ATV completely around, coming to a sudden stop facing the demons.

"Is he crazy?" she said, at the same time she turned their ride around.

"Chains, Sheriff, I'm trusting your aim," Duncan said from his vehicle. "Don't let me down."

Then he took off, charging right into the swarm.

"He's crazy," Natalia confirmed, right before accelerating to join him.

Hayden stood slightly on the back of the vehicle, resting his gun hand on Natalia's shoulder and using it to steady his aim. They were rapidly approaching the trife, tearing toward them, drawing sharper hisses as they neared.

A demon dove at them from the left, and he shifted his pistol, firing and hitting it in the thigh, the force just enough to knock it away. He pivoted again, adjusting the weapon forward, firing three rounds into oncoming traffic, hitting a trife and sending it tumbling to the ground.

Casey fired into the masses, her finger steady on the trigger, a spray of rounds that cut them down one after another. Duncan was tense on the controls in front of her, cursing loudly at the trife as he prepared to dive into their midst.

"Come on you grepping bastards!" he cried. "I'm not dying today!"

The trife cleared a path around him as he barreled through, not willing to get crushed to stop the vehicle. They reached out for him as they passed, claws extended, aiming to cut him to ribbons.

Casey swung around, letting the rifle fall away as she drew a pair of pistols from her lap, firing into both sides of the mess, knocking the demons away one after another.

Hayden and Natalia poured in behind them, riding right on their tail, close enough that if Duncan crashed they would crash too. Hayden added his fire to Casey's, at the same time holding the ATV tight between his legs and letting go of Natalia, extending the claws of his replacement and slashing it toward any appendages that came too close.

They whipped through the line, punching out the other side within seconds, forcing the trife to stop and change their momentum and putting fresh distance between them. Hayden retracted the claws, grabbing onto Natalia again as they hit a rise in the terrain and bounced over it, the ATV losing the ground. They came down hard, the vehicle rocking on its wheels and nearly tipping before they got it settled.

Duncan was gaining ground ahead of them, leading them toward a line of trees in the distance. They chased along behind him, still keeping an eye on the trife at their backs.

Some were still giving chase, but most had given up now that they were behind, not finding the small group of humans worth sacrificing the reproductive cycle over.

They continued to add distance between themselves and the trife, slowing slightly as they reached the trees to navigate more cleanly through. Duncan led them on a winding path into the woods, cutting across piles of dead leaves and shorter vegetation, bouncing over roots and leading them back toward the north.

They broke loose of the treeline, coming out beside the road and their original path when Duncan's ATV came to a sudden stop, almost causing Natalia to collide with him a second time.

Hayden opened his mouth to yell at him to be more careful.

Then he saw why the man had stopped.

There was something in the road ahead of them, big and boxy and armored, a huge eagle and star logo emblazoned on the side. A half-dozen soldiers were arranged around it, positioned across the roadway. Each one of them was wearing dark armor like nothing Hayden had seen before. Each one of them was holding a big, mean rifle, trained on the two ATVs.

"Shit," Duncan said, slowly raising his hands.

Hayden stared at the soldiers for a moment before following suit.

They had intended to go to Lewis-McChord.

It seemed Lewis-McChord had come to them.

15

ONE OF THE SOLDIERS RAN FORWARD, CLOSING THE GAP between them and the blockade. They tapped the side of their helmet, and when they spoke their voice was loud and clear, amplified to reach them.

"Don't just stand there, lollies," the man said. "Get the hell in the truck, or we're all going to be trife food in the next thirty seconds."

Duncan looked back at Hayden, confused. Hayden didn't understand it either. He could hear the trife behind them though, hissing and regaining the idea that they could kill the humans.

"You want to die, you sit there and wait to die, but this train is leaving the station, right now!"

The soldier turned his back on them, walking purposefully toward the truck.

"Hayden?" Natalia said, glancing back at him.

Hayden looked at the trife. They were gaining momentum, resuming the chase.

A crack from the top of the armored truck and one of them fell.

"I don't understand it either," he said. "But we can't stay here, and they haven't tried to take our guns."

She nodded and climbed off the ATV. Hayden did the same, handing her the PL90 and unlashing the pack from the vehicle. Duncan and Casey followed his lead, quickly gathering their gear. Six more rounds lashed out from the soldiers, cutting down another group of trife.

"Pick up the pace, lollies!" the lead soldier shouted, not even bothering to turn around.

Duncan and Casey started to run, Hayden and Natalia right behind them. The sound of the trife horde was getting louder, the masses heading their way.

They reached the side of the truck, the soldiers around them changing formation and closing in on the vehicle, pausing every few steps to fire on the trife. Every round produced a kill, each one perfectly placed. There was no fear in their movements. No hurry. They weren't like the Scrappers.

They were real soldiers.

The four of them reached the other side of the truck. A heavy door was open there, the leader standing in the frame. He had already removed his helmet, revealing an older man with salt and pepper hair, a nasty gash along his cheek that nearly mirrored the one Hayden had received.

"Come on in, lollis. Mi casa e su casa."

He moved aside, allowing them into the truck.

"Let's go, team!" he shouted, getting the attention of the soldiers. They broke positions, slipping behind the truck, reaching the door and climbing in, one after another. The soldier on the rooftop was last, swinging down on muscular arms, grabbing the door and slamming it closed behind him, only moments before a trife crashed into it.

"Move out, Sixteen!" the leader said.

The truck groaned and then started to move. Hayden

looked down the length of it. A long column, with benches on either side. The soldiers grabbed their spots, sitting tight against the sides. A cockpit up front, where another soldier was behind a large wheel, driving the vehicle. Past them, a thick windshield, trife jumping up to it and scraping their claws against it. Their sharp fingers skipped off the transparency, unable to make it through.

The truck shook as it bounced back onto the road, catching trife with the grill, knocking them down and crushing them beneath its wheels. The horde was coming at it from the side, the demons hitting it from the left, one after another, rocking it with each blow.

"Fuckers are trying to knock her over," the lead said. He looked back at Hayden. "Can you believe that? Rico, do something about that, will you?"

One of the soldiers reached under the bench, pulling out a laptop. She opened it up, a pair of small thumbsticks popping up as she did. She put her fingers on it, making delicate movements despite the action of the truck.

"Fire in the hole!" she said, tapping on the base of the laptop.

Hayden heard the whistle outside, and then the thump of the explosion. The truck rocked once, a little harder, before settling, the trife attacking it eliminated.

"Nice shooting, Rico!" the soldier behind him shouted, slapping the woman on the shoulder.

The truck sped along the road, free and clear of the creatures. The leader positioned himself in front of Hayden, his eyes falling on the scar on his cheek. He smiled, producing a row of clean, straight white teeth.

"Name's Sergeant Bennett," he said, putting out his hand. "And you are?"

"Duke," Hayden said, meeting Bennett's gaze. "Sheriff Hayden Duke. Are you from Lewis-McChord?"

Bennett nodded. "We were. Scout Team Seven."

"Hoo-rah!" the soldiers behind him shouted.

"Sheriff," Bennett said. "That's an antiquated term, isn't it? A man of the law. It's been a long time since anyone's used that title. Hell, it's been a long time since there's been any law anywhere outside Lewis-McChord, and that's Space Force law."

"Hoo-rah!" the soldiers shouted again.

"What do you mean were?" Duncan asked.

His voice was shaky. He was nervous about being in the truck. Nervous about being with these soldiers. Hayden wasn't comfortable either, but he was doing a better job of hiding it.

What the hell was going on here?

"Were," Bennett said. "Past tense. How'd you hear about Lewis-McChord, anyhow, Sheriff? We aren't exactly common knowledge to the outside world. Keep a low profile, and all that shit."

"We were in Ports," Natalia said. "Were we talking to you?"

Bennett's smile faded in a hurry. His eyes locked on Natalia. "Ports," he said coldly. "You were in Ports?"

"Two days ago. Someone from Lewis-McChord told me you were in trouble. That you were locked down by the trife. But that doesn't seem to be true."

Bennett stared at her. His face was stone, his expression flat. Hayden reached out, putting his hand on Natalia's shoulder. He couldn't have cut the sudden tension in the air with his claws.

He glanced at Duncan. The scavenger was shaking, his hand on the pistol hidden beneath his robes. The soldiers hadn't taken their weapons. They hadn't made a move for their packs. They didn't now, either. They weren't worried about the four of them. They weren't threatened by anything they might try to do. Why should they be? They were armed and armored and trained to be warriors. Trained to kill trife. Trained to kill who knew what else.

Bennett started to laugh.

It was rough and deep and choppy. A hard coughing chuckle that only made the tension worse. The smile returned to his face, and he shook his head.

"Fucking-A," he said, looking at them. "That bitch is still alive."

"Who?" Casey asked.

"We call her Doctor Frankenstein," Bennett said. "She did this. She screwed this whole thing up. The whole damn war, with her stupid ideas. Control the damn trife? You can't control the damn trife. You can't keep a virus in line by subduing it. It needs to be eradicated. Shit." He turned, punching the wall beside them. "Son of a bitch."

Hayden stared at the soldier. None of them knew what he was talking about.

"Jack," Duncan said. "My partner's name was Jack. He was captured at Lewis-McChord, three years ago. You sent us a message. You told us to come. Do you know anything about that?" His voice raised in volume as he spoke, the anger coming out past the fear.

Bennet turned back to Duncan, unconcerned with his tone of voice.

"Three years, lolli? Three fucking years? Do you have any idea how many of you Doc Frank's had us collect in the last three years? This is war, lolli. War like you've never seen it before. War like nothing your uneducated ass is even capable of understanding." Bennett paused, shaking his head. "It doesn't matter anyway." He turned to look at Natalia. "She wasn't lying to you, ma'am. Oh, she's lied before. I think ninety percent of the words out of her mouth are lies. That's her typical M.O. But not this time.

"Lewis-McChord is gone. The trife Doc Frankenstein thought she had under her control? She didn't have shit. They destroyed everything. The only reason we're still alive is because we were out on patrol. We were the lucky ones if you can call it that. And the poor bastards to the south? They're completely fucked."

"What do you mean?" Hayden asked. "What did you do?" He stared at the soldier, his anger building. "What the hell did you do?"

Bennett started laughing again.

"We made monsters, Sheriff. Monsters to fight monsters. Monsters to kill monsters. Those trife are heading south to test themselves, the way Doc Frankenstein taught them to do. They're heading south to kill the goliaths and anything else that gets in their way."

16

"So," Casey asked, breaking the tense seconds of silence that followed the Sergeant's statement. "Are we prisoners?"

Bennett glanced over at her. He licked his lips and shook his head slightly.

"Damned if even I know what you are," he replied. "We've been tracking you since you wiped out that group of trife a hundred klicks back." He pointed at the sky. "Drone. You know how to kill trife, and that's exactly the kind of people we're looking for. Lewis-McChord fell two weeks ago. We went back to take a look-see, but not all of the trife went south. They left a guard there to keep the place quiet. I guess they don't like being experimented on."

"Neither do people," Duncan said. "But that never bothered you, did it?"

"Lots of things bother me, lolli. But I keep my mouth shut and follow orders. That's what Spacers are born and bred to do."

"You keep calling us 'lolli,'" Natalia said. "What does it mean?"

"Lolli," Rico said while the other soldiers laughed. "Short

for lollipop. Because you stand stick straight in one place while the trife come to eat you up like candy."

Bennett smiled. "Maybe that isn't fair to you four. You made it within twenty klicks of home base without dying."

"We would have made it further if you hadn't been blocking the road," Duncan said.

"Look, I get it," Bennett said. "Doc Frankenstein took your friend, and you're pissed about it. Hell, I would be, too. You were heading to Lewis-McChord to do what? Rescue him? I don't want to be the bearer of bad news, but your friend is long gone. The people we took, they didn't survive more than a few weeks at best."

Duncan's face paled, and he slumped to the floor. "Son of a bitch," he said, lowering his head into his hands. Casey knelt beside him, putting her arms around his shoulders. "I don't understand any of this," he cried.

"If we aren't prisoners, then what are we?" Hayden asked.

"I don't know. Recruits, maybe? We've scouted the base, but we're only one squad, and we can't carry enough firepower to get back in."

"Scout Team Seven," Natalia said. "What happened to One through Six?"

"Dead, I think. We've been trying to raise someone for the last week. All we get is dead air. We don't have a hardlined network link in the truck like the Spacer bunkers do. If Command thinks we're offline, they might not send back a resupply."

"Resupply?" Hayden said. "From where?"

Bennett didn't answer right away. It was clear he was weighing his options. His hand rose to his cheek, absently feeling the line of the scar. Was their shared wound going to be the tie that bound them?

"Sixteen, find somewhere quiet to park the truck," Bennett shouted to the driver.

"Yes, sir!" he replied.

"I think we need to have a little history lesson. Both of us. In the meantime, let me introduce you to my squad." He turned to face the length of the truck.

"You already know Rico." She waved with a gloved hand. "The mug next to her is Killroy." He moved his finger to the other side. "Shelby and Hot Dog. And the tour guide is Sixteen."

"Hoo-rah!" they shouted.

"Your turn, Sheriff."

Hayden motioned to Natalia. "This is my wife, Natalia. That's Duncan and Chains."

"Chains?" Bennett said. "You have a Spacer's call sign. Why do they call you Chains?"

"It was more self-explanatory before," she said.

"Brace!" Sixteen shouted.

Bennett reached up, holding himself against the roof of the truck. Hayden figured it would be a good idea to do the same, planting his replacement against the ceiling. Natalia and Casey grabbed onto the nearest wall right before the truck bounced hard, shaking everybody up and sending Duncan crashing against the side.

He sat up, clutching at his shoulder, giving Bennett a dirty look.

"When Sixteen says, brace, you damn well better brace, lolli," Bennett said in response.

The truck rumbled to a stop.

"Rico?" Bennett said.

"We're clear, Sarge," she replied.

"Plant the drone for recharge," he said. "Killroy, you're on guard."

"Yes, sir," Killroy said.

"The rest of you buckets gather your shit and get the hell

out of my truck. I want to talk to this group in private. You see a bug; you kill it dead."

"Yes, sir!" they replied.

Killroy opened the heavy door, tossed his rifle onto the roof, and then pulled himself up after it. The other soldiers in Scout Team Seven abandoned the truck, ranging out around it.

Hayden looked out through the windshield. They had stopped in an open area on the other side of a small stream, putting some water between them and the trife just in case they had kept following.

Once they were out, Bennett pulled the door closed. The moment he had, Duncan sprang up, pistol in hand, pointing it at the Sergeant.

"That was a stupid move," Duncan said. "I'm going to-"

Bennett moved faster than Hayden could believe, stepping forward and slapping the weapon from Duncan's hand before he even had time to pull the trigger. He spun around the large man, quickly bringing him into a tight choke hold.

"Do you think trife are the only thing that's been modified over the years?" he said. "I could break your fucking neck before you could blink, lolli." He shifted his grip, shoving Duncan forward and into the door. "That's your one and only warning."

"How many trife are still loitering at Lewis-McChord that you need our help?" Casey asked.

"I didn't say I needed your help. I said we could use a few extra bodies. I'd rather not risk my squad if I don't have to."

"You mean you'd rather risk us?" Natalia asked.

"In a sense."

"You said we needed a history lesson?" Hayden said.

Bennett nodded. "You start, Sheriff. I want to know who you are, and where you came from."

"You already know that," Hayden replied. "Sheriff Hayden Duke. We came up from the south."

"That's cute, really. And I'm in the mood for obtuse answers." He stared at Hayden.

"The Pilgrim," Hayden said. "Have you heard of it?"

Bennett nodded again. "Eight ships, Sheriff. That's how many we had. Five of them made it. Three didn't. The Pilgrim and the Dove on the West Coast. The Freedom on the East. The Chinese got three out. The Russians, seven. The Japanese two. Koreans, one. India got fucked. Or so the history goes. But, our history says that the Pilgrim was over-run, all souls lost. You're telling me that isn't true?"

"It isn't true. Metro is alive and well inside the ship. Fifty-thousand of us."

"Do they know they never left Earth?" Bennett asked.

"No."

He laughed. Hayden was getting used to that.

"It's better off that way, isn't it, Sheriff? So what exactly are you doing here?"

"One of the secured hatches glitched," Natalia said. "It opened. The trife and the Scrappers were waiting."

"Shit," Bennett said. "That's a raw deal. Let me guess, they grabbed you, and your action hero husband came after you?"

"Yes."

Bennett clapped his hand on Hayden's shoulder. "You are a bad man, aren't you, Sheriff? Or maybe a good man, depending on how you use the words. You'd make a great Spacer."

"Do you know about King and the Scrappers?" Hayden asked.

"Some. We've got limited satellite access, so we keep an eye on things around the globe."

"How does it look?"

"About as good as it probably feels."

"King brought Nat to Ports to access the Space Force mainframe. He got access to the master code."

Bennett's left eyebrow went up. "You're shitting me?"

"No. He has it. He's going to use it to get into the Pilgrim. He wants the equipment there."

"Son of a bitch."

Bennett didn't look happy about that. At all.

"What?" Natalia asked.

"The master code hasn't changed. It can't be changed. If he uses it to get access to the Pilgrim, he'll get access to everything."

"I know."

"No, you don't know. I'm not just talking about your hidden city. I'm talking about the entire Spacer network. All of the communications. All of the positions. Everything."

"He already has the positions," Natalia said. "It was part of the terminal output at Datalink Portland."

Bennett looked even less happy.

"Why does it matter?" Hayden said. "What harm can he do?"

"Maybe none. But the potential is there, and we don't like loose ends. Fucking data scientists, they never should have given up that intel. They were convinced all hope was lost."

"I think you need to give us your side of the story, Sergeant," Hayden said. "Unless you're planning on killing us now that you have ours?"

"I'm not going to kill you. We don't kill our own, and the citizens of the Pilgrim are our own."

"And the citizens of Earth aren't?" Duncan asked. "Because collecting them for experiments is the same thing."

"Are you going to keep droning on about this?" Bennett asked. "Because I don't need it, especially now. If you want to be part of this, shut your mouth. Otherwise, get lost."

Duncan stared at him but didn't move.

"Earth isn't our planet anymore," Bennett said. "Which means that no, you aren't one of ours."

"Aren't you from Earth?" Natalia asked. "The people at Lewis-McChord?"

Bennett looked at her and shook his head.

"No ma'am."

"WHAT DO YOU MEAN, 'NO MA'AM?'" NATALIA SAID.

"History lesson," Bennett replied. "You want to sit?" He waved to the empty benches.

Hayden moved to the bench to sit. Natalia joined him. Casey and Duncan took the other side, while Bennett stood over them like a schoolteacher.

"I'll give you the quick and dirty version, as I remember it from my schooling," Bennett said. "Somebody sent the trife to destroy us. We fought them. We lost. We built a bunch of ships. Generation ships. They were supposed to go to different places, far enough away that with any luck, the assholes who sent the trife wouldn't find us. But the governments of the world came together last minute and decided to redirect all of the ships to the same place instead. Proxima Centauri. Four light years away."

"Twenty-four years to reach it at the Pilgrim's maximum velocity," Natalia said.

"That's right," Bennett said. "What are you, an Engineer?"

"Yes."

"I should have guessed. You have that look about you."

"What look?"

"Like you know more than everybody else, but you're smart enough to pretend to be humble."

"I don't know more than anybody else, and I'm not pretending."

"See? There it is." He smiled. "Where was I? Oh yeah. So here we had seventeen ships, with an average colony size of forty-three thousand. That's close to a million folks on this new world, plus plenty of tools to start colonies there. So we did. Fast-forward two hundred years. We reproduced and expanded into a colony one hundred million strong. We figured out how to fold spacetime. We started building a war machine."

"Against who?" Hayden asked.

"Therein lies the problem," Bennett said. "We don't know."

"I'm confused," Casey said.

"About we don't know? We know somebody sent the trife. They're too perfectly engineered to be an accident. We know they have to be out there, somewhere. We've got ships looking for them. Scouts."

"And you decided to come back to Earth and hang out in secret instead of helping the people here?" Hayden asked.

"Yes and no. Lewis-McChord has been occupied by Space Force personnel since the war started. They were the ones working on what they called the Goliath Protocols as a means to keep the trife under control until they could figure something else out. They had a city, too, like the Pilgrim. It's all underground. All self-contained. Most of it's empty nowadays. We have a crew of science-types and a crew of soldiers, and that's it. But that's where the tech for your Metro originated. We had to keep it secret though. Could you imagine how many people would have come up north to escape the trife?"

"Maybe because they were killing us?" Casey said.

Bennett put up his hands. "I get it, kid. I do. But let me finish my lesson, and then we can do Q and A, okay?"

Casey sat back, understandably angry.

"So, from what I understand, the Spacers at Lewis-McChord were working on a solution, first to neutralize the trife, and then to destroy them. They produced the goliaths and set them loose on the world. Only they fucked something up because the big guys think people are trife, too. The original scientists, they thought it was a terrible mistake. But the powers that be? They saw it as an opportunity."

"To fight fire with fire," Natalia said. "To create killing machines of their own."

"Bingo," Bennett said. "You'd make a good Officer. When we came back to Earth, we saw what it had become. A wasteland, where the trife were the dominant species, the goliaths were holding their own, and humans had wasted the last hundreds of years fucking each other over, instead of trying to come together to survive. Back on Proxima, you've got people who used to come from all over the world living and working and loving together. We've got our own set of problems, but we managed to unite over our common enemy, and rebuild our civilization."

"Wait a minute," Casey said.

"I told you, kid-"

"No. Shut the grep up for a second. You're telling me you assholes made a conscious decision to abandon us?"

"Not abandon us," Duncan said. "Use us."

"To grepping use us?" Casey said. "You could have kept fighting the trife, but instead you've been stealing innocent people and experimenting on them? Who the hell is the real monster here?"

"Chains," Hayden said.

"No. Damn it, Sheriff. Do you have any idea what I've

been through? What so many people here have been through? You left us behind and then when you were strong enough to return, you come back and treat us like we don't matter? Like we're more like the trife. Like we're not even the same grepping species as you?"

"You aren't," Bennett said, flatly. "You aren't the same species."

"How can you say that?" she shouted.

"We're at war, kid. Against an enemy we don't know. An enemy we can't find. What we do know, is that they know Earth is here. Let's just theorize that we did come back. We spent all our resources driving the trife back off the planet, and then tons more resources trying to rebuild and return some sense of order to this place. The enemy sees this, and then what? Maybe they send more trife. Maybe they send something even worse. Or maybe they just have another virus to throw at us, and wipe out ninety percent again? How does that help anybody?"

"But we're humans, too," Casey said. "We're your people that you left behind."

"The colonists on the Pilgrim, yes. The rest of you? No. You've regressed into something else. Maybe it was the trife that caused it, but it happened all the same."

Casey opened her mouth to argue again but decided against it. Knowing her experience, could she convince Bennett or even herself that her community was civilized?

"You have a responsibility to the people you abandoned," Hayden said.

"You don't even know this so-called enemy will ever come back," Natalia said. "Or if they exist at all. You claim someone sent the trife, but you can't find them. How can you be sure they're still around?"

"I can't answer that," Bennett said. "Look, I understand why you're pissed. I don't make the decisions. I follow orders. I'm telling you what I know. What they taught me in school and during basic. We'd be inhuman to say we don't feel compassion for Earthers, but the bigger threat is still out there, and it doesn't make sense to sacrifice what we've rebuilt."

They fell into a prolonged silence. There was nothing to say and at the same time too many things to say. Hayden sat with the new information, trying to process it in with everything else. But he didn't need logic to know what was right. What the Space Force was doing? That wasn't right.

"Let me try to sum this up," he said. "The colonists on the Pilgrim don't even know they're on Earth. They're unaware, and they're in danger. That danger comes from a man named King, who happens to think he's a god and has an intention of subverting the survivors of this world to his rule. Which wouldn't be terrible overall, except he's a selfish despot who uses the darkest, most violent part of society to control the weak. And then we have the escaped trife, an army of them in the thousands, that are making their way south to prove their mettle against the goliaths, who are also going to kill as many humans as they find on the way. Finally, we have the Space Force base at Lewis-McChord, which those same trife destroyed and left in a currently unknown state. Is that about right?"

"Sounds right to me, Sheriff," Bennett said.

"That's right," Natalia agreed.

"Here's what I'm thinking. Sergeant, you said the people on the Pilgrim are in essence honorary, what do you call yourselves?"

"Centurions," he said.

"Honorary Centurions. That means they deserve your protection, does it not?"

"As far as I'm concerned, it does."

"But even if we take this truck south right now, it'll take

how long to get back to the Pilgrim?" Hayden asked. "Chains?"

"It depends on the average speed, but no less than a day or two."

"Which will put us three days behind King. I can only imagine what he and the Scrappers can do to the Pilgrim in three days."

"You want to get back into your base, right Sergeant?"

"I do."

"We want a faster trip south. You have starships, don't you?"

"A starship, Sheriff. One. Assuming the trife didn't tear it to shreds."

"Would they know what it is to attack it?"

"Probably not. How do you know about it?"

"Recon," Duncan said. "I've been watching you for years. I saw what you bastards were doing."

Bennett ignored him. "You're suggesting we work together to reclaim the base, and then I give you a ride south to the Pilgrim?"

"And help us defend it," Hayden said.

"And then?"

"And then we stop the trife."

Bennett shook his head. "I can't do that."

"Can't or won't?"

"Protecting the Pilgrim is one thing, Sheriff. I can make that fall inside of my operational scope. Protecting the Earthers? That's something else."

"Are you grepping kidding me?" Casey said. "Do you even hear yourself speak? You created those trife. You made them better killers. You won't take responsibility for that?"

"I agree Doc Frankenstein shouldn't have tried to control them. It's her fuck-up for making the effort when she should have been focusing on extending the Goliath Protocols. A fuck-up one that's going to have seismic effects for the Earthers and our test programs."

"Test programs?" Hayden said.

"What do you think Earth is now, Sheriff?" Bennett said. "It's a test bed. A massive petri dish. It's where we come to try new ideas to do what your wife said: Fight fire with fire. I told Frankenstein the trife idea was one of her worst, but she followed through regardless."

"And now innocent people are going to die," Casey said.

"Innocent people have already died," Duncan said.

"That's what happens in war," Bennett replied.

"You can't hide behind that, Sergeant," Natalia said. "Not when it's staring you in the face."

"I can, and I will." He bit his lip, his stoned face breaking for the first time, his expression suddenly pained. "I have to. I can't live with myself any other way. None of us can."

"Then do something about it," Hayden said. "This one time. I'm not asking you to try to change the whole world, but at least give these people a chance. Take responsibility for the monsters you created. Help us save the Pilgrim and then help us save more innocent lives. Please."

Bennett stared at him, their eyes meeting. He traced the scar on his cheek with his finger again. Then he nodded.

"I'm not making any promises, Sheriff. But I'm not saying no. We restore order at Western Command, we cut off the Scrappers at the Pilgrim, and we figure it out from there. That's the best I can do right now. Deal?"

"Deal."

18

The truck stopped a second time, two kilometers from the central access road to enter Lewis-McChord proper. At that stop, Bennett and Killjoy dug through a locker and produced a fresh set of body armor for Natalia, fresh charges for Hayden's PL90, and advanced weaponry for everyone else.

"Be careful with these," Bennett had warned them. "Whatever you think of Earther society, they aren't ready to handle technology like this."

Hayden had gripped one of the laser rifles before passing it to Casey. It was lighter than anything he had held before, and fit his grip almost perfectly. She had said the same thing when she took it from him, before marveling that it carried nearly two hundred shots.

How could it be that the Spacers couldn't defeat the trife? With firepower like this, why were they bothering to try to change the demons into their weapons or create new kinds of monsters instead?

He had a feeling he knew the answer:

Fear.

Fear of an enemy they had never met, and couldn't get a read on. Fear of the possibility that if they did meet, not matter what they did, they would find themselves completely outclassed and quickly dead.

Fear of the unknown.

He understood that fear. In some ways, he had felt it the moment he stepped out from behind the secured hatch, leaving Metro behind and entering a brand new world. He had felt it again when he emerged from the Pilgrim, and then from the structure leading out into the world when he had seen a goliath for the first time.

He had good reason to be afraid. Fear helped him stay alive. It made him cautious. It made him alert.

Would it help the Centurions, too?

It wasn't helping the people of Earth. Not so far, anyway. The Centurions didn't want to get involved again, their fear of losing the planet a second time overriding their sense. Could he convince Bennett to forgo his mission directives to do the right thing?

He wanted to believe he could.

They were armed and ready when the truck stopped a third time. They had already passed through the gate at the perimeter of the base, or at least where the gate had once been. The entire thing had been trampled into the ground by the trife horde, knocked down and destroyed and left behind. Through the windshield up ahead, Hayden could see the remains of large buildings, many of them smoldering and wrecked. There were bodies strewn around as well, both human and trife, though he didn't see anything living up ahead.

"All right, Squad!" Bennett said, speaking out loud for their benefit.

Scout Team Seven had intercoms in their helmets and didn't need external sound. But there were no helmets for the four of them. Each one was custom molded for the wearer's head. The only reason Natalia had armor was because Rico had a spare and they were almost the same size.

"Hoo-rah!" the squad members replied in unison.

"Here's how we play this. Sixteen's going to drop us off at the center of the compound. We'll split into two groups. Sheriff, you, me, Rico, and your wife are going to make a line for the entrance to the underground complex to the east. Our mission is to secure the facility. Shelby, Hot Dog, Killjoy, Chains, and Duncan will head west to the hangar. Your mission is to recover and secure the Tokyo. Any questions?"

"I'd like to go into the complex with Natalia and Hayden," Casey said.

"That's a request, not a question," Bennett replied. "Request denied."

"But-"

"Chains," Hayden said. "We made a deal, remember?"

"Is it a coincidence he's splitting Duncan and me up from you? No offense, Sheriff, but Sarge here has already stated he doesn't give two shits about us Earthers. How do I know his lackeys aren't going to off us as soon as you're out of sight?"

"I'm offended by that remark," Bennett said. "I'm a soldier, but I'm also a person."

"Am I?" she retorted. "You said I wasn't not long ago."

"Chains," Hayden repeated. "Do you want to come with me? Natalia can go with the others."

She shook her head. "I'm not going to separate you from your wife again. All I'm saying is, be careful how far you trust this man and his squad. Just because they talk a good game, we don't know them."

Bennett smiled. "That's good advice," he said. "But if we wanted to kill you all, we could have done that already. Or we could have left you to the trife, and let them do it."

"Can you trust we won't kill you, Sergeant?" Duncan asked.

"You even try, scavenger, and you'll be dead before you can think too much about it," Shelby said.

Hayden glared at Duncan. He was the biggest wild card in their newfound alliance. He was surprised the man wasn't begging to go into the underground facility, ostensibly to search for his lost partner.

Was he planning to make trouble?

Was Casey's warning accurate?

They had undertaken the journey north with the expectation that they would find allies at Lewis-McChord. Then he had learned the missives they had received in Ports were most likely a lie, only to have that truth turned on its head with Bennett and his squad's appearance. To be sure, he had no idea what to believe, anymore. He had no idea what was true and what wasn't, or how those truths might shake out in the end.

"Any other questions, comments or stupid objections?" Bennett asked, locking his eyes with Duncan. When nobody moved, he turned back to Rico. "Put the bird in the air."

"Yes, sir," Rico said, opening her laptop. She put her thumbs on the controls, guiding the drone from the top of the truck.

Hayden saw it zoom past the windshield, zipping out toward the compound.

He had made the best decision he could. Now they all had to live with it.

"Sixteen, be ready to move on my mark," Bennett said to the driver.

"Yes, sir," he replied.

The Sergeant watched Rico navigate the drone. She watched the display, her face tight as she looked down on the dead.

"No sign of trife, Sarge," she said. "Lots of bodies, but it looks like they all headed south."

"We were here sixteen hours ago, Rico," Bennett said. "You saw them, too."

"Yes, sir."

"So where the fuck did the bugs go?"

"Good question, sir. I'm-"

"Oh, shit!" Sixteen shouted from up front. "Brace!"

There was no hesitation from any of them. Even Duncan got himself stable in an instant. It was a good thing, too, because that was all the time they had. Not that it helped much. Something hit the side of the truck, something big and heavy enough to knock it off its wheels and onto its side.

Hayden fell forward, catching himself on his replacement hand, planting it on the side of the vehicle, which was now the floor. He grabbed for Natalia, missing her and watching her hit the truck on her side. Rico was thrown backward, rolling over as the laptop tumbled from her hands. It landed in front of him, giving him a limited view as the drone recognized it was no longer under control and began to sink toward the ground.

It was facing the truck, offering a surreal third party glimpse into the future.

Trife, hundreds of trife, were suddenly pouring toward them from behind the truck and out of the ground, where they had been hiding in wait only seconds before.

19

"Regroup!" Bennett shouted, getting his feet under him. "Fire at will!"

The first of the trife slammed into the windshield, throwing large claws at it with enough force to leave a crack across the length of it. It hissed and bared its teeth as it drew back its arm again.

An invisible bolt burned instantly through the glass, a pinpoint of light that put a sudden hole into the trife's head, stabbing right through its brain and causing it to fall. Another demon replaced it right away, hitting the transparency a second time and widening the crack.

More laser rifle bolts followed, tiny holes made in the glass with each shot fired. The tight lines crossed through the trife, knocking them back.

"There's too many," Hayden said.

"And we're grepping trapped in here," Casey added.

"Shut up and keep shooting," Bennett replied.

The trife hit the windshield again, the cracks spreading and growing. Sixteen was on the ground beside the driver's seat, digging his sidearm out of its holster, rising and turning to face the onslaught.

Another hit and the windshield shattered. Sixteen opened fire, smaller plasma rounds burning into the trife closest to him, causing them to scream and fall back. One of them managed to get a shot in at him, and its claws caught an edge on his armor, sinking beneath and pulling him toward the outside as it died.

"Shit!" Sixteen shouted, suddenly frantic. His plasma pistol discharged into the trife, but it was momentum pulling him, not muscle.

"Grab him!" Bennett shouted as Killjoy rushed ahead. He dove for the soldier's outstretched hand, just missing it as the trife grabbed the scout and finished taking him away.

They heard his screams as he was torn to pieces.

"No!" Rico shouted. "Son of a bitch."

"They grepping ambushed us!" Casey shouted, shifting her aim and pulling the trigger on her laser rifle. A small red flash ahead of it indicated a shot had been fired. Further ahead, another trife died.

"We can't stay in here," Hayden said.

Killjoy scrambled back from the front of the truck, firing into the trife as they pressed their way inside.

"The only way out is through," Bennett said. "They tipped us onto the other door."

Rico grabbed the laptop from the ground, dropping to the floor and cradling it in her lap. "Standby," she said.

"Killjoy, move back," Hayden said, easing his way forward. He turned the dial on the side of the PL90.

"Scouts, hold your fire!" Bennett ordered.

Hayden assumed Casey and Duncan would be smart enough to do the same.

The trife stopped dying in front of them. They climbed into the truck, their leathery faces looking almost pleased.

"Ten seconds!" Rico said.

Hayden pulled the trigger, sending a gout of superheated gas outward toward the creatures. It decimated everything in its path, burning through the seats and controls at the head of the truck in seconds, pouring into the trife and forcing them back.

"Five seconds!" Rico said.

He took a few steps forward to extend the reach of the throw, the trife winding up back outside the vehicle. He watched the counter tick down. Only three seconds left.

It was enough.

"Fire in the hole!" Rico yelled.

Hayden stopped shooting, ducking down and turning his face away. A whistle came from nearby, a projectile launched from the drone. It hit the ground close to the trife and detonated, throwing them away from the truck, and sending dirt and debris pouring through the blown-out windshield.

Hayden let it smack against him, removing the spent cartridge from his rifle and digging into his pocket for a replacement.

"Go, go, go, go, go!" Bennett shouted.

Hayden charged ahead, leading them out. He used his replacement to clear some of the jagged window around the frame of the truck before squeezing through and getting out into the open.

The trife had been thrown back by the drone, but they recovered quickly. One of the creatures dove toward him in a long leap through the air. It was bigger than the ones in Ports and had more ridges along its frame. He dropped back as it approached, falling onto his rear at the same time he brought up the plasma rifle, holding down the trigger and burying the trife in superheated gas.

He rolled aside as the remains hit the ground.

Then the Spacers were there, emerging from the truck

and opening fire, forming into a circle near one another. Rico moved out behind him, escorting Natalia to his side before turning to cover them both.

"These are not the bugs we left here three weeks ago," Bennett commented, getting a better look at the trife.

"Big mothers," Killjoy said.

"Break east," Bennett said. "Stay in formation."

The entire group started moving, remaining in a circle with a full field of fire. They started gliding east, one step at a time, laser rifles emitting constant red line projections to warn friendlies of the fire, while the invisible beams pierced the creatures around them.

The trife died by the dozens, charging in and going down like a wave collapsing on rocks. Scout Team Seven was responsible for most of the kills, though the others managed to get a few good shots in here and there.

"Sarge, I don't know if we have enough ammo for this," Shelby said, removing the battery pack for her rifle and placing in a fresh one.

They were halfway to the main compound, easing ever closer to the broken buildings and rotting corpses. He didn't know which structure led into the underground facility. Was it even a good idea to try to get there?

"Maybe we should head for the starship?" he asked, getting close to Bennett.

"We don't leave men behind, Sheriff," Bennett replied. "We need to know if anyone's alive down there."

"If we go in there, we might not make it back out."

"Roger that. It's the way its gotta be."

Hayden didn't argue. He aimed the plasma rifle and fired, a single shot bursting out and punching through a trife's chest.

They kept going. The trife didn't relax their attack, and they were getting ever closer, putting the pressure on the group to hit them faster and faster, before they could get in an attack of their own. They covered the ground between the truck and the compound, moving into the main area.

Hayden was sweating and tired. Duncan had lost his robes somewhere, shedding them to cool off. Even so, his clothes were drenched in sweat and grime, and he looked ready to surrender and fall. Casey and Natalia looked tired, too, but the Spacers? They hadn't broken a sweat. Their breathing was easy. It was as if they weren't in the middle of a firefight at all.

"Incoming!" one of the Spacers shouted.

Hayden didn't know what they meant until a sudden shade fell across them. His eyes darted up, just in time to see a group of airborne trife dropping toward them from above.

"Shit," he said. He had started to think all of the flying demons had gone south.

He turned the dial on his rifle, swinging it toward the sky.

Too late. The trife came down on them hard, crashing into their midst. One of them tackled Natalia, throwing her to the ground. He spun toward it, only to see it bounce off her without attacking, throwing itself at Casey instead.

She slammed it in the face with the butt of her rifle, the blow sending it reeling toward Killjoy. The large man had exchanged his rifle for a sidearm and a humming knife, and he drove the weapon into the creature's neck. The pitch of the hum increased, pulling the blade through the demon and removing its head.

"No lasers in close combat!" Bennett shouted, likely for their sake. "You're liable to burn a friendly."

The same went for plasma. Hayden dropped the weapon completely, digging his claws into an incoming trife and ripping them out.

Bennett caught one of the fliers in his hands, turning and

bringing its head under his arm and twisting. A sharp crack and he let go, the trife dead.

"Sarge!" Shelby shouted.

She had been knocked down like Natalia, and two more of the trife had joined in their attack. They were hitting her armor, trying to get their claws and teeth through.

She screamed as they succeeded.

Bennett pulled a sidearm, aiming and firing in one impossibly quick motion. Three rounds, three kills. Hayden could hardly believe it. The trife dropped around Shelby, and Bennett rushed over to her. By his expression, he knew the man was too late.

"Break east!" Bennett shouted, pointing toward a smaller building a few hundred meters away. "Inside! Get inside! Killjoy, Rico, cover fire, everything you've got left. Hot Dog, take point. Hot Dog!" He slammed his fist into the ground. "Fuck!"

Hayden grabbed Natalia's arm, pulling her along. Casey and Duncan were with him, though Duncan's shirt was stained with blood. Killjoy and Rico were a meter ahead, on one knee and facing back toward the main trife force, waving them ahead.

"Move it, lollies!" Bennett screamed. "I lose my scouts because you dawdled, I kill your sorry asses!"

Hayden ran past the two Spacer soldiers. As soon as they were out of the field of fire, Killjoy and Rico opened up, a massive salvo that shredded two more lines of the trife.

They kept running. Bennett came to a stop, waving them past, pulling a second sidearm from somewhere. Every round he fired was a perfect shot, even when he spread the weapons to two disparate targets.

How?

He had said the trife and goliaths weren't the only things the Spacers engineered. Was the Sergeant even human?

They made it to the building. Hayden went in first, claws out and pistol in hand. He pushed through the open door and into the windowless space, his only hint at the imminent attack a sharp hiss from his left. He threw his hand up in front of his face, catching the trife claws on his metal appendage, putting the pistol against it and pulling the trigger. The trife collapsed.

The building was little more than a short, open floor with a heavy blast door beyond it. The door was sealed, reminding him of the Pilgrim.

If the door was sealed, that meant the trife hadn't gotten inside.

They ran up to it. There was a small control panel on the left side, a keypad just like the ones on the boxes in the strands. Natalia stopped in front of it, reaching out for it and quickly entering a code. The master code.

The door clanked and then began to slide open.

Casey shoved the muzzle of her rifle through the opening, watching for trife. Hayden covered the rear, while Duncan doubled over, coughing up blood and vomit. Bennett was in the frame of the outer door, silently guiding Killjoy and Rico back through their helmet comms. He didn't need to shout at them right now.

"It's clear," Casey said behind him.

"Go," Hayden replied. "Duncan, go!"

The scavenger stumbled toward the doorway, entering with Casey. Natalia stayed by Hayden's side.

"Nat, go," he said.

"I'm not about to go through another hatch like that without you," she replied.

He nodded, firing his pistol at a trife that tried to jump Sergeant Bennett from the side. The Sergeant seemed surprised the creature had nearly taken him off guard, staring at it for a moment as it writhed on the floor.

Then Rico was at his side, the two of them rushing back toward the open hatch.

"Inside, lollies," Bennett said. "Master code, huh? Shut the door."

Natalia and Hayden moved through the hatch. She began entering the code to close it, while Bennett and Rico fired back at the trife moving into the building. Rico's rifle went dry, and she pulled out her sidearm, firing round after round into the demons. Bennett's sidearms came up empty, too, and he stepped back, ready to punch the creatures in the head if he had to.

He didn't. The door changed direction, sliding closed and locking with another loud clang. A short whirring noise followed, and then the floor they were standing on started to vibrate as the entire module started to descend.

"Geez, that was intense," Casey said, leaning back against the lift. "I thought we were dead for sure."

"Too many of my people are dead," Bennett said, slamming his fist into the door again. "Too damn many."

"I'm sorry," Natalia said.

He looked at her, eyes barely visible through the helmet. He pulled it off, still glaring her way. "Not your fault," he said sharply, obviously upset at losing most of his squad.

Duncan's coughing drew their attention. The scavenger was sitting against the wall, his shirt completely stained with blood, a large gash down the side of it. Rico rushed to him, kneeling beside him and tearing it away from the wound. It was long and deep.

"We can't fix this," she said.

Duncan looked at her, and then up at Hayden. He had tears in his eyes. He opened his mouth to speak.

He died before he had the chance.

20

THE REMAINDER OF THE GROUP FELL INTO A SHORT SILENCE, AS each of them worked to calm the flow of adrenaline and the aftershock of the fight. Hayden held Natalia in his arms while she leaned into him, exhausted and frightened. He glanced up at Bennett, whose expression proved how angry he was at the outcome of the attack.

"Shit," Casey said, shaking her head. She didn't say anything else.

"At least the facility isn't overrun," Rico said. "Maybe they couldn't get out, but the trife didn't get in."

"Not much comfort against what I just saw," Bennett said. "Those bastards were bigger and meaner than the last round. Either they're mutating again, or these are the next generation, grown full-size in less than a week."

"Do you think your Doctor's experiments caused it?" Natalia asked.

"I don't know," he replied. "Either way, I don't like what it means for us."

"Why?" Casey asked. "You can just go back to your planet,

119

where everything is awesome. You don't have to live here with the monsters. I do."

"Even if I responded as the callous asshole you think I am; the fact remains that we've spent a hundred years trying to build a better weapon, and this is proof that we've failed, miserably. Our advanced weapons didn't mean shit against their numbers and evolved size and strength and intellect. How long do you think they were preparing to hide in the dirt like that?"

"A couple of days at least," Hayden said. "If I had to guess."

"Yeah. Fuckers knew we were coming back," Bennett said.

The lift thudded as it came to a stop, the wall on the opposite side sliding away and revealing a long corridor behind it. A man in a uniform was leaving a room further down, and he froze and looked back at them, surprised by their sudden appearance.

"Don't just stand there," Bennett shouted to him. "Get Colonel Orten." The man started running away from them, while Bennett laughed. "Damn desk monkeys."

"What are you going to do about Duncan?" Casey asked.

"They'll send a med team for him," Rico said.

"Not much they can do for dead, though," Bennett said.

They moved out into the corridor, traversing the length of it. They passed multiple doors on either side as they walked, and Hayden stared through the window of each. They were offices, where men and women in uniform were manipulating displays. He had no idea what they were doing, but the calm simplicity of it made him jealous.

They were nearly at the end of the corridor when a stout woman with short gray hair intercepted them. She wasn't wearing a uniform, instead dressed in loose, white pants and a shirt, a long white cardigan over it.

"Doctor Franklin," Bennett said flatly. "Where's the Colonel?"

This was Doctor Frankenstein? She looked like a kindly old grandmother, not a mad scientist.

"Dead," she replied sharply. "Just like the rest of the units stationed here. I asked for trained, optimized replicas. Is this the best Proxima Command can do?"

"I'm the best Proxima can do," Bennett said. "And I damn near died trying to get in here. Most of my squad didn't make it."

"Don't get so emotional, Sergeant," she said. "Command will make you some more subordinates." Her eyes shifted, landing on Hayden. "You brought me new subjects?"

"Are you out of your mind?" Bennett said. "Have you learned nothing from your failure?"

She looked back at him. "Failure? What failure? This generation is the strongest yet."

"We can't control them."

"That's not your problem, Sergeant. I know you don't agree with our work here, but you follow orders, you don't give them." She looked at Hayden again. "Are you the resources from Ports? Let me guess, the Sergeant here told you he needed help getting back to base? A clever excuse, Bennett. Like you need help. You're top of the line."

Hayden stared into the woman's eyes. He didn't see any sign of compassion there. She didn't care who they were, or where they had come from. She just wanted to use them for whatever experiments she was conducting. And Bennett had led them right into the trap?

He glanced at the Sergeant. He didn't believe that. Bennett was a hard man, a soldier's soldier, but his motives were clean.

"I follow orders from Colonel Orten," Bennett said. "If he's dead, I follow the chain of command. You're a civilian. You aren't in the chain."

"Considering we've run out of soldiers, I'm the next best thing," Franklin said. "You will listen to me."

"Oh? How are you going to enforce that statement?"

"You were out scouting when the last delivery arrived, Sergeant," she said. "I have a new toy to play with. Do you want to meet it?"

Bennett and Franklin stared one another down. The Sergeant seemed to know what she was referring to, and he was hesitant to continue to challenge her.

"You can't harm them," Bennett said. "It's against protocol."

"You're going to try to convince me they're Centurions?" Franklin said. "Don't be stupid."

"Sheriff Hayden Duke, of the generation ship Pilgrim," Bennett said. "His wife Natalia, and their daughter-"

"Casey," Casey said, realizing Chains wouldn't make her sound like she was with them.

Franklin drew back in surprise, staring at them. "You're full of shit," she said.

"My morality filters were adjusted to meet your goals, Doctor," Bennett said. "If I'm lying, it's only because you wanted it that way as part of my operational directives. I personally think lies are for dirty sacks of crap, and I wouldn't stoop to it unless I were under orders. Which I'm currently not."

His eyes burned into her. She stared back at him for a moment, and then backed down.

"If you're from a generation ship, you would have an identification chip," she said. "Bring them to the lab. I'm going to scan them. If you're telling the truth, that will prove it, and I might even apologize."

Hayden held up his replacement hand. "Excuse me, Doctor," he said. "I'm not entirely clear what exactly is happening here in reference to your exchange with the

Sergeant, but one: I lost my identification chip when a damn Scrapper cut off my hand. Two: I'd sooner cut your throat out than let you harm a hair on my wife's head."

Franklin smiled. "Are you threatening me, savage? I don't take kindly to threats." She turned away from him, dismissing him like he was nothing. "I have the full support of Command on this one, Sergeant," she said to Bennett. "That's why they sent me something a little more effective to help keep this location under control. Hell, it's the only reason anyone in here is still alive. Unlike you, they believe in the work we're doing here."

"I lost five people getting in here," Bennett said.

"Inferior product, clearly," Franklin said.

"Product?" Rico replied. "You bitch."

"Rico!" Bennett snapped.

She straightened out, coming to attention. "Sorry, sir."

"I've been monitoring their actions, Sergeant," Franklin said. "Observing how they react and evolve. I saw them dig those trenches. I knew you were headed for a reckoning. To be honest, I'm impressed any of you survived. Three or four more generations, and that may not be the case."

"You're killing what's left of this world," Casey said. "The world you came from. How do you live with yourself?"

"Quite easily," Franklin said. "Millions of years ago, life emerged from the ocean to dry land. Did we return to the ocean or did we fish it for our sustenance? Did we use its abundance to meet our growing needs or preserve it as some sort of ancestral home? The Earth is our ocean now. We require its resources to forward our goals. To preserve our way of life. The universe doesn't stop evolving. Neither do the trife. Neither do we."

"Doctor-" Bennett started to say.

"Take them down to the lab. I'll determine if they're really from the Pilgrim or not. If so, they have nothing to worry about from me. I'll honor the protocols. If not, I have samples that have been waiting for a host."

Bennett didn't look happy, especially after she had admitted she expected them to die in the ambush, but he complied.

"Sheriff," he said. "Turn over your weapons. You will come with me. Don't make me use force."

Hayden met the Sergeant's eyes. He turned his sidearm over in his hand, holding it out. Bennett took it.

"Natalia," Hayden said.

She did the same, turning over the guns she had left. She had nothing to fear from Franklin anyway. Her chip was still intact.

Casey took a couple of steps back as Rico approached her, but there was nowhere for her to go. She handed her weapon over, too.

"I'll be down shortly," Franklin said. "I'm just going to get some lunch."

Bennett looked like he wanted to snap her neck. Instead, he moved ahead of Hayden, Natalia, and Casey, while Rico took up the rear.

"This way," he said.

"Oh, and Sergeant," Franklin said after they had taken a couple of steps. Bennett paused and turned his head. "Welcome back."

"BENNETT, WHAT'S GOING ON?" HAYDEN ASKED AS THE Sergeant led them through the complex.

"Yeah, don't you hate Doctor Franklin?" Casey asked.

"I do," he replied. "Believe me. I despise that horrible excuse for a Centurion. But I'm a soldier, Sheriff. I follow orders. You know what that means."

"You follow orders from your superior," Hayden said. "You said she isn't your superior."

"She isn't my superior," Bennet said. "Not directly. But she has the support of Command, which means it's my duty to fall in line behind her. I don't have to like it; I have an obligation to do it. I'm sorry, Sheriff. There is a bright side. Once we convince her you're from the Pilgrim, she won't have a choice but to help me figure out how to help you. Even a bitch like Franks isn't going to let the savages hurt the colonists."

"I don't have my chip," Hayden said.

"She has other ways of testing, I'm sure. I wouldn't be too worried about that."

"I would," Casey said. "I'm not from the Pilgrim, which means I'm screwed."

"We'll see about that," Hayden said.

"We get her to do you last," Bennett said. "Maybe she'll decide not to bother. Looking at you, I think you could pass for their kid."

They reached the end of a long corridor and turned left. They went another twenty meters to a second sealed hatch. There were no soldiers left to guard it, so a smaller man in a lab coat was doing the job.

"Sergeant Bennett?" he said, seeing them. "You're still alive?"

"Disappointed, Gersh?" Bennett said, smiling.

"They make you grunts better and better each iteration, don't they?" Gersh replied.

"Didn't keep me from near getting my eye torn out," Bennett said. "Doctor Franklin asked me to bring these three down here for testing."

"New subjects?" Gersh said, looking at them and smiling. It wasn't a pleasant smile.

"No. They're from the Pilgrim. The colony survived."

"Bullshit," Gersh said, his expression changing slightly. He seemed suddenly in awe of them.

"It's true," Natalia said. "Your boss is making us prove it."

"I'll be damned."

He turned and tapped his wrist against the control panel beside the door. It slid open.

They entered the lab. It was familiar to Hayden because he had been in one just like it before, on the Pilgrim. The central station leading to different corridors, down which he knew he would find additional rooms for medical treatment, a larger laboratory filled with equipment, a freezer, and an operating table. He had no question there were cells down here too, to contain the subjects while they reacted to whatever Doctor Franklin injected them with.

"Research module," he said.

"You've seen one before?" Gersh said.

"On the Pilgrim. I met one of the scientists there. She was being held in stasis. Special Officer Jennifer Kazlaski. What do you think? Is she a savage or a Spacer?"

Gersh's face turned red. "I'm supposed to stay with the door."

"Run along then, little mouse," Rico said.

"I'll bring you to Pod One," Bennett said. "Franklin can figure it out after that."

He brought them past the workstations in the central area. The workers there looked up as they crossed, but only for a moment. Hayden's eyes trailed to one of the displays. It looked like a magnified blood sample.

The Pod was a simple treatment room. An adjustable chair in the center, some cabinets on the side. It wasn't really big enough for all of them, but Hayden felt like Bennett put them there on purpose, because he knew it would annoy Franklin. That was fine with him.

"Sergeant," Natalia said. "Doctor Franklin called you and Rico replicas. Does that mean-"

"It does," Bennett said. "We've got two types of people on Proxima. The ones that are born, and the ones that are made."

"Made?" Casey said.

"Like the goliaths are made," he replied. "Printed, for lack of a better word, though the actual processing is a bit more complicated than that. Replicas like Rico and me, we're soldiers. Grunts. Sent in to do the dirty work, so the other kind of people don't spend twenty years maturing just to go out there and die. We take two years to go from a design on a computer to a real living thing."

"And you're okay with that?" Hayden asked.

Bennett smiled. "I don't remember anybody asking me if I wanted to be a replica before I was a replica."

"You're okay with being forced to be a soldier?" Natalia asked, clarifying his question.

"It isn't so much forced," Bennett said. "I'm a copy of someone else, who was also a lifelong grunt before the Centurions invented us. I've been modified, of course. Every generation is altered slightly, both in appearance and in overall sequencing. Direct copies don't work because without a unique identity; we go insane. At least, that's what I've heard, and based on my own experience, I believe it. But, we're considered human. We have the same rights. We pay taxes. We have free will, for the most part."

"We're better than regular humans," Rico said. "Sarge is being humble. We're faster, stronger, have better stamina, heal quicker."

"That only matters down here," Bennett said. "Nobody's trying to kill you on Proxima."

"Usually," Rico said. "It's not a utopia. There's still crime. We still need law enforcement."

"Replicas?" Natalia asked.

"Yup," Bennett replied.

"They can't make you strong enough to defeat the trife," Hayden said.

"The human body has limitations."

"But if they can make replicas, why do they need to experiment on the people here?" Casey asked. "Why not use copies?"

"I don't think the regular humans would like it very much if the replicas staged a rebellion," Bennett said. "And that's exactly what would happen if we weren't treated equally. That's a fight nobody wins."

"It didn't sound to me like Doctor Franklin was treating you equally," Natalia said.

"Frankenstein is a bitch," Rico replied. "Bigoted, jealous, whatever you want to call it. She thinks because she's a scientist, because she knows how to build us, that makes her better than we are."

"It's not that," Bennett said. "She just thinks she's better than everyone, savage, replica, or otherwise."

"I heard that."

Doctor Franklin turned the corner. She had a dark wedge of some kind in her hand, most of it chewed away.

"Rico, you're dismissed," she said.

Rico looked over at Bennett. It was obvious she would destroy the Doctor if he let her.

"Hit the barracks, Rico," he said.

"You'll have plenty of space," Franklin added, teasing the fact that all of their comrades had been killed by the trife.

"You could have brought them to Lab A," Franklin said. "This room is a little small."

"What was I thinking?" Bennett said.

"Follow me."

She led them out of the Pod and down the hallway, finishing her meal as she went. She was unaffected by anything that had taken place on the surface. The death of the soldiers, the loss of a lot of good men and women. Made or not, they had died protecting her, and she didn't even care.

She led them into the main area of the lab, a mirror image of the place where Jennifer had tried to betray him, knocking him out so she could attempt to negotiate with the Scrappers. His eyes danced around the room, finding the freezer, the samples, the machines, and equipment.

"Do you have stasis chambers down here?" Hayden asked.

Franklin glanced over at him, raising an eyebrow.

"Yeah, I know what they are," he said.

"You could have found them anywhere."

She went over to a cabinet and took out a small device. Hayden recognized it right away. He used to carry one on his uniform.

"Give me your wrist," Franklin said, looking at Casey.

"Uh." She froze, not sure what to do.

"Here," Natalia said, sticking her arm out. "Scan it."

Franklin's gaze lingered on Casey, and then she turned the device and ran it over Natalia's wrist.

"Natalia Duke," Franklin said. "Lead Engineer." She looked up at Natalia with newfound respect. "You aren't lying?"

"I never have been."

"This is your husband?" she motioned to Hayden.

"Yes."

"You lost your hand to a Scrapper?" she said to him.

"Yes. The Scrappers want to get into the Pilgrim," Hayden said. "They want the guns the Space Force left behind. They have the master code, and they're on their way. Best case, they're going to expose the colonists to the trife contagion. The scanner just confirmed we are who we say. Can we please start doing something about helping them?"

Doctor Franklin shook her head. "You haven't proven you're one of them."

"What?"

"I don't know how you wound up outside, Mrs. Duke," she said. "It could be you married a savage? It would be the logical thing to do, for protection out there. He looks capable."

"Damn it!" Hayden said. "I came from the Pilgrim. You're being a stupid, stubborn, arrogant pain in the ass."

Doctor Franklin shoved her finger out at him. "You watch your mouth," she said. "I can have you killed with just a word."

She glanced at Bennett. Hayden wasn't sure if the soldier would comply with that order as quickly as she seemed to think he would.

"If you're recently off the Pilgrim, you may have the contagion. All three of you might." She retreated to another cabinet, opening it up and removing a glass container from it, filled with a reddish liquid.

"What is that?" Natalia asked.

"This is the inoculation for the trife contagion," she replied. "We escaped exposure, and never developed our own immunity. We wouldn't be able to operate here without it."

"You have the cure?" Hayden said. He had tried not to worry about what might happen in the future while they were still in so much danger now. He never imagined there was any kind of cure for the disease.

"Of course. We aren't savages."

"I may be pregnant," Natalia said. "Will it hurt the baby?"

"Pregnant?" Franklin said."No, it won't harm the child. If it needs inoculation, it will be protected, too. I can test you to see if you're pregnant."

She retrieved another small device and used it to load a shot of the liquid. Then she went to another cabinet and took out a different device.

Hayden glanced at Natalia. They were going to find out if she really was pregnant or not? He had already accepted the outcome whatever it was. It was still making him nervous.

"You'll have to remove the armor. In the meantime, I'll need a blood sample from both of you." She put the device down and retrieve two syringes. She went back to Casey again. "Hold out your arm."

"I don't want you to stick me with that thing," she said.

"I wasn't asking," Franklin replied.

Casey didn't move.

"Sergeant, a little help?"

Bennett hesitated for a moment and then approached Casey. She looked at him pleadingly, but there was little he could do.

Natalia started removing her armor, unclasping and unzipping it. She tried to do it quickly, to distract the Doctor, but she wasn't fast enough.

Casey put out her arm. Franklin jabbed it and quickly extracted a vial of blood. She pulled back without a word. No comfort. No apology.

"Now you," she said to Hayden.

He already had his arm out. She took the sample.

"If Natalia doesn't have the contagion, will the inoculation cause a problem?"

"Clearly not a doctor," Franklin said impatiently. "Not at all." She handed the two vials to Bennett. "Don't lose track of which one is which."

He didn't reply.

She turned back to Natalia. Her arms were bare by now.

"This one will register changes consistent with pregnancy," she said, showing her the first device.

"We have that one on the Pilgrim," Natalia replied.

"This is probably a newer model," Doctor Franklin said. Lift up your shirt."

Natalia lifted it to expose her stomach.

"Trife?" Franklin asked, seeing the bandages.

"Yes. I've heard they won't attack pregnant humans?"

"That depends on how long they've been pregnant. Trife have an extraordinary olfactory system. It goes beyond scent, to the point that their noses filter and identify specific chemicals. But like with people, some are higher functioning than others. You could be three weeks pregnant and still be attacked. You're fortunate. A few inches to the left and you might have lost whatever chance of pregnancy you have."

Natalia's eyes snapped toward Hayden at the response. He

had accepted that Ghost was the father. But now, maybe he wasn't? His heart started thumping harder, and he suddenly became more impatient for the results of the test.

Doctor Franklin put the device against her stomach. The seconds seemed to pass too slowly, each one a relative eternity. Only five of them ticked off before the device was finished with its readings. Hayden realized he was holding his breath, but he wasn't going to exhale. Not yet.

Franklin glanced up at Natalia. A small smile extended from her face. "Yes. It looks like you are pregnant."

Natalia looked at Hayden again. They stared into one another's eyes, with a renewed sense of excitement over the prospect.

Of course, they had to get out of this mess first.

"Do you know how long?" Natalia asked.

"Not from this device. I'd need to run more tests. Let me finish up with this first."

Doctor Franklin didn't seem concerned with the results one way or another. It was a fact to her, with no emotion behind it. She put that device down and picked up the other one, jabbing it into Natalia's arm, the reddish fluid draining from it.

"How is that?" she asked.

"It didn't hurt at all," Natalia replied. She was still beaming from the idea that the baby might not be Ghost's after all.

"Good."

"Doctor Franklin, I promise Hayden and Casey are part of my family from the Pilgrim," she said. "What's the harm in believing me when I tell you that?"

"I know you want to protect them," she replied. "I understand why, especially now. But I have samples that need hosts, and hosts are getting harder to come by. One of our mission parameters is to stay out of sight. Nobody is supposed to know we're up here. The abundance of trife and the lack of goliaths make that part easy, but it also makes getting new resources difficult. You're an Engineer, Natalia. I expect you understand the importance of what we're doing here. Successful mutation of the genome means a future for our kind. A future for your baby. Failure means eventual extinction."

"But you're talking about my husband and my daughter," Natalia said.

"If it were my family, I would be willing to make that sacrifice," Franklin replied.

Natalia looked at her like she had two heads. Hayden didn't blame her. He couldn't believe the Doctor had just made that statement.

"Obviously, you have no idea what it means to love someone," Natalia snapped.

"I know what it means to love my people," Franklin snapped back. "All one hundred million of them on Proxima."

"Not the replicas," Casey said.

"If your companions aren't Centurions, the path forward is clear," Doctor Franklin said, ignoring her last statement. "Regardless of your emotional ties."

She grabbed the vials of blood from Bennett's hands and brought them to one of the machines. She stuck them in it, hit a switch, and then turned on a nearby display.

Five seconds later, she turned around.

"Neither one of you have the contagion," she announced. "No contagion. No identification chip. Sergeant, take them both to holding."

"Sergeant, did you hear me?" Doctor Franklin said when Bennett didn't react. "I said, take them to holding."

The Sergeant looked at the Doctor, and then at Hayden. He was hesitating, which was a good sign. He didn't want to bring them in. He knew it was wrong. But what would win out in the end - justice or duty?

"Sergeant!" Franklin snapped a third time. "Don't make me make the call. You'll spend the rest of your shitty fake life regretting it."

Bennett glanced at her, and then at Hayden. He looked defeated. What the hell was this "toy" the Doctor had mentioned?

"I'm sorry, Sheriff," he said.

"No!" Natalia said, moving between Bennett and Hayden. "You can't do this. I'm not going to let you."

"If I don't have the contagion, it's because I'm immune," Hayden said. "One of the ten percent. I can't get it."

He always thought he would be relieved to find out he wasn't going to die that way, and now it turned out it would be the reason he and Natalia and their baby were torn apart? Over his dead body.

"Sergeant, call Rico for backup," Franklin said, ignoring them both. "I'm done here."

She headed for the door. Hayden threw himself toward her, caught before he could take two steps, the Sergeant's left hand on his throat, his right hand grabbing and holding the replacement. Even unaugmented, Bennett was stronger than his mechanical hand.

"Sheriff, don't."

Casey came up behind him, grabbing his sidearm from his holster. Bennett's hand moved fast, releasing Hayden's neck, swinging back and slapping the gun from Casey's hand. He rotated on one leg, back-kicking her into the wall.

"Please," he said. "I don't want to hurt any of you. Rico, I need you in Lab A, asap."

Doctor Franklin watched the altercation with a sick smile on her face. A very sick smile. Looking at her face, he was certain that she knew the truth. She knew he was from the Pilgrim.

She just didn't care.

"You bitch!" Natalia said, trying to grab her.

Doctor Franklin backed away, barely making it clear as Bennett pulled Natalia back. He was struggling to keep all three of them neutralized, but so far he was successful.

"Damn it, Sergeant!" Hayden said. "You know this is wrong. You know this is bullshit. You saw what she did to your people. She let you walk right into a fucking trap. She let them die to prove - I don't even know what the hell she was trying to prove!"

Bennett shook his head. "I can't, Sheriff. I just can't. I have a duty."

"To be this bitch's tool?" Casey said. "That's what you are, right? A replica. A grepping tool to be used. Free will my ass."

She tried to hit him again. He caught her fist, turning her arm until she shouted. He let go.

"You don't understand," he said. "None of you do."

"How can they?" Doctor Franklin said. "They're savages. Pilgrim or not. Maybe the protocols are a mistake? Maybe it doesn't matter if the colonists haven't been outside? Being cooped up all of those years, maybe it made them just as regressed as the rest of them? Imagine what I could do with that many subjects. I could probably solve this war once and for all."

"What war?" Hayden said. "You've never even seen the enemy."

"I know who the enemy is," Natalia said. "Advanced Civilization? Not even close."

Hayden's chest heaved, his face red with anger. He squeezed his hand, extending his claws.

"Get out of the way, Sergeant," he said.

"Sheriff," Bennett replied. "You can't beat me."

"I'd rather die trying to escape than die as some fucking experiment," he replied.

"No!" Natalia said. "Can we all just calm down and talk about this?"

"There's nothing to talk about," Franklin said. "I'm sorry, Natalia."

Rico appeared in the doorway, gun in hand, pointed at Hayden.

"Back off!" she shouted.

"And there's the other one," Franklin said. "Good doggy. I've got more important things to do than be part of this."

She cleared the doorway, intending to leave. Hayden caught Bennett's eye again. Hayden held his mechanical hand ready to strike. He didn't think he would connect, but he had to try. He couldn't just let them do this.

"I trusted you," Hayden said.

"I know," the Sergeant replied.

"Sergeant, please," Natalia said. She had tears in her eyes. "Rico? Please."

"Franklin, wait," Bennett said, bringing the doctor to a stop.

"Are you questioning my authority again, Sergeant?" she said. "I don't have time for your emotional bullshit. I have samples to prepare. Do your fucking job!"

Hayden could see the conflict on the Sergeant's face. The replica's eyes darted around the room, looking at each of them.

"Rico," he said.

She tossed him her sidearm. He caught it, pointing it at Doctor Franklin, his decision made.

"I'm taking the Toyko, and I'm getting them out of here," he said. "You know this man is a colonist from the Pilgrim."

"Is he?" Franklin said. "Prove it, Sergeant. Beyond a shadow of a doubt, prove it."

"You've lost sight of everything we should be doing here."

"That isn't your call, Sergeant," Franklin said. "Command has my back."

"Then maybe Command has forgotten what it means to be human, too? Funny that I should have a better comprehension of it than you do."

"You aren't taking them," Franklin said. "I'll give you three seconds to drop that weapon and fall back into line, and then I call for backup. One. Two."

Bennett pulled the trigger. The round cracked from the pistol, a spark of blue light catching it directly in front of Franklin's forehead a split second later.

"What the?" Casey said.

Franklin smiled as three more rounds hit the forcefield in front of her.

"You bitch!" Rico shouted, rushing toward Franklin. She

tried to punch the woman, her hand hitting the same energy barrier. She cursed as she drew it back, her knuckles burned.

"I'm the bitch?" Franklin said. "At least I know the meaning of loyalty." She continued to back away, protected by the energy shield. "Command's going to hear about this, Sergeant. Your root genome is going to be dishonorably erased. You too, Private."

Hayden noticed the other scientists in the area were moving into the hallway and running away, clearing the area as quickly as they could.

What the hell had Doctor Franklin called for?

He didn't have to wait long to find out. The floor started to vibrate in a quick tempo, shifting under his feet. Something was coming from down the hallway, through the hatch into the Research module directly to them.

"Hayden," Natalia said.

He looked back. She had picked up Bennett's gun, and she tossed it to him. He caught it, preparing to use it.

Against what?

It entered the doorway to the lab, filling the entire frame as it came to a sudden stop. It was a lustrous metallic, smooth and sleek, with no sign of joints or seams. It was humanoid in shape, seven feet tall and slender. Its face was a blank sheen with a series of blinking lights along its chest. It was a roid like the Butcher, but hundreds of years more advanced.

And they were supposed to fight it?

"Stand down, Sergeant," Franklin said.

Bennett kept his gun leveled on the Doctor even though he couldn't hit her through the shield.

"Just let them go," he replied. He glanced at the roid. It was motionless in the doorway.

"No," she said.

Then the roid was charging toward Bennett, hands out to grab him. The Sergeant swung the gun toward it, snapping off four quick rounds. They scuffed its metal face but didn't do any lasting damage.

"Shit," he said dryly, diving away as the machine reached for him.

It turned to track him while he rolled back to his feet, lifting its hand so its palm was out. The metal split in the center, rolling away. An instant later, a ball of superheated gas poured out of the opening, heading directly for the Sergeant.

He reacted immediately, twisting his body to avoid the plasma. It slammed into the wall with a heavy hiss, making a deep mark on the metal.

"Geez," Casey said. "We have to do something."

"Run," Bennett said. "Run now! Rico, lead them out!"

"Come on," Rico said to them.

Bennett charged toward the roid, firing his gun into its face. It didn't react to the bullets at all. It reached out for him again, missing as he ducked beneath its grasp, positioning himself so it would turn its back on them.

"Run!" he shouted again.

Rico started for the doorway. Natalia looked at Hayden, and he nodded. They had no other choice.

"Go," he said, grabbing Casey's arm and pushing her behind Rico. They broke for the exit, all four of them, while Bennett did his best to keep the roid distracted.

It didn't work. It sensed their movement. It put its other hand out, firing a wave of plasma toward the doorway. Hayden had no idea how Rico managed to get under it, but it passed over her head, hitting the wall and burning into it.

A second ball was already on its way. It caught Rico in the chest, hitting one of the armor plates and digging in, the force throwing her backward. She hit the wall hard, slumping there.

"No!" Natalia said, rushing to her side. She flicked her

head back to where Doctor Franklin was standing, a smug smirk resting on her elderly face. "Stop this!"

"Nat, we have to go," Hayden said, catching up with her.

The roid had put its focus back on Bennett, storming toward the Sergeant while he did his best to get away. It was going for the soldiers but not them. Why?

He knew why. Franklin didn't want to hurt Natalia, and what good would he and Casey be as test subjects if they were dead?

"Hayden, no," Natalia replied. "They shouldn't have to die for us."

"It was their choice."

"It doesn't matter."

"We can't stop that thing."

"Maybe we can," she said. "It just depends on whether or not it can hear."

"Hear?"

She stood up, walking back toward the roid.

"Nat?" Hayden said, rushing to join her.

The roid had caught up to Bennett, wrapping a slender hand around his neck, holding him up and back against the wall. His gun was on the floor beside him. His eyes shifted as they approached. He looked angry they hadn't abandoned him.

"What are you doing?" Franklin said. She was standing nearby, watching them with a mixture of confusion and amusement. "You can't stop it."

"I said to run," Bennett managed to eke out with what little air he had remaining.

"SH13LD-012," Natalia said, reading the serial number along its back, lightly etched into the metal along with the USSF logo. "Access override-"

The roid's arm shot back toward her in an effort to stop her from talking. Hayden barely got between them, taking the hit instead. He was thrown backward by the blow, hit with enough force to send him to the ground, a fresh pain blossoming in his chest.

Natalia stood her ground. Her lips were moving. She was saying something to the roid.

It opened its hand, letting Bennett fall to the floor. The soldier gasped for air, clutching at his throat. It turned around, facing Natalia.

She raised her arm, pointing toward Doctor Franklin.

It started to move.

"No!" Franklin shouted, furious. "You can't do this. You're mine."

The roid walked toward her, ignoring her complaints. She was frozen in place, pressing at something behind her ear. She removed it a moment later, practically screaming into it. "Stop!"

The roid didn't stop. It reached out to her, sparks flying as its hand hit the energy field. It didn't draw back. It didn't feel pain. It pushed against the shield, sprays of light exploding around its hand as it sank into and through, grabbing Franklin's arm.

It held her fast while the force field ran out of power. She slumped in its grip.

Bennett was back on his feet. He grabbed his gun from the floor, walking briskly toward the Doctor and putting the weapon to her head.

"I should kill you," he hissed.

"Sergeant, no," Natalia said. "It's over. That isn't what we do."

He glanced back at her, nodded, and holstered the gun, moving to Rico's side.

Natalia returned to Hayden, holding out her arm to help him up. He winced as he rose. "Damn, that thing is strong."

"Are you okay?" she asked.

"I've gotten worse. Just one more bruise to add to the collection. What did you do?"

"I gave it the master code. Bennett was right. It does control everything."

"That's a serious flaw in the design, isn't it?" he asked.

She smiled. "Yes, it is. But software is like a building. Sometimes you can't change the base without tearing everything else down first."

"So they screwed it up a long time ago?"

"And probably never saw a need to fix it. The code is supposed to be lost."

"How did you know it could hear you?"

"I didn't."

Hayden's smile faded. "Nat, if this hadn't worked-"

"It doesn't matter now," she replied. "It did work."

2 3

"WHAT ARE YOU GOING TO DO THEN?" DOCTOR FRANKLIN said. "If you aren't going to kill me. What do you want?"

Knowing they didn't intend to end her life had restored some of her fiery defiance. She stood with the roid behind her, its hand on her shoulder, staring angrily at Bennett and Hayden.

"We want what we've always wanted," Natalia said. "To stop King from getting into the Pilgrim. We didn't have to come to conflict. You created it with your stubbornness. You know Hayden is a colonist, and you were going to use him anyway."

"You shouldn't be using anybody," Casey said. She pointed at the roid. "Look at that thing. You could probably wipe out the trife with enough of those if you wanted to."

"Do you know how much a single Shield costs?" Franklin said. "It took three years and the loss of most of the soldiers in Lewis-McChord to get Command to send one down. The trife are exponentially less expensive to produce."

"All it costs are some savages, right?" Casey said.

"Okay, that's enough," Hayden said. "King is on his way to the Pilgrim. Hell, he's probably already there by now. The trife are marching south. They may have reached Sanisco and are killing innocent people as we speak. You have a ship, and we need it to get there as soon as possible."

"And then what?" Franklin said. "All five of you are going to take on two armies by yourselves? You should let me try my sample on you. It'll enhance your strength, regenerative capabilities, and senses. It's in an advanced stage of testing, so it may not kill you."

"Maybe we can take your little pet, too," Casey said.

"You can imagine the Shield has massive power requirements. It's meant to be defensive and needs a recharge after a couple of hours."

"I have an ally waiting for word from me," Hayden said. "She has two dozen soldiers with advanced weaponry. Not this advanced, but she has Marine Corps rifles and armor."

"My trife will tear them apart," Franklin said. "They've been engineered to kill goliaths. And if this generation doesn't succeed, I'm betting the next one will."

"What do you mean?" Natalia said.

"You still don't get it, do you?" Franklin said. "I'm this close to a solution that will keep us safe from our enemies."

"You can't control them," Bennett said angrily.

"That was nothing more than bad luck, and you know it."

"It's not bad luck. All of the trife's power was tied up in one man. If you can't see how dangerous that is from every angle, you're even crazier than I already thought."

"My husband was a good man."

"Better than you," Rico said. She had removed her armor, revealing a dark bruise that covered nearly her entire stomach but thankfully no other damage.

"What happened to him?" Natalia asked.

"He died," Franklin said. "Heart attack in the middle of the night. Too big and too sudden for me to stop it." She was more angry than sad when she said it as if his death was more of an inconvenience to her work than it was emotionally difficult.

"The trife were imprinted on him," Bennett said. "They learned to communicate with him through hand gestures. They wouldn't listen to anyone else, and they knew when he was dead. That's when they started attacking the base. They took out everyone except us, and only because we weren't here."

"And they're getting smarter," Rico said. "You saw that. What the hell do you think, Doc? Letting them evolve out of control?"

"If they can kill the goliaths, I can get them under control," she said. "We just need to imprint the next generation. Maybe use multiple mentors."

"I don't quite get it," Hayden said. "What's the endgame there? You make an army of killer trife, and then what?"

"And what happened to trying to make them sick, like they made us sick?" Natalia asked.

"It didn't work," Franklin replied. "Every virus we gave them killed half at best, and then the next batch were completely immune. Every damn time. The directive now is to make them our weapons. When the enemy shows up, or when we find them, we pick the army up and send them to their planet. We give them back what they gave us, only bigger and badder and more deadly."

Natalia glanced at Hayden. He knew what she was thinking. Ghost had told her the same thing. They had to be the biggest and baddest to survive. Neither one of them believed that.

"What if there is no enemy? Or what if you never find them?" Natalia asked.

"At least we'll be ready."

"And what about Earth?" Casey said.

"Earth is their breeding ground," Franklin said. "Don't tell me you're upset by that. It's been that way for almost four hundred years. Nothing changes there."

"We won't have the goliaths anymore if your trife kill them all."

"So?"

"We'll be killed off completely."

"The goliaths were only created one hundred years ago. You survived before that."

"Barely."

"And you will again."

"Sergeant, maybe I can talk to your Command?" Hayden said. "Maybe I can talk some sense into them?"

Bennett shook his head. "There's no time. Messages go back and forth on the starships. It's the only way to communicate. It takes a week to travel from here to Proxima."

"They won't listen to you anyway," Franklin said. "Why should they? Earth is ancient history."

"Not for us, it isn't," Casey said.

Franklin sighed. "I know you don't want to hear this. None of you do. You've made that clear. You've even managed to turn my soldiers against me. Earth is lost. It's over. The people from the Pilgrim, if you save them, they can be transported to Proxima. The savages have to live with the hand they've been dealt. That's how it is, and there isn't anything you or I can do about it. I know you think I'm a bitch, and in a lot of ways I am. But there's a reason for it. I have a mission, a duty, to save as many people as I can. Yes, some have to be sacrificed for me to complete that mission, but I hold it sacred because of what it means to the greater good."

"You're choosing one group of humans over another," Hayden said.

"Is that really so wrong?" she snapped. "My planet is more important than your planet. Is that what you want to hear? Because that's the truth."

"Then it's a shame you lost this one," Hayden said. "Because we're making a new truth. How far are you willing to go, Sergeant?"

"What do you mean?" Bennett asked.

"You helped us because you were adhering to one protocol over another. But what if I tell you I want to do something that may be outside of your ability to rationalize?"

"You have something in mind, Sheriff?"

"A few things. One, we need to destroy the nest here."

"No!" Franklin said. "You can't."

"You don't get to decide anymore, Doc. You said it yourself, the next generation will be smarter and meaner, and they'll only get stronger after that. We have to stop it now."

"Sheriff, you need to be careful," Bennett said. "If you go too far, Command might decide to rescind their decision to stay hidden. You can't stand up to an attack from Proxima."

"At least if they did attack, the people here would know their death sentence is being written by their own damn kind."

"I'm sorry. I can help you recover the colonists from the Pilgrim. I can't help you do that."

"Fair enough."

"You're still outnumbered, Sheriff," Franklin said. "Even if you stop the Scrappers, you won't be able to handle my trife. So why resist? Help me finish my work, and maybe good things will come of it in the end."

"That option's off the table, so stop mentioning it."

Franklin closed her mouth, but her eyes burned into him.

"I want to know more about the Goliath Protocols," Natalia said.

Hayden glanced over at her. He knew that tone of voice. It was the same tone she took every time she thought she had a viable idea.

"What are you thinking, Nat?"

"Monsters to fight monsters," she replied. She turned to Franklin. "What do you know about it?"

Franklin shook her head, refusing to speak.

"Shield Twelve, I need Doctor Franklin's compliance," Natalia said.

The roid's hand closed tighter on Franklin's shoulder, causing her to cry out.

"Damn it," she said. "Fine. I'll tell you what I know. It isn't going to help you."

"I'll be the judge of that," Natalia replied.

"Sheriff, we can start getting organized in the meantime," Bennett said. "Weapons, armor, and supplies."

"We may need medical support, too," Hayden said.

"I'm sure we can convince a few of the other non-combatants here it's in their best interests to come along for the ride. You should stop by and get some treatment, too. You and Rico. You both look like shit."

"Yes, sir," Rico said.

Bennett turned back to Franklin. "Just so we're clear, Doc. As of this moment, I'm in charge of Lewis-McChord."

"You are not," Franklin said.

"Natalia, can you do me a favor?" Bennett said.

"What do you need, Sergeant?" Natalia replied.

"Since you have the master code, can you arrange for Doc Franklin to be locked out of higher level systems, such as producing recordings to send back to Command?"

"If you can show me how."

"I can."

"Then, yes."

Franklin looked at them both, her face turning red. She didn't speak.

"Chain of command, Doc," Bennett said. "You're out of it."

"We've got a lot to do, and we're already on borrowed time," Hayden said. "Let's get to it."

24

"What is that?" Hayden asked.

They were assembling near the lift that would take them back outside. Hayden, Casey, Bennett, Rico, and two of Lewis-McChord's medical staff, Petrov, and Shihab. A small transport, similar to the ones in Metro that had been stripped for parts, was sitting to the left of the corridor, stacked with crates of guns, ammunition, and as many medical supplies as the base could spare.

Hayden and Casey had been fitted for the Spacer's black body armor; a modification made to Hayden's by the medical team that covered his arm but left his replacement hand exposed. Helmets had also been provided, taken from inventory and quickly remolded to better fit their heads. Hayden's was somewhat tight against his skull, a little too small. Casey's was almost too loose to wear, her frame and head smaller than most. Neither of them were wearing the helmets right now. They both found them confining, but he knew they would be useful once the fighting started.

He felt pretty good, all things considered. Petrov had treated his wounds, binding the gash on his face and taping his ribs, as well as providing oral medication that had helped relieve more pain than he even realized he was in. He watched Natalia and the Shield approach, Doctor Franklin riding a second transport with some strange apparatus piled onto it.

"This is part of the Goliath Protocols," Natalia said, patting the stacked electronics.

There were multiple pieces, all of it reminding him of the systems on the Pilgrim. It was old technology, especially compared to the Shield standing beside it.

"It hasn't been used for a while," she continued. "I had to dig it out of storage after I persuaded the Doctor here to tell me where it was."

He knew what she meant by persuaded, glancing at the roid.

"What does it do?" he asked.

"If it's still functioning properly, it will give us a little more control over a goliath."

"A goliath? Singular?"

"We only have equipment for one. And that's assuming it works."

"Right." He looked at Doctor Franklin. "Can we trust her?"

"If she screws us, she dies," Natalia said. "We can trust her as far as she values her life."

It was strange for Hayden to hear her speak that way. She was the compassionate one. The one who always believed in the best side of people. Maybe she hadn't been able to find one in Doctor Frankenstein.

"I'm complying," Doctor Franklin said. "I'm curious to see if this plan of yours will be effective. Every action is an opportunity to study and learn."

"If that's how you rationalize it, that's fine by me," Hayden said. "Sergeant, are we just about ready?"

"We are, Sheriff," Bennett replied. "Now that the Shield is here."

He picked up a helmet from in top of the stacked crates and handed it to Natalia. Bennett had already explained how it worked to them while she was locking Franklin out of the base's administrative systems.

The whole thing was simple enough to use, especially since they would be sticking to one channel. Anything they said would be broadcast. Anything they saw would be marked on a grid for everyone else. With the rifles plugged into the system, the onboard computers would assist in their aim, triangulating coordinates. As if Sergeant Bennett needed the help to be a better shot.

"Send it up," Hayden said.

Bennett nodded, tapping his identification chip against the lift's control panel. It slid open and remained that way while the Shield made its way in. Natalia took its place watching over Franklin, putting on her helmet, plugging it in, and then drawing her sidearm and pointing it at the scientist.

Hayden grabbed his helmet and slipped it on, connecting it to the armor. Casey did the same. The world changed in front of his eyes, numerous overlays appearing in the corners of the transparency.

The lift closed with only the Shield inside. They waited while it rose and opened again, dropping the roid off on the outside, leaving it to take on the trife alone, at least for a few minutes. Their goal was to stay clear long enough to get their bearings and start making their way across the compound to the hangar where the starship Tokyo was waiting.

The lift returned, the door opening ahead of them. There were three dead trife inside, with three crushed skulls.

"Move out," Bennett said, his voice loud and clear in the helmet.

He led them into the lift, with Rico at his side and the medics and Doctor Franklin in the middle.

"I don't have time to babysit you up there," Natalia said to her. "If you run-"

"I'm not going to run," Franklin replied. "I don't want to die."

"Good doggy," Rico said, looking back at her and drawing a scowl in return.

"Rico," Bennett said.

"Sorry, sir," Rico replied, even if she wasn't.

"Here we go," Bennett said as the lift neared the top. "We make a straight line for the hangar. Conserve ammo as best you can. Let the Shield do most of the work."

"Roger," Rico said.

"Pozz," Hayden and Casey said.

The lift stopped. Time seemed to stop with it. Hayden could hear every thump of his heart reverberating through his body. He could feel the adrenaline pouring in. He had to get Natalia safely to the ship. He had to protect his family. Nothing else mattered.

The doors in front of Bennett and Rico began sliding open. Bennett positioned himself in a crouch at the center, and Hayden's helmet began to flash targets as the networked systems communicated with one another. There were only a few, and they vanished almost as quickly as they appeared.

"Move out!" Bennett shouted, stepping out into the enclosure, weapon up and ready to fire.

Hayden could see past the others to the scene ahead. A dozen dead trife littered the floor, the Shield moving further out into the open to confront them. He could see its silver body flashing as it moved and the dark blobs of trife attacking it, trying to find a way to bring it down.

They sprinted through the small building, pausing when they reached the doorway. Bennett and Rico scanned the exterior, the targets lighting up on Hayden's helmet. There were too many of them to make out individual forms.

"Shit," he heard Petrov say, voice tight with fear. It was probably the medic's first experience beyond the safety of the base.

"Straight line, full speed," Bennett said. Then he was racing forward again.

The transports were programmed to follow behind him. Petrov and Shihab stayed close to them, using the cargo for cover as they crossed the field. The hangar was only a hundred meters distant, but with nearly four hundred trife between it and them, it seemed like a million kilometers.

"Sheriff, left flank," Bennett said.

Hayden turned his head in time to see a group of trife moving up from that side, impressed with how easily the Sergeant had read the grid and the fact that the helmet had picked up the creatures before he did. He rotated their way, still running forward, the rifle's reticle appearing in his helmet's display even though he had it pressed against his side. It allowed him to shoot from the hip, six plasma bolts in succession, six solid hits that dropped each target.

'Nice shooting, Sheriff," Bennett said. "Stay alert."

Hayden looked forward again. The Shield was up ahead, almost at the hangar, dead trife on the ground like bread-crumbs along a path. The creatures were realizing the roid was an impossible target and were shifting back to the humans.

Bennett and Rico opened fire, laser rifles scoring quick kills in rapid sequence, trife after trife falling to their assault. Hayden's HUD started thinning out, the demons dying at a rapid pace. They covered the ground quickly, careful not to trip on dead trife and maintain their momentum.

The Shield circled back, retreating behind them as a larger group tried to come up from the rear. Hayden and

Casey turned around, walking backward, monitoring the trife as the Shield engaged them, its speed and weight and power more than enough to crush them with single blows. They spread around it in a wider berth, hissing as they charged the line unimpeded.

"Bennett," Hayden said, realizing there were too many for them to take on alone.

The lasers started crossing from his rear as the Sergeant and Rico fired back into the masses, thinning the herd. Hayden and Casey added their firepower, the helmet's systems assisting their aim, guiding the rifles and giving them clean kills with nearly every shot.

"Incoming!" Natalia shouted, at the same time more targets started popping onto the HUD, positioned on a vector from above them.

"I hate the flying bastards the most," Bennett said. "Sheriff, switch the PL90 to auto and give 'em hell."

Unlike the last time, they were prepared for the airborne attack. Hayden flipped the switch on the side of the rifle, rotating to aim upward. A flock of trife was swooping in toward them, claws out and ready to tear into them.

He depressed the trigger, grinning as the weapon fired bolt after bolt of plasma up toward the creatures. Superheated gas slammed into torsos and wings, sending the demons tumbling from the sky.

He didn't get all of them. They dove in toward the group, suddenly stopped in their tracks as the Shield moved in beside them, leaping into the air, letting the creatures hit it straight on, grabbing them and crushing their necks. The transports moved through right before the Shield came down, landing hard and bouncing back to continue the defense.

He ejected the charge, grabbing a replacement from his pocket and slipping it in. They were almost to the hangar.

They reached it half a minute later. The trife were approaching more cautiously now, trying to find a less deadly approach. Bennett made it to the door, slapping his wrist against the control pad. It started to open, and he stood on the side and waved them through.

"Good work, Sheriff," he said as Hayden moved past. "Nice work, Chains."

"Savages my ass," she said in reply.

They finished entering. Bennett hit the pad on the other side, closing the door again, him and Rico remaining near it and firing into the trife to prevent them from entering. A few managed to slip through, but they fell quickly to shots from Casey and Natalia.

The door slammed closed with a loud clang.

"Clear!" Bennett shouted.

They had made it.

Hayden turned, eager to get a look at the starship.

He looked back at Bennett, confused.

"What the fucking hell?" Bennett said.

25

DOCTOR FRANKLIN STARTED LAUGHING.

"What the hell did you do?" Bennett said, drawing his sidearm and pointing it at her head.

The Tokyo was supposed to be in the hangar.

It wasn't.

The starship was gone.

"I sent the Tokyo to orbit as soon as you started bitching that you needed it," Franklin said. "I wasn't taking any chances."

"Call it back," Bennett said. "Now!" He shouted in her face. She didn't flinch.

"How would you like me to do that from here?" she asked. "Bring me back to the main facility, and I'll consider it."

"Are you out of your damn mind?" Bennett said. "We were lucky to make it here without any casualties. We aren't going back."

"You're as trapped here as the rest of us," Rico said.

"There's a terminal connected to the satellite uplink right there," Bennett said, waving toward a small console in the corner. "Bring it back."

"No," Franklin said.

"Gloria," Doctor Shihab said. "We volunteered to be part of this mission, to help the colonists trapped on the Pilgrim. You have no right to hold them hostage."

"Who's being held hostage?" Franklin said. "Sergeant Bennett has seized control of Lewis-McChord against regulations. He has no right to lock me out of administrative access."

"I disagree," Petrov said. "He explained the situation to me. You're out of line, Gloria. You have been for months."

"Really?" Franklin said. "I'm out of line? You didn't question me when my studies were going well. Then Paul dies, and I turn into the monster?"

"You let the scout team walk right into an ambush. Then you sent the Tokyo to orbit and left us stranded here," Petrov said. "And you can't see a problem with that?"

Doctor Franklin reached into a pocket, retrieving a small device with a brown liquid in it.

"The more promising of the two samples," she said, looking at Hayden. "Take the sample, and I'll call back the Tokyo."

"She's completely lost it," Rico said.

"Nobody is taking that," Natalia said. "I have the master code, remember? Sergeant, show me what to do, I'll call it back."

"Not this time," Franklin said. "The satellite uplink doesn't use the same base software. It's nowhere near complicated enough to need it. There is no master code. Do you think I'm stupid?"

"Yes," Casey said. "How about we throw her outside with the trife?"

"You don't have anything to bargain with, Franklin," Bennett said. "Call the Tokyo back, or I put a bullet in your head."

"Go ahead. You can all stay stuck here while the colonists on the Pilgrim die. Or you can take the fucking sample!"

"Nat, there has to be a way to override it," Hayden said. "Master code or not."

"Maybe, but how long will it take?" she replied.

"Damn you, Gloria," Shihab said. "Command is going to hear about this. All of it."

"Fine. Let them. But what if my sample is good? What if I can make the Earthers strong enough to stand up to the trife? Isn't that worth trying for?"

"That isn't what you want it for," Rico said.

"Does it matter? Take the sample, Sheriff."

Hayden glared at Doctor Franklin. What choice did he have? They needed the ship. They needed to get back to the Pilgrim. They couldn't wait another hour. It might be too late already.

"Damn it," he said. "Fine. You win. I'll take it."

"Hayden," Natalia said. "No."

"Forget it, Sheriff," Casey said, cutting in front of him. She pulled her helmet off. "If you're going to stick someone, you can stick me."

"Casey, no," Hayden said. "I'm not letting-"

"You don't get to decide," Casey said. "Just like you didn't get to decide with Jake. He died for you, not because of you. Because he believed in who you are, and what you're trying to do. So do I. You have a wife with a baby on the way. You need to do everything you can to be here. I don't have anybody."

"You have us," Natalia said.

Casey smiled. "I do. And I'm grateful for it. I thought I was content before because I didn't know what happy was. I'm happy now. No matter what happens." She looked back at Franklin. "Now stick me with that shit, and let's get on with it."

Hayden opened his mouth to protest again. He didn't have a chance. Doctor Franklin stuck the device against Casey's neck. It emptied in seconds.

"Grepping hell that hurt," Casey said, rubbing the spot as Franklin pulled the device away. "So what happens now?"

"It'll take an hour or two to work its way through your system," Franklin said. "You'll probably get very tired, and then you'll feel a lot better. There's no question about that. The only question is whether you'll survive for long once the changes take hold."

"Fine. Now call the grepping ship."

Franklin smiled, hopping off the transport and making her way to the terminal.

"Reload and get your asses ready," Bennett said. "The trife might try to come in with the Tokyo."

Hayden checked his rifle, dumping the half-used cartridge and putting in a fresh one. Natalia and Casey did the same for their weapons. So did Bennett and Rico.

"Any idea how much juice the Shield has left?" Rico asked.

Natalia looked at the roid's back. "Twenty percent."

"You can tell from its ass?" Rico said.

"The lights," Natalia said.

Franklin typed something on the nearby terminal. A few seconds later, yellow strobe lights distributed around the hangar started to flash, a too perfect voice announcing its arrival.

"Caution. Starship incoming. Clear the landing field. Repeat. Caution. Starship incoming. Clear the landing field."

They were already clear, still near the heavy side door to the hangar. An echoing clang sounded from the rooftop above, and then it began to slowly twist open from the center, a massive shutter that enclosed the space.

It had only opened a few meters when the first of the trife appeared on the edge of it, looking down at them from fifty meters up. Bennett fired at it, a laser bolt pinning through its head and causing it to tumble to the floor below.

"Lock and load!" he growled, keeping his aim fixed on the roofline.

Hayden pointed the PL90 upward, waiting for more of the trife to appear. They were hanging back while the roof continued to move aside, waiting for more space to maneuver and approach from all sides.

Tense seconds passed. Doctor Franklin returned to the group, positioning herself near the transports and doing her best to hide.

"This is your fault," Natalia hissed at her as she crouched between the equipment. "We should have been in the fucking transport when the roof opened."

"It was worth it," Franklin replied.

The trife didn't risk looking down this time. They leaped into the opening, one after another, two hundred of them in one large mass dropping toward the ground below.

Hayden opened fire with the rest of the soldiers, the targeting systems in the helmet and armor helping correct his aim and keep him steady while he released bolt after bolt of plasma. Three dozen trife died before they made it to the ground, the rest absorbing the shock by rolling on their frames as their legs hit, still with enough force it would have left a human unable to move.

They bounced back up, charging toward the group, the Shield rushing out to meet them.

It was a near mirror of the battle outside. The soldiers laid down heavy fire while the Shield grabbed at the trife, crushing whatever body parts it happened to get a hold of. The tighter quarters made the action more frantic, and the trife started to gain ground, closing in on the small group.

A growing whine from above signaled the approach of the starship, but Hayden didn't have time to look. He ejected a used plasma cartridge, meaning to change it out before realizing he didn't have time. He slapped the weapon on the back of the armor, drawing his sidearm and squeezing his hand. Claws and explosive rounds would have to do.

He shot the nearest trife, taking a step back, pivoting and shooting another. A third nearly reached him, but the HUD threw up a red marker and a piercing squeal on his right, and he turned that direction and slashed at the head of the trife with his claws, cutting clean through its neck.

He looked away, finding Natalia nearby. She had switched out her rifle too, using her sidearm to bury slug after slug in the closest trife, knocking them down only a few meters away. He rushed over to join her, adding his firepower and putting more ground between them and the demons.

The whine above them converted to a rumble. Hayden risked a glance up, finding the belly of the Tokyo was only a few hundred meters above.

"Rico, as soon as she touches down get your ass on board," Bennett said. "Prep for launch."

"Roger that, Sarge," Rico replied.

"Help!" Shihab shouted.

Hayden snapped his attention toward the doctor. A trife was standing on top of the equipment, ready to drop down on him.

Its head snapped sideways, a bullet crossing through its skull, knocking it away. Shihab's terrified eyes turned toward Natalia, a meek smile crossing his face.

"Shield's out!" Casey announced.

He spun to find the roid standing motionless off to the side, the lights along its back all out. The trife were gathered near it, and realizing it was dead began to separate to retarget them.

"No. Nooo!"

Hayden turned again, just in time to see Petrov's neck

163

sliced open by trife claws. The woman crumpled to the ground, gushing blood, the demon standing over her while it looked for a new target. He aimed and fired in one smooth motion, his explosive rounds entering its chest and detonated, blowing out its innards.

"Rico, go!" Bennett shouted.

The Tokyo had entered the hangar, dropping steadily toward the floor, a trio of landing gears extending from its body. Hayden recognized it from the picture Duncan had shown him, though it was much more impressive in person. The metal that composed its outer hull was smooth and sleek, like the Shield, with no sign of seams. It had a long fuselage and stubby wings that drooped at the ends, reminding Hayden of the eagle on the USSF logo. There was no obvious cockpit to be seen, everything managed by cameras from deeper inside. A large, gold eagle and star emblem was painted on the side, along with a serial number and the name "Tokyo" in script near its pointed nose.

A ramp was opening near its center. Rico was already running for it, trife dying on both sides of her as Bennett laid down cover fire, clearing her path to the ship.

She leaped onto the ramp, rolling to her feet and continuing up.

"Let's move, people," Bennett ordered, beginning his advance.

Hayden could see the trife jumping onto the top of the ship, trying to use it as cover as they approached the group.

"Careful not to shoot up our ride now, Sheriff," Bennett said, cautioning him and the others.

They continued toward the ship. The gear hit the ground with a heavy thud, the shocks flexing and absorbing some of the impact. The belly dipped toward them, never coming close to their heads, before flattening out, the ramp directly ahead.

Bennett stopped in front of it, waving to the others to get on board. Shihab went up first, shaken and in tears. The transports, Doctor Franklin, and Casey followed, and she walked up backward, still shooting at the trife that dropped into view. Natalia went next, with Hayden joining Bennett as the last two to climb in.

"Go ahead, Sheriff," Bennett said.

Hayden had taken two steps up the ramp when Rico's voice cut across the comm.

"Sarge, get on board. We need to go. Now!"

The grid in Hayden's helmet changed, picking up the targets she was identifying from her vantage point on the ship. Another large group of trife were outside the hangar, approaching rapidly.

Another large group was inside. Trife jumped down from the wings and rushed in from the sides of the ship, hissing as they charged the ramp. Bennett and Hayden backed up the ramp as they opened fire, cutting down the first line but only slightly slowing their approach.

They made it to the top, where the others were standing.

"Go, Rico!" Bennett shouted.

A heavier rumble and the Tokyo started to rise. The trife leaped from the ground, bouncing onto the ramp. Bennett tried to shoot them, his rifle failing to fire, its battery spent. He turned it in his hands, using it to bat the trife, his powerful arms knocking them back with solid blows.

They continued to climb.

"Rico, bring up the damn ramp," Bennett said.

"I can't Sarge," Rico replied. "Not as long as the sensors are reading something on it."

"Shit," Bennett said.

Two more trife vaulted the gap, landing on the ramp. They had nearly reached the top of the roof, where even more of the demons were waiting to make the jump.

Hayden depressed the trigger on his pistol. It clicked, finally out of rounds. He glanced over at Bennett, who had crouched into a fighting posture.

The trife hissed at them, watching them carefully, remaining on the ramp.

"Hayden, you're blocking my line of fire," Natalia said. "Duck."

Bennett glanced back. "I have a better idea," he said.

Before anyone could react, he flexed his legs and jumped, his strength carrying him to the two transports.

And Doctor Franklin hiding between them.

He reached back, grabbing her by the shoulders as she shouted in surprise.

"Sergeant? What are you doing?"

"Cleaning up your mess," he growled. "You were right. I should have killed you when I had the chance. I don't like to make the same mistake twice."

And then he threw her, shoving her down the ramp and into the trife. She screamed as she tumbled into them, nearly knocking them off balance as the first caught her, looking down at her and hissing but not sinking its claws into her.

He cursed when he saw she didn't have enough momentum to knock the demons off, snapping up Casey's sidearm from her armor and firing two quick rounds into the trife's heads.

They stumbled backward, still clutching Doctor Franklin in their grasp. She looked back at him, terrified, opening her mouth to speak as they finally tripped off the ramp.

"Rico, close it," Bennett snapped.

"Roger that."

The ramp rose up, slamming closed and sealing with a light hiss. For the first few seconds, nobody said a word. Then Rico held Casey's pistol out to her. She took it, smiling at the Sergeant.

He nodded back before turning his attention to Hayden, who was staring at him in shocked surprise.

"You know I did the right thing, Sheriff," he said, pulling off his helmet.

Hayden followed suit, his eyes shifting to Casey. She was hard to see under the helmet, but he thought her face looked pale. Was she sweating?

"Yeah," he said. "I guess you did."

"Rico," Bennett said. "Set a course for the reactor. We've got a nest to exterminate."

26

"I THOUGHT YOU DIDN'T WANT TO DESTROY THE NEST?" Natalia said.

"That was before. As far as I'm concerned, Frankenstein broke more protocol in an hour than I can in a lifetime. You back me up on that Shihab?"

The doctor nodded. He was visibly shaken by the whole thing. "Yes, Sergeant. She was more out of control than I realized."

Bennett glanced at Hayden. "There you have it. Come on into the cockpit if you want to see the show."

Hayden looked at Casey. She had taken off her helmet. Her face was red. Her hair damp. She didn't look good. Franklin had told them this would happen.

"Shihab, can you take care of her?"

The doctor looked at her, realizing he had a patient. He nodded, appearing relieved to have something to do. He took her by the arm, speaking softly to her and guiding her to a seat on the side of the craft. He put her in it and then returned to the transports, picking one of the crates off it and bringing it to her.

"I'll take care of her," he said. "I've done this for Franklin's subjects before."

"Thank you," Hayden said. He was worried about her.

"I'm going to stay with her," Natalia said.

"Pozz," Hayden replied.

"Let me give you the grand tour, Sheriff," Bennett said. "This here is the loading deck. Cargo and what have you."

Hayden looked around. The deck was mostly empty space, with markers on the walls to help arrange the pallets and crates that could be loaded into it, and wire straps buckled to the sides that would be looped through to keep them steady during flight. There were a couple of seats in the front corner, either for guards or extra passengers. They looked like they could be easily detached and stowed if they needed the extra room. That's where Casey and Natalia were now. A stairwell led up higher into the ship. Bennett waved him toward it.

They climbed to the next level. It was more comfortable and plush. A carpeted floor. Rows of spaced, padded seats. It was sterile and fresh and clean. The seating went forward and back from the stairs, bending around a curve at the center of the ship. Four pods split them on either side at the forward and aft quarters, and there was a heavy door with a control pad all the way up front.

"It probably looks comfy to you, Sheriff. But she seats one hundred in an emergency, and for a week-long ride, it isn't that grand. The Tokyo is more of an orbital transport, meant to bring us up to a bigger capital ship waiting in deep orbit, out of sight from the ground, but she can make the fold herself if she needs to."

"What's behind the door?" he asked, pointing up front.

"Sensor arrays, mainly. Only a ship's engineer can access it." He laughed. "Or your wife, I guess. This way."

He led him around to the center of the curve on the port

side. There was another door there with a control pad on it. He tapped his wrist against the pad, and the door slid open.

Three steps down brought them into the cockpit. Rico was sitting in the front and center, surrounded by screens and placed ahead of a flat control panel, though she had a different helmet on her head with wires leading to the ceiling. Her chair had a joystick on either side of it, with numerous buttons on each that carried out various functions.

Hayden looked at the screens. They showed the view from a number of different cameras, but they seemed more for observer's benefit than the pilot's. He could see the ground moving quickly below them, the trees little pricks of green and brown below.

"She's built more like a fighter than a transport, owing to her size," Bennett said. "And she has a few guns, though we haven't had much opportunity to use them. The helmet gives Rico a full view of the outside, following her head movements. Plus other HUDs and overlays that feed information from the sensors. You're lucky Rico didn't die out there. Sixteen was the only other qualified pilot."

"It's incredible."

"You were on a starship your whole life, but this is the first time you've been off the ground," Bennett said, smiling. "Shit, Sheriff. I don't know what to do about all of this. I feel for you and your wife. I feel for Casey, especially now. I don't like the idea of innocent people dying. But I don't want to be a traitor to my people, either."

"You aren't betraying them to help clean up a mess," Hayden said, echoing the Sergeant's earlier statement.

"Roger that," he said.

"We're approaching the reactor," Rico said.

Bennett's eyes locked on one of the displays. Hayden

followed them, seeing that a large clearing had opened up below. A dark grey hemisphere was in the center, and the dark shapes of trife were around and on top of it.

"There it is," Bennet said.

"Can you hit the nest without destroying it?" Hayden asked.

"No. But don't worry about the scientists. Our backup batteries will last two years with the skeleton crew manning the place, and only the research labs, medical, the kitchens, the barracks, and a handful of apartments are still active, anyway. Plenty of time for Command to send fresh batteries, or build a new reactor, or whatever they decide to do with the place."

"What are you going to tell them about why you destroyed it?"

"The truth. We lost control of the xenotrife, they became too great of a threat to the base, and we neutralized it. Losing ninety-eight percent of the military assets will do wonders to drive that point home."

The Tokyo was drawing closer to the hemisphere. A steady thrumming sound echoed through the ship, increasing in pitch as the ship slowed to a stop, hanging in the air.

"We're in position, Sarge," Rico said. "I need to dip the nose."

"Better hold onto something, Sheriff. Rico, give me a second to go secure the hold."

"Yes, sir."

Bennett left the cockpit. Hayden watched the trife on the reactor as they responded to the presence of the ship, spreading out and looking up at it. A group emerged from the inside, through a dark portal at the base of the structure, spreading their wings and taking off.

"You see that, Rico?" Hayden said.

"Yup," she replied. "Sarge, are you ready? We've got bogies coming up to meet us, and the guns don't point down as far as they should."

Bennett's voice sounded through speakers in the cockpit. "Roger. We're secure. Do what you need to do."

"Hold on, Sheriff," Rico said.

Hayden grabbed the back of her chair as the front of the starship angled downward. The flying trife were getting close. He heard a light rumble on both sides of the cockpit, and then a line of plasma tore through the group from twin cannons on the ship, cutting them down and clearing the air.

Rico adjusted the Tokyo laterally, the motion reminding Hayden of Duncan's boat on the open water. Then her thumbs depressed on the joysticks, sending a pair of plasma streams out and into a single point at the side of the reactor. The superheated gas burned through the metal structure, digging a hole in the interior.

Hayden stumbled forward a step as the pitch of the whine around them changed, the Tokyo beginning to back and rise away from the reactor. Rico was steady at the controls, and even though her face was covered by the helmet, he could see the tense concentration in the veins of her neck.

Below them, trife started pouring out of the reactor, moving slowly in the familiar lethargy of their reproductive process.

"Time for the show, Sheriff," Rico said.

Then she depressed the triggers again, guiding two bolts of plasma perfectly through the hole she had made. He assumed they hit something on the inside, but nothing happened for the first few seconds, except that Rico increased their velocity away, the ship vibrating, working hard to carry them backward at that speed.

Then the inside of the hemisphere lit up in a flash of

orange and white. It cracked and rumbled below, a shock-wave spreading out beneath it. The hemisphere held a large portion of the detonation, but a gout of fire shot up from the plasma hole and spat out from the exit, enveloping the trife nearby and reducing them to ash.

A few seconds later, it had all subsided, leaving a column of smoke pouring out of the top of the reactor.

"Scratch one nest," Rico said.

"Roger that," Bennett replied. "Nice work, Rico. Bring us into orbit."

"Yes, sir."

"Orbit?" Hayden said. "What about the Pilgrim?"

"My word is gold, Sheriff," Bennett said, apparently able to hear him in the cockpit from his position. "But we have a No Contact Protocol. We can't just drop in and show the locals there are spaceships flying around out here."

"They have a right to know how they've been abandoned."

"Says who?" Bennett replied. "The Tokyo is not part of your war, Sheriff. We'll go in secret; we'll get out secret. We stop the Scrappers from getting Inside, and then we can see about arranging a rescue without the Earthers ever knowing we're here. That's as far as I'm willing to go. Take it or leave it."

"How are we going to stop the trife that moved south from here without this ship?" Hayden asked.

"I never promised I would help you with the trife."

"You just destroyed the nest."

"It was a threat to Lewis-McChord. And I was able to destroy it without breaking the NCP."

"I can tell them about you," Hayden said. "I can tell them all about Promixa, Lewis-McChord, everything."

"But will they believe you? There's no shortage of madmen among the Earthers. I think you already know that. Besides, you're one of us. Why don't you just save your people and go to Proxima with them? You don't need to protect everyone."

"Yes, I do. Whether you help me or not."

"Why?"

"Because Earth needs someone to champion justice and law and order. Earth needs a Sheriff."

"How is she?" Hayden asked, approaching the seats in the hold where Natalia and Casey were sitting.

Doctor Shihab was slumped against the transport, physically and mentally exhausted, his eyes closed.

"Stable," Natalia replied. "Sleeping."

Hayden looked at her. They had gotten her out of the body armor while he was in the cockpit with Rico. The light cloth undergarments they had given her were soaked with sweat, and clinging to her small frame. Without the chains, without the leather, she looked more like a child than ever. She seemed peaceful enough for the moment at least.

"Doctor Shahib says this is normal," she continued. "She'll be out for an hour or two. When she wakes up, she'll be more alert than ever."

"Does he know what the sample is supposed to do?"

"He said they were trying to increase human endurance. RHR, he called it. Rapid Healing Response. He said it's a carryover from work being done before the generation ships left Earth. The program was discontinued for a long time, but Doctor Franklin convinced Command to reinstate it. She insisted there wasn't a single clear path to victory."

"I don't necessarily disagree with that statement, just her idea of what it means."

"Me, too. And victory over what? That's my biggest problem with all of this. The Spacers are using Earth to find a way to fight an enemy they've never seen. An enemy they can't identify. They have no way of knowing if any of their efforts will be effective."

"I know."

Casey groaned slightly. Both of them looked over at her. Natalia put her hand on her forehead.

"She's not as hot as she was before," she said, shaking her head.

"What is it, Nat?" Hayden asked.

"I'm angry with myself for letting Franklin use that damn sample on her. I should have tried to find a way to crack the uplink."

"You were right. It would have taken hours that we don't have. I shouldn't have let her take it for me. That selfish part of me made me hesitate. I don't want to leave you behind, especially now. It was such a relief to learn I'm not carrying the contagion."

"You're allowed to be selfish sometimes."

"With this? No. I screwed up, and now she's paying for it."

"It was her choice."

"Then we have to both stop beating ourselves up, right?"

She smiled. He had maneuvered around her with logic, and she knew it.

"There are no windows on this thing, but maybe you felt it," Hayden said. "The Tokyo is in low-Earth orbit. It's pretty amazing. Just like the videos on the PASS. You can't see the destruction from this high up. Just the green and whites and blues and browns. You'd never know how lousy the situation is on the ground." He paused. It was still difficult sometimes to come to terms with everything they had been through. "Bennett won't bring the ship anywhere near where there might be any people."

"I suspected he wouldn't," Natalia said.

"You did?"

"Yes. The Sergeant reminds me of you, and not just because of that scar on his face. He could almost be your replica."

"I don't know about that. Bennett's trying to stay within the guidelines of his duty, and I respect that. I can't say I did the same trying to get to you. I cut off Malcolm's hand to get his identification chip."

He hadn't told her that before. She was as shocked as he would have expected.

"Did you kill anyone?" she asked.

He shook his head. "No. I wounded Malcolm and Hicks and Bradshaw. Malcolm killed Wilson because she tried to help me. He killed a lot of people trying to keep Metro safe."

"I'm sorry, Hayden. She was always loyal to you."

"Too loyal." Hayden lowered his head to his human hand. The tears were welling in his eyes. "Sarah, Francis, Jonas, Jake. His father, Hank. Duncan. They all died trying to help me get to you. Jake and Hank gave me this hand because they said the world needed more good men. I'm not a good man, Nat. I'm not."

She leaned forward, reaching out to him. Putting her hand on his face and making him look at her.

"Yes, you are," she said. "We all do things we aren't proud of. But like you told me, we're doing the best we can with the situation we're in. Your heart is in the right place, or you wouldn't be saying the things you're saying now. You didn't give up on me. You haven't given up on the Pilgrim, and I know you aren't going to give up on the innocent people out there. The people King and his Scrappers are abusing."

Hayden nodded, reaching up to cup Natalia's face. "I don't know how we're going to stop an army of trife without Bennett's help. Wiz's soldiers aren't going to be enough."

"I already thought of that, remember?" she said, pointing over to the second transport. "One thing at a time, but when the time comes, Bennett may be able to help more than you or he knows."

"And what about you?"

"What about me?"

"I think you should stay here. On the Tokyo."

She shook her head. "You're kidding, right?"

"Come on, Nat. I'm serious. Stay here with the ship. Stay safe."

"While you go out there and die? No. I'm not doing that, Hayden. I can't believe you would even ask me to."

"What else am I supposed to do? I don't want you to get hurt. I don't want you to lose another chance to be a mother."

"Without a father? Without a husband? That's not what I want. It never has been. You know that."

"I'm scared for you," he admitted.

"I'm scared for you," she replied. "But in this case, I hope that makes us stronger."

"I hope so, too."

She put her arms around his neck, pulling herself close. "We'll survive this."

He put his forehead against hers, looking into her eyes. "You're beautiful, you know."

"So are you. And you're better than what your fear is trying to make you. Fight for what you know is right. Be the Sheriff you were born to be. Whatever happens, we can both be proud of that."

He put his lips to hers. One kiss to seal their resolve.
"We've got a lot to protect," she said.
They did. He wasn't going to lose her. Not again.
Not ever again.

28

THE ROUTE BENNETT MADE THEM TAKE WAS ANYTHING BUT direct, causing the ride down from orbit to last nearly two hours. The upside of the delay was that Casey was awake by the time they were nearing the surface. Doctor Shihab guided her to the cockpit, where Natalia, Bennett, and Hayden were standing behind Rico, watching the displays while she guided the ship.

"Wow," Casey said as she entered and saw the screens.

The Tokyo was only a few hundred meters up, hugging the mountainous, barren terrain on its approach to the Pilgrim, covering a desert land nobody would want to live in, and only the most robust survivor could remain in for long. Coarse plants lined jagged rock, both of them assuming shades of brown that continued as far as Hayden could see.

He had tried to describe the Pilgrim's location to Bennett, only to be assured that they knew where the ship's launch site was. The reason they had never been to it was because they had always assumed it was overrun and lost, not overrun and secured.

"Casey," Hayden said, smiling when he saw her. "How do you feel?"

"Pretty good, all things considered. I don't have horns or anything, do I?"

"Not so far." He felt a fresh pang of guilt that she had taken the sample instead of him. He didn't tell her that. He knew what she would say.

"See? It isn't all bad." She pointed at the screen. "Trife nest."

Hayden eyed the display. They had passed half a dozen nests and thousands of trife already. The nests were wedged in the crags of the hills, likely out of reach of the goliaths. They had passed one of them already, too, gaining altitude to travel beyond its reach, though the Tokyo's airborne status meant the giant hardly paid any attention to it as they went by.

Seeing so many nests, and so many trife had shaken Hayden's hope they could accomplish anything lasting and positive here. Maybe it would be enough to help the colonists of the Pilgrim escape this hellscape for the relative comfort of Proxima Centauri? Maybe Bennett was right, that he and Natalia should head there too, and leave the people of Haven, Sanisco, Lavega, and others to fend for themselves?

"Lots of trife nests, Chains," Bennett said. "That's the way your world is."

"It doesn't have to be," she replied. "You have the resources to stop it."

"Not alone, I don't. Everybody's lost hope on Earth, whether they live here or not."

"That's because they haven't met Hayden yet," Casey said. "That's because King is running things, and he's an asshole. I think things can change."

Maybe not. The Space Force had abandoned them. Someone had to stick around to help.

"Rico, ETA to the drop point?" Bennett said.

"Fifteen minutes, Sarge," she replied.

"Let's head back down to the hold. Chains, are you in on this?"

"I'm in," she said without hesitation.

"You're sure you're okay?" Natalia asked.

"I feel fine," she replied. "I feel the same as I did before Franklin stuck me. Where is she, anyway?"

"You don't remember?"

"No. The last thing I remember is her jabbing that needle into me."

"She's gone," Bennett said.

"Good riddance," Casey said.

"There's another one," Rico said. "Starboard side."

Bennett's head turned to the proper display. The others found it too. It was still hazy in the distance, but the size and shape were unmistakable. Another goliath, large and hairless, its mottled skin nearly blending with the brown backdrop. It was moving away from them, giving chase to a group of trife desperate to avoid its sweeping reach. They drew closer to it as it bent over, knuckles scraping the ground as it caught two of the demons in its grasp, bringing an oversized hand to its mouth and dumping the creatures in.

"It isn't so scary, seeing it from up here," Casey said. "I remember one time, a goliath passed through Carcity. We stayed hidden and silent. It didn't help the poor bastards who had ducked under one of the old buses. It stepped right on it, crushed the grepping thing flat to the ground, pressed it so hard the blood couldn't even escape the wreckage."

"That's some story, Chains," Bennett said. "Were you close to the victims?"

"One of them was my half-sister."

"Damn. I'm sorry to hear that."

"It's okay. So many people die out here, you get used to it.

You get numb to it. If she hadn't died, I don't know if I would have left when I did. It worked out for the best."

"Even now?" Hayden asked.

Casey looked at him, face tight. "I told you, Sheriff. My choice. My decision. Drop it."

"Rico, can you mark its location somewhere?" Natalia asked. "That one may be promising, especially if it's the closest to the Pilgrim."

"Can do," Rico replied.

They stayed far away from the goliath as they passed it. The giant was moving in the same general direction as they were, leaving Hayden to wonder if it might make an appearance near the Pilgrim and create another round of turbulence for the residents of Metro.

Bennett turned away from the monitors, motioning the others to follow. He led them back down to the hold, where Shahib was unpacking the rest of the medical gear and setting up a mobile triage station. He would be ready to patch up anyone who made it back to the starship. With any luck, he wouldn't be needed at all.

"Grab your gear," Bennett said. "Make sure you have enough magazines, cartridges, and batteries. Hopefully, we'll get lucky, and there won't be any trouble. But somehow I doubt it."

"You aren't worried about the Scrappers seeing us in your gear?" Hayden asked.

"Not so much. Could be someone found this stuff laying around somewhere and claimed it. Besides, I can't care about it if I'm dead."

"Pozz that," Hayden said.

"Once we're clear of the Tokyo you're in charge, Sheriff. I'll do what you say."

"Thank you."

"You'll be an honorary Deputy," Casey said. "Just like me."

"You aren't honorary," Hayden said. "You're the real deal."

"Big things come in small packages," Bennett said. "That's an old saying, but it suits you, kid."

Hayden set about organizing his gear, refreshing the cartridge in the PL90 and putting a new magazine in his sidearm. He loaded the pockets of the armor with additional ammunition, taking nearly half of what they had brought for his armaments. Then he pulled the networked helmet back on, connecting it to the suit and waiting for it to boot up.

Natalia, Casey, and Bennett did the same. They hadn't been finished long when Rico's voice pierced their shared comm.

"Prepare for touchdown," she said. "Boots on the ground in two."

The ramp clicked and hummed, beginning to drop. A gust of warm air swept into the hold, wrapping itself around them. Dust followed, kicked up by the ship's propulsion. Gravitoelectric generators, according to Rico. Though he hadn't seen it, she claimed the Pilgrim was resting on a sled lined with the technology, which would have been used to carry the massive generation ship from the launch site through the planet's atmosphere, and beyond the gravity well before being jettisoned. According to the pilot, the sleds of the other generation ships were still up there, circling the globe in a high orbit.

Hayden watched the clock in the top left of his helmet tick off the seconds as the Tokyo drew nearer to the ground. The ramp hit the dirt at exactly the two-minute mark, and Bennett ran forward and down, rifle up and ready as he emerged into the barrens.

Hayden, Casey, and Natalia followed behind him, out onto a small plateau fifty meters above the base of the landscape.

"Rico, keep the Tokyo safe," Bennett said. "You have to bug out, then bug out, but make sure you come back."

"Roger that, Sarge."

"Command is yours, Sheriff," Bennett said. "The Pilgrim should be just over the other side of the ridge there, about ten klicks from our current position. We've got six hours until sundown. That should be plenty of time to get there before it gets dark."

"Pozz," Hayden replied. "Everybody stay close. Remember, even if King hasn't arrived yet there are going to be Scrappers on site, and we're going to be outnumbered. We survive and succeed by being smarter than they are."

"That shouldn't be too hard," Casey said.

"No it should not," he agreed. "Stay sharp."

He glanced over at Natalia. She was already looking back at him.

They were going home.

29

HAYDEN KNEW THEY WERE IN TROUBLE THE MOMENT THEY crested the ridge of the rocky hill that backed the Pilgrim's launch site.

It was nearly dark, and a line of ugly clouds had filtered in behind them as they navigated the back side of the ridge that kept their approach out of sight. If he were superstitious, he might have taken the appearance of the heavy clouds as an omen for what was to come. As it was, he had barely paid it any mind and hadn't thought about it again until he saw the situation below.

It had been a little over a week since he had fled the torn and dented structure he was now looking down on with Natalia, Casey, and Bennett from their perch nearly half a kilometer away. It hadn't changed much since the last time he had turned his head to look. The roof was peeled away, sitting awkwardly against the side of it. The walls were battered and dented inward. Massive impressions had been made beside it and around it, leading across the depressed collapse of earth where the Pilgrim was resting.

There were trucks sitting outside the building. A dozen of

them. Scrappers were standing around them, a couple of them wearing Marine Corps armor Hayden was willing to bet had come from the cache beneath Metro. They were all carrying Marine Corps rifles.

Someone jumped out of one of the trucks. They were dressed in faded clothes, their hair ragged, their face scared. They tried to go back into the building. They had tried to go back to the Pilgrim. One of the Scrappers shouldered his rifle and fired, and the person fell face-first into the dirt.

The Scrappers left them there like that.

"Hayden, they're taking them," Natalia said, softly and painfully through the shared comm.

It sure looked that way. The trucks were loaded with colonists, and as he opened his mouth to respond, their engines started coming to life, one by one. A rumbling echo sounded in the valley, one that would surely be loud enough to draw the goliath they had flown over in the Tokyo if it remained stationary for long.

"We have to do something," Natalia said.

It didn't. Headlights pierced the dimming landscape. The Scrappers around the trucks retreated to them, grabbing the sides and climbing up. Then the convoy was underway.

"We're too late," Hayden said, biting his lip in an effort to hold back his emotion. They were too fucking late.

"Stay smart, Sheriff," Bennett cautioned.

The Spacer Sergeant was right. He couldn't help them by letting his feelings guide his decisions. He stayed silent while the trucks vanished into the dusty horizon, following the same path Ghost had taken.

"Casey, where do you think he's bringing them?" Hayden asked.

"I can't begin to guess, Sheriff," she replied. "You said there are fifty-thousand colonists in Metro?"

"Give or take."

"Each of those trucks can carry one hundred. Two if they cram them together. If they bring them to Haven, it's twelve hours there and back."

"Unless they have a lot more trucks, they can't have moved more than ten thousand," Natalia said.

"And what are they going to do with them?" Casey asked. "That's too many new mouths to feed."

"And why are they traveling at night?" Hayden said.

Casey gasped. "Geez."

"What is it?" Hayden said.

"If you were King, and you got access to a city inside a starship but you had limited resources, what would you do?"

"Separate the wheat from the chaff," Bennett said. "Figure out who has value, and who doesn't."

"And then what?"

"Dispose of the chaff," Bennett said.

The statement made Hayden's blood run cold.

"And if I didn't want to waste ammunition," he continued. "I would load them into trucks."

"And drop them in the middle of nowhere in the middle of the night so the trife will take care of the problem," Hayden said, finishing the thought.

"No one could be that cruel," Natalia said.

"You met King and Ghost," Hayden replied. "You don't think so?"

"We can't catch up to them," she said, her voice breaking. "That son of a bitch."

"There are still people to save in there," Hayden said. "There have to be. We need to focus on them."

"Pozz that," Casey said. "You want to go down now, or you want to wait for full dark?"

"It might help to wait," Bennett said. "The helmets have night-vision. It will give us an edge."

"What if more trucks come?" Natalia said.

"We'll disable them, and the Scrappers driving them," Casey said.

"Sheriff, it's your call," Bennett said.

Hayden's eyes shifted, locking on the colonist face-down on the ground near the building. He couldn't see into the damaged structure from this angle despite the missing roof, but he was sure there were guards posted near the lifts to the underground hangar.

"I'm not waiting. We have no idea what's happening in there. Casey, are you still feeling okay?"

"I feel great, Sheriff," she replied. "Better than I have in a long time."

Just like Franklin had said. But what would happen when the crash came?

He stood, climbing over a larger stone and dropping down. The others followed without question, staying close and bringing their rifles into a ready position.

They picked their way down the slope at an angle, taking a path that would bring them to the intact side of the outer structure. It took nearly half an hour to make the trip, but they made it down without being spotted, pressing tight against the side of the building and take a moment to regroup.

"Bennett," Hayden said. "You're the best shot. I want you to take point. Sweep into the building, kill anything that moves."

"Pozz that, Sheriff," Bennett said.

They started creeping along the side of the building, single-file. They had taken a dozen steps when Casey's voice broke the comm.

"Trucks," she said. "Coming this way."

"I don't hear anything," Hayden said.

"Helmets have augmented external mics, and I don't hear anything," Bennett said.

"They're coming, Sheriff," she said. "I'm sure of it."

"I believe you." He scanned the hills nearby. "Bennett, head up there, find a good spot."

"Pozz," the Spacer replied, changing direction, running quickly back up the slope.

"They couldn't have brought them very far if they're coming back already," Natalia said.

"Unless it's a fresh group," he said. "Maybe they're rotating? It doesn't matter. They come back here; they're coming back to die."

THEY WAITED AT THE EDGE OF THE BUILDING FOR THE TRUCKS to return. It was another two minutes before the microphones in the Spacer helmets were able to pick up the noise of the engines, and two more after that before the trucks faded through the haze and into view, raising a fresh cloud of dust behind them. There were ten of them this time, a fresh load of trucks. One of them had a huge trailer on the back of it, easily big enough to carry three or four hundred colonists, and the sight of it made Hayden sick and angry.

Bennett's vantage point was feeding them a raft of information on targets and positioning. There was a driver behind the wheel of each truck, a guard on the passenger side, and two more in the back. Forty Scrappers in total. The biggest trouble was that as soon as they attacked, the rest of the militia anywhere near the Pilgrim would know about it.

But not all. Their transceivers didn't reach down into the ship. If they were fast, they could get to the entrance before word reached whatever forces were already inside.

"Wait until they get out," he said to the others.

"I've got a clean shot, Sheriff," Bennett said. "I can take out all ten drivers before they make it all the way in."

Hayden considered the approach. Having the Sergeant take out all of the drivers with pinhole-sized laser blasts to their heads did have a certain appeal.

"Okay," he said. "We move on your mark. Do it."

"Pozz that," Bennett said. He was still affirming the order when the rear truck started to lose its speed, the driver already dead.

"That's one," Casey said.

"How?" Hayden asked.

"I don't know. I can hear a lot better. Smell a lot more. Must be the crap Franklin gave me. Two. Three."

Hayden watched the trucks. He was taking them out from the rear forward, to make sure the loss of control of one truck wouldn't mess his aim up on the next.

"Four. Five. Six."

He was snapping off bolts at nearly one per second, making instant adjustments and firing the rifle. He had turned off the flash of light at the muzzle that signaled friendlies of the shot, making the weapon completely silent and invisible, but no less deadly.

"Seven. Eight."

The front two trucks had gotten word from somebody at the back, or maybe they had seen the prick of light the laser gave off from a more direct angle. Either way, they slowed to a stop, all of the Scrappers jumping out and looking for cover.

"Come on," Hayden said, charging out from the side of the wall.

He didn't have the best line of sight on the Scrappers, but Bennett did, and his networked system made up for his vision, helping aim his PL90. He fired a pair of rounds, watching them burn past the truck's large cab and hit something he could barely spot.

Natalia and Casey ran out with him. It only took a few steps for the latter to start bounding ahead, moving faster than any normal person could. Faster than Bennett, even. She got to the back of the first truck, diving and sliding on her back with her weapon pointed to the rear, shooting the two Scrappers waiting there, rolling back to her feet and running toward the second vehicle. Bullets kicked at the ground around her, one of them cracked off her armor, but she didn't slow at all.

"Sheriff, the building," Bennett said.

Hayden slowed and spun. A group of Scrappers were running out of the building behind them, just starting to bring revolvers to bear. One of them fell, a hole appearing in the side of his skull.

A second toppled over.

They realized they were getting hit from the side, and they moved to retreat into the structure.

Hayden's eyes flicked to the threat display in the helmet. Casey was charging through the line of trucks, downing the Scrappers single-handedly.

"Me and Nat are heading into the structure," he said. "Bennett, Casey, back us up when the trucks are clear."

"Pozz," Casey said. "Should only be a minute."

He felt a pull in his gut. Guilt, because at the moment he was selfishly grateful for what Doctor Franklin had done.

They entered through the twisted metal of the doorway. The interior hadn't changed all that much since the last time he had been through. The Scrappers had erected tents to stay out of the elements, and they had stuck mainly to the corners and shadows to avoid the goliaths. There were bloodstains on the cracked cement floor and the walls, mingling with trash and offal. A dark tarp was resting in the center of the room, a pale, dead hand sticking out from beneath it.

Scrapper, or colonist? Hayden wasn't sure he wanted to know.

There were live Scrappers inside, too. His HUD lit up nearly a dozen. He and Natalia continued ahead, into the hail of bullets that rained in on them. They let the helmets help guide their aim, firing single rounds into unprotected targets, dropping the Scrappers one at a time. He was aware of the slugs cracking off his chest padding, and he felt the pain of one that hit his less-protected arm. It didn't have the force to punch through or do more than leave a bruise.

They walked together, side by side, along the left side of the structure. He could see the lift he had emerged from up ahead, and a larger one beside it that was used for the vehicles. There was no sign of colonists. The trucks had returned, but there wasn't another group waiting to go. He hoped it wasn't because they were done culling the city.

They were halfway to the lifts when Casey and Bennett joined them, firing at the remaining Scrappers from the rear. It took all of thirty seconds to clear the room.

"The tents," Bennett said, turning and sweeping the area. Hayden knew the helmet could do infrared, but he wasn't sure how to activate it. Of course, the Sergeant knew, and he had seen people inside.

He pointed to one of them. Hayden walked over to it, leading with his rifle. He stuck his head in.

A woman was lying on some blankets. She was naked and bleeding from her thighs. Unconscious, with thick bruises around her neck. He could tell by the smoothness of her skin and the clothes beside her she was from Metro.

"Fucking bastards," he cursed. He didn't have time to attend to her. He left the tent, angrier than before.

"What did you find?" Hayden asked Bennett.

"Let's just kill them, Sheriff," he replied.

Hayden nodded. He walked over to one of the dead Scrappers, pushing aside his robes until he found a transceiver. He picked it up. Nothing but static at the moment. He tucked it into his armor, replacing a cartridge for it and refreshing his rifle. Then he went to the lift.

"Stay ready. We don't know if they managed to radio anyone down below or not."

"Pozz," the others said.

"Nat, how are you feeling?" he asked.

"I'm okay, Hayden," she replied. "A little shaken to see things like this. But at least we're going to stop it."

"You've got that right. Casey? How are you holding up?"

"I feel great," she replied.

For now.

He found the button on the lift and slapped it. The cage closed around them, the mechanism humming and shaking as it started to bring them down.

"THIS IS EXCITING," CASEY SAID, AS THE LIFT RUMBLED downward into the subterranean hangar.

"I wouldn't call it that," Natalia replied. "Not with so many of our people dead."

"Oh. Geez. I'm sorry," Casey said. "I wasn't thinking. I feel wired. Twitchy, even."

"It's okay. I understand."

"When we get to the bottom, there's going to be a long ramp that leads directly into the Pilgrim," Hayden said. "The bridge is down a corridor to the right. I'm not sure how to get back to Metro from there."

"I know how," Natalia said. "Pig brought me out directly from Section C up to here, and then I was taken outside to wait for Ghost."

"You remember it?"

"I memorized the route, in case I had a chance to escape, to try to get back. It was stupid, considering the door can't be opened from this side."

"It wasn't stupid," Hayden said. "The door can be opened, and it gave you something to occupy your mind."

"I kept hoping you would come. At the same time, I was terrified you would come."

"I felt the same way. I'm not scared right now. I'm too pissed to be scared."

They rode the rest of the way in silence. Hayden lifted the PL90 as the bottom of the shaft faded into view. The others followed his lead.

He looked down through the open-grated floor, his helmet calling out a target at the same time that target started firing up at them, a rapid-fire staccato of rounds that could only have been launched from a Marine Corps rifle.

"Shit," Hayden said, aiming his weapon down.

The rounds sparked off the metal below them, ricocheting through and bouncing off the metal. One of the slugs skipped off the wall and hit his transparent faceplate, the angle and velocity enough to put a small crack in it.

Too close.

Sergeant Bennett dropped to a knee, sticking the muzzle of his rifle through the floor, but the shooter backed up, getting out of range of the weapon.

"I guess they know we're here," he said.

"Is everyone okay?" Hayden asked.

"Yes," Natalia replied.

"I got hit in the leg," Casey said. She leaned over. "What the grepping hell?"

"What is it?" Hayden asked nervously, spinning to check on her. There was a small hole in her armor near the back of her knee, one of the weakest spots in the suit. She had her finger in it, and when she pulled it away, it was clean.

"It didn't break the skin," she said, surprised.

She looked up at Hayden, flinching when the gunfire started again, bullets punching up from below. The target appeared on Hayden's HUD, vanishing a few seconds later. The shaft fell silent again.

"Got him," Bennett said.

The silence only lasted a few seconds. The lift reached the bottom, where a squad of Scrappers was already waiting, having taken defensive positions behind nearby equipment Hayden assumed was being brought to the surface. They opened fire on the lift the moment the bottom of it came into view, once more sending a barrage of slugs through the bars of the cage and into their armor.

Hayden turned his head away, positioning himself in front of Natalia. He could feel the rounds hitting the back of his armor, skipping off the thicker plates or being absorbed by the softer ballistic material. It pressed in when it hit the soft padding, like a hard jab to the spot that sent waves of pain from the location though it didn't break the skin.

"Geez!" Casey shouted, curling up to make a smaller target. Dozens of rounds were entering the cage. For the Scrappers, it was like shooting ducks in a barrel.

Except the ducks were mostly bulletproof, and had guns, too. Sergeant Bennett especially was unfazed by the return fire. He calmly crouched beside Hayden, taking aim and firing, his laser rounds taking down three of the Scrappers in quick succession. The other three were wearing Marine Corps armor that seemed impervious to the lasers, at least where they were covered by the heavier plating.

Hayden had seen how plasma affected the armor, too. It could burn into the thick material, but it didn't burn through, at least not straight away. He put the PL90 on his back, switching to his sidearm. He was still a better shot with a pistol.

"Aim for the neck," he said. "Near the shoulder."

The Spacer armor was more protected there, with a high collar that covered the vulnerable joint.

"Pozz that," Bennett said, shifting both weapon and aim.

He squeezed off a round that struck one the Scrappers

below the helmet, a spray of blood launching back from his wounded neck as he stumbled and collapsed. Hayden fired three shots of his own, the last of which struck the second Scrapper. The third was smarter. He turned sideways and lifted his shoulder, covering the weak spot and shooting back across his body. One of the rounds hit Bennett's faceplate, scuffing it instead of cracking it.

"Son of a bitch," he cursed, shooting back.

The Scrapper ducked below the nearby crates, hiding from the return fire while the lift stopped and the doors rolled open. Casey sprang out without a word, running forward and punching the center of the equipment. It was thrown back and into the Scrapper, hitting him hard and knocking him into the wall. She drew her sidearm and fired it point-blank into his neck.

"Clear," she said.

"That sucked," Bennett said, looking over his armor. "I don't know if these things were ever tested against such heavy firepower."

"Wiz said the Marine Corps version lost integrity after enough hits," Hayden said. "Could be these do, too."

"I should have read the fucking manual."

"Let's go."

They sprinted away from the lift, past the small station at the edge of the ramp. Hayden hadn't gotten a good look at the outside of the Pilgrim during his exodus. He didn't get a chance yet, either. There were more Scrappers at the airlock, leaning out past the metal rim. Their attack drove all four of them back behind the control station, grabbing for their rifles to return fire.

"So much for the element of surprise," Bennett said. "These assholes really are a problem, aren't they, Sheriff?"

"They sure are," he agreed.

"Sheriff," Casey said. "I've got them. Cover me."

"Casey-" Hayden started to say.

"I've got them. I don't know what's going to happen to me when this wears off or when this is going to wear off, but we should use every tool we've got."

Hayden stared at her, hesitant. Not because she wasn't right. But he didn't want to lose her. Not her. Admitting what Franklin had done, accepting it, and using it, only drove the knife of guilt deeper.

"Damn," he said. "Okay. On my mark."

"I'm ready."

"Sergeant, Nat, are you ready?" he asked.

"Pozz," they replied.

Hayden counted two more of his heartbeats. Then he leaned out around the corner, sending a line of plasma bolts racing across the distance.

"Now!" he shouted.

Casey darted around the corner, sprinting across the ramp at full speed. Natalia and Bennett emerged with Hayden behind her, firing around her, enough blasts that the Scrappers were smart to stay under cover. They stuck their rifles out and fired blindly, shots echoing through the cavernous hangar.

Hayden cursed as one of them hit his helmet again, the force causing the existing crack to web out from the center, blocking his view.

"I need to lose the bucket," he said to the others before abandoning the comm. "I can't see."

He pulled the helmet off, throwing it angrily to the side. He felt more exposed, and yet more free than before. The assisted aiming of the system was great, but he would always prefer his eyes.

Casey raced down the ramp at a speed Hayden could barely believe, making it to the airlock within ten seconds. He winced when he saw her enter the space, the Scrappers firing on her point-blank as she grabbed one, throwing him into another, drew her pistol and fired it seven times, pop, pop, pop, pop, pop, pop, pop.

The enemy position fell silent. Casey turned around, falling to a knee, but waving them in.

"Shit," Natalia said, seeing the condition she was in.

Casey grabbed her helmet, pulling it off and throwing it aside. Even from a distance, Hayden could see the blood on her forehead.

They ran across the ramp to her. Hayden only took a moment to put his eyes on the Pilgrim's exterior. So much of it was cloaked in darkness, but he could see the rise of it, the angles and lines along the sides. The ship was blocky and rough, not smooth and sleek like the Tokyo. It was utilitarian and functional, a result of its rushed to completion nature. Still, it was impressive. That humankind had managed to build something so large and so advanced in such a short time. For some reason, it seemed even more incredible from the outside than it had living in it.

They came to a stop at Casey's side. Her armor had multiple holes through it, unable to absorb the rounds with maximum exit velocity. She had a bullet wound to her head, another three in her chest, a few more in her legs. There was blood, but not as much as Hayden would have expected. He glanced over at her helmet. It was as destroyed as his.

"Grepping hell," she said. "Bastards."

Hayden looked over at the Scrappers. They were in much worse shape than she was.

"Casey, are you hurt?" Natalia asked.

"I don't think so," she replied. "It hurt when they did it, but it's starting to feel better."

Her forehead already had a patch of pink skin where the wound had been seconds before.

"Rapid Healing Response," he said. "Your body's putting itself back together in a hurry."

He wished he could be happy about it, but his mind was drawn back to the video Jennifer had shown him. Whenever they altered the human genome, the improvements were temporary. The human body was built on ages of evolution. Quick changes didn't have good results in the end.

Had Doctor Franklin solved the problem? She thought maybe she had. He could only hope she was right.

"I'm okay," she said, getting back to her feet. "We need to keep moving."

Bennett picked up one of the Marine Corps rifles and a pair of magazines. "Might as well conserve ammo," he said. "Laser rifle is shit against their armor, anyway."

"Nat, you should grab one, too," Hayden said. She was already swapping out her guns, putting the laser rifle on her back. "Which way to Metro?"

Natalia moved to the other side of the airlock, scanning the corridor before moving into it and pointing.

"This way."

3 2

THEY RAN DOWN THE CORRIDOR, WITH CASEY TAKING POINT. She slowed at each of the intersections, taking just long enough to spin her rifle down each corridor before going through.

The loss of the two Spacer helmets was sure to make things more challenging. Without the networked feeds of data, they needed to speak externally, and they wouldn't all get the extra sensor readings from the system, having to rely solely on their eyes for contact and aim. They were also more vulnerable now. Hayden especially. He wouldn't heal like Casey.

They reached one of the stairwells. Casey pushed it open slowly, aiming downward. Their route had been clear so far, leaving Hayden to wonder what path the Scrappers were using to get the colonists out. The larger vehicle lift, most likely. He didn't know how to get out to the hangar floor from the ship. At least, not yet.

Natalia directed them, telling them how far down to go. They traveled the stairwell without incident, dropping ten levels before exiting out into another corridor.

"I don't know how you know where to go," Casey said. "Every hallway looks the same."

"I made it a point to remember," Natalia replied. "Besides, I'm more accustomed to this than I am the world outside."

"I can't even imagine."

They made it a dozen meters before they came across the first dead trife. It was splayed out on the floor, bullet wounds in its head and chest. A handful more were nearby in a similar state, riddled with bullets. Hayden guessed they had been dead for a few days, already.

Had King sent the Scrappers to clean out the nest right after he left? Ales had said they recovered the Marine Corps module, which made it likely.

"There's something up ahead," Casey announced quietly, coming to a stop. "Scrappers, and colonists I think."

"How do you know?" Hayden asked.

"I can hear them talking. I can't make out the words, but they have funny accents like yours."

"Leading another group out?" Bennett said. "They know we hit the trucks."

"We hit the drivers," Hayden said. "They could have more."

"No," Casey said. "It sounds like they're moving away. Further into the ship."

"Towards Metro," Natalia said. "If they know we're here, they could decide to separate the chaff more quickly."

"There are only four of us," Hayden said. "Why would they be that worried?"

"Whatever it is, we need to be careful," Natalia said. "For us and for the colonists."

"Agreed," Hayden said. "Casey, lead us toward the voices. Get us close, but not too close."

"Pozz."

They started forward again. Casey was going slower,

pausing to listen every few steps. She led them through the corridors, turning left at a t-junction. Hayden looked around as he entered. It was familiar.

"I've been here before," he said.

"Section C," Natalia replied. "They are going back to Metro."

A loud clanging thud sounded from up ahead, echoing in the hallway.

"They closed the hatch," Natalia said.

"Yeah," Casey agreed.

"They probably don't know you have the master code," Bennett said.

"I don't know," Natalia replied. "Ghost saw it. If he knows I'm here, he'll probably assume I saw it."

"He may not know you're here," Hayden said. "He left you for dead, and under most circumstances, you would have been. With that armor on, you could be anybody."

"He left you for dead, too," Natalia said. "He told me that if you survived, maybe that made you a god like him and King. He seemed to get a thrill out of that element of chance, as slim as the odds might be."

"Which is probably why he didn't kill you either," Hayden said. "Goddess."

He could just make out her smile through the faceplate.

It took them another few minutes to reach the hatch. They passed the room where Hayden had met Pig on the way, the sight of it returning the memory. It wasn't painful because Natalia was here. Besides, the Scrapper had gotten what he deserved.

Casey leaned out around the corner, pointing her rifle and then looking back at them. "It's here. We're clear."

They spilled out into the end of the short hallway. The secured hatch was ahead of them, thick and large and imposing. Part of Engineering was on the other side, and the city a little further in than that. Were the Scrappers waiting for them there, lined up and ready to fire at anything that came through the hatch?

"Maybe we should go back around, through the hatch I used," Hayden said. "I'm pretty sure I remember how to get there from here."

"Do you want to take more time going around?" Natalia asked.

He considered for a moment. "No. Whatever's happening in there, I want to stop it as soon as possible."

"Me, too," she agreed.

"We'll cover you," he said.

She walked over to the door, to the control panel. Hayden, Bennett, and Casey took positions nearby, getting down prone and aiming at the door. They were ready to shoot as soon as it started to move.

"Stay behind it as long as you can," Hayden said.

Natalia glanced back at him, flashing a thumbs-up. Then she started entering the code.

"If Ghost doesn't know she's here, he will once that hatch opens," Bennett said.

"If Ghost is here," Hayden replied.

"Odds he isn't?" the Sergeant asked.

"Low," he admitted. "He has to be here, somewhere. Maybe on the other side of that door."

The idea of facing off against the Courier again excited him. He wanted a chance to pay him back for leaving Natalia for dead.

Natalia entered the last of the alphanumerics. A green light shone from the panel, and the sealed hatch began to open.

33

HAYDEN LOCKED HIS EYES ON THE HATCH, REMAINING PRONE and motionless, rifle ready, while the hatch finished its motion, revealing the passage ahead. He expected Bennett to start shooting first, the sensors in the helmet able to pick up targets much sooner than he could get a solid visual on them. But the Sergeant didn't start shooting. He didn't need to.

There was nothing. No ambush. No Scrappers. The position was clear.

"I don't get it," Casey said.

"I don't trust it," Bennett replied.

Hayden pushed himself back to his feet. "It doesn't matter. We keep going. I know the way from here."

They were inside Engineering, near the waste disposal system's massive pipes that ran to the processing unit a level above. The place where he had first heard signs of life from the other side of the hatch, though he hadn't been able to make the connection to the noise at the time.

They followed the corridor back down, taking it slow and steady until they reached the central Engineering control center, the room of displays and computers where Natalia had once held court. The room was deserted, a few cups of water resting filled on desks next to uneaten nutrition bars, while others were broken on the floor. Papers were scattered there with them, as if they had tried to run, too. Some of the displays had bullet holes in them. There was more than one slick of blood.

"Damn it," Natalia said in a soft voice, seeing the state of the room.

Hayden's gut clenched. It had taken too long to get back here.

"Casey, do you hear anything?" he asked.

"No," she replied. "I don't know where they went."

"Into Metro, then," he replied.

"Or they're staging an ambush," Bennett said. "Waiting for us to come out."

"That's a risk we have to take," Hayden said. "We're almost there."

They passed through Engineering, into the corridor leading out to Metro. It was long and slightly curved, and they took it a little faster than before, moving with a fresh purpose. Hayden didn't care if they came out into an ambush. He would kill the Scrappers before they killed anyone else.

They neared the end of the hallway. The artificial daylight from the atmospheric generators poured in through the open hatch at the end. Hayden could see the faded brown of the park beyond it, in the same condition it had been a week ago. The first column of blocks was visible in the distance. There was no sign of an ambush. There was still no sign of the Scrappers at all.

"Where are they?" Natalia asked.

"They could nail us from the top of the blocks," Bennett said. "We're open targets trying to cross from here to there."

"We have to cross," Hayden said. "We make a break for the

Law Office first. There's a hidden lift into the underground there. If they're taking colonists out, I bet they're going that way to a lower airlock and out to the hangar floor."

"If they're taking colonists out, they aren't going to get very far," Casey said, referring to the downed drivers.

"Which might entice them to shoot first and worry about how much ammo they have later," Bennett said.

"Right. We start there. We can come up at them from behind and take them by surprise."

"What about the rest of Metro?" Natalia asked.

"What about it?" Hayden replied. "We need to kill the Scrappers that are in here, plain and simple."

"We need to find Ghost," she said. "If he's here, he's in charge. If we take him out, then-"

"Then someone will take his place," Hayden said. "Everyone wants to be in King's favor. Some of them think he really is a god and is going to reward them after they die. Some of them just want the power that comes with being his new best friend. We need to take them all out, and if we're going to do that, we need to be smart. I want to get at him as much as you do, love, but not at the expense of more of our people."

Natalia nodded. "Okay. I'm with you."

They reached the end of the corridor, looking out into Metro. There were no obvious signs of occupation on the streets. There was no sign of anything on the streets. They were empty. Deserted. Everything was quiet, as though the entire city was abandoned. Hayden knew that wasn't the case. That couldn't be the case. The Scrappers had the remaining colonists holed up somewhere.

How many had they already killed?

"On my mark, we run as fast as we can to the first line of blocks. We go into the strand, there." He pointed at one of the narrow alleys. "From that one, we can cross over two more blocks and then turn right, take the strand to the Law Office. Got it?"

"Pozz," the others replied.

He glanced at Casey. She could outpace them easily in her current condition. "If you aren't sure, stay behind Nat or me."

Then he moved to the center of the corridor, set back a little, with Natalia beside him.

"Whatever happens, keep your head down and keep running," he said. "In my experience, most of the Scrappers are lousy shots."

"Not Ghost," Natalia said.

"I think he's got better things to do than sit up there and wait for us."

"Ready?"

"Yes."

"I love you."

"I love you, too."

Hayden drew in one more deep breath, filling his lungs for the sprint. "Go!" he said, and then he burst forward, out into the park.

They made it about twenty meters before the shooting started. The bullets echoed in the enclosed space, sharp and loud. They spit into the ground around them, one after another kicking up small bits of flooring while the group charged ahead. Hayden felt a round hit his hip, caught by the Spacer armor. He raised his mechanical hand over his head in an effort to protect it, glancing over to make sure Natalia was with him.

She wasn't.

He came to a sudden stop, turning in the midst of the gunfire, finding her on the ground a few meters away. She had tripped, or been hit in the leg, and was regaining her feet. A bullet skipped off her helmet as she rose.

"Go!" she shouted at him.

Of course, he wasn't going to listen. He ran back toward her, while Bennett stopped close by, bringing up the laser rifle and firing. The opposing salvo lessened slightly in response.

"I've got you covered," Bennett said.

Hayden reached Natalia, grabbing her arm and helping her along. Bennett fired again, and another Scrapper must have died because the stream of slugs decreased once more.

They resumed the sprint, reaching the edge of the blocks and entering the strand. He looked up as he did, just in time to see a Scrapper on the rooftop of the closest block lean over to fire down at them.

An invisible bolt shot up at the Scrapper. A hole blossomed on his forehead, the dense beam of light burning instantly through his brain. He jerked once and toppled over, falling into the alley beside them with a sickening thud.

"Come on," Hayden said, guiding them through the strands, moving quickly.

They raced along the alley, reaching the end of the first block and drawing up at an intersection. He leaned out into it, pulling back when heavy fire started chewing up the sides of the blocks.

"If they hit the pipes," Natalia said, cutting off.

"Then what?" Hayden asked.

She brought up her rifle and fired into one of the exposed pipes. A hiss of steam followed, pouring out of the hole and creating a curtain between them and the Scrappers.

"They'll damage the venting system," she said, smiling. "Which only matters if you're in space."

"Nice," Casey said.

"Bennett, can you see through that?" Hayden asked.

"Pozz," the Sergeant replied, adjusting something on his helmet. He stepped out into the center of the intersection, switching out the laser rifle for the Marine Corps machine gun. He brought it up, snapping off bursts of three rounds, one after another with slight adjustments in his aim.

One of the Scrappers came charging through the steam, face covered by a nitrous oxide mask, screaming as the vapor scalded him. He pointed his revolver at Bennett. The Spacer slammed it aside with the stock of the rifle and then reversed course, batting the Scrapper in the head.

The man crumpled to the ground. Bennett lowered the rifle, firing a single round into his head. Then he looked at Hayden.

"We kill them all, right?" he asked.

"Right," Hayden replied.

"Clear," Bennett said.

34

THEY STOOD AT THE EDGE OF THE STRAND, LOOKING ACROSS AT the Law Office. A pair of Scrappers in helmetless Marine Corps armor were standing outside, turning left and right as though they knew Hayden and the others were there, and they were nervous about when they would appear.

They didn't have to be nervous for long. Hayden fired one round. Bennett fired the other. Both Scrappers dropped, their heads snapping back from the force of the slugs.

They had killed almost two dozen of King's militia already, most of them trying to intercept them in the strands, for some reason thinking they could get the drop on Hayden where he was most comfortable. There was still no sign of colonists or any clue where they were being held, but the fact that the Scrappers were guarding the Law Office at all was a good sign.

Hayden glanced at Bennett. The Spacer was scanning the area, letting the helmet search for targets. When he was satisfied, he pointed across the split. "We're good to go, Sheriff."

"Pozz that. Let's move."

They crossed the split together, staying close, with

Bennett guarding the rear. They made it to the two bodies without incident. Natalia put her wrist to the closed Office door, unlocking it. Hayden pushed it to the side while Bennett covered the rear and Casey covered the front, allowing him to make a space for them to enter.

They ducked into the front of the Office. Hayden's eyes crossed over the desks of his deputies. Bradshaw. Hicks. Wilson. He felt a new flare of anger, both for what they had done to him and for what he had done to them. He couldn't help but feel responsible that the Scrappers had gotten into Metro. The deaths of the colonists were on his hands, at least in part.

He started walking toward the rear. He didn't know if there was a means to operate the hidden lift behind the station from above, but if the Scrappers had led the colonists to it, there was a good chance it was still down. If nothing else, he was certain Casey could take the fall and bring the lift up to them.

He was passing Wilson's desk near the back when a Scrapper exited the small block of cells on the right. He seemed surprised by their appearance, the heavy prison door dampening the earlier sound of gunshots from outside. He drew back, drawing his revolver.

"Don't," Hayden said, four rifles all being trained on the man at the same time.

The revolver fell from his hands, thunking to the floor.

"Who the grep are you?" he said.

"Shut up," Hayden said. "Where are the colonists?"

The man's eyes tracked to Hayden's mechanical hand. His expression changed. Recognition. He licked his lips, and then smiled, revealing a grin with few remaining teeth.

"You're still alive," he said. "Ghost thought it might be you."

"Where is he?" Natalia asked.

"Bridge," the man replied. "Not that it's going to help. What, just the four of you?" His laugh was rough. "You're all grepping dead. You aren't getting out of the Pilgrim alive."

"Where are the colonists?" Hayden asked again.

"Dead, most of 'em," the Scrapper said. "Took 'em out to feed the trife. Got off on the screams. Especially the little ones. I love the little ones if you know what I mean."

Hayden closed his fist, extending his claws. "Where are the survivors?" he shouted angrily.

"Far as I know, there's a group still down toward the ass end, that's the ones Ghost says we should keep. There's one last group heading up to the surface. That's the ones Ghost says we don't need. If you see little Kyle in that group, tell him Baker says hello." His grin widened.

"You're a dead man," Hayden hissed. "You and the rest of King's soldiers."

"Good luck on that, Sheriff," Baker said. "You're nothing. A little piece of shit. Four black turds, about to get squashed. You can't grep with a god." He started laughing again.

"Sheriff, forget him," Casey said. "Lock him up or kill him or whatever, but we need to move."

"Yeah, Sheriff," Baker said. "Don't just stand there, lock me-"

A loud crack, and then a spread of blood began to bloom from Baker's chest. He glanced down at it, still laughing as he fell to his knees. He looked over at Bennett and then fell forward onto his face, dead.

The Spacer holstered his sidearm. "Decision made," he said.

"Hayden, let's go," Natalia said. "We have to stop them from bringing those colonists out."

Hayden stared at Baker, a sense of hopelessness creeping in. One group left in Metro? One group on its way Outside?

How many dead? How many tortured? How many abused by assholes like this?

"We're too late," he said softly. "For all of them."

"No, we aren't," she replied. "Snap out of it, Hayden. I need you. The colonists need you. If you want to feel guilty, do it later."

He looked at her, struggling against the rising tide of despair. He was the Sheriff. He was supposed to protect these people.

He had failed.

Miserably.

"Damn it, Hayden," Natalia said. "Not now."

He closed his eyes. She was right. He couldn't do this now. He was still the Sheriff of Metro. He still had a job to do. He opened them and nodded. "I'm okay."

"We'll both hurt later," she said.

"Later," he agreed. "The lift is this way."

He turned away from Baker. Away from the prison.

"Hello?" someone shouted from the cell block, the sound barely making it through the reinforced door. "Hello? Is someone out there?"

Hayden rushed to the door, grabbing it and pulling it open. The others trailed behind him as he entered. A hand was wrapped around the bars of the cell to his left. He turned to face it, a mix of guilt and relief flooding through him.

"Well, I'll be," Malcolm said, staring out at Hayden. "Welcome home, Sheriff."

"GOVERNOR," NATALIA SAID. "YOU'RE ALIVE."

Malcolm's head turned toward her. He didn't recognize her with the Spacer helmet on. "Do I know you?"

"It's Natalia Duke," she said.

His eyes returned to Hayden. "I don't believe it," he said. "You found her."

"I told you I would," Hayden said.

"Sheriff?" another voice said from further down. "Hayden, is that really you?"

Hayden turned toward it. Hicks' face was planted against the bars. Bradshaw was beside him. He looked back at Malcolm. The Governor's suit was torn and filthy, and he had pinned the cuff of his sleeve over the stump of his missing hand.

"Shit, Malcolm," he said. "I'm sorry for what I did. I really am. But-"

"Forget it, Hayden," Malcolm replied. "It doesn't matter now. A hand is nothing compared to what these assholes have done to the city."

"I came to stop them."

Natalia turned to a control panel on the wall and started entering the master code.

"You're too late for that," Malcolm said. "They've been here for three days. They were prepared. We weren't." He shook his head. "This is my fault, Hayden. All of it. I didn't know. I didn't know we never left Earth. All of these years. I could have-"

"There was nothing you could have done," Hayden said. "You were trying to protect us. To follow the protocols you were given. I don't blame you for that, and nobody else can, either."

Natalia finished entering the code. The cell doors clicked, unlocking. Malcolm pushed his open, emerging beside Hayden. Hicks and Bradshaw joined him. They were still in their uniforms, dirty and sweaty. Hayden could see the bulge of bandages around the areas where he had shot them.

"I killed people, Hayden," Malcolm said. "The citizens in Block Thirty-two. Wilson. For nothing. It was all for nothing. I cut them down in cold blood. I thought I could keep this place safe. I expected aliens, not people. It was supposed to be sealed, with only one way out. How was I supposed to know? How was I supposed to stop this?"

"How do you think I feel?" Hayden said. "I cut off your hand. We were both doing what we thought we had to do."

"And look where it's gotten us."

"It isn't over yet, Malcolm. There's a group being led up to the surface. There's another group somewhere in the upper blocks. We can still save them."

"How?" Malcolm asked.

Hayden held out his Marine Corps rifle toward Hicks.

"We do our jobs," he said.

Hicks took the weapon and nodded. "I'm ready, Sheriff."

"Bennett, give Deputy Bradshaw your rifle," Hayden said.

Bennett tossed the Marine Corps weapon to the other deputy. "Welcome to the party," he said.

"Malcolm, Hicks, Bradshaw, this is Bennett and Chains."

Casey waved at them. Bennett gave them both a curt nod.

"Can you carry a gun?" Hayden asked.

Malcolm held out his hand. Hayden passed him his sidearm.

"I'm not a good shot, but at least I'm not left-handed," the Governor said.

"First, we're going to stop them from taking the colonists out," Hayden said. "Then we're going to come back and deal with the rest of them."

"What about the man in white? The one who calls himself Ghost?"

"You know him?" Natalia said.

"He was there when they stormed the city. They came in through Engineering. Hundreds of them. The colonists were terrified. His people shot a few of them, a dozen maybe. That was all it took. We aren't soldiers, you know?

"He asked for the Governor, so I went out to meet him. He saw my missing hand and started laughing. He said he knew you and Natalia." He glanced over at her. "He said you're the reason he was here. That you got him Inside."

Natalia nodded somberly. "I did. I'm sorry. You don't know what he did to me-"

"It's okay," Malcolm said. "I'm not trying to blame you, Nat. You didn't leave Metro. You were taken. I get how Ghost operates. I experienced it firsthand. Hell, you came back to do something about it. I can't say I would have done the same. I'm pretty sure I wouldn't have."

"He told me Metro and the Pilgrim belonged to a man named King. He told me to hand over the engineers and the doctors, and anyone else who was critical to the city's operations. I hesitated at first. Of course, I did. So he killed a resident. Every time I tried to think before I spoke, he killed another one. I stopped thinking after that. I gave him everything he asked for. I wanted to be defiant, but I couldn't. Not when he was shooting people right in front of me. I used the loudspeakers to gather the doctors, the nurses, the engineers. Everyone he wanted. If they came too slowly, he killed people. They learned in a hurry, too. He had the entire city under his thumb in a few hours. All it took were a couple hundred dead colonists. When I was done, he locked me up in here."

"And didn't kill you," Casey said. "Why is that?"

"He said it was because the people know me. They'll take me seriously."

"Ghost said that?" she asked.

Malcolm looked surprised. "Yes, why?"

"What about you two?" Casey asked, glancing at Hicks and Bradshaw. "You're telling me Ghost didn't think the only trained, uniformed officers in the city were enough of a threat to get rid of?"

They looked back at her but didn't say anything. Hayden noticed the way their faces hardened, their expressions gaining a measure of tension. He didn't like it. At all.

"Malcolm, what's going on?" he asked.

The Governor raised the sidearm he had been given, pressing it against Hayden's head before he could react. Hicks and Bradshaw brought their rifles up as well, catching them unprepared.

"I'm sorry, Sheriff," Malcolm said. "I told you. It's too late. The colony is gone. Metro is dead. You ended it. You and your wife. Watching Ghost kill the people who put their faith in me, I learned real fast. You do what you have to do to survive. You make sacrifices to protect as many as you can."

He tilted his head, then, tapping at the collar of his suit.

Hayden noticed there was a badge pinned beneath it, out of sight.

"Ghost, it's Malcolm," he said. "Are your men in position?"

"They are," Ghost replied. "Do you have him?"

"I do," Malcolm said. "He walked right into it, just like you said."

"Bring them to the split. I'm on my way down."

"Yes, sir." He tapped the transceiver again.

"Grepping bastard," Casey said. "I knew it was your voice I heard in the corridor, you and your two stooges here, I bet. This son of a bitch has been in prison all of twenty minutes, Sheriff."

"What did he promise you, Malcolm?" Natalia asked angrily. "What do you get in return for this? More people are going to die because of you."

"More people are going to live because of me," Malcolm replied. "He gave me a thousand lives to set you up and turn you in. A thousand more colonists."

"What about the contagion?" Hayden said. "If you know about it, then you know that thousand is hardly worth anything. Most of those people are going to die."

"Unless they get the cure," Bennett added.

"Cure?" Hicks said. "What cure?"

"My people have a cure for the contagion," Bennett said. "We can treat anyone who survives."

"What?" Malcolm said. "Who are you?"

"Sergeant Noel Bennett," he replied. "Space Force."

"Space Force?"

"There's a lot you don't know," Natalia said. "More than we have time to explain. The point is, you're on the wrong side. You still have a chance to get on the right one."

Malcolm kept the gun against Hayden's head. "You're lying."

"No," Natalia replied. "Where do you think this armor

came from? I had the disease, Malcolm. They cured it. They saved my life, and my baby's."

"Baby?" Malcolm said.

"Yes. I'm pregnant."

He stared at her. Hayden could see his resolve was breaking. He wanted to do the right thing for the people of Metro. Now he wasn't sure what that was.

"Help us, Malcolm," Hayden said. "You don't have to turn us in. What do you think will happen if you do? He'll kill them anyway if he doesn't want them. He'll kill you, too, once he's done with you."

"Ghost is on his way down," Malcolm said. "There are three squads of Scrappers waiting outside this office, and he's bringing three more."

"Good," Casey said. "More assholes to kill."

"Governor," Hicks said. "If the Sheriff's telling the truth..."

"Have you ever known me to lie, Hicks?" Hayden asked.

"No, sir," Hicks replied.

"Come on, Malcolm," Hayden said. "We can take them on together."

"And then what?" Malcolm said. "Things go back to the way they were before?"

"No. That's stupid. Nothing can go back to the way it was before."

"I can get your people out of here," Bennett said. "Back to Proxima Centauri with the rest of the descendants of the generation ships, if that's what you want."

Malcolm hesitated for a moment before finally lowering the pistol. "I'm not sure what that means, but I can't very well turn a pregnant woman over to that asshole. I saw what his soldiers did to some of the others. You know, Ghost is going to kill me for betraying him."

Hayden smiled. "Not if we kill him first."

HAYDEN MOVED SLOWLY, MAKING SURE TO HELP MALCOLM keep the pistol pressed against his head as they moved out of the Law Office and into the split.

The Scrappers were waiting there, nearly twenty in all, arranged in three groups surrounding the Office. Only a few of them were in Marine Corps armor and carrying the more powerful rifles. The squad leaders, Hayden guessed. The others were in the familiar brown roughspun robes, six or seven of them wearing nitrous oxide masks, all of them brandishing less impressive revolvers. They trained the weapons on him as they came out, ready to fill him with holes.

Hicks and Bradshaw came out next. Hicks was holding Natalia. Bradshaw was holding Casey. Bennett had a different mission, but nobody was going to tell Ghost that. At least, Hayden was hopeful they wouldn't. He still wasn't completely certain he could trust Malcolm and the deputies. Not after they were ready to hand them over to the Scrappers in the first place. They were taking a risk, a big one, to walk out unarmed and dependent on the Governor's honesty.

"Hold your fire," one of the squad leaders said to the other Scrappers, sensing them getting antsy. He left his group, walking toward Malcolm. "Where's Baker?"

"Dead," Malcolm replied. "He got careless."

"I never liked that grepper anyway," the leader said. He looked at Hayden. "So, you're the invincible Sheriff of Rottingham." He laughed at his joke. None of the others understood it. "Yeah, well, you ain't so invincible now, are you?"

"We'll see," Hayden replied. "I got out of Ports. I can get out of this."

The squad leader laughed. "Yeah, right. You'd need a grepping miracle, and you aren't the one with the god on your side."

"If you really think King and Ghost are gods, you're dumber than you look," Casey said.

"Shut your mouth, bitch," he replied. The Scrapper started walking toward her.

"Oversergeant, get back in line," Ghost said, emerging from one of the nearby strands. He had another dozen soldiers with him, trailing at his back.

Hayden turned his attention to the Courier. He was wearing the familiar white suit, but his head had been shaved, and he had a makeshift white patch over his eye that hadn't been there before.

"Sheriff Duke," Ghost said. "We've never been formally introduced." He walked over to Hayden, holding out his hand. "I'm Ghost."

"That's not a name," Hayden said, refusing to put his hand out.

"It's the best you're going to get," Ghost replied, withdrawing the hand. "I just wanted to tell you that I admire your work." He glanced at Malcolm's stump of a hand. "And your determination. There are very few people who have survived the situation I left you in. Both here not all that long ago, and in Ports."

"I'm resourceful like that."

"I'm sure you are."

"You didn't have that eye patch the last time I saw you," Hayden said. "Right before you nearly put a hole in my head."

"You shouldn't have moved," Ghost said, clearly amused by their conversation. He reached up and tapped the patch. "I have your wife to thank for this. When I arrived back at Sanisco without her, my father was, shall I say, a little less than pleased."

"And he took your eye?"

"He wanted more than that, but he still needs me. I wish he could return it to me, all things considered, but I'll have to settle for gratitude instead." He glanced over to Natalia. "You remember what I told you, don't you? It is as it should be. The fate of humankind, decided by the gods of our kind. King, me, you, your husband." He put his hand on Hayden's shoulder. "Did she tell you about us, Sheriff? Did she tell you that she initiated it? That she practically begged for it?"

Hayden didn't waver. "She told me enough."

"I can only imagine the scene when you burst through the door to save her before the trife could have their way. It must have been very heroic. I admire you for that, Sheriff. In a different world, maybe we could have been friends."

"I don't think so," Hayden said. "You're too much of an arrogant asshole."

Ghost smiled before drawing back and punching him in the gut. The armor absorbed most of the blow.

"I haven't seen any like that down here," the Scrapper said, eyeing the armor. "Where did you get it?"

"A friend," Hayden replied.

"Not that one, I'm sure," Ghost said, pointing toward Casey. "I can smell a desert rat from a mile away." He paused, tapping his index finger against his lip. "Wait. Don't tell me. He came with a starship, right? The Tokyo?"

Hayden bit his lip, surprised Ghost knew about the ship and trying not to betray it. He must have failed because the Scrapper laughed.

"You can't hide things from a god, Sheriff," Ghost said. "Especially a god with the Space Force master code. Did you know the Tokyo has an automated flight system, and it can be activated remotely through the proper channels? No? I didn't either until the Pilgrim's sensors started registering a nearby transponder. I didn't know what it meant, but I've found Mae to be incredibly agreeable to my requests. She filled in the blanks for me. She helped me override the commands and call the little birdie home."

Hayden didn't respond. He could only imagine what Ghost had done to the Engineer to get her help.

"What I really came down here for was Natalia. Mae is agreeable, but she isn't your wife, and we have a lot of preparations to make."

"What kind of preparations?" Natalia asked.

"A question," Ghost replied, smiling. "What do you think we're all doing here?"

"Besides slaughtering innocent people?" Casey said.

"I thought you wanted the weapons?" Hayden said.

"We do want the weapons," Ghost replied. "But we want something much more valuable than that. We want the Pilgrim. We want to repair it. And we want to get the fuck off this shitty, trife-infested shithole of a planet."

"You're crazy," Natalia said. "The Pilgrim has been sitting here for almost four hundred years. Most of the systems are breaking down and falling apart. Even if you managed to get this ship into space, it could lose something critical at any time."

"A risk I'm willing to take," Ghost said. "We don't belong here, any more than you belong here. This world was left behind, sacrificed to the aliens and the humans who were too unimportant to be loaded onto a generation ship in the first place."

"What do you mean?" Hayden asked.

"Oh, you don't even know the history of your own ship, do you, Sheriff?" Ghost said. "The people loaded onto the ships by the USSF? They were all considered very important persons. Scientists, engineers, doctors, the well-educated and well-heeled. Upper crust, save for the soldiers brought along to protect them. It was a fucking joke, one that nobody was ever supposed to learn the punchline to. The ships would have been long gone by the time any of the rank and file were the wiser for it. Except they didn't all make it. You're

Sheriff now. What was your father? His father? What was your first progenitor's position on the ship? In the city? They only wanted certain kinds of people. The rest of us got screwed."

"None of us had anything to do with that," Hayden said.

"I'm not blaming you. I'm making a point. King and me, we deserve to be out there with those people. We deserve to be living in the stars. I saw the orders, the one transferred to the Pilgrim so long ago, the one that nobody was alive to read, redirecting the ship to a different destination. Proxima Centauri. The Tokyo came from somewhere. Was it there?"

"They won't accept you there," Hayden said. "You don't belong."

"Fuck you to tell me who belongs, Sheriff," Ghost shouted. "You don't decide that!"

"I don't have to," Hayden replied. "The Centurions will decide. They'll kill you for what you did to the real colonists."

"Not if I kill them first. I've got weapons, thanks to you. I've got the ship, thanks to you. I've got three thousand Scrappers ready to go to war."

Hayden stared at Ghost. He couldn't believe the man was serious. He wanted to bring the Pilgrim to Proxima Centauri, land the ship and start shooting? He was going to die, and he was going to take the remaining colonists with him.

"Now, if you'll excuse me, Sheriff," Ghost said. "Bring her over."

Hicks started walking Natalia toward Ghost. A slight buzzing noise started to rise from behind the Law Office. Hayden glanced back at Malcolm.

It was time.

Except Malcolm shook his head.

"No," he whispered. "I won't, Hayden. You cut off my hand. You made me kill those people. I can't forgive you for that." His eyes shifted back to Ghost. "Ghost. Sir. It's a-"

Hayden tore himself from Malcolm's grip, throwing back his head as the Governor pulled the trigger. The muzzle flash burned the side of his face as the round exploded past, zipping out and hitting one of the blocks.

He turned on Malcolm, so many emotions roiling through him at the same time he couldn't find the words to speak them. He acted instead, closing his fist, extending his claws, and bringing them down and through the traitor's other wrist, severing his remaining hand.

Malcolm fell to his knees, screaming. Hayden whipped around a second time, pain blossoming in his shoulder as a knife sprouted from it, finding a hole in his armor and sinking into his flesh.

Something started whining behind him, and the Scrappers in front of him began to die.

The rounds from the drone ripped through the groups of enemy soldiers, tearing them to pieces the same way it had torn up the residents on top of Block Thirty-two. A dozen of them were dead within seconds, the rest scrambling to readjust their aim to fire on the killing machine.

Hayden shifted his attention back to Ghost. The Courier was still facing him, hand out from releasing the knife. Hicks was right next to him, having already released Natalia and bringing the rifle Bennett gave him up toward the Scrapper.

Ghost saw him, spinning without hesitation, using the remaining knife to cut into and through Hicks' unprotected neck. Hicks collapsed almost instantly.

Rounds continued to spew from the drone, tearing up the floor of Metro and sawing into the Scrappers. Most were trying to run, to escape the killing machine. Bradshaw had seen what happened to the Governor and had turned back to face it, aiming and firing his rifle up at the drone. It only took a few short bursts to hit something critical, and the machine started to smoke and lose altitude, spinning and sparking as its machine guns wound down. Casey was on him an instant later, recovering from his betrayal and slamming him into the side of the head with a hard punch that brought him to the ground.

Ghost was reaching for Natalia, hand out to grab her. Not again. Hayden rushed toward him, claws out, charging as hard as he could.

The Courier's hand landed on Natalia's forearm, and he tried to drag her into him, to get the knife on her throat. She bucked away, punching with her off-hand, hitting him because he couldn't see that side of his face. The blow caused him to release his grip, and she fell back and away.

Then Hayden made it to Ghost, slashing hard with the claws. The Scrapper deflected them with his knife, turning and punching the one already in Hayden's arm. He cried out in pain, losing feeling in his arm momentarily, his hand falling limp.

Ghost pulled a sidearm, firing at point-blank range, the rounds hitting Hayden's armored legs. One of them made it through, creating a stinging pain in his calf and causing him to stumble.

He expected Ghost to move in for the kill, but he didn't. He broke away from the fight, dashing back the way he had come.

Back into the strands.

Hayden forced himself up, the pain of the shot subsiding. It didn't have enough energy left after piercing the armor to do much damage. He took two steps toward Ghost before noticing there were still a few Scrappers nearby, and they had realized the drone was down.

He grabbed the revolver attached to the back of his armor, turning and firing, hitting one of the Scrappers in the shoulder, right before a shot from Casey hit them in the chest.

One down.

He spun and aimed at a Scrapper already aiming at him, staring at the muzzle flashes and hearing the bullets whiz by as he pulled the trigger, his round hitting the man in the chest.

Two down.

He spun again, finding a third Scrapper to his left, charging toward Natalia. He couldn't get a shot off past her without risking hitting her instead.

He didn't need to worry. Casey intercepted the soldier, hitting him with her shoulder and sending him tumbling away. He rolled and tried to get up, but she had already targeted him, firing three rounds into his body.

Three down.

Hayden turned in a full circle, looking for Scrappers. There were none left, at least not here. Nearly two dozen had died within seconds.

But Ghost had gotten away.

"Damn you, Hayden," Malcolm cried from somewhere behind him. "This is your fault. All of it."

Hayden ignored him, finding Hicks on the ground. He knelt beside him, feeling for a pulse. There was none. He rolled him slightly, retrieving his PL90 from Hicks' back. Then he stood up, closing his eyes. The price of loyalty was always too damn high.

"He's dead because of you," Malcolm said.

Hayden turned back on the Governor, storming toward him, his fury threatening to boil over.

"Because of me?" Hayden shouted. "We had a fucking plan. You were supposed to help us. Now Hicks is dead, and Ghost is gone, you selfish, self-righteous son of a bitch."

"Hayden," Natalia said, trying to get his attention.

"You didn't just betray me, you worthless piece of shit," Hayden continued. "You betrayed everyone in Metro."

"Hayden," Natalia said again, more insistently.

"I saved them," Malcolm replied. "I kept my end of the bargain. Ghost knows that. He'll spare them. I did what was right for the people."

"Bullshit. You did what was right for you."

"Hayden!" Natalia shouted. "We have to go."

Hayden looked at her. Then he turned his head in the direction she was pointing. There were Scrappers running down the split. At least fifty of them.

Damn it.

"Chains, let's go," Hayden said. "This way."

He turned back to Malcolm, staring down at him. "I hope you enjoy whatever's left of your life, Governor," he said.

Then he joined Natalia and Casey, running toward the rear of the Law Office and the underground garage where Bennett was already waiting.

THE LIFT WAS UP WHEN THEY REACHED THE GARAGE, BUT A word from Natalia to Bennett and it started to lower, carrying them into the space beneath Metro where the USSF munitions were being stored.

They only let the lift drop halfway before jumping from it, falling the last few meters and letting their armor absorb the hit. It was painful but necessary, the lift reversing course and rising into place as the Scrapper reinforcements arrived on the scene, getting only a few quick, wild shots through the space before it was sealed off to them.

Hayden stood up, his shoulder numb again from the hit. He grabbed the handle of Ghost's knife, clenching his teeth and grunting as he pulled it out. Blood spilled from the wound with it, soaking his hand as he sought to keep the pressure up.

"You need to take off the armor," Natalia said. "So we can wrap something around it."

Hayden nodded. He pulled the PL90 from his back and handed it to Casey. Then he unclasped the armor, and she and Casey both helped him shrug it off his upper torso. His undershirt was already stained with blood.

Bennett rushed out of the nearby drone control vehicle, hurrying to them. He had found a medical kit inside the thing, and he flipped it open to reveal plenty of bandages and sanitizing gel. He placed it calmly on the ground beside Hayden.

"Take off your shirt, Sheriff," he said.

Hayden did as he was told. Bennett smeared the gel on the wound, wiping it and the blood away with a cloth. He reached into the kit and pulled out another device, which he pressed against the cut. He ran it down the wound, leaving adhesive behind that held the damage closed. Then he quickly threw a patch over it.

"Another couple of inches to the right, and you would have lost the use of that hand of yours," the Spacer said.

Hayden didn't respond. He was already moving to the lockers along the wall. He pulled a few open. They had been cleaned out, save for a few basic utilities. He pulled on the first one he found. It was tight, but it was good enough.

"Ghost knows about the Tokyo," he said.

"I know," Bennett replied. "I was listening in on Natalia's comm. This is a problem, Sheriff."

"This whole thing is a problem," Hayden said.

"Your man fucked us. We would have had them all dead to rights."

"It was a risk. We can't linger here. Ghost can open the lift from the bridge, and then the others will come."

"If they aren't already," Natalia said. "What are we going to do?"

"Three options," Hayden replied. "Try to catch up with the colonists and get them free. Go after Ghost. Head deeper into the splits and try to clear the Scrappers from Metro."

"The last one isn't going to work," Natalia said. "We can't

go back out this way, and circling around will take too long. Ghost left them alive for a reason. He won't go killing them now."

"Especially if King wants them," Casey said. "I kind of like the fact that he took Ghost's eye."

"If Ghost has the Tokyo, what does that mean?" Hayden asked.

"The Tokyo has a fold drive," Bennett said. "If he could figure out how, he could use it to go to Proxima direct."

"Without his army?"

"He just might be crazy and or dumb enough to do it. If Command thinks the Earthers know about them, they might decide to cleanse the settlements."

"Cleanse the settlements?" Casey said.

"Blast them from orbit. Make sure nobody survives who might know we're out there."

"Geez," Casey said.

"Hayden, we can't let the Scrappers lead the colonists out to be slaughtered," Natalia said. "I want to stop Ghost too, but we can't."

"What does it take to figure out how to use the fold drive?" Hayden asked, looking at Bennett.

"It would just depend on if they could get onto the ship past Rico, and then how long it would take them to torture Rico enough that she would talk."

"Estimate?"

"Depends on their methods, but Rico's a Spacer and a replica. She's tougher than your average grunt. It could take days."

"Or they could decide to come back here with more Scrappers," Casey said.

"Unlikely," Hayden replied. "Don't forget, there's an evolved trife army pouring toward Sanisco. King's going to have his hands full already."

"He might be looking to escape it," Natalia said. "Even his high tower won't save him if the trife storm it."

"We have to stop them from taking the colonists," Hayden said. "That's a lot of lives at stake. Once we free them, we can send them somewhere to hide."

"You're asking Rico to bear the brunt while we do this, Sheriff," Bennett said.

"I know. What would Rico tell us to do?"

Bennett paused a moment and then smiled. "She'd say to help the colonists. She's always been selfless like that."

"Then that's what we'll do. We're in a good position from here."

They all turned at the sound of boots heading toward them from the connecting corridor. Bennett's laser rifle was in his hands before Hayden could react, and the Spacer fired as the first of the Scrappers entered the space, killing them before they knew what was happening.

He leveled the revolver toward the exit. He only had three bullets left for the gun. Casey was holding his PL90, aiming it at the entrance. A stream of plasma launched from the weapon, catching the next two Scrappers that entered.

Then she was running ahead, taking off like a dart in the direction of the enemy. Bennett trailed her, while Hayden and Natalia brought up the rear.

They entered the corridor. Hayden stopped when he reached it, turning at the sound of a hard thunk. The lift was starting to come down, and he could see at least a dozen feet standing on it.

"We've got trouble from the rear," he said. "Don't slow down."

Not that he thought Casey had any intention of slowing. He could see her again now that he was through the garage's hatch, up ahead and shooting at the pair of Scrappers trying to intercept them.

"Hayden, wait," Natalia said.

He froze, spinning back to the garage. She had stopped at the door and was entering the code to close it.

He shifted his eyes to the Scrappers. The lift was halfway down, but they weren't willing to jump the rest of the distance. She finished inputting the code. The door started to slide shut.

"That won't hold them for long, but it will slow them," she said, running to catch up to him. "Thanks for not letting Ghost grab me, by the way."

"I told you, love. I'm not losing you again."

She smiled. "Just be careful, okay? You don't have any armor protecting you anymore."

Hayden hadn't given it much thought, but she was right. He couldn't afford to get shot now.

"Pozz that."

She took his hand and squeezed it. They sprinted after Casey and Bennett together.

HAYDEN LED THEM THROUGH THE SHIP, HEADING FOR THE Marine Corps module and the hangar beneath it. They ran into light resistance along the way, Scrappers appearing from adjoining corridors, likely guided by Ghost from the bridge, using the same sensors Hayden had used to track the trife. None of them did much damage or stayed alive for very long. The combination of the trained Spacer soldier and the genetically enhanced Earther was too much for the ragtag militia to manage in small numbers.

They reached the module quickly, going in through the formerly sealed hatch and entering the barracks area. The ancient Marine soldiers were still where Hayden had left them, though the broken door had been jammed open all the way. Moving out into the armory, he was taken aback by the sheer volume of dead trife littering the floor around them. Hundreds of the creatures lay mingled with a few dozen Scrappers, the remains of a battle even larger than the one he had escaped. It hadn't been easy to take the module, but King's militia had managed to do it.

There were no weapons remaining inside. No ammunition. No armor. They had picked the entire place clean, not stopping to collect their dead. The smell was horrible, the visuals nauseating. They moved cautiously to the edge of the hole in the center of the floor and looked down. What had once been a huge trife nest was visible below, scarred and torn and filled with pieces of trife.

"It looks like they dropped a bomb on it," Bennett said.

It did. Hayden looked further back, to the massive loaders that were meant to dismantle and transport Metro to its new location on its new world. It was a purpose they would never get to serve. There were boxes of tools and rags positioned near them, the evidence of Scrappers trying to make the behemoths function. Looking the other way, past what was left of the nest, Hayden could see they had managed to open the large hangar doors. There were dim lights beyond it, and a heavy, wide ramp leading down to the floor of the inner cavern.

"This way," Natalia said, spotting a ladder that had been installed on the other side of the room, beside a makeshift pulley system the Scrappers had used to lower their treasure.

The group circled the hole, reaching the ladder.

"I'll go first," Casey said, slipping onto it before anyone could object. Bennett slotted in behind her.

"Ladies first," Natalia said, moving in front of Hayden. "If anyone is going to get shot, it'll be me."

He didn't argue. She had a point. Her armor could take the hits. His flesh couldn't.

They descended quickly. Casey hit the floor and turned, scanning the hangar. Bennett reached the bottom and did the same. He raised his hand, indicating the area was clear.

Where the hell were the colonists?

Hayden had expected them to be somewhere along this

route, though he imagined the Scrappers knew how to reach the hangar proper without going through the Marine Corps module. If they were already off the ship, were they already loaded onto the trucks and on their way out to be fed to the trife? Had it been a mistake to head into the ship, rather than wait for the group to arrive? Could they have taken on the Scrappers herding the colonists if they had?

They were committed to where they were, and there was nothing they could do about it. It pissed him off that Ghost should have been taken care of and wasn't because of Malcolm. He had been remorseful for what he had done to the Governor. He had thought they could put it behind them for the good of the many. Did Malcolm really believe he was doing the greater good in hoping Ghost would spare lives for his cooperation? Or had he only been convincing himself he was?

Either way, they had missed a chance to save lives and stop the bleeding.

They ran across the hangar, past the remains of the trife and the demons' nest, slowing as they neared the ramp leading into the outer hangar floor. A large metal brace crossed the ramp a few meters ahead of them; the side of the massive sled designed to carry the ship into orbit. It was hanging too low for the loaders to get out past it, but then King didn't want to take them out, he wanted to take them up. He wanted to get the Pilgrim back into space, to escape an Earth overrun with trife and goliaths. Why had he cleared out the Marine Corps weapons then? Hedging his bets in case he couldn't find a way inside?

There was a trio of Scrappers at the base of the ramp, but they were facing the other way, watching something ahead of them. Hayden couldn't see what they were looking at past the side of the sled, but he was thankful they didn't know he was there. Had the sensors in the hangar been damaged in the destruction of the nest? Did Ghost know they were there?

A round of quick shots from Bennett's laser rifle dropped the three guards one after another before they could react. After the last shot, the Spacer slung the rifle on his back.

"Out of charge," he said, drawing his pistol.

"How much is left on the PL90?" Hayden asked. He had left the rifle with Casey while she ranged ahead.

She checked the display. "Ten bolts," she replied. "Not much."

Even though they had made it this far, they were slowly being whittled away. It was only going to get tougher going forward.

"Nat, what do you have?" he asked.

"One hundred shots in the rifle," she replied. "The pistol has fifteen rounds and two magazines."

"Pass the rifle to Bennett," Hayden said.

She held it out to the Spacer. He took it and tipped his head. "Thank you, ma'am."

"Come on," Hayden said.

They made their way down the ramp, to the floor of the outer hangar. It really was a cavern, the space for the starship hewn out of hard rock, the ground below them also stone. Whatever had carved it had chewed the floor, leaving it slightly rough for better footing. There were smaller rocks and piles of dirt and debris nearby, pours of the earth above their heads that had collapsed at the passing of the goliaths. How stable was this area? Would one more goliath passing cause it all to cave in?

Hayden stopped at the bodies of the Scrappers, quickly going through their pockets and retrieving bullets. He reloaded his revolver and took a second from the dead.

"Sheriff, look," Casey said, pointing.

Hayden turned the other way, looking back past the

ramp. He could see the shadows of the Pilgrim's belly, sharp angles and spears of sensors stretching out toward the floor. He could see more of the sled sitting around it. Further in the distance, he could see the backs of hundreds of people, shuffling toward the large lift at the far end.

"There they are," he said softly.

It was hard to spot the Scrapper guards in the dim light and range, but he was certain they hadn't been spotted, either. The laser rifle was as silent as it was deadly.

"Bennett?" he said. The Spacer helmet's optics could zoom in on the group.

"At least six at the rear," he said. "Probably more in front. I can hit them from here."

"Without hitting any colonists?" Natalia asked.

"Most likely. It's nearly a kilometer shot, though. It's going to drain the rifle in a hurry to increase the output that much."

"Let's try to get closer," Hayden said.

"We don't have a lot of time," Natalia said. "They're almost at the lift."

"Scratch that," Bennett said. "They are at the lift. They're herding them in to send them up. They probably have more soldiers topside waiting for them."

"They might not," Hayden said. "We took out the trucks."

"A fact I'm sure Ghost is aware of," Natalia said. "He has enough Scrappers to send a new crew."

"Is there another way up?" Hayden asked.

Bennett kept looking ahead. He pointed to the left of the group. "Looks like there's an emergency stairwell over there."

"Pozz that. We need to get closer. When the colonists are in, we hit the Scrappers down here and then take the emergency stairs up. We have to get to the top before the lift does."

"Then what?" Casey asked. "We send them back down? It may not be safe in here."

"I know it isn't safe in here," Hayden said. "No, we aren't going to send them back down. We have to bring them somewhere safe."

"Outside?" Natalia said. "There is nowhere safe."

"There is one place."

THEY MOVED TO THE SIDE OF THE CAVERN, STAYING TIGHT AND hugging the wall. Bennett kept his enhanced vision on the colonists as they were being loaded into the lift, setting a pace that would get them there in time.

There was no real cover down here, save for a few remaining trucks that the Scrappers had yet to repair, and they were all too far away to be of use. They were counting on the Scrappers staying distracted, focused on pushing the people into the huge car that would carry them to the surface.

Now that they were getting closer, Hayden could see the Scrappers himself. There were over a dozen, each of them armed with more powerful Marine Corps rifles that were better for keeping the prisoners in line.

He could see the colonists better, too. They were disheveled and tired, faces downcast and posture slumped. Defeated. Hopeless. How many others had they already seen taken, never to return? Did they already know they were going to their deaths? Did they know how it was going to happen?

There were at least a thousand of them shuffling into the lift. Men, women, and children. Hayden didn't recognize any of them, but by the looks of them, they had come from the middle strands. They were the cleaners and clothiers, the farmers and teachers and counselors. King didn't think he needed any of them on his ship? He didn't know the first thing about what it took to keep the colony running or the value of their roles.

Or maybe he just enjoyed killing them.

The Scrappers moved behind the line as the colonists were almost boarded. They cursed and commented, waving their guns and getting in their faces. One of the Scrappers grabbed a girl from the line, pulling her away and throwing her to the ground. He dropped to his knees over her, grabbing at his robes. One of the other prisoners stopped and turned back, breaking from the group to protect her.

The gunshot echoed loudly in the cavern, the sound of it causing the colonists to duck their heads and push harder to get onto the lift. The colonist fell forward to the ground. The girl screamed. The Scrapper laughed above her, reaching for the bottom of her dress.

Bennett glanced back at Hayden. They had been hoping to wait for all of the prisoners to be loaded and on the way up. They couldn't wait. Not now.

He nodded.

The Spacer kept the laser rifle at his hip, using the helmet to adjust his aim from the position. The Scrapper pulled the girl's dress up past her hips. He leaned over her, grabbing her face. An instant later, a small burn mark appeared in the back of his head. He slumped onto her and didn't move.

She screamed louder.

It took the other Scrappers a few seconds to realize the man had been shot. A couple of them pointed at him and laughed, enjoying the chaos. The others shouted at the colonists, telling them to keep moving or more of them would die.

Bennett shifted the laser rifle and fired. One of the laughing Scrappers stopped laughing, crumpling to the ground.

The others saw it. Two of them screamed louder at the colonists to get on the grepping lift. The others searched the dim cavern for the source of the laser.

"Go," Hayden said.

Casey, Bennett, and Natalia charged from the shadows, opening fire on the Scrappers as they did. The Scrappers saw them, most of them returning fire as they approached. A couple of the soldiers turned their rifles on the colonists instead, opening fire into their backs. Screams echoed in the cavern, shouts of fear and fury.

Scrappers died. Colonists died. One of them made it onto the lift, and he hit the controls to close it, leaving a dozen prisoners and the rest of his squad behind.

Hayden continued the charge behind the others. He flinched each time he saw a Scrapper round hit Natalia's armor, but the material held fast, protecting her from the slugs. She shot back at the enemy, her aim not as sure as Bennett's or his own. It didn't matter. The Scrappers fell to the onslaught, unprepared for the attack.

It was over by the time Hayden reached the girl, grabbing the dead Scrapper and throwing his body off her. She was on the ground and in tears, no more than twelve or thirteen.

"It's okay, sweetie," Hayden said. "It's okay. It's Sheriff Duke."

"Sheriff?" someone said beside him. He turned his head. Another colonist was standing there, looking at him in surprise.

"That's right," Hayden said. He could tell they recognized him. "It's going to be okay. We need to get up, all right?"

The girl was looking at him. She nodded. He held out his human hand, and she took it.

"What the hell is happening here, Sheriff?" the other colonist asked. "I don't understand any of this."

Hayden helped the girl up. She smoothed her dress, tears still running down her face.

"I don't have time to explain," he said. Three of the other colonists had survived, while a dozen more were dead on the ground ahead of the lift. "We have to stop them from taking the others."

"Taking them where?"

"It doesn't matter where." He caught the girl's eyes. "I'm going to bring you somewhere safe. All of you."

"They took so many of us already," the man said. "Nothing is what we thought it was, is it, Sheriff?"

Hayden glanced over at him. He was an older man. He looked exhausted. All of them did.

"No, it isn't. But there's still hope." He scooped up one of the discarded Marine Corps rifles. "We're heading up those stairs over there. Follow behind us; we'll meet you at the top. Okay?"

The man nodded. Hayden held out the rifle toward him.

"I don't know how to use that."

"Point this end at the threat, and squeeze this," Hayden said.

The man took the weapon. He was uncomfortable holding it, and Hayden doubted he would hit anything if he did have the resolve to use it, but having the rifle in his possession seemed to calm the other colonists.

Hayden hurriedly grabbed another rifle from one of the other dead Scrappers before rejoining the others.

"We don't have any time to waste," he said. The lift had already cleared the opening and was rising slowly and loudly up its shaft. He turned back to the colonists. "We're getting out of here."

41

THEY HIT THE STEPS HARD, RUNNING AS FAST AS THEY COULD. Hayden's body was tired. His arm was burning from Ghost's knife wound, his calf was sore from the bullet that had slammed into it, and his head hurt where Malcolm's shot had grazed him.

He wasn't going to let any of it stop him. Seeing the Scrapper attack the girl below. Seeing the fear and exhaustion on the faces of the people of Metro, the people he had sworn to protect, had bolstered his resolve and was feeding him strength now.

The emergency steps were simple and narrow, a tight iron spiral that rose up close to the large machine lift that was bringing the colonists to the surface. They had to take it single-file, and Casey had gone out ahead, bursting up with energy like none of this was any effort at all.

Bennett was behind her, and as they rose he started slowing, his head turning and shifting, his hand smacking the side of his helmet. Hayden could tell when they were near the top because the air was getting warmer, and that was when the Spacer finally came to a total stop.

"Chains, hold up," he said, getting her attention before she burst out into the open.

"What is it?" Hayden asked, coming up beside him.

"I've got contact with Rico," he said. He didn't sound happy about it. "That fucker remote called the Tokyo over the ridgeline. She's parked half a klick from here, the ship's controls are locked, and I'll give you one guess who's coming to the door."

"Ghost?" Natalia asked.

"Hoorah," Bennett replied. "And enough Scrappers to make sure Rico doesn't do anything stupid. It seems the master code can bring the ship to the Pilgrim, but not out to a position it can't identify, which means they need a pilot to get back to Sanisco."

"Can she hide?" Hayden asked.

"She'll try, but they'll find her. The Tokyo isn't designed for smuggling."

"What about Shihab?" Casey said.

"Hopefully they won't bother looking for him. Rico will stash him somewhere."

"We need to get out there before the lift makes it up," Hayden said. "Does she know the deal?"

"Pozz," Bennett said. "She'll stall him as best she can to keep him out, but no guarantees. She suggested offing herself, but I told her we'd be along." He looked Hayden in the eye. "And we'd better be along, Sheriff. I'm not losing Rico to this."

Hayden nodded. He could tell how much the Sergeant cared for her. Were they more than soldiers together? "We'll be along," he said.

"Pozz," Bennett replied.

"Casey, we're ready," Hayden said, putting the rifle's display up near his eyes, ready to start shooting.

"Here we go," Casey said.

She pushed the door open, immediately firing her remaining bolts from the PL90 and then dropping the weapon. She dashed toward the Scrappers near the lift, drawing their fire as the rest of them moved out into the area.

Hayden could see the rounds hitting her, most of them smacking into her armor. Even if the slugs made it through, the healing factor Franklin had given her would clear the wounds in seconds. Still, a shot to the head and a bullet in the brain could probably keep her from getting up.

She seemed to realize the same thing at the same time. Her hand went up to cover her face, and a split second later a bullet hit it, knocking it back from the force. She didn't slow her approach, reaching the Scrappers as Bennett and Hayden aimed and fired, dropping a pair of the soldiers nearby. She reached her target, a heavy fist slamming them in the stomach and lifting them from the ground. A second punch to the head dropped them.

Hayden turned his head, finding another group of Scrappers approaching from outside. "Bennett!" he shouted, getting the Spacer's attention.

Bennett looked over, immediately shifting his aim and starting to shoot. The Scrappers tried to take cover behind the nearby tents, but the Sergeant's helmet and laser were both able to pierce the nylon, reaching through and cutting them down, forcing them to break the cover and shoot back.

Hayden aimed and fired, aimed and fired, sending short bursts at the enemy. The Scrappers moved to a prone position in response, lowering their profiles to him. It didn't help against the advanced Space Force weaponry, and Bennett's laser blasts burned them dead where they lay.

It was done within seconds. Twenty Scrappers lay dead on the ground, most of them taken out by Bennett.

M.R. FORBES

"My word," one of the colonists said, seeing the lopsided outcome. "Sheriff, those are some new deputies you've got."

Hayden smiled. They sure were. He appreciated Sergeant Bennett's efficiency, and at the same time, he resented it. If one Centurion soldier could do this kind of damage, what could they do with one hundred? One thousand? There would be no trife on Earth. There would be no King. No Ghost. They could reclaim their planet if they were so inclined.

But he had forgotten.

Proxima Centauri Command had no faith in Earth and its inhabitants.

He still did.

The lift appeared behind the steel bars of the cage containing it. Hundreds of faces looked out at them. There was still fear in their eyes, but when they realized the Scrappers were dead, and a few of the colonists who had been with them were standing there, armed, that fear started to fade, at least a little.

"Sheriff," Bennett said. "The Scrappers are in the Tokyo."

"Is Ghost with them?"

"I don't know. Rico doesn't have visual. The door was opened from the outside. That's as good as I've got."

"Pozz that."

The lift shuddered to a stop, the cage sliding upward to allow the colonists to flee. They started piling out, looking down at the dead Scrappers with a measure of gratefulness. As they exited the lift, a shout rose from the side, and a moment later the remaining Scrapper who had tried to join them to escape was pushed out into the open.

"Kill him," the colonists said, the dictate starting with a few and growing quickly.

Hayden put up his hands. "Hold up. Hold on. I'm sure some of you know me. I'm Sheriff Hayden Duke. Me and my

252

people are the reason you're free, but if you want to stay free, we need some kind of order. First, we don't kill defenseless people, even assholes like this one."

Most of the crowd quieted at that. A couple of the colonists grumbled. The Scrapper stood between them, terrified.

"Second, we can't stay here. We can't stay with the Pilgrim. I know a safe place, but it's not going to be easy to get to it. There are vehicles out there. They can take you. I need drivers. A dozen volunteers. If you're good with machines, you're probably a good fit."

"Where the hell are we, Sheriff?" one of the colonists asked.

They didn't know?

"Earth," he replied.

He heard the collective gasp.

"We aren't supposed to be on Earth," one of them said.

"What happened?" someone else said.

"Okay. Okay. There's no time for that now. We're still in danger. I need volunteers. I'll explain everything later."

Colonists started spilling forward. Nearly fifty gathered within seconds, and Casey quickly explained how to drive. Hayden quickly split them into groups of three. If one of them couldn't figure out how to work the truck, maybe the others could.

"Sheriff," Bennett said. "Rico's caught."

"Damn it," Hayden replied. "They hurting her?"

"I don't know. They took her communicator. I've lost contact."

He looked worried. Hayden didn't blame him.

"We're out of time," he shouted. We make a run for the trucks. Drivers in the cab up front, everyone else in the backs."

"What about this guy?" Casey asked, pointing at the Scrapper.

Hayden stepped up to him, getting in his face. The man was shaking with fear.

"You stand here, and you don't move until we're gone. You got it?"

He nodded.

Hayden looked at Casey.

"Lead them out," he said. "Be-"

Hayden froze. So did the rest of the colonists. They waited a moment, suddenly tense.

Another moment confirmed it.

The ground was starting to shake.

"Turb," one of the colonists said.

"Go," Hayden said to Casey. "Go now. Bennett, keep an eye out for Ghost. Let's move!"

Casey started running, down the row of tents toward the trucks beyond. Night had fallen, and it was still cloudy. The only available light was coming from small lamps near the building, and something else on their left. The Tokyo, if Hayden had to guess.

The colonists got into motion behind her, a herd of people stampeding toward the vehicles. Bennett ran at their side, rifle up and ready, scanning the area with the enhanced view of his helmet.

Natalia stopped beside Hayden. So did the girl they had saved.

"Sheriff," she said in a small voice. "I just wanted to say thank you."

"You're welcome," Hayden replied. "Now go. Don't lose the group."

She nodded and ran off, joining the others.

"What are you picking up?" Hayden asked.

Natalia was still wearing the Spacer helmet, and receiving

data from Bennett's gear. "Clear so far. The Tokyo is out there."

"The Scrappers have it."

"Then why hasn't it left?"

"Good question. We can't worry about it now. We made our decision. Rico made hers. We'll catch up to her in Sanisco."

Natalia kept looking at him, hesitant about something. It only lasted a moment.

"You're right. Let's go."

They started moving behind the colonists, keeping an eye out for trouble.

The ground shook again, the intensity increasing. Hayden glanced over his shoulder as they cleared the edge of the building, searching for the goliath in the darkness.

"At least the strength of the vibration helps figure out how far away it is," he said. He turned his head the other way, toward the light of the Tokyo.

Natalia was there, running. Sprinting as fast as she could. Not toward the trucks.

Toward the ship.

4 2

"Natalia!" he shouted, a sudden chill rushing through him, a kick of fear and confusion. "Nat! Where are you going?"

He started running after her, trying to chase her. She was a faster sprinter than him in the best of times, and now? The Spacer armor helped her stamina and strength. He was exhausted. There was no way he could keep up.

"Nat!" he shouted again. He didn't understand. What the hell was she doing?

The ground shook a little harder beneath his feet. He looked back at the colonists. They had made it to the trucks and were starting to pile in. Casey was coming back his way.

"Casey, stop her!" he shouted, pointing at Natalia. Why was she going up there? Was she planning to give herself to Ghost?

Had she been on his side the entire time?

Casey didn't change direction. She kept running toward him.

Hayden stared at Natalia, frozen. He couldn't believe she

would do that to him. Not for one second. She had something else in her head. Some other plan. But what? What was she thinking, that she had abandoned him after they had sworn to stick together?

"Casey, that way," he said again.

She didn't listen. She charged at Hayden, getting within a few meters and leaving her feet, diving toward him.

He heard the crack from near the Tokyo at almost the same moment Casey hit his side, pushing him away. The heavy slug of the sniper rifle caught her in the hip, the force of it tearing through muscle and bone as she came down on top of him. His back flared in pain from the impact, and he looked up at her with fresh surprise.

"Grepping hell that hurts," she said. "Son of a bitch."

She complained, but she didn't hesitate. She grabbed Hayden, rolling him to the left, just before another round hit the ground beside them. She kept them moving, tumbling away. One more round hit his mechanical hand, and then the shooting stopped.

"Damn it," Casey said, groaning. "I can feel the grepping muscles pulling back together. This is grepping sick."

The area ahead of them lit up, the truck headlights turning on. Hayden shifted his head up and back. He could just barely make out the dim silhouette of the goliath coming their way. It was close. Too close.

"Go," Hayden said. "Tell them to shut off the lights and be _"

The lights on the trucks started going out. Bennett must have already given those orders.

Hayden looked back to the Tokyo. He saw Natalia there, near the side. He saw another figure rise from the short wings, holding a large rifle. He jumped down beside her.

Ghost.

A fresh light appeared from below the ship. The access ramp. Ghost stood beside Natalia. It looked like they were talking.

"Casey, get off me," Hayden said, trying to get up.

"Sheriff, stay still, or it will see you."

"Casey, get the hell off," he repeated.

"No!" she said, holding him down. She was so much stronger than she looked.

They walked to it together, climbing up and in. The ramp started to close. Hayden watched it with tears in his eyes. Damn it, Nat.

"Casey, get off," he said again.

"No. I'm not letting you get up and run after the Tokyo like a fool. She's gone, Sheriff. Whatever her reasons."

"I know. I don't understand it, but I have to trust Natalia that she thinks she's doing the right thing. But we have to get those trucks to Crossroads in the middle of the night."

"So?" she said.

"So except for Bennett, none of those people has ever seen a trife before, nevermind killed one."

"So?"

He pointed back at the goliath. "We need to clear the path."

She looked at the giant, and then back at him. She smiled. "Oh." She looked up, into the building behind them. "I've got just the thing." She rolled off him, holding out her hand to help him up.

He stared at her. There was a massive hole in her armor near the hip, large enough that the round must have nearly taken the leg off. But she was standing.

"I know, right?" she said. "I should have been dead a few times already. Maybe Franklin was onto something after all?" She smiled, a hint of pain still visible on her face.

"At what point does victory take precedence over morality?" Hayden asked.

"Whatever that means. Are you coming or what?"

Hayden heard the Tokyo begin to whine. He glanced back as it started to lift from the ground. Whatever Natalia was up to, he hoped it was good.

He took her hand and let her pull him up. She ran back toward the Scrapper camp, so he followed, finding the goliath again as he did. The ground was shuddering with each of its steps, and he could make out its outline despite the darkness. It was only a few hundred meters away, a gap it could close in seconds.

"Where are we going?" he said.

She reached one of the tents, pulling back the flap. "In here."

He ducked inside. She came in behind him.

"We need to bait it, not hide from it," Hayden said.

Then he noticed the tent wasn't empty.

The vehicle in front of him was black and silver, chrome and polish. Two wheels sat on either end of a narrow, sleek chassis with flames painted down the side. A bar crossed the chassis at the front, rising from the forward wheel into a shape that was clearly a handle. The sharp angle ahead of it reminded him of a trife claw, but it bled easily into the overall shape of the thing, giving it a menacing appearance.

"What the hell is that?" he asked.

Casey smiled. "This, Sheriff, is a classic, twenty sixty-seven Harley Davidson, and it appears to be in near mint condition. I noticed it with the Spacer helmet sensors on the way in. I wonder where they got it?"

"You know how to use it?" Hayden asked.

"Did you forget who you're talking to? Get on."

She slipped her leg over the seat and reached down, pressing a button in front of the handlebars. The machine roared to life, vibrating softly as he threw his leg over it and settled behind her.

She did something on a small display between the handles, and the engine noise got louder.

"This ought to keep biggie interested," she said.

She kicked up the bar preventing the bike from falling over and turned the handle, twisting her wrist as she did. The synthetic motor noise changed to a louder roar, and the back wheel of the bike spun, trying to find purchase on the ground and shifting them to face the flap.

Hayden could smell the goliath now, so close its fetid stench was wafting down at them. He could hear its low grumble, and he knew it had to be close.

The motorcycle kicked forward, and Hayden instinctively wrapped his arms around Casey to keep from being thrown off. The front wheel hit the flap and pushed it aside, and then they burst out and through.

"Shit," Casey said, shifting on the bike and adjusting the throttle, sending it into a tight left turn and darting ahead.

They barely avoided the goliath's monstrous hand as it reached out toward the source of the noise, sweeping through the tent where they had been only seconds earlier.
They scooted ahead, the headlight flashing on and lighting up the worn dirt path ahead of them.

Hayden could see into the cabs of a few of the trucks. He could see the colonists' terrified faces as they stared at the monster coming their way. They didn't dare move or make a sound. It probably hadn't taken much for Bennett to convince them of that.

"Don't lose it," Hayden said in Casey's ear.

"Pozz," she replied, slowing and revving the motor, the sound of it echoing across the landscape.

The goliath took another step, vibrating the ground

beneath the bike. It groaned as it started to reach for them again.

"I said don't lose it, not let it eat us," Hayden said.

Casey laughed, and then pulled the motorcycle ahead.

The chase was on.

43

NATALIA RAN UP THE SLOPE.

She didn't look back.

She couldn't bring herself to look back.

Not that she needed to. She could picture Hayden behind her, watching her flee, confused and worried and scared. She hated to do this to him. It was the next-to-last thing she wanted. Making sure he survived, making sure the colonists survived, that was the only thing she wanted more.

So she ran. Away from her husband, and toward the only other man she had ever let near her body. A man she had come to hate more than words could describe.

It didn't make sense on the surface. Ghost wanted her. More specifically, he wanted her talent as an Engineer. He wanted her to help him get the Pilgrim off the ground and into space. And she was going to give that to him?

Not if Hayden held up his end, despite her apparent betrayal. There was a part of her that was certain he would accept her decision fairly easily, even if he didn't agree with it. They knew one another too well. He would know she wasn't changing sides. He would know he always had her love.

So what was she doing?

She saw a muzzle flash ahead, from the top of the stubby wings of the starship. She recognized it by its size and shape as the sniper rifle Ghost carried. She risked a glance back. If Hayden died, she would rather die with him.

She saw him on the ground, Casey above him. They were both moving. A crack and another round hit the ground near them.

She tore off her helmet, throwing it away, drawing her sidearm and putting it against her head while a third shot rang out.

"Ghost!" she shouted. "Stop shooting! You kill Hayden; I kill myself."

His face appeared over the edge of the wing, looking down at her. He smiled, getting to his feet, bringing the weapon with him. He put it on his back and jumped down.

"Natalia," he said. "This is highly unexpected. A good surprise, to be sure."

"Shut up," she replied. "I'm here to bargain."

"Of course, you are. For your husband's life?"

"For more than that. If you want to get the Pilgrim off Earth, you need me."

"I wouldn't use the word 'need,' but it certainly would help." He paused a moment, considering. "What do you want?"

"There's a mass of trife headed for Sanisco. The same one that attacked Ports."

"I'm aware."

"I want you to help us stop it."

"What? Why would I do that? The tower is secure. King is safe."

"Innocent people are going to die."

He laughed. "This is what I mean about the fate of the world in the hands of gods, Natalia. We determine who lives and who dies through our manipulations. You're a benevolent deity. You want to save them. But from what? If this group doesn't kill them, the next one will."

"This group is different. You must have recognized that."

"Stronger. Bigger. And two different types are working together. They were similar to the group we met out near the checkpoint."

"Similar but not the same. That was an earlier iteration."

"Iteration?"

"It's a long story. The deal is, you help me stop the trife, I help you get into space. That's fair, isn't it?"

"How do you know I'll hold up my end?"

"Because I'm going to give you something you want, but don't know you want, to help you fight them."

His smile grew. "Now that is a statement I can enjoy. I'm not even going to ask you what it is yet. We have a deal."

He motioned toward the ramp of the ship.

"Are you sure your father will back you on this?" Natalia asked.

"He'll have to if he wants you." He pointed to his eye. "This is proof of how much he wants you. Tell me, Natalia. Are you pregnant?"

She froze. Only for an instant, but it was long enough. He knew the only reason she would be alive was if she were with child, or incapable of having a child.

"Is it mine?" he asked.

"No," she replied. "Even if it's your sperm, it isn't your child."

"Your husband isn't going to save you, Natalia, if that's what you're thinking. Besides that goliath, there's a huge trife nest between here and, well, anything. He'll lead your people right into it. Right to their deaths."

"You left him for dead once before. How did that turn out?"

Ghost shrugged. "We'll see how many lives he has, then. If he turns up again, I'll make sure to finish the job."

He started toward the ramp, turning his back on her. She could have shot him. She could have killed him. She didn't.

She followed.

44

GHOST BROUGHT HER UP THE RAMP AND INTO THE STARSHIP. A group of Scrappers were waiting there, along with her Engineering second-in-command, Mae. The woman's face lit up at the sight of Natalia before sinking again when she realized she was there willingly.

A glance to the right revealed Doctor Shihab's fate. He was cuffed to the transport carrying the medical equipment, but otherwise unharmed. A doctor would be too valuable to waste. Especially one from Proxima.

"Mae, are you okay?" Natalia asked.

Mae nodded, but it was forced. She didn't look great. A bruise near her eye was the only surface damage. That didn't mean there weren't more elsewhere.

"Let her go," Natalia said.

The Scrappers looked at her like she was crazy until Ghost intervened.

"Let her go. She's off-limits."

The Scrappers did as Ghost said. She stumbled over to Natalia, wrapping her arms around her. "I can't believe you're here."

"It's going to be okay," Natalia whispered. "I promise."

"Enough reunion," Ghost said. He looked at the lead Scrapper, an ugly woman with a large scar across her forehead. "What about the pilot?"

"She won't cooperate," Scar replied.

"I'll get her to do what you want," Natalia said.

"You're making yourself very useful already," Ghost said.

"Just remember our deal. It'll be worth it."

"Where is she?"

"Upstairs," Scar said. "She won't give us the code to the bridge."

"I have the code," Ghost said. "If you two will come with me."

Natalia took Mae's hand, leading her behind Ghost, forward to the steps leading up the next level of the Tokyo. The Engineer was cold and clammy, her body shivering with fear. She clutched Natalia's hand with a vice grip, terrified to let go.

They climbed the stairs behind Ghost. Rico and the Scrappers were right at the top. She was being held by two of the largest soldiers Natalia had seen. One of them was larger even than Oversergeant Grimly. They looked like they were straining to hold the Spacer replica still.

"What's your name, pilot?" Ghost asked, approaching her.

"Fuck you," Rico replied.

Ghost glanced back at Natalia and then punched Rico in the gut. She didn't react at all.

"Impressive. They breed you differently out there, don't they?"

"I repeat, fuck you," Rico said.

"Rico," Natalia said, moving from behind Ghost and into view.

"What the hell are you doing here?" Rico said.

"I made a deal with Ghost. He's going to help us with the trife problem if we help him with the Pilgrim."

"Are you out of your mind?"

"No. I know what you said earlier. We have a chance to save a lot of lives, but I need you to do what Ghost says."

"Is this the Sheriff's idea?"

"No, it's mine."

Rico shook her head. "Damn. For an Engineer, you sure are stupid."

Ghost laughed at that. Natalia clenched her teeth. "We need to stop the trife that are moving south. We need this ship and the equipment on it to do that."

"You want me to fly these assholes back to Sanisco?"

"Yes."

Ghost drew a knife, pressing it against Rico's neck. "Or I can kill you," he said.

"Go ahead," Rico replied. "You can sit here and rot forever."

"Rico," Natalia pleaded.

The Spacer looked at her. She stopped struggling against the Scrappers. "Fuck. Fine. I'll do it. Whatever you're thinking, you'd better be right."

"What's the alternative?" Natalia asked. "We'd all die, anyway."

"True."

"Let her go," Ghost said.

The two Scrappers released Rico's arms. She turned on one of them, punching him hard enough in the jaw that it cracked against the blow, and he crumpled to the ground. The other one reached for her, and she put up her hands.

"Just wanted to show you that I could," she said, stepping over the fallen soldier toward the bridge.

Ghost, Natalia, and Mae followed behind her. Ghost whistled as he entered the bridge.

"Amazing," he said.

Rico dropped back into the pilot's seat, leaning forward to activate the controls. Ghost stared at the whole setup like a child watching a magic show, a huge grin on his face.

"Here we go," the pilot said, using the joysticks to bring the ship off the ground.

"Unbelievable," Ghost said.

Natalia looked at him, tempted to go for one of his knives and stab him right then and there. Even past his amazed expression, she could tell he was watching them like a hawk, ready to react if they did move to attack. Besides, the still-standing Scrapper had positioned himself right by the entrance, ready to interrupt if needed.

And, despite her growing reservations about her plan, she still needed him.

The Tokyo drifted quickly into the sky, rising a thousand meters above the surface within seconds, and continuing upward.

"What are you doing?" Ghost asked.

"Minimum viable altitude," Rico said. "I have to get to a certain height for efficiency, or we'll burn up the reactors in no time."

"You know how to get to Sanisco?"

"We have full satellite imagery of the entire planet," Rico said. "We've been watching for a long time."

"Watching and doing nothing," Ghost said. It was a fact to him, not an emotional wrongdoing like it was for Casey.

"Not exactly nothing," Natalia said.

The Spacers had created the goliaths. The goliaths had helped stop the total annihilation of humankind. Of course, the reasons were in no way benevolent.

The Tokyo continued to rise, getting through the clouds. Then it slowly accelerated forward, taking only a few minutes before starting to descend.

"Can you go a little north?" Natalia asked. "Find the trife?"

"Roger," Rico said, making small adjustments to the flight path.

They cleared the clouds less than a minute later, still a few thousand meters up. Sanisco was visible as a spot on the landscape. The trife were visible too. They were a black, undulating stain on the surface, heading steadily toward the city.

"If I had to guess, I would say it'll be about nine hours before they get there," Rico said.

"That should be enough time," Natalia said.

"Enough time for what?" Ghost asked.

"For Mae and I to set up the equipment while you talk to your father about defending the city from the trife."

"Equipment?"

"Yes. We're going to catch a goliath."

THE MOTORCYCLE ROARED DOWN THE ROCKY HILLSIDE WHERE the Pilgrim had been constructed, along the worn road for nearly ten kilometers before reaching a somewhat paved connecting road. They moved in fits and starts, slowing to keep the goliath close enough that it would continue trying to grab them and then speeding up to escape.

They had gone another ten kilometers or so when they came across a truck on the side of the road, similar to the ones trailing further behind them, back and away from the goliath's senses. It looked like it had been stopped there intentionally. There were more tire tracks all around the area, along with crushed vegetation. Casey slowed the bike as they reached it, looking back over her shoulder for the goliath. It was hard to see in the darkness, but it was always easy to hear, and its smell wafted a good hundred meters ahead of it.

"If I had to guess, they led the colonists out through there," Casey said, turning the front of the bike to get the headlights on a worn area in the brush.

A building was visible behind it, rising out of the darkness. It was cold stone and metal, rusted and cracked.

"Looks like an old power station," she continued. "It may have been feeding the launch site at one point. There could be an old reactor down there, still giving off radiation."

Where there was radiation, there were trife.

"The driver probably got hit before he could make it back to the truck, so they left it."

The ground shook behind them, the first hint of the goliath's odor signaling its approach.

"Whatever happened, I'm glad it's out of sight," Hayden said. He couldn't imagine the colonists driving through a mass graveyard of their former neighbors. He didn't want to see it himself, either. "The trife seem satisfied, let's -"

He hadn't finished the sentence when the first trife burst through the space in front of them, hissing and throwing itself at them. Hayden drew his revolver, firing in one smooth motion. The bullet hit the trife in the shoulder, the force knocking it just far enough off course. It landed on the left side of the bike, turning on its hind legs to face them and catching a set of claws to the side of its head.

"Hold on," Casey said, spinning the bike and twisting the throttle.

They spit dirt into the wounded trife's face, bursting away from it.

"Not too fast," Hayden said. "We need them out in the open."

Casey went a few hundred meters and slowed again.

"Watch the flanks," Hayden said.

This was the hard part he had known was coming. Bring the trife out for the goliath to dispose of, without letting the trife or the goliath catch up to them. He had to trust in Bennett to keep the convoy on track and out of danger, and the colonists not to panic and do something stupid.

Hayden held the revolver in his right hand, his replacement gripped tightly around Casey's stomach, ready to release at any moment. He pressed his legs against the side of the bike, holding on as tightly as he could.

The trife poured out of the landscape from their side. Hayden didn't shoot at them without thought, saving his remaining rounds for the ones that got too close. He wouldn't be able to reload while they were moving, and he only had one other gun to exchange.

Casey steered the motorcycle expertly through the thick, weaving from side to side to get a few extra centimeters on each of the oncoming trife, managing to thread the needle as they zipped past. They heard harsher screeching behind them when the trife realized they were caught out in the open, and then they heard the goliath grumbling and crunching, grabbing the demons and bringing them to its awful mouth.

They continued along the road, rattling over ruts and breaks and holes, the bike's suspension somehow managing to handle the rough terrain. The trucks would have an easier time, made for heading off-road and taking challenging paths.

The trife continued to emerge, but now they were coming from the other side, hissing and scrambling to return to their nest and escape the goliath. It had fallen further back, slowing to feed, and the sudden appearance left Casey and Hayden right in the way of the retreating stampede.

"Grepping hell," Casey said, looking to their right.

Hayden fired at a trife that got too close, hitting it in the head and knocking it down. There were dozens more coming, certain to cross their path, too many to stop. It was like a wave against a rock near the shore, an inevitable collision that couldn't be prevented.

"Hang on," Casey said. "I'm dropping it."

She slowed almost to a stop, pulling the bike to the left. Hayden kept his grip on her, letting her guide him as they fell. They hit the ground, the motorcycle landing on top of them, the weight pressing down. Almost immediately, trife began hitting it, climbing over and past on their way anywhere but where the goliath was.

Hayden put his mechanical hand over his head to protect it, watching through fingers as they trife crashed over them in the hundreds. The nest had to be huge. He could only hope that meant it was the largest threat between here and Crossroads.

If there was another run of trife like this, there was no way they would make it, goliath or not.

Casey was beside him, bearing most of the weight of the bike. She howled as it pressed down on her, head shaking from side to side. At first, Hayden thought it was because she was in pain, but after a few seconds, he realized it was something more.

The sample was doing something to her.

The last of the trife bounced over the bike. Hayden turned his head back, searching for the goliath. It was close enough to smell, and he saw the silhouette of a huge hand reach down and grab one of the trife a few dozen meters away.

"Casey, stop moving," Hayden said, looking back at her.

She didn't listen. Her whole body started to convulse, and her eyes met his. They were filled with pain and fear. A line of white spittle spilled from her lips, running down the side of her face.

Hayden's heart thumped in his chest, fear of his own filling him. The smell of the goliath was growing stronger, but the ground hadn't shuddered. Its hand was near. Reaching down to them?

"Casey, stop moving, please," Hayden said.

Her eyes narrowed, and her body was suddenly still. He looked up, searching for the giant's hand to blot out the sky and the dim light coming down from the moon and stars. He found it a moment later, hovering over them a dozen meters up. The creature groaned in apparent decision, and then the hand moved away.

"Too close," Hayden said.

The ground shook, shaking them with it. The thrash of vegetation accompanied it, suggesting the goliath was moving into the trees, probably following the trife toward the nest. Good. They had the opening they needed to get through.

"Casey, we can go-" Hayden turned his head back.

Casey was still.

For a moment, he thought she was dead.

Then she gasped out a breath, wheezing hard. That was followed by a sharp cough.

"Sheriff," she said softly. "Shit, Sheriff. I'm sorry."

"For what?" he replied. "The goliath is moving away; we're clear for now."

"The sample. Whatever the hell. She gave me. It's not. Working anymore."

"What do you mean?"

"The bike. The weight. The fall. Broke my ribs. I think my lung. Is punctured. Grepping hell. It hurts."

She had tears in her eyes.

"I'll get it off you," Hayden said. He shifted his mechanical hand, positioning it under the motorcycle. "Help me push."

He had to get it off her, to get it off him.

She pushed, and he pushed, using the strength of the replacement to help lift the bike off. Hayden stood with it, pushing down the stand. He could hear the rumble of the trucks in the distance, getting closer. He could feel the vibrations of the goliath's steps diminishing, moving further away.

He could hear the hisses of multiple trife at the sudden intrusion.

Once the motorcycle was stable, he turned back to Casey. Her arms had fallen limp at her sides, and now that she was prone, the blood was flowing out through the damage to the back of her armor.

The wounds weren't fresh. She had taken them back at the Pilgrim. She had known they weren't healing and hadn't said anything until now.

"Damn it, Casey," Hayden said, kneeling beside her. He clenched his teeth against the sudden pain of the truth. "What the hell am I supposed to do?"

"Take the bike," she said, gasping for air. "Make it to Crossroads. Go to Sanisco and kill the grepping King."

"Without you? No. You're coming, too."

She smiled. "You know I'm not, Sheriff. I wish I were. It was worth it. It was all worth it. You're a good man, Sheriff Duke. A good man in a bad world. It needs you more than me."

"Bullshit. You're a good woman. I wouldn't be here without you."

"I know." She tried to laugh but failed. "Do me a favor?"

"What?"

"When King is dead. Go to Carcity. Find my brother. His name. His name is Paul. Get him out of there. Or. Or kill the grepping Mayor. I don't care which. Help him for me, will you? Do what I couldn't."

Hayden wiped at his eyes, the tears welling in them. "I will."

"If you can ride a horse, you can ride a motorcycle. Turn. Turn the grip for throttle. Other hand for the brake. Lean into turns. Or try not to turn. That's it."

The rumble of the convoy was getting louder. Hayden

glanced in the direction of the sound, spotting the headlights closing in.

When he looked back, Casey was dead.

He stared down at her for a moment before putting his hand over her eyes and pushing them closed. The tears dripped off his cheeks and onto her.

He stayed with her until the trucks arrived, the lead vehicle in the convoy coming to a stop a meter behind him. Then Bennett was at his side. The Spacer put his hand on Hayden's shoulder.

"She was a real fighter," he said. "She would have made a great Spacer."

"She wouldn't have had to die if you people were doing a damn thing to help down here," Hayden replied sharply.

"I'm helping," Bennett said.

Hayden looked up at him. He nodded. "Help me put her body in the truck. She shouldn't have to rot out here."

Bennett didn't say anything. He helped Hayden pick her up and carry her to the back. The colonists didn't question it. They made space, helping them place her inside.

Then Hayden turned to Bennett.

"Let's end this," he said.

THE TURRETS OUTSIDE CROSSROADS WERE STILL OFFLINE WHEN Hayden and the convoy arrived. Hayden had figured out how to turn off the motorcycle's synthetic motor noise by then, reducing its passage to a soft whine instead of a loud roar. That didn't mean they approached silently. The trucks were electric, but the number of them made a din regardless. By the time they pulled to a stop, Wiz was standing outside the hastily repaired gate into the garage, flanked by her soldiers, dressed and ready for war.

"Who the grep are you?" she snapped as Hayden approached on the bike.

Two dozen Marine Corps rifles were pointed at him, but he didn't waver. He rode slowly, coming within two meters of Wiz before rolling to a stop.

"Sheriff?" she said, once he was close enough to be recognized. "Where the hell did you come from? Did you find your wife?"

She didn't motion for her soldiers to stand down, instead leaving the rifles pointed at him. He kicked down the stand, turned the bike off, and dismounted.

"I found her," he said. "And I lost her again."

"You should get some handcuffs."

He would have smiled, but Casey's death had left him in a dark mood. He wanted to get to Sanisco now. Tonight. He knew it wasn't going to happen. They had been lucky to make it all the way here in the dark. There had been two more pockets of trife along the road, and it had taken the help of some of the braver colonists with the guns they had captured to help deal with the problem.

"I came to ask you to keep the promise you made to me," he said. "We need to move on Sanisco at first light."

"Promises are a tenuous thing out here, Sheriff," Wiz said. "You should know that."

"How many soldiers do you have, Wiz?" Hayden replied. "Is this all of them?"

She didn't reply. He knew it probably wasn't all, but it likely was most.

"I've got over a thousand people in the back of these trucks. How many of them do you think you can kill before they overpower you?"

She pursed her lips.

"And," he continued. "How are you going to give the order to start shooting, if you're already dead?"

A red dot appeared on Wiz's forehead. It was a necessary bit of showmanship to bring his point home.

"You wouldn't," she said.

"I would if you plan to renege," he replied.

She put her arms out, lowering them toward the ground. Her soldiers lowered their guns. "I'm a woman of my word. Let's get your people out of the elements. You're lucky you aren't swimming in trife already."

"Luck has nothing to do with it."

He turned around and motioned to the drivers, who opened their doors and jumped out. One from each truck circled to the back, alerting the other colonists. They started climbing out of the truck.

"Who are they?" Wiz asked.

"Pilgrims," Hayden replied.

Wiz smiled. "Cute. So you came from your ship? Where are the rest?"

"Most of them are dead. The Scrappers were bringing them out to the trife, save for those King deemed important. He wants to take the Pilgrim."

"What do you mean, take it?"

"He wants to launch it."

"That's ridiculous. And send it where?"

"I don't know," Hayden lied. "That's what Ghost said."

"You ran into Ghost, then?"

"You could say that."

"How the grep did you make it here from there? There's a huge trife nest out that way."

"Goliaths do have their uses."

"You tamed one?"

"I wish. That may not be impossible, though."

"Now I'm curious."

"We can talk more inside."

Bennett walked over, stopping beside him.

"Hello, gorgeous," Wiz said, looking at him. He had removed his helmet, leaving his face visible. "And you are?"

"Bennett," the Spacer replied. He looked at Hayden. "They're bringing her out."

"Who?" Wiz asked.

Hayden turned around. A group of colonists were carrying Casey's body in a sling, holding her off the ground.

"Oh," Wiz said, seeing who it was. "Damn. What a waste."

"I want her handled with respect," Hayden said.

"I'll have my people put her to rest near the turret."

"Thank you."

She pointed at four of her soldiers. They left the line and took the sling from the colonists.

"Take her over to the southwest turret and bury her," Wiz said.

"Yes, ma'am," they replied.

"Is Jake with you?" Wiz asked.

Hayden shook his head. "He didn't make it, either."

"But somehow, you always seem to," she replied. "I hope it was worth it."

"I'll make it worth it."

She turned back to her soldiers. "Sally, show the pilgrims in, give them whatever food and water we can spare."

"Food? Wiz, we don't have enough for this many. We-"

"Did I ask you?" Wiz said, glaring back at her. "Just do it."

"Yes, ma'am," Sally replied. She shouted to the colonists. "All of you, follow me!"

The lead colonists looked over at Hayden for confirmation. He nodded. Then they started moving toward the soldier. He noticed the shuffle was gone from their steps. They were stronger now, growing in confidence after surviving the journey.

"You want to go to Sanisco, Sheriff?" Wiz said. "How many of them can fight?"

"A dozen, at least," he replied.

"A dozen? Out of over a thousand?"

"They aren't soldiers. They've never been exposed to real violence before today."

"I don't suppose you still have the Butcher?"

Hayden shook his head.

"Of course not. How they hell have you lived this long?"

"To be honest, I don't know."

"As good of an answer as I could expect. Let's go up to my office so we can talk."

"Pozz that."

Wiz started walking away, leaving Hayden and Bennett to follow. The rest of the Crossroad's guards fell in line behind her, and then took positions near the gate as they entered the garage. Wiz led them across the first subterranean floor, which was conspicuously absent of travelers.

"Where is everyone?" he asked.

"Gone," she replied. "I kicked them all out after I tried to grab you and failed. I know King is pissed at me, and I know he'll do something about it as soon as he finds the time. I didn't want them to get hurt."

"You left them to fend for themselves out there?"

"I sent people out to tell them not to plan on stopping here. It's the best I can do. I don't want to be responsible for them when it comes to King. Whatever that means to you, the good news is I have food for your people."

"Thank you."

"Don't thank me. I'll expect payment once you take over for King."

"Take over for him?"

"Unless you want me to fill his shoes. You can't depose a ruler and not pick up the slack. You'll cause more chaos than you prevent."

"I guess I'll owe you, then."

"You're damn right."

They reached the stairwell, taking it to Wiz's office. Hayden noticed most of the supplies from the captured Marine Corps module had been organized there.

"So, Bennett," Wiz said. "That armor you're wearing. I've never seen anything like it before."

Bennett opened his mouth, but Hayden put up his hand.

"I found Natalia in Ports," he said. "When I got there, it was being overrun with trife. But these aren't your normal trife. They're evolved. More intelligent. More deadly. They forced Ghost and the Scrappers to leave."

"But you didn't?"

"Not until I had my wife. She uncovered coordinates to USSF caches around the country. One of them was up north, near some place that used to be called Seattle. Bennett's a Collector. We found him near the cache, and together we found the cache. The armor was part of it."

"Where's yours?"

"I lost it fighting the Scrappers. They shot the hell out of it."

"I can imagine."

"We found something else there," Hayden continued. "An airship. A transport of some kind. It was still functional."

Wiz raised her eyebrows. "You were able to fly it?"

"My wife was," Hayden lied. "We used it to make a quick trip back to the Pilgrim. We got into a scuffle with Ghost. He took Natalia, and he took the airship."

"To Sansico?"

"Yes."

"That's pretty grepping unbelievable."

"I know. But it's true. We need to get to Sansico."

"Why? You know King wants to be on the Pilgrim. Why don't you wait for him there?"

"Because the trife horde that attacked Ports didn't stop there. It's headed south toward Sanisco, and then on to Haven."

"And then here," Bennett said.

"My question stands," Wiz said.

He shouldn't have expected her to understand. "The trife will kill everyone in the city. Everyone in Haven."

"That doesn't affect you. Your wife has an airship. She can get out."

"That's not the point. We need to stop the trife."

"Stop the trife, and kill King? You're out of your grepping head."

"Maybe not. I have a few tricks up my sleeve. Do you know that expression?"

Wiz nodded. "I've heard of it."

"Good. You do your part, and we might be able to change a small part of this world. You could do something good for someone beyond yourself for once."

"Who says I want to?"

"I don't remember giving you a choice."

Wiz laughed. "Touche, Sheriff. Tell me what you need from me."

THE SUN WAS ALMOST RISING BY THE TIME GHOST RETURNED to the Tokyo. He had left it, Natalia, Mae, Rico, and a number of Scrappers on the rooftop of King's tower, vanishing for hours while he went to speak to King. Food had been brought to them during the night. A feast unlike anything Natalia had seen before. A celebratory feast from the leader of the Scrappers, in thanks for the promise of getting the hell off the planet Earth.

She didn't eat any of it. She had no appetite at all. Not when she knew Hayden was out there, fighting to reach Crossroads with the colonists, and from Crossroads to join her here. Besides, she had work to do. A lot of work.

The equipment Doctor Franklin had presented her with was old. Over one hundred years. It had been stored in one of the closets of Lewis-McChord's research module for almost as long. When assembled, it consisted of a clockwork enclosure around a seat, a bunch of electrodes, a wired cap, and a pair of heavy goggles with displays inside the lenses. It came with a second piece. The more important piece. The one that had driven her decision to leave her husband behind.

For all intents, it looked like a high-tech spear. It had a sharp point that led back into a tube that was wrapped with electronics, with a set of fins at the end which also acted as a transceiver and wirelessly connected the spear to the enclosure. As Doctor Franklin had explained it, the tool had been used sparingly not long after the goliaths had first been developed and released into the wild, one of the many tests they had done to determine the best use for the giants they had made.

They were tests that, while successful, had been determined to be of limited use. The entire piece of tech was thrown in the closet and forgotten.

Until now.

"Are you sure this thing will work?" Mae said.

Natalia was grateful for the Engineer's presence. She would never have finished the reconstruction and testing in time without her. And the work had helped Mae take her mind off her circumstances and focus on something she loved.

"I have no idea," she replied. "It looks like it works."

She had the printed manual for the device beside her. It was nearly one thousand pages thick, and there hadn't been time to do more than scan it. All of the diagnostics they had done checked out, on both the enclosure and the spear.

"I guess that's the best we can hope for, isn't it?" Mae said. She paused a moment. "Can we hope, Nat?"

"Yes," Natalia replied. "There's a lot of reason to hope, or I wouldn't be here."

Mae nodded. "I can't get used to all of this."

"It takes time," Natalia said. "I'm not that used to it, either. I'm just going through the motions and hoping for the best."

"I like that approach."

"Are we almost ready?" Ghost asked, sneaking up on them from the ramp into the ship.

"Where's Doctor Shihab?" Natalia asked instead.

"He's seeing to some of our injured," Ghost replied. "Believe me; we have no intention of harming him. Are we almost ready?"

"Yes," Natalia replied.

"Good. The trife are getting close."

"King is on board with this?"

"For your cooperation, yes. And also because once the trife are done in Sanisco, they'll threaten the farms further south. We're assuming the Pilgrim will need a resupply of food?"

"And water," Natalia said.

"Then it's in our best interests to deal with the trife now, especially if you have a means to aid in that mission."

"So you get to keep your other eye?"

Ghost smiled. "I'm sure you're enjoying that outcome. For now, I do."

"Why didn't you kill him? You didn't have to let him hurt you."

"He's my father. He saved my life. That's worthy of respect, isn't it?"

Natalia couldn't argue. Her parents were both gone, but she had honored them during their lives, becoming an Engineer when she wanted to be a Doctor and following in her father's footsteps.

"We have a number of people out at the edge of the bridge," Ghost continued. "If King had dealt with the nest there earlier, this would have been easier. They're cleaning it out now to get in position to start shooting when the winged bastards start carrying the others over. I'd rather let the incoming trife deal with our resident aliens, but we can't wait that long to engage."

"I agree." Natalia stood up. "Mae, can you run through the diagnostics one more time, and then keep everything ready?"

"Of course," Mae replied.

Natalia walked up to Ghost. "Let's go to the bridge."

Ghost followed behind her. She could feel his eyes on her back. What did he feel? Anger? Desire? Nothing? She was doing her best to keep her emotions in check, too. She was worried sick about Hayden and Casey. Worried sick about the colonists. Knowing she was trying to save them was the only thing allowing her to keep going.

They went up the steps to the top level of the Tokyo, and then back to the bridge. Rico was already there, along with a half-dozen Scrappers guarding her. She turned in her seat as Natalia and Ghost entered.

"We're ready to go?" she asked.

"Pozz," Natalia replied. "We need to find a goliath."

"It shouldn't be hard," Ghost said. "There's one that wanders east of here, on the other side of the water. Do you think goliaths can swim?"

"They're big enough they don't have to swim," Rico said. "And the bay isn't that deep."

"How do you know?" Ghost asked.

"Satellites, remember?"

"Then we head west," Natalia said. "Do you think your Scrappers can hold the trife back for now?"

"They're doing their best. It will take time for the trife to cross the water."

"Rico, let's go," Natalia said.

"Roger," Rico replied. "Hold on."

The ship whined to life, a soft thrumming gaining intensity as they started lifting away from the deck. Natalia could see Sanisco down below the base of the tower. It was quiet for now, but it wouldn't stay that way much longer. She turned her head to see through the display facing north. She could see the small shapes of hundreds of humans approaching the base of the fallen bridge, and the small sparks of muzzle flashes as they fired on the trife there. Looking across the bridge, the dark mass from the prior night was closing in, nearly at the edge of the bay.

"We have to hurry," she said.

"We are," Rico replied, the Tokyo begin to accelerate forward.

Natalia turned her head the other way, to look to the south. The display for the starboard facing cameras was dark.

"What happened there?" Natalia asked.

Rico glanced over. "I don't know. The display is malfunctioning, I guess. It happens sometimes, even on our ships."

For some reason, she doubted that.

THEY LEFT CROSSROADS BEFORE DAYBREAK, JUDGING THE BEST time during the night to make their exodus from the secure structure and out into the wild. Wiz had organized her entire entourage for the journey. Every soldier in the place was armed and outfitted, along with the colonists who volunteered to participate in the attack. A few others were given rifles to defend the waypoint, just in case.

Two trucks, four cars, and one motorcycle traveled along the cracked brown highway. Thirty-three soldiers, sixteen colonists, one Spacer, and one Sheriff. It was a poor army compared to what King could throw at them.

Then again, King was going to have troubles of his own. Bennett was certain the trife would be closing in on Sanisco soon if not already, and Hayden was certain the Tokyo and Natalia would still be there when they arrived. After a considerable amount of thought, he had a feeling he knew what his wife was planning. It was crazy, foolish, and ingenious if she could make it work. It didn't ease his worry or leave him feeling any better about the fact she had left him without a word, but he had to have faith in her.

It had served him well so far.

The convoy had reached Haven by the time the sun started to pierce the sky, rising high enough to split through the damaged buildings that composed the city.

Wiz brought the car at the front of the line to a stop while a pair of Scrapper guards manning a checkpoint approached, pointing guns at her as they drew close to the vehicle.

"What is this?" one of them asked, nervously looking back at the rest of the convoy.

"A bad day to be a Scrapper," Wiz replied, smiling.

"What's that supposed to mean?" the guard asked.

The two rounds hit the two guards in the head only a split second apart, fired by Bennett from over a kilometer away, well out of sight of the target.

Ghost wasn't the only one with a high-powered rifle.

Wiz glanced at Hayden and then started the truck forward again. The rest of the convoy followed.

They stopped a few hundred meters in, the soldiers jumping out of the vehicles and moving into the streets of the city. Hayden and Wiz abandoned their car. Hayden pulled his revolver. They made their way along one of the streets, staying near the outer perimeter and looking for Scrappers.

Hayden remembered a few of the guard positions from his first visit, and the Collector seemed to know them as well. They sprinted across a narrow street, getting a good angle on one of the lookouts. Wiz took her time aiming, finally releasing a round that dropped the Scrapper there. A moment later, more gunshots starting ringing out.

"Here we go," Hayden said in response to the attacks.

They sprinted through an alley and over a pile of rubble to an open, cracked stairwell leading up to a defunct second floor. Hayden ascended it quickly, finding a pair of guards at the top, weapons out and scanning for the source of the activity. They both turned toward him as he crested the stairwell.

They both died before they could do much else.

"Clear," Hayden said, reaching the bodies and crouching beside them.

The Scrappers had reacted quickly to the initial shots. He could hear the rumble of engines as cars were dispatched from their current location and sent out to meet the threat. He spotted one of them crossing an intersection a few blocks down, a van carrying an untold number of King's soldiers toward the fight.

It was crossing a second intersection when a hole suddenly appeared in its windshield, and the van started rolling to a stop. The crack of Bennett's rifle caught up to the slug an instant later, and then the Scrappers inside started piling out.

"Do you see it?" Wiz asked through her communicator.

"Yes, ma'am," Sally replied. "We're on it."

A squad of Wiz's soldiers appeared around a stack of debris, opening fire on the van and its cargo. Three Scrappers fell before they could hurry to cover and start shooting back, forcing their people to evade.

"They need backup," Hayden said, turning and heading down the steps.

Wiz followed, running with him across the street and into a space between two piles of debris. They took a wide path, intending to circle behind the van and take the Scrappers by surprise.

The Scrappers took them by surprise instead. A car appeared around the corner, enemy soldiers leaning out the window and opening fire. Bullets sprayed the ground ahead of them, and they dove over a short wall just in time to avoid being hit.

"Damn, that was close," Wiz said.

"How's your aim?" Hayden asked.

"Fine. How's yours?"

He crouched and turned, gripping his revolver and popping up from behind the wall. The car was still there, the Scrappers out of it and walking in their direction. They exchanged fire, the Scrappers bullets whipping past him or taking chips out of the stone in front of him. His rounds hit their mark, dropping the soldiers, and leaving the car.

"Not the brightest of the bunch, are they Sheriff?" Wiz said.

"I don't think they've ever been challenged before," he replied. "Head back around that way."

"Where are you going?"

"I'm taking the car."

"You know how to drive?"

"It can't be harder than a horse or a motorcycle."

They split up. Hayden ran to the car, slipping behind the wheel. He pulled on the safety strap and pressed on the accelerator, putting the vehicle in motion. The street ahead of him was clear, the residents of Haven noticeably absent, remaining hidden during the sudden attack.

He drove down the street, braking sharply to make a hard right turn and cross three more. A second Scrapper car passed in front of him without slowing, the driver thinking he was one of them. A moment later, shots rang out from that direction, and he heard the car crash into something.

He turned right again, finding the van in front of him, the remaining Scrappers pinned down behind it. One of them waved to him, and he slammed on the accelerator again. If they wanted his intercession, who was he to deny them?

He rocketed toward the van. The Scrappers tried to run when they realized he wasn't going to slow, but it was too late. He slammed into them with the car before slamming the car into the van, the impact rattling his frame and squeezing him tight against his harness.

He settled back, detaching the belt, throwing the door open and climbing out. The Scrappers were all on the ground. One of them pulled his revolver and tried to aim. Hayden didn't give him a chance.

Wiz cleared the corner while her other soldiers emerged from cover and rushed to him. They quickly regrouped, the popping echo of gun battles still ringing out from other parts of the city. The fighting wasn't over, but if this side of the city were any indication, it would be soon. The Scrappers were murderers and degenerates playing at being organized soldiers. Wiz's people were the real thing.

"We need to keep going," Hayden said. "How far to the Impound from here?"

"Three blocks north," Wiz said. "Why?"

"I left something there last week. I want it back."

"Then let's go get it."

Hayden followed Wiz and two of her squads across the three blocks, drawing nearer to some of the most intense shooting. They came out on the far end of the firefight, behind the Scrappers who were firing on Wiz's squad and the Pilgrim volunteers. Two of the colonists were dead in the street between them, along with four Scrappers.

Hayden wasn't eager to shoot anyone in the back. At the same time, this wasn't an arrest. This was war, plain and simple. He aimed his revolver and fired, hitting one of the Scrappers in the back. The rest of Wiz's people joined him, and the city's defense was whittled down further.

The end of that shootout left only one other somewhere further north, where the shots were coming at a more relaxed pace.

"Sally, go find the source of that gunfire and neutralize it,"

Wiz said into her comm. "Take Alpha and Beta squads with you."

"Roger," Sally replied. "On it, Wiz."

Wiz turned to Hayden. "They'll be clear in no time. It seems King sent a few too many of his Scrappers out to the Pilgrim. Haven is ours."

"Which doesn't mean anything right now," Hayden said.

He looked down the street, finding the garage leading into the Impound.

"It's a start, Sheriff," Wiz said. "And a good opportunity to get your people's hands dirty."

"Or dead," Hayden replied.

He walked over to the dead colonists, leaning over them and pushing their eyes closed. They wouldn't have time to bury them.

Wiz joined him there, picking up their rifles and taking their extra magazines from them. They couldn't afford to leave the valuable weapons and ammunition behind. In fact, her other soldiers were already looking through the Scrapper's robes.

"You could have taken Haven anytime," Hayden said. "With the weapons you collected and the people you have."

"I wouldn't be so sure. Ales had a tank and a Butcher, remember?"

"How could I forget?"

"We softened them up once already. It cost me. Hopefully, it will be worth it."

"For all of us."

"Yes."

Hayden continued to the gate leading into the Impound. The guard, Billy, was in the street in front of it, his chest bloody. Hayden winced at the sight of him. He was too young to have gotten caught up in this.

He bent over him and took his keys.

"You fighting King?" someone said, coming up behind him.

Hayden turned around. An older man was standing there. He had a weathered face and few teeth, and he was holding an old shotgun.

"I am," Hayden replied.

"You can have my gun," the man said. "I'm not the man I used to be, but I can still pull the trigger."

Hayden shook his head. "No. Stay here, protect the other residents. There's an army of trife coming. I'm going to try to stop it, but-"

The man nodded. "That's the way it is, ain't it? No matter how much good you try to do, the trife will always come and fuck it up." He cackled hoarsely. "I'll round up the others. We'll be ready if they come."

"Stay hidden."

"We'll try. Ain't always possible. Say, didn't I see you with Hank Jackson's kid, Jake, not too long ago?"

"Maybe," Hayden said. "I was here about a week ago. Passing through."

"Where is that boy?"

Hayden shook his head. The old man lowered his head somberly.

"That's the way it is, too."

"I'm passing through again, on my way to Sanisco. Wish me luck."

He lifted his head, the smile returning. "Good luck, Mister-"

"Sheriff," Hayden said. "Sheriff Hayden Duke."

"Good luck, Sheriff."

Hayden turned back to the gate. It took him a few tries to find the right key.

"Hey, mister."

A small, familiar voice got his attention. He spun around

again. The girl he had bought the star from was standing there, her mother clutching at her shoulder.

"Can I help you, miss?" Hayden asked, crouching.

"You killed the bad men," she replied. "I know you like these."

She held a second badge out to him. It was almost identical to the first, except some of the silver had worn off, exposing the dark plastic beneath.

"It's yours," she said.

He took it, pinned it to his shirt, and nodded. "Thank you, miss."

"Abigail," she said. "You can call me Abbey."

"Thank you, Abbey. Now run along with your mom. Go and be safe. There's a storm brewing."

49

THE TOKYO SHOT OVER THE LANDSCAPE. RICO KEPT THE starship low despite the Spacer's desire to keep the truth of their existence quiet, forced to stay near the deck in order to spot the goliath nearby.

Not that it was much of a concern. The area west of Sanisco was light on settlers, as most of the survivors tended to stay close to the main population centers from Sanisco south to Haven, and then west to Lavega. There were probably wanderers down there, Collectors or simple loners, but the former would know better than to mention seeing anything out of the ordinary, and the latter would never be believed.

And there were trife. Not great amounts, but pockets that stretched across the vacated areas, enough that Natalia had to wonder how many covered the face of the planet. A trillion? More? When she saw what the Spacers were capable of, she wondered how they could leave the planet to its own devices. When she thought about how numerous the trife must be, she wondered how they could even think to ever cleanse the Earth.

It took five minutes to head two hundred kilometers west. It took another three to come across a goliath.

It was walking east, tracking a group of trife ahead of it. They were rushing toward a hillside, desperate to escape.

It also wasn't alone.

A second goliath walked beside it, a little bit shorter than the first. It had a vague appearance of being female to the first's male, because while the creatures were genderless it had the suggestion of breasts on its chest, and its hips took on a wider profile. She had been under the impression all of the goliaths were constructed from the same genetic mold, but clearly that wasn't true. She had also thought the creatures were loners themselves, sticking to their own predetermined range.

Clearly, not true either.

"Well, we found one," Ghost said. "Two, actually. Now what?"

"Come with me," Natalia said. "Rico, get us close to the bigger one."

"Roger," Rico said.

The Tokyo drifted lower, remaining a few hundred meters above the goliath's reach, and staying a couple of kilometers back. Natalia had to admit she was fascinated by the creatures, and by watching them chase down the trife. They seemed to have an extra-sensory perception, able to put their hands where the trife would be before the trife got there and making up for the fact that they were larger and less nimble. They could gather nearly a dozen into their hands with each sweep, picking them up and tossing them into their toothy mouths, grinding and swallowing in seconds.

Natalia brought Ghost back down to the hold.

"Mae, did everything check out?" she asked.

"Yes, Nat," Mae replied. "All of the systems are registering as online and operational."

"Perfect."

Natalia reached down and picked up the spear. It was already locked inside its launcher; essentially a battery-powered railgun.

"You'll only get one shot," Natalia said, holding it out to Ghost. "I'm here because I know you can make it. I don't know if anyone else can."

Ghost took the device, balancing it in his hands and getting used to the weight of it. "You want me to shoot it?"

"That's part one," Natalia said. "You need to hit it in the base of the neck, here." She came close to him, putting her face near his and putting her hand on the back of his neck.

"How do you feel about being this close to me?" he asked.

"I'd like to take your other eye," she replied, backing away. "Here." She showed him on her neck, too.

He smiled, amused by her response. He thought she was an idiot for giving herself up for this.

"What's part two?" he asked.

"Succeed with part one first, and then we'll worry about it," she replied. "Rico, can you hear me?"

"Roger," Rico said, her voice coming out of a speaker somewhere on the wall. "I read you."

"Lower the ramp."

"Roger."

The ramp started dropping from the belly of the Tokyo, allowing cool air to start flowing in. The ground was visible beyond it, a thousand meters below.

Ghost didn't hesitate. He turned and walked down to the edge of the ramp, positioning himself in a crouch with his body pressed against the mechanics that opened and closed it for stability.

Natalia went halfway down herself, her heart racing at

the height. She scanned outside, finding the goliaths to their right.

Ghost looked back at her, flashing her a thumbs-up.

"We're ready for approach!" Natalia shouted so Rico would hear.

The Tokyo started to turn and accelerate, slowly enough the inertia didn't knock them over. She brought the goliaths directly ahead of them. The creatures had slowed in their pursuit of the trife, turning to face one another.

They grumbled and growled at one another. The Tokyo moved in toward them, taking a wide path around, vectoring to take position behind the back of the larger one.

Ghost had his head turned slightly, his good eye looking down the spear, preparing to take the shot.

A warning sound triggered in the hold, and the ramp began to lift. Ghost threw himself backward, further up it, as the Tokyo yawed hard to the right, shuddering and shaking as the engines gained power.

Natalia was thrown from her position, tossed across the hold and into the side, hitting it hard. Mae was knocked off-balance as well, grabbing for the edge of the enclosure and holding on.

"Rico, what the fuck?" Natalia said, her whole body aching from the impact.

"Small problem," Rico replied. "I think they're onto us."

"What?" Natalia said.

"The smaller one threw a trife at me from over the other one's shoulder."

"That's impossible."

They weren't supposed to be intelligent. They were organic machines. Created and programmed to complete a task: eat anything on two legs that moves.

"Tell that to the trife. A missile's a missile. I barely got out of its way."

"What are they doing now?"

"Watching us."

"I don't understand."

"I don't give a shit either way. This plan isn't going to work."

"We don't have time to find another one." Natalia turned to Ghost. He was at the base of the now-closed ramp, looking back at her.

"Lower the ramp," he said. "We're trying again."

He enjoyed the challenge too much to give up.

"Roger," Rico said. "I can't stay steady if they keep throwing shit at me."

"I'll deal with it," Ghost said.

The ramp lowered again, the Tokyo moving to make another run. This time, Ghost wrapped his arm around the hydraulics so he couldn't be thrown out. Natalia braced herself as well, more prepared for the ship to make sudden movements.

The Tokyo swiveled, slipping sideways like a boat on water, turning to face the goliath. It kept moving to the side, the massive creature already spinning in an effort to face them. The smaller one rumbled louder, sending a large hand up toward them that forced Rico to pull back and away.

"Fuck!" Ghost cursed as they retreated. "Get me a damned shot!"

The Tokyo whined harder, rising up and away from the giants.

"I'm going to drop in and swoop past," Rico said. "Breaking as I reach the bottom of the curve. You'll only have a half-second to make the shot."

"I'm ready," Ghost shouted. "Do it."

The Tokyo continued to ascend, the air coming into the hold getting colder as they climbed. Ghost shifted position again, bracing himself for the fall. Natalia moved to one of the seats with Mae, strapping herself in.

Her stomach rose to her throat as the bottom fell out of the ship. She shouted in fear and strange excitement, struggling to keep her eyes on Ghost as they tumbled out of the sky. The whine of the ship and the rush of incoming air was deafening, and she couldn't believe the Scrapper thought he could make the shot like this.

But his head didn't move. His eye didn't move. He kept it open despite the intake of air, focused solely on the goliath as they tumbled behind it.

She saw the smaller one pacing ahead, rushing toward them and swiping at them. She felt the ground solidify, the Tokyo slowing suddenly, the g-forces pressing her down. She heard a light snap, and then she was pushed back in her seat as the ship accelerated away.

A few seconds passed in silence. She leaned her head back, trying to catch her breath.

Then Ghost was beside her. "Did I hit the right spot?" he asked.

She unbuckled herself and hurried to the equipment, looking at the simple diagnostic display.

"I can't believe it," she said, glancing back at him. "You did it."

He nodded as though the outcome was never in doubt, and maybe in his mind it wasn't. "Show me part two."

50

Hayden didn't care that Casey's car was loud. He was determined to drive it into Sanisco, to bring it up to King's tower and ram it through the despot's face.

He had seen the Tokyo shoot past, a matte silver bird of prey headed out for breakfast. They were still twenty kilometers out of the city then, far enough their arrival wasn't imminent, and close enough they might have been visible on the ship's bridge.

But the Tokyo didn't change course. It didn't hunt them down. No Scrappers emerged from the city to confront them, either. They avoided detection through no effort of their own. There was no point in being subtle. Not now. The objective was to reach King at all costs.

Bennett was riding in the car beside him, having given up the motorcycle, leaving it back in Haven. He had the high-powered Marine Corps rifle cradled in his lap, his hand resting lovingly on it. The Space Force didn't have guns like these anymore, he explained. They didn't bother with high-velocity projectiles since they had perfected laser and plasma. He said there was something about bullets that made their use feel more personal.

They were still a kilometer outside of the city. The Tokyo had been gone for fifteen minutes, and from the increasing pitch of crackling echoes from the other side of Sansico, they were fairly certain the trife were on the verge of launching their assault.

Bennett lifted the rifle, shifting himself to lean out the window and peer through the scope. It had better zoom than his helmet, allowing him to get a clear view of the city at a distance.

"The tower blocks a lot of the view on the north side," he said. "But I'm pretty sure those are flying trife in the air out there, dropping off their land-bound brethren. If I had to make another guess, I would say the Scrappers are falling back." He shifted the rifle slightly, looking closer in. "Oh, that's interesting."

"What is it?" Hayden asked.

"Looks like the residents are trying to get out, and the guards on the gate won't clear the exit for them."

A series of pops sounded, closer than the rest.

"Shit," Bennett said. "They just started shooting civilians."

"What?" Hayden said. He had been hoping to wait until the trife got deeper into the city to make their move. It was a frightening prospect, but their plan was to thread through the demons to the tower, hole up in there with King and whatever Scrappers made it that far, and wait for the Tokyo to come back.

If it came back. There was no way to confirm it had gone hunting and not to the Pilgrim, at least not until they got inside. They were playing a hunch, both that Rico wouldn't agree to bring King and Ghost to the ship, and that Natalia had goals of her own in mind. Goals that King would only agree to because he thought it would be the best thing for him. In his discussions with Bennett and Wiz, they had concluded that King would need supplies to get the Pilgrim off the ground. He couldn't imagine the leader of the Scrappers making the twenty-year journey without all of the comforts of home.

That would mean stopping the trife horde.

That would mean giving Natalia's plan a chance.

"We can't stay here and let them die," Hayden said.

"No we cannot," Bennett agreed.

Hayden dipped his head, tapping his communicator. "Wiz, the Scrappers are killing the civilians trying to escape the incoming trife."

"Why the hell aren't they going underground?" Wiz replied.

"I don't know. Does it matter?"

"I know, I know. You want to help them. We're ready to move, Sheriff."

"You have the rocket?"

"It's my last one."

"And this is what we were saving it for."

She sighed. "Roger."

The convoy started to move behind them. Hayden glanced over at Bennett. "You're clear to shoot whenever you feel like it."

"Pozz that," Bennett replied, squeezing the trigger. The gun bucked against his shoulder, and a kilometer away one of the Scrappers shooting civilians fell from his perch.

Hayden started the car and slammed on the accelerator. They lunged forward, gaining speed as they moved down the road toward the barricaded entrance to the city.

"I think we've got their attention," Bennett said. Bullets were scraping the ground ahead of them, fired too soon.

"We're just getting started," Hayden said.

Wiz's cars spread out behind them, a wedge pattern of

reinforced steel raising a cloud of dirt behind it, a cloud that helped cover the trucks at the rear from view. They had advanced half the distance when the incoming rounds started making contact with the vehicle, pinging off the forward armor and sending up sparks. One of the trucks stopped behind them, and even though Hayden couldn't see it, he knew what was happening:

Wiz would be climbing out of the passenger side of the cab, a long cylinder strapped to her back. She would hop onto the roof, plant the cylinder's tripod, and quickly bolt it down into the sheet metal. Then she would use the cylinder's computer to set the target and range. Then she would fire.

They drew closer to Sansico as all of this was taking place. The wall of spent vehicles was rising over them, the Scrappers manning it firing down. An armored car blocked the front, keeping traffic from flowing through.

Not for long.

He heard the thunk of the cylinder over the roar of the engine, and then the hiss and whine of the rocket motor that propelled the explosive forward, sending it zipping over their heads as a red and white streak. It slammed directly into the armored car and exploded, the force of the detonation going up and out and throwing wrecked cars and Scrappers everywhere, and putting up a wall of smoke in front of them.

Bennett pulled himself back into the car, grabbing his helmet off the floor and shoving it on.

"You've got warm bodies fifty meters past the smoke-screen," he said. "Most likely civilians."

"Pozz," Hayden said. "Is there a way around?"

"Once you get into the smoke, slow down and turn left."

"Pozz."

They didn't slow until they were crossing onto the city and entering the wash of smoke. Hayden slammed on the brakes, turning the car to the left and easing forward. Wiz's soldiers did the same, moving more cautiously to avoid hitting civilians. Fortunately, the explosion had either killed or scared the shit out of all the Scrappers on the wall.

Hayden made it through the hazy air without hitting anyone, accelerating again as he found the path ahead clear. He moved into the city while Bennett swapped the larger rifle for a smaller one, returning to his position halfway out the window.

They raced along the street, turning right and speeding up. There were residents standing on the side of the road, men and women in tattered clothes, children in nothing at all. They had heard the explosion and came out of hiding, and when they saw him entering, when they saw they weren't Scrappers, they waved.

Bennett waved back at them while yelling at them to hide. They scooped up their children, quickly retreating inside.

"Sheriff, what's your position?" Wiz asked, still in range of the transceiver. "You've got two of my squads trailing you."

"Turned west, heading north toward the tower. You?"

"Coming up from the east. I can see the trife from here. Scrappers are going to run right into us."

"Let them go through if they want to run. Kill them if they want to fight."

"Roger. That was the plan."

Hayden glanced back over his shoulder, finding Wiz's troops behind him. They clung to their cars, weapons out and ready for use.

It seemed like they were winning, for the moment at least.

It was an illusion.

They were a trio of small boats about to get smashed by a huge wave.

51

THEY HAD COVERED TWO MORE BLOCKS WHEN THEY NEARLY collided with a second car as it turned the corner, heading in the opposite direction. It was one of the open-framed Enforcer cars, loaded with nearly a dozen Scrappers, each of them with terrified expressions on their otherwise rough faces.

Hayden jerked the wheel instinctively, cutting away from the vehicle and nearly slamming into a pile of rubble on his right.

"You're going the wrong grepping way, mate!" one of the Scrappers shouted as they went past.

Hayden reached the corner and turned his head to the left.

"Sergeant, I've got targets," he said to Bennett.

The Spacer turned to look.

"Fuck me," he said.

A line of trife with no end was rushing down the street toward them, large and mean. The group at the front rushed toward the car as he opened fire, cutting them down.

"Get us the fuck out of here, Sheriff!" he shouted.

Hayden pressed down on the accelerator, and the car lurched away from the trife. The demons chased behind, slowing to change direction and giving Bennett time to reload and start shooting again. Wiz's cars kept coming, hitting the bodies as they fell, crashing through and over them, the armor shoving the creatures out of the way. He heard a scream when one of Wiz's soldiers was grabbed and pulled from a car.

"Wiz, we have contact," Hayden said.

"Same here, Sheriff," Wiz replied. "We're two blocks from the tower."

Hayden leaned forward, craning his head to see out the windshield and up. The tower was closer than he realized.

"Looks like we're close, too."

He jerked back as the car hit something in front of them, looking down in time to see the trife go up and over the car, and a second get impaled on the spiked grill in the front. There were more coming from ahead, trying to cut them off.

"We're out of fucking time!" Bennett said, sending bursts into the creatures and knocking them down, one after another. The soldiers behind them started shooting too, steady streams to cut into the demons.

"We aren't there yet," Hayden said, reaching another corner. "Hold on." He turned hard, forcing Bennett to grab the edge of the car door to stay attached.

They raced toward the tower, getting ever closer. He could hear more gunfire now, coming from the same direction, the Scrappers likely fighting to keep the trife from entering. They had found a break in the horde, a clearing that carried them to the next street over. Hayden looked in the rearview mirror.

Wiz's squads were gone.

The cars were there, the soldiers in them pulled out,

buried under a pile of trife that were tearing through their Marine Corps armor and ripping them apart.

"Sheriff, look," Bennett said, pointing up.

Hayden looked out the top edge of the windshield as the Tokyo went streaking past. It started shooting a moment later, a stream of plasma fire stretching from its guns to the trife on the ground.

His heart jumped into his throat, racing hard. Natalia!

They turned right at the next street.

Hayden brought the car to a stop.

A tank was there, blocking the road. The hatch at the top of it was open. A trife was climbing out.

Hayden threw open his door, grabbing his rifle and jumping out. Bennett picked up the larger rifle and did the same.

"Think we'll make it?" the Spacer asked.

"We have to."

They ran, sprinting toward the tank. The trife on it spotted them, jumping down at Hayden, only to have its chest blown open by Bennett's rifle. Hayden stepped around it, shooting a second and clawing a third.

They reached the tank, getting to the other side. The fighting was heavy here, Scrappers on the steps firing out at the trife, while more of their comrades retreated inside. Hayden found Wiz, the rest of her soldiers, and the colonists on the other side, hiding beneath one of the trucks, watching and waiting. The trife were running past them so far, but it wouldn't last forever.

"How do you suppose we get through that?" Bennett asked.

A trife hissed beside them. The Spacer turned, using the rifle as a club and bashing it hard in the face, breaking its neck. Another came at them, and Hayden shot it, along with a third and fourth. The tide was catching up to them, leaving them stuck in the middle.

"Make a run for it," Hayden said. "That's all we can-"

He felt searing heat, and then blasts of plasma were detonating around them, hitting the trife between them and the tower hard, some of the strikes catching the Scrappers and clearing the field. The Tokyo passed low overhead, climbing up and away to make another run.

"Fucking Rico," Bennett said, smiling.

"Let's go," Hayden said, rushing across the wide street. He looked to where Wiz was hiding. She was pulling herself out from cover along with the rest of their troops.

They all ran for the tower together. The remaining Scrappers were regrouping, realizing suddenly the trife weren't the only ones attacking the city.

A hail of gunfire cut them down in a hurry, Wiz's soldiers making quick work of the remaining group.

They met at the steps, scaling them together. More trife were entering the area, and when Hayden looked back over his shoulder, all he saw were hundreds of dark spots with sharp claws and large teeth charging at them from everywhere.

"Wiz!" he shouted.

She glanced back and then started speaking into her comm. There was a cement barrier up ahead, right before the door into the tower. They vaulted over it, her soldiers stopping on the other side, turning and getting into a line behind it, using it as cover as they took over for the Scrappers they had killed.

Bennett, Wiz, Hayden, and a dozen colonists and soldiers moved through the doorway and into the lobby. A pair of Scrappers were hiding behind one of the desks, and they popped up and started shooting, cutting three of the colonists down before the rounds from Bennett's rifle punched through the wood of their cover and into their bodies.

"How do we find King?" Hayden asked.

"Do you think killing King will be close to enough?" Wiz replied angrily. "Have you taken a look outside, Sheriff? Every human in the path of these things is going to die. Every grepping one!"

Hayden locked eyes with her. Maybe she was right. Maybe it didn't matter if King was dead or not. Would it, if everyone else in the area were dead, too?

"I'm not giving up," he growled. "My job is to protect people. From King, from the trife, and from whatever the hell other threats come around. My wife is out there, and she's put all of her faith in me getting to the top of that fucking tower. And that's what I'm going to do. You got me this far. If you want to bail now, be my guest."

Wiz shook her head. "You're either unbelievably grepping naive, unbelievably grepping stupid, or unbelievably grepping genuine. We haven't had that around here in a long, long time, Sheriff. Not as long as I've been alive."

"Does that mean you're coming?"

"No, but-"

She stopped talking, her ears perking up as the ground rattled slightly beneath their feet.

"Is that?"

They froze, waiting. The ground rattled again.

"She did it," Hayden said, unable to contain his sudden excitement. "She did it!"

"Did what?" Wiz asked.

"You might be the Wiz, but I told you, I have the trick up my sleeve."

"On second thought, Sheriff. I think I will come."

52

RICO GUIDED THE TOKYO BACK AROUND, SWOOPING DOWN toward the city and releasing one last volley of plasma from the ship's guns. The superheated gas blasted into the trife, killing hundreds instantly.

It was nowhere close to enough.

"I can't spare any more shots," Rico said, looking over her shoulder at Natalia.

Natalia wanted to tell Rico she did a great job because her strafing runs had gotten Hayden and the others into the tower. She couldn't say anything about it with the two Scrapper guards standing on either side of her.

"Mae, how is Ghost?" she asked instead, using the ship's comm to call down to the Engineer.

"He has a smile on his face," she replied.

"I bet," Natalia said.

She glanced up at the displays, finding the first goliath right at the edge of the bay and heading directly toward the tower. The second goliath, the smaller one, wasn't far behind.

Even though Natalia knew what was supposed to happen, she had been surprised when the GCS worked exactly as

314

intended, allowing Ghost to gain full neurological and musculoskeletal control over the giant through the wireless interface between the spear and the enclosure.

She was doubly surprised when he had started walking toward Sanisco, and the other goliath had followed.

It was as if they were a couple.

"I think they just realized he's there," Rico said, spinning the starship back toward the goliath. The trife had changed direction, breaking up and swarming to the north and south, finding a path that would bring them around to the giant.

"Engineered to kill goliaths," Natalia said. "Let's hope this works."

The goliath were good at eating regular trife, but these weren't regular trife, and trying to eat them wouldn't be enough.

The demons slowed as they neared the goliath. Ghost had brought the giant to the first street at the edge of town, a massive foot coming down on top of an abandoned building, crushing it easily. The creature rumbled loudly, looking out at the oncoming aliens, hands raising in a freakish martial pose.

Could the goliath handle the sheer numbers of the creatures, even with Ghost driving?

They were about to find out.

The trife stormed toward the goliath, charging at it from both sides. It was almost comical to watch them as Ghost turned the massive organic machine north, lurching forward and stepping on dozens of the demons, swinging its other foot back and following through, kicking hundreds more out of its path. The trife coming up from the south had no idea what to make of the behavior, expecting the goliath to try to scoop them up. They froze their advance while the north flank that had evaded the blows started scampering up the goliath's legs.

Ghost swung the giant's leg to the side, crashing it into a taller building, crushing the trife against the stone and steel. He stamped a hand toward the ground, flattening dozens more, kicked back and knocked a separate group of creatures aside.

In seconds, he had killed nearly five hundred at least.

There were still thousands more.

Another grumble stole Natalia's attention from Ghost's goliath. The smaller creature was climbing out of the water, splashing onto the shore and moving toward the trife. They reacted to it immediately, the southern mass splitting into another branch of three lines of trife and rushing toward the creature.

The goliath reached out to them, grabbing a few and pulling them up to its mouth. As it did, the other trife jumped onto it, quickly climbing it and slashing at it with their large claws. Hundreds of the demons poured up the goliath's legs, even as it finished devouring the first group and reached down for more. It ignored the trife already on its body despite the assault, and despite the blood that was already spilling from a thousand small wounds.

Ghost's goliath was faring infinitely better. It moved the way he would move. Its feet kicked out at the trife, its hands plucked them from its body or slapped them harder into it like it was crushing flies.

The mass of xenotrife below him realized it was being massacred, turning and trying to escape. His goliath turned with it, facing south toward the smaller giant.

That one was slick with blood. The trife had reached its head, and one of them was climbing onto its eye, slashing at the soft tissue. It howled in pain and frustration, one hand reaching up for the demon, the other still trying to collect more of the trife to eat.

"Nat," Mae said, her voice panicked. "We have a problem."

53

THEY BOARDED THE LIFT, STARING AT THE CONTROL PANEL.

"Which floor?" Bennett asked.

The door was still open, and the trife were on their way. They leaped the small barrier, ripping into Wiz's soldiers with newfound fury.

"Something pissed them off," Wiz said. "Just pick one."

Hayden didn't know how many floors were in the building, so he entered 1-0 on the control panel. Bennett stuck his rifle out and fired a few rounds.

A dozen trife dashed across the lobby toward them, one of them managing to get its claws between the closing doors. Hayden fired his revolver into its head, knocking it back.

Then they were on the rise, ten people in total. Hayden, Bennett, Wiz, and six of her soldiers. Only one colonist remained. A man named Harris. He was one of the youngest of the volunteers, and his face was pale and frightened.

"We have no idea what we're coming out to," Bennett said.

"Or what floor King is on," Hayden replied.

"Does it matter?" Wiz said, pushing in front of him to look at the lift's control panel. "The trife are in the building.

If he wants to leave, there's only one way out." She pointed up.

"Good point," Hayden said. "Can you get us to the top?"

She nodded, tapping the panel. They went right past the tenth floor, continuing their ascent.

A loud detonation sounded from somewhere below. A few seconds later, the lights inside the lift went out, and the whole thing came to a stop.

"Shit," Bennett said, flicking his helmet light on and illuminating the cab. "Power went out."

"You think?" Wiz said.

"Sounded like they blew a transformer or something."

"On purpose?" Hayden asked.

"If I had to guess."

"They really want to get us."

"It might be my fault," Bennett said. "If they recognize the armor."

"I didn't even think of that," Hayden replied.

"Yeah, the older iterations, they didn't have much loyalty to one another. Things change, I guess."

The lift was motionless. Trapped in the shaft. There was no obvious way out of it.

"It should have an emergency backup," Wiz said, tapping the control panel. It still had power. "Enough to carry us to the next floor."

She got it working.

"Do you hear something?" Hayden said.

Bennett sighed in his helmet. "They're climbing the shaft."

"All this to get to King, and we might not even make it that far," Wiz said.

"We'll make it," Hayden said. "We have to."

The lift came to a stop, the doors opening. They were on the thirty-fifth floor.

"How many more?" Hayden asked.

"Thirteen," Wiz replied.

"Not too bad," Bennett said.

They looked back as the lift began to shift in the shaft, hit by the trife climbing around it.

"Can they get through the cables?" Wiz asked.

"Not likely," Bennett replied.

"Where are the stairs?" Hayden said.

The floor was dusty, old and abandoned. There were no Scrappers living up here. Hayden could feel the breeze of a draft from somewhere on the outer perimeter, likely pouring in through broken windows and cracked facade.

"This way," Wiz said, pointing to an old, worn sign.

A sharp snap, a loud hiss, and the lift began to fall behind them.

"What the fuck?" Bennett said. "Keep going. You two, with me."

He grabbed Harris by the shoulder, turning him around. Bennett and his new squad started shooting, firing on the trife as they continued to back away.

Wiz led Hayden around the corner to the stairwell. She threw open the door, cursing when she heard the rumble of trife coming their way.

"Grepping hell. We need to move fast. Bennett, hurry your ass up back there!"

"Pozz!" the Sergeant shouted.

Echoes of gunfire drowned out the sound of the demons. Shouts of pain rose above it from behind Hayden, the trife making it to the soldiers. Bennett turned the corner, Harris slung over his shoulder. The colonist was bleeding heavily.

Hayden stood in the doorway between the corridor and the stairs. Wiz was already on her way up. Bennett kept moving backward, dropping the Marine Corps rifle and drawing his sidearm. He fired single rounds into each trife that came near, headshots that dropped them in an instant.

"Bennett," Hayden said as the Spacer reached him. "Put him down."

"We don't leave anyone behind," Bennett said.

Hayden winced. "He's dead."

Bennet dropped Harris to the ground, looking down at his motionless eyes. "Fuck!"

"Come on."

They went through the doorway, letting it close behind them. They started to ascend.

The door slammed open seconds later, the trife pushing it aside. Judging by the noise, a second group was close and ready to join them.

They scaled the steps as fast as they could. Bennett was still moving fairly easily, though Hayden noticed the soldier had a spot of blood near his neck. Had he been hit? Hayden was struggling to keep going, each step burning up his legs.

They made it two floors before the trife were almost on them, close enough they could see their arms as they turned the corner to the next set of risers.

Bennett stopped, quickly reloading his sidearm and pulling a knife from his boot.

"I'll keep them back," he said. "You go on ahead."

Hayden froze. "No. You need to survive this. Somebody has to get the colonists to Proxima."

"Rico can do it," Bennett said. "She's got my back. Don't stand there and argue, Sheriff. I owe you this. You and all the Pilgrims, and all the Earthers we left behind."

He fired two rounds into the first trife to turn the corner. More followed.

Hayden didn't have time to argue. He slapped the soldier on the shoulder and then continued to climb.

He heard the gunshots behind him as he forced himself to run, finding more strength in the Sergeant's sacrifice. He made one floor, another, another. He caught up to the last of

Wiz's group on the forty-seventh floor. Wiz had already gone out to forty-eight.

He reached the exit, nearly falling through it and catching himself against the wall. He was in the middle of a small, secondary area that led to another door. It had a small glass window in the center of it, but the window was cracked, and fresh blood was dropping from the shards.

What the hell?

He ducked low, along with the two soldiers with him. Sally was one of them. She looked frightened.

"We lost Wiz," she whispered to him.

What? Hayden clenched his teeth. "How?"

Something moved in front of the doorway, visible through the shattered glass. It was big and dark and metal. It hit the door hard, throwing it inward at them.

Hayden ducked away, getting low on his stomach as the door slammed into the one behind it and fell over, nearly on top of him. By the time he looked up, the roid had Sally in its grip, and it broke her neck with barely any effort, dropping her lifeless body to the floor.

"You are intruders. You are not welcome," it said, its head turning toward Hayden.

Hayden rolled to his knees, bringing up his mechanical hand and catching the roid's as it tried to grab him. The replacement was just strong enough to turn the arm aside, and only for an instant. He dove past it, rolling over the glass, feeling shards cut into his back on the way past. He grunted in pain, getting to his feet behind the roid and drawing his revolver. He fired it into the thing's back, hoping it would be weaker than the front. What else could he do?

It wasn't. The roid turned, facing him.

"You are not welcome," it repeated.

"Pin, hold on a second," a voice said from behind Hayden.

The roid froze in place. "Yes, sir."

Hayden spun slowly until he was halfway between the roid and a small, stocky man in a suit. The man had a gun in his hand. A laser pistol. A half a dozen Scrappers were with him, along with a pair of women in too-little clothing. Hayden found Wiz, too, her body slumped near the door, her head blown half-off. She should have waited for them, instead of rushing ahead alone.

"You must be King," Hayden said.

"And you must be Sheriff Duke," King replied. "You only had your eyes opened to the reality of the Universe a week ago, and people are already whispering your name from here to grepping Lavega. Pin, grab him."

Hayden was too slow avoiding the roid this time. It wrapped a heavy metal hand around his replacement, holding it tight. He didn't bother to struggle against it. He couldn't get free.

King turned sideways and pointed. "Look outside, Sheriff," he said. "What do you see?"

Hayden looked past the man. A row of windows gave him a view out to a small deck and then the landscape below. The trife hadn't gotten that far south yet, so what he saw was mostly brown and green.

"What am I looking for?" he asked.

"Exactly," King replied. "There's nothing. Grepping nothing. Oh, I tried. I tried to make this shithole livable. I tried to make the Earth something more. I spent the last twenty years at it. Do you know what I got in return?"

"No."

"Assholes like you, who think they know better. What do you know, Sheriff? About this world? About how to survive in it? About how to thrive in it?"

"I know better than to treat people like things. There's strength in unity. There's-"

King aimed the laser pistol and fired, burning a hole

through Hayden's good hand. The fist clenched on its own, the damage messing up the nerves.

"Bullshit," King said. "There's strength in control. These people need to be controlled. They grepping want to be controlled. Before I came along, they barely managed."

Hayden remembered the former Mayor of Haven. Somehow, he doubted King's version of the truth was the right one.

"And they're doing great now?" Hayden said. "They're naked. They're hungry. And they're victims to you and your soldiers."

"You're just like your grepping wife, aren't you, Sheriff. No damn respect. The next time your sentence doesn't end in 'sir,' or 'your highness,' I start burning out other parts of your body." He turned back to the window. "Fear is a great motivator, Sheriff. It's allowed me to clear fifty kilometers of highway to the east. Twenty to the south. It's allowed me to get smelters going, to start making weapons to fight the trife. It's allowed me to raise a military force of over three thousand, and drive nearly ten-thousand people to start doing real, useful labor."

"Fine, sir," Hayden said, his hand still burning. "I don't understand the point of this conversation, sir."

"The point is, you came here to kill me because I'm a threat to your people on the Pilgrim. But I'm not the threat, Sheriff. I'm their salvation. I'm their messiah. I'm their god, who's going to lead them home to the Promised Land where they belong. Where we belong. I respect you, Sheriff. I respect that you made it all the way here. I don't want to be your enemy. Kneel before me. Kiss my ring. Be one of my disciples. You can go home with your people. With your wife. We can all get away from these grepping trife once and for all. I'm a fair ruler. I'm a just god."

Hayden stared at him. Where were the trife, anyway?

They should have reached this floor by now. Or had they given up pursuit once they finished Bennett off?

There was a soft whine from outside, and the Tokyo flashed past the window, slowing and rising out of view.

Hayden only noticed now how the ground was shaking, the building he was standing in shivering with it. The goliath. How close was it?

"Your wife is something else, isn't she, Sheriff?" King said. "A goddess of another kind. I proved my benevolence to her. She's agreed to help me, to cooperate fully with no resistance. Why don't you do the same? I could always use someone like you, and the Pilgrim is going to need its Sheriff."

Hayden closed his eyes. Natalia was on the Tokyo with Ghost. With the Scrappers. He was stuck here with King. Trapped. Everyone around him was dead. Gone. Bennett. Casey. Wiz.

How did he ever think they could pull this off?

He opened his eyes. "Okay," he said. "Let me go. You win. I'll join you."

"You'll join me, what, Sheriff?" King said.

"Your Highness," Hayden replied.

"Pin, bring him over," King said.

The roid lifted him by his arm, carrying him across the floor to where King was standing.

"Put him down."

The roid lowered Hayden to the ground, pushing on his shoulder to force him to his knees.

King put his pistol against Hayden's head. "You even think of trying to stab me, and you'll be dead before you can twitch." He put out his other hand. A large ring rested on it.

Hayden leaned forward and kissed it.

"Thank you, Sheriff. Unfortunately, I have doubts about your loyalty, considering you've only submitted to me under extreme duress. I'm afraid I'll have to terminate our agreement, effective immediately. Pin, dispose of him."

"Yes, sir," the roid said, grabbing Hayden again before he could move. The machine lifted him by his shoulders, carrying him in the direction King had motioned.

A broken window on the east side, away from the deck.

"Have a nice trip," King said, smiling. "I'll see you next fall."

Hayden glared back at him, at the same time catching movement in the corner of his eye.

Someone was standing in the doorway. His face was bloody, but he was still upright.

Bennett.

The Spacer lifted his pistol toward King, who saw him at the same time Hayden did. He was already diving out of the way.

"Pin, help me!" King shouted.

The roid didn't spare any pretense. It threw Hayden forward.

Right out the window.

54

"WHAT IS IT?" NATALIA REPLIED.

"Ghost. Something's happening to him."

Natalia wasn't sure it was really a problem, but she turned to one of the guards.

"I need to get down there."

The guard nodded, following her as she fled the bridge and descended the steps into the hold. She rushed to the enclosure, where Ghost was convulsing.

"What the hell?" she said.

"I don't know," Mae replied. "He just started shaking."

"What the grep did you do to him?" the Scrapper asked, drawing his revolver.

"Don't be stupid," Natalia replied. "We didn't do this. Shit. We need to get him out of the chair. Help me pull him out, will you?"

The Scrapper nodded, holstering his gun and lifting Ghost while Natalia and Mae removed the goggles and electrodes connected to his body.

"What the fuck are you doing down there?" Rico said over the comm. "The goliath is freaking out."

"Freaking out how?" Natalia asked.

"It's chasing after the trife near the other one."

Natalia paused. She couldn't quite believe it. "Get him out of the way. I'm strapping in."

"Nat," Mae said. "You can't."

"I can. I think I know what happened."

Her eyes trailed from Mae to the big Scrapper. He had an unconscious Ghost in his arms, the revolver on his hip exposed.

She only hesitated for an instant. There was no future if they didn't get this right.

She went for it, grabbing it out of its holster as the Scrapper figured out what she was doing. He dropped Ghost to the floor, reaching for her.

She pulled the trigger, firing a round into his arm, and a second into his chest. He stumbled back in shock, falling to his knees.

There were two other Scrappers in the forward seats. They saw the commotion and started to rise. They didn't make it far. Four more rounds knocked them both off their feet.

"Nat?" Mae said, terrified at the violence.

"Rico, seize the day," Natalia said, certain the pilot had heard the ruckus.

"Already done," Rico replied. "The bird is ours."

"What about him?" Mae asked, pointing to Ghost.

She pointed the revolver at his face, hesitant to pull the trigger. Why, after everything he had done? She steeled her resolve and fired.

The hammer clicked, the cylinder empty.

"I'll get another one," Mae said.

"I need to get the goliath under control. Grab a revolver from one of the bodies and keep it pointed at him."

"Yes, ma'am."

Natalia jumped into the enclosure, unzipping her armor, grabbing the electrodes, and placing them on her skin while Mae retrieved a gun and held it pointed at Ghost. If he woke up, would Mae be able to keep him still? Would she be able to shoot him if needed?

If he woke up. He was out cold, with no sign of regaining consciousness.

Natalia picked up the headset, sliding it over her head, enveloping her senses in darkness.

"Mae, start the uplink."

"On it," Mae replied.

Natalia knew the moment she entered the comment to reinitialize the control protocol. Her entire body began to tingle and stiffen. A billion neurons fired at once, a brief moment of intense agony. Then she settled back in the chair, and the perspective of her vision had completely changed.

"Wow," she said.

She was seeing as though she were the goliath, looking back at the smaller giant from one hundred meters up. Her body was huge. Her hands were huge.

She was crawling in trife.

She acted as though she and the goliath were one and the same, moving the way it would move. She slammed its leg into the side of a building, crushing dozens of trife. She reached up and grabbed demons climbing toward its head. She stepped on more of them at her feet.

But something was off with the system. She noticed it immediately. There was a pull. A resistance. A pain. The goliath was hurting. Not physically. Emotionally. It was crying out in deep rumbles directed at the smaller one, the one she had labeled a female.

It was hard to imagine. It was hard to believe.

The goliath was in love.

"It's okay," she said. "I'm going to help you."

She directed it toward the other one, fighting the trife like a human, instead of grabbing them to devour like a goliath.

She batted the creatures away from the other goliath with massive hands. She picked them off, trying to get it clear. It was wounded and in pain. Its left eye was a bloody mess. Hundreds of the demons were scaling it like ants.

She felt her goliath stop resisting as she gave in to what it wanted. A new freedom of movement carried her forward, and she reached out, grabbing the smaller goliath around the waist and lifting. Then she carried it, in long steps back to the water.

She leaned down, pulling the goliath with her, back off her shoulder, laying it into the bay. The trife hissed and screamed as they hit the water, the ones on its back crushed against the bottom, the ones on its chest left trying to swim and failing. They washed off it like dirt, floating desperately away.

The smaller goliath grumbled. A gentle, thankful sound.

"I helped you, you help me," Natalia said, reaching out and taking the smaller one's hand. "Watch me."

She didn't know if the other one would learn, but she helped it back to its feet, and as she moved back toward the city she knew it was following.

She crushed hundreds of trife, satisfied when they started to scatter at her feet, breaking apart and attempting to run. She slammed her open palms down on top of them, crushing dozens more. She looked back and saw the second goliath was doing the same.

"That's right," she said. "That's right."

They moved into the city, edging closer to the tower. The trife were routed, desperate to run, scattering in every direction. As she neared the tower, she saw the demons running out, pouring from the structure like water as they made their escape.

She kept going, walking toward them, getting close to the tower.

Something appeared in front of her. A small form that exploded from the side of the building, its arc of travel carrying it out and down.

A sharp whine came from the goliath's mouth as she realized what it was.

Hayden.

THE AIR WAS COLD AND CRISP.

It seemed strange to Hayden that he would notice that as he pinwheeled his arms, like that would slow the descent to his certain death.

He could see the ground below, still far away, but there was nothing in between him and it that would keep him from being smashed on impact. He didn't feel much fear at that moment. What he felt was anger and sadness. Anger at King for betraying him. Sadness that he would never see Natalia again. He would never see her baby, either. Would Ghost play the father?

He tried to keep his eyes open as he fell. Why not? He didn't want his last few seconds to end in darkness. He wanted to take his end head-on.

He was aware of the goliath to his left, so close he felt as though he could almost reach out and touch it. It was an ugly thing, mottled skin, and twisted bones. It was uglier from this angle.

Strangely enough, it was watching him.

Even stranger, he saw emotion in its eyes. Human emotion. Ghost was in control of the giant, after all.

But the emotions were wrong. He saw fear and desperation, and why would Ghost give a shit if he splattered on the hard ground below?

Should he reconsider closing his eyes?

The wind buffeted at him. The ground was getting closer in a hurry. But the goliath wasn't standing still. It was reaching out, stretching its hand toward him. A moment later, the ground vanished, replaced with mottled flesh coated in a slick of blood and mashed pieces of xenotrife.

His breath caught in his chest. He closed his eyes. An instant later, he hit the flesh, the pressure of the fall mashing him tight into the palm, pressing him deep into something with a little bit of give. The hand descended at the same time, further cushioning the blow.

He opened his eyes. His whole body hurt. His ribs were probably broken.

He was alive.

The smell was nearly unbearable. He picked himself up, heart racing as the hand rose toward the giant's face.

It stopped at eye level. The thing was smiling at him.

"Nat?" he asked.

It nodded.

He would have laughed, but there was no time.

"Forty-eighth floor," he said, pointing. "King."

He needed to get up there. He needed to help Bennett, and kill that asshole would-be god once and for all.

The goliath grumbled, and the arm started to rise. He turned to face the tower. His right hand was almost useless; the laser shot leaving it clenched. His left?

He clenched his hand. The claws sprang out.

It was still working just fine.

He rose toward the window, the hand reaching as high as

it would go. He saw the Tokyo to the north, circling toward them. Natalia was so close, and still so far.

He was almost there. He could see over the edge of the floor, into the room.

There were King's Scrappers, all of them dead.

There was the roid, moving toward the corner.

There was King, his back to Hayden, facing the roid. He had picked up a nasty looking ax from somewhere.

Where was Bennett?

Past the roid, if he had to guess. Holding his own against the machine because that's how tough the Spacer was.

He flexed his legs, preparing to jump as the hand approached the window.

He ran forward, pushing off the edge of the palm, leaping in at the leader of the Scrappers through the window.

One second too late.

King smelled the hand approaching and started to turn, eyes wide when he saw Hayden coming at him. He brought his ax up in a two-handed grip, using the handle to block Hayden's claws as they slashed down toward his head.

The force of the impact still knocked the stocky man backward, and he tripped over one of the dead Scrappers. Hayden stumbled a step before recovering, dancing forward and dropping onto King, claws headed for his throat.

Something hit the side of the building, hard. It shook everything violently, sending his punch wide. King jabbed up at him with the head of the ax, hitting him on the side and knocking him off.

They rose at the same time, facing one another.

"I knew it was too easy," King said, spitting out a line of blood. "Come on, then."

Hayden gathered his footing, looking out the window. The goliath was grumbling, but the pitch of it had changed. Natalia wasn't controlling it anymore.

What happened to her?

The thought nearly cost him his head. King charged him, swinging his ax. Hayden got his claws up just in time, the impact sending up sparks, the blade cutting one of the daggers away. King's body slammed into him, knocking him back and leaving him on the ground, with King on top.

"Still too easy," King said, swinging the ax down.

Hayden shifted his head to the side, the blade hitting the tile right next to his ear. He punched up with his bad hand, hitting King in the temple. He punched him again, and again, until King recovered, slamming the handle of the ax against Hayden's face and breaking his nose.

Hayden cried out in pain and anger, grabbing King's arm with his mechanical hand and using its strength to pull the man off him. He threw him to the side, rolling over and getting up, using his sleeve to wipe the blood from his face.

King got up too, facing him and laughing. He was enjoying this. Enjoying the challenge. Maybe he thought he couldn't lose?

Hayden looked past King. Bennett was on the roid's back, clinging to it and reaching into a now-open service cover and grabbing for the wires there. King's laser pistol was on the ground a few meters away.

King saw it too. They both went for it at the same time, meeting in the middle. Hayden's claws met King's ax again, slashing at the man and blocked again. Hayden punched King on the side of the head. King hit Hayden in the nose. They both roared in pain, stumbling and falling near the gun.

The Tokyo appeared behind them, whining loudly as it dropped onto the deck and settled.

Neither one of them paid it any mind. They charged one another again, King's ax waving ahead of him like a deadly banner, Hayden trying to find a way to get his remaining pair of claws through the defense.

The ax came in fast and hard. Hayden blocked it, barely, turning and slashing with his claws. King bounced back, narrowly avoiding the blades before pushing the attack, ax swinging toward Hayden's head.

Hayden ducked below it, avoiding the forehand, and anticipating the backhand.

He didn't try to avoid it, though. He did the opposite, throwing his right arm out into the blade's path. It connected, digging deep into his arm and sticking in the bone.

King's face turned white as he realized what Hayden had just done.

Then it turned red, Hayden's claws slashing through King's throat and spraying his blood on them both.

He fell on his rear as King stumbled sideways in front of him, clutching at his throat. He made it a few steps before falling over.

He didn't move again.

56

Natalia lifted the goliath's hand, raising it toward the window, Hayden standing in the massive palm.

King's roid had thrown him out the window, and now she was bringing him back up to face the machine again?

She had to be crazy.

Then again, he had asked her to, and she trusted him, crazy or not. Besides, she knew that look in his eyes. He was going to do what he came to do or die trying.

She lifted the goliath's head, watching as Hayden jumped from her massive hand back into the tower. Then she looked down, finding the trife below. What was left of the horde was scattering, fleeing in every direction. The other goliath had recognized the retreat and followed dutifully after them, crushing them beneath its feet. With any luck, none of the demons would survive to build a new nest.

She intended to stay where she was, to be ready in case Hayden emerged from the tower again. She considered trying to scale the building, like in that movie she had seen on the PASS in Metro, but the tower's condition was

336

anything but pristine, and she wasn't sure it would stay upright.

"Rico," she said, the words coming out as a grumble from the goliath. "We need to land. Hayden's in trouble, and we're the only ones left to help him."

She couldn't hear Rico's response. Not while she was hooked into the enclosure.

She shifted the goliath's attention back up, watching the tower. Her nerves were starting to fray, not knowing if Hayden was alive up there. She examined the side of the building again. Maybe she could climb-

Something grabbed her, pulling her roughly from the enclosure. The electrodes were still attached at first, and the movement caused the goliath to stumble and fall into the side of the tower.

Then the headset was torn away from her eyes, the wires leading under her armor ripped off as she was dragged out of the seat and onto the floor. She shuddered, her muscles tensing and flexing in response to the sudden extraction, paralyzed and still.

Ghost was standing over her, holding one of his knives in hand.

The end of it was dripping blood.

Mae?

"The only reason you're still alive is because of what you have in your belly, Natalia," he said. "Did you plan for me to have a seizure like that? Did you expect me to get knocked out? Or maybe you thought your bitch subordinate would have the guts to shoot me? You thought wrong."

He was angry. Furious. He knelt down over her.

"You're mine, Natalia!" he shouted. "So is this ship. So is the Pilgrim. It's over!"

He reached over her, grabbing at one of the electrodes

337

and yanking it free. He pushed her over onto her stomach, taking her hands and pulling them together.

"I'm sure if the guards down here are dead, the guard with the pilot is dead, too," he said. "I need to go deal with her, and then I'll be back for you."

Natalia's face pressed into the floor, her muscles only now beginning to come back to life. She wiggled her fingers, desperate to do something to stop the Courier.

Like she could, even if she were healthy.

Ghost started wrapping the wire around her left wrist. She tried to shake it away, but he squeezed harder.

"Don't move!" he yelled. "I've had it with you. I've had it with your grepping husband. You're going to carry my baby to term, Natalia, and when he's born, I'm going to grepping kill you. Do you understand? The minute he's in this world, you leave it!"

Tears welled in her eyes. She could almost stand to be stuck with him if only to raise Hayden's child. She yanked her hand again, getting it away from him. She tried to roll over, but he sat on her back, pushing her down harder.

A shuddering whine from the Tokyo signaled a shift in the craft's vector. It rolled to the side, yawing sharply enough to throw Ghost off her back. She reached out, somehow managing to grab the edge of the enclosure and hold on.

Ghost slammed into the wall across from her, falling back to the floor as the Tokyo straightened out. Had Rico seen what was happening down here? Had she made the maneuver on purpose?

He was up in an instant, coming for her again.

She rolled over, surprising him by being able to kick up at him, hitting him in the chest, and knocking him back. The Tokyo whined again, rotating quickly, the momentum pulling him to the side. Natalia held onto the enclosure, making it to her feet, the shock of the disconnect clearing from her system.

She looked to her right. The bodies of Mae and the Scrappers had been thrown around with the hard maneuvers. Mae's throat was cut, the revolver she had been holding was a few meters away from her body.

She dove toward it.

Ghost's foot appeared ahead of her, kicking it away. It didn't go far, hitting Mae's corpse and getting stuck.

Natalia rolled away from him as he tried to jump on her, managing to get her fist up and into his face. He shook it off, reaching for her neck with his free hand.

"Maybe I don't need an heir after all," he growled.

The Tokyo shuddered violently, rocking enough that they both bounced. Natalia was prone on the ground and didn't move much. Ghost was thrown off his feet, falling backward.

She pushed herself on her back, looking for the gun. She reached back and grabbed it. The handle was slick with blood. She flipped her head back toward Ghost. He was holding his knife by the blade. He threw it at her, hitting her in the shoulder. She gasped in pain but didn't drop the gun. He produced another knife, charging at her as she aimed.

She pulled the trigger.

The revolver clicked. Empty.

"Not this time, bitch."

Ghost smiled like a feral animal. There was no humanity left in him. No sign of his earlier calm demeanor. This was his true nature. A monster.

The starship's ramp started to open.

Neither of them noticed.

Natalia used her free hand to reach over, grabbing the knife in her shoulder as Ghost lunged for her. She pulled it out, groaning in pain as she slashed at him, catching his chest. His counterattack sliced along her stomach, leaving her in more pain. His leg fell on top of her right arm, pinning it down while he kneeled beside her.

"I'm going to cut it right out of you," Ghost said. "How does that make you feel?"

She tried to slash him again. He caught her wrist, squeezing until she dropped the knife. He held her hand, too strong for her to resist. He turned the knife in order to stab downward.

"Just. Grepping. Die!" he howled, his face twisted in anger, his good eye wild.

"You first," Hayden said.

He pressed his metal fist against the side of Ghost's head and squeezed.

The knife fell from Ghost's hand, clattering on the floor beside Natalia. His body would have slumped onto her, too, but Hayden was holding it up with the replacement. He grunted as he threw Ghost's corpse back and away from her, and then retracted the blades.

"Hayden," Natalia cried. "Oh, Hayden."

She couldn't believe how horrible he looked. His shoulder was soaked with blood. His hand had a burn hole right through it. His face was bloody and sweaty.

She doubted she looked any better.

"Nat, are you okay?" he said, his eyes falling on her bleeding arm. When he saw the cut on her stomach, his whole face froze. "Did he?"

"It's okay, Hayden," Natalia replied. "It isn't deep."

He held out his replacement hand. Natalia took it, and he lifted her to her feet, taking her in his arms, kissing her and holding her tight. Her tears poured onto his cheek, and she could feel the warmth of his on her face.

"King?" she asked.

"Dead," he replied.

She had figured as much, but hearing him say it was still a relief.

"Where's Casey?" she asked.

Hayden's body tensed. He pulled away from her, fresh tears springing to his eyes.

"She saved my life."

"And mine," Natalia said. "And theirs." She touched her stomach.

"Sheriff, you alive in there?" Bennett's head appeared above the base of the floor. He relaxed visibly when he saw them. "Yup. Still alive. Both of you." He climbed into the ship, looking around, his eyes stopping on Ghost. "What a fucking mess. Asshole. Hey, Rico! Where are you?"

"I'm here," Rico said.

She was at the base of the stairs. Bennett's face lit up when he saw her, and he rushed to her, taking her in his arms.

"You are one badass Spacer," he said. "You know that?"

"So are you," she replied.

He held her for a moment, looking into her eyes. He smiled. "Well, why not?" Then he leaned forward, putting his lips on hers. She melted into him, returning the kiss.

"Should we break them up?" Natalia said after a few seconds.

"No," Hayden replied. "He disassembled King's roid on his own. I'm not getting in his way for anything."

She laughed. It felt good to laugh. It felt better when Hayden laughed, too.

The two Spacers broke apart a moment later.

"So, Sheriff," Bennett said. "We killed the bad guys. We crushed the aliens. What's next?"

"The hard part."

THREE MONTHS LATER

"THAT'S THE LAST OF THEM," BENNETT SAID, STANDING ON THE dusty plateau near the Pilgrim's launch site.

The Centurion transport lifted effortlessly from the ground to the sky, before a flare of energy at the rear of the rectangular craft carried it up and out of sight.

Hayden and Natalia stood beside the Spacer, watching the last of the colonists who had decided to relocate to Proxima Centauri begin their journey to a new life.

It was a journey they had already started. A journey that had seen them become the defacto leaders of a small region of what had once been the western United States of America. The United Western Territories, as they had decided to call it. It was a bit more of an unorthodox colony than they or any of the original passengers on the Pilgrim had likely expected, but it was something, and it was worth fighting for. It was worth staying for.

And they weren't the only ones who stayed. Out of the fifteen-thousand remaining colonists, over half had decided to stick with their Sheriff. Over half had chosen Earth, trife and all, instead of a faraway place where maybe life would be more comfortable, but not necessarily any less complicated.

It wasn't an easy life. It would never be an easy life. But things were changing. Hope for the future was growing, like the small bump in Natalia's stomach that bulged out just enough beneath her light armor that everyone knew it was there.

"Has there been any decision from Command?" Hayden asked, glancing at the Spacer.

Bennett nodded. "It took some time, as you know. I came this close to being court-martialed before the powers that be came to their senses." He held his thumb and forefinger so they were almost touching. "That's why you hadn't seen Rico and me in a while before this."

"And now you're the official liaison," Natalia said.

"Unofficial official liaison," Bennett replied. "Command is taking baby steps on this one. NCP is still in effect for most of the world. But, since you've got pilgrims down here, and they're legal citizens of Proxima Centauri, just like you two, it left those high and mighties in a bit of a spot." He laughed.

"They're going to send supplies?"

He nodded. "Yup. Armor, guns, and tech. Limited amounts based on budgetary considerations, but enough that between you and your new friends, you should be able to hold your current territory and expand it a bit."

Hayden smiled at the Spacer's mention of new friends. He was referring to the two goliaths that had chosen to stick close to Sanisco. Two massive guardian monsters who had decided they didn't want to eat people after all. It was a strange development, but according to Natalia, she had formed a bond with the male through the interface, enough that she had used it a few times since to work on learning to better communicate with the creature.

That was another spot for the Space Force to figure out. They had created the goliaths as biological machines. As weapons. But somehow, at least two of them had grown beyond their original programming and started learning to think for themselves. In a sense, they had created a new form of life. It was their responsibility to protect it.

"And if the aliens who sent the trife show up?" Hayden said.

Bennett shook his head. "We aren't there yet, Sheriff."

Hayden nodded. He didn't expect Proxima Command to go that far, that fast, even if he was certain it was the right thing for them to do. "It's a start."

"Pozz that," Bennett said. "I like your new hands, by the way. Very sleek."

Hayden held up his hands. "I forgot you hadn't seen them."

A month at Lewis-McChord had given him and Natalia time for their other wounds to heal, but King's laser had destroyed the main nerves and muscles leading to his right hand, leaving it useless. He had been surprised when Doctor Shihab had come to him with an offer to modernize both prosthetics, but the doctor's parents were that grateful to him for saving their son's life and they were wealthy and influential enough to make it happen.

The new limbs were a lighter, stronger alloy, matte black, smooth, and in correct proportion to his body. He didn't need to have the armor he wore outside Sanisco altered anymore. It slid right over the replacements, for the most part hiding his injuries. It had been tough to give up Hank's hand for sentimental and practical reasons. But while the new prosthetics didn't have the long claws on the wrist, what they lacked in sharpness they made up for in overall strength. He hadn't needed to so far, but he could use them to crush a trife's bones with little effort.

Besides, the older prosthetic wasn't going to waste. He had handed it down to the new Governor of the UWT. Malcolm was an asshole, and he had made some questionable decisions, but Hayden couldn't argue the man was ultimately loyal to the colony, and he knew how to lead and how to administrate. They needed that as much as anything, and a fresh start was a fresh start.

For everyone.

"How's Rico?" Natalia asked. "I was hoping she would be coming back with you."

"Rico put in for early release from Space Force," Bennett replied. "She's transferring to the private sector."

"Too much excitement?" Hayden asked.

Bennett laughed. "Not exactly. Centurion law forbids the kind of fraternization Rico and me had in mind, so we solved the problem. I just happened to draw the wrong straw, so I'm here instead of her."

They all laughed at that.

Barking in the distance drew Hayden's attention. He looked back to the tents near the entrance to the Pilgrim's hangar. Gus had emerged from one of them and was loping their way.

"Gus, you mangy old coot!" Hayden shouted, leaning down as the dog reached them.

He rubbed its side while it nuzzled against his legs. Natalia had refused to leave Lewis-McChord without the dog and had forced the new base Colonel, a woman named Salil, to give them a ride back to Duncan's former home.

"Yeah, anyway I'm hoping to get permission to bring Rico back with me once we're married. A liaison does have his privileges. In the meantime, you're stuck with just me."

"Are you staying long?" Natalia asked.

"A week. Just to make sure the first shipment arrives as currently scheduled. Then I'll be alternating two weeks in, two weeks out. After the cluster-fuck Dr. Franklin caused, I'll also be in charge of making sure our gene-heads stay smart."

"No more human samples?"

"Not under my watch. To be honest, I'm not sure what we're going to do about the trife and their masters in the long-term. Most of our work here has been a bust."

"Maybe they'll never come back," Hayden said.

"Maybe they don't exist in the first place," Natalia added.

"I hope either one of you is right," Bennett said. "Until then, we do the best we can. Hopefully, in time, we can convince more and more people that Earth is still worth fighting for."

"Do you really believe that?" Natalia asked.

"I have since I met you two. You're the most stubborn, ornery, genuinely good people I've ever met, and I'm proud to know you."

"You aren't so bad yourself, Sergeant," Hayden said.

"Oh, I didn't tell you. It isn't Sergeant, anymore. It's Special Officer. That puts me at a level high enough I can boss everyone else around."

"No more Doctors telling you what to do?" Natalia asked.

"No, ma'am."

The three of them fell into a short, comfortable silence, looking off into the distance, where the haze of the transport's thrusters was still visible. Hayden put his arm around Natalia's waist, resting his hand on the small bump of her stomach. She tilted her head to rest it in the crook of his shoulder.

"So, I guess that's it, Sheriff," Bennett said. "You keep doing what you're doing. I keep doing what I'm doing, and we hope for the best."

"At least the people here are starting to have some hope," Hayden said. "But this isn't it. Not yet. You said you're here for a week?"

"Pozz. Why?"

"I have a promise I still need to keep."

THREE MONTHS LATER

THE SETTLEMENT SEEMED TO APPEAR OUT OF NOTHING, forming from within the haze of dust and heat that permeated the landscape this far east.

It was exactly how Casey had described it. There were piles of cars everywhere, junkers of every shape and size, from the smallest cube to the largest rectangle and everywhere in between. The bigger vehicles had cloth covering the broken windows and decorations of different types laid out in front of them, proving people lived there.

The ride from Haven hadn't taken long. Less than a day, with a stop at Crossroads to check on the restoration. Hayden had put Deputy Hicks in charge of the waypoint, and one of the Pilgrim's former Engineers was helping to restore the guns to their former glory. Bennett promised he would do what he could to get ammunition sent down for the weapons, especially since the location was vital for transporting goods between the Pilgrim and the cities beyond. More than five thousand of the colonists had decided to stay on board the starship and continue living in the cubes. They would be able to utilize the resources onboard to produce food, clothing, and other important goods to deliver throughout the UWT, a prospect that excited Hayden every time he thought about it.

It was hard for him to get excited right now. Every kilometer had brought his mood down a little more, and reaching Carcity was more of a sad occasion than anything else.

He shouldn't have to be here. He especially shouldn't have to be here because Casey was dead.

But he was. He had promised her before she died that he would find her brother and make sure he was safe, one way or another. He wouldn't have made the promise if he wasn't going to keep it.

He slowed the car as he entered. There were a few residents already outside, and they stopped whatever they were doing to look at him. Maybe they recognized the soft rumble of Casey's car. Or maybe they just didn't get many visitors.

The convoy rolled to a stop behind him. Three former Enforcer cars laden with new lawmen. Deputies, all of them, save for Bennett, who was watching from the back.

He stopped the car, turned off the engine, and opened the door. Natalia did the same on the passenger side. They climbed out together.

A woman crossed a dirt path ahead of them, between a large, faded yellow vehicle and the large maze of cars in the center of the village. Hayden eyed the pile of vehicles, picturing Casey and her brothers and sisters hiding in the midst of the rusted steel while the trife surrounded them, searching for humans who may have left themselves exposed.

He remembered what she had said about the Mayor. He fought to keep himself calm.

"Can I help you, traveler?" the woman asked, looking him over.

He was wearing a long coat over his dark Spacer body

armor and one of Ghost's white hats, the plastic badge pinned to the front of it. Natalia said he looked like Roy Rogers, and he couldn't completely disagree.

Her eyes shifted from him to Casey's car. He knew by her face that she recognized it.

"My name is Duke," Hayden said. "Sheriff Hayden Duke."

The woman's expression changed. Not fear. Relief.

"I've heard of you," she said. "Word is you killed King."

"That's right," Hayden replied.

"You in charge now?"

"Yes and no."

He didn't feel like explaining how he intended to convert the Territories into a democracy once he had the necessities under control.

"Oh. What brings you here, then, Sheriff?"

"I'm looking for someone. Did you know Casey? She also went by-"

"Chains," the woman said. "My sissie's girl. She always was a spunky one. Left here with that car a few years ago, I ain't seen her since. You buy that somewhere?"

"No. I inherited it."

"What do you mean?"

"From Casey. We were friends. She." He paused, fighting to keep his voice from breaking. The hardest part of all of this was dealing with the guilt he felt over the people who had helped him and hadn't made it. "She died."

The woman's face fell. "Oh. Oh." She looked at him. "I better tell my sis."

"Hold on," Hayden said. "We're looking for her brother, Paul. I'm sure you know him?"

"Everybody knows everybody here, Sheriff. It's all relative in Carcity."

The words were a punch to his gut. Casey had said the

same thing, but her tone had been full of vitriol. This woman said it like it was a way of life. A mantra.

"What do you want with him?" she asked.

"I want to make sure he's safe."

"How do you mean, safe?"

"I've heard things about your Mayor. And about how things are run around here."

The woman opened her mouth to speak. Hayden heard a crack, and then a bullet hit his armor in the chest. He looked down at it, and then up in the direction of the source. His deputies fanned out behind him, drawing their guns.

"You want to come out?" Hayden said. "Or do you want to die where you're standing?"

The answer was another round that hit Hayden's armor. Hayden glanced back, noticing Bennett hop off the car at the back of the line and start moving around the other side of the maze.

"Get the grepping hell out of here!" a man shouted. "We don't want you here, telling us how to live our lives."

Hayden looked at the woman. "Is that the Mayor?" he asked.

"Yes."

Hayden wasn't surprised.

"What do you want?"

She bit her lip, trying to judge him from what little she knew and compare him to the Mayor. She glanced at Natalia, noticing her bump.

Natalia smiled at her.

"I want my kids to be safe," she said at last. "Isn't that what any good mother wants?"

"Is he alone?" Hayden asked.

"No. He's got a few others who want what he wants."

Hayden motioned to his deputies.

"See if you can grab them without killing anyone," he said.

"You don't want to kill them?" the woman asked.

"It's not about what I want. You can't have law without justice."

"I don't understand."

"I know, but hopefully one day you will."

The deputies started toward the building. More cracks of gunfire pierced the air, rounds smacking into their armor.

It stopped suddenly, replaced with shouts and grunts. The deputies were only reaching the vehicle when Bennett came out, holding a short, thin man by the throat.

He hadn't even seen the Spacer enter it.

"You can't do this," the man complained, just barely able to breathe beneath Bennett's grip.

"I can, and will," Bennett said. "The rest of them are waiting for you inside."

The deputies moved past him, entering the vehicle. Bennett brought the Mayor to Hayden and shoved him forward.

"Here you go, Sheriff," he said.

"Thank you," Hayden replied.

The Mayor spit on Hayden's shoes. "Grep you. You think you can drive in here and change what is. I've been in charge of Carcity for twenty years now. My pa was in charge afore that. This is my city."

"Not anymore," Hayden said. "This city is being annexed to the United Western Territories. It falls under UWT law effective immediately." He stared at the Mayor. "We don't tolerate people like you."

"People like me?" the Mayor said. "You son of a bitch." He moved forward, throwing an awkward punch.

Hayden caught it in his replacement hand, putting enough pressure on it to make the Mayor cry out. Then he let it go.

"You're lucky we're in desperate need of laborers. You

and whoever else was involved with the abuse of the minor residents here will be relocated to help clear the road east." He looked at the woman again. "Half of my deputies will stay to help you get integrated into the Territories."

The woman nodded. He could see the change in her already, just from knowing she and the rest of the Carcity residents were out from under the Mayor's thumb.

"Thank you, Sheriff," she said.

"You're welcome," Hayden replied. "Paul?"

"He'll be safe now, Sheriff. I promise. As safe as anyone can be out here. Say, you going to get rid of the trife?"

"We'll see."

"Better to start with the real monsters, first, eh?"

Hayden smiled. "Pozz that."

"Things are going to change, ain't they, Sheriff? Things are going to get better?"

"For good people, yes," Hayden replied. He glanced over at Natalia. She looked at him lovingly, nodding her head. "For bad people? They'd better find somewhere else to go.

"There's a new Sheriff in town."

Other Series in the Forgotten Universe:

Head to mrforbes.com/forgottenuniverse to see all of the books.

Earth Unknown (Forgotten Earth, Book One)

mrforbes.com/earthunknown

Sheriff Duke returns in the follow-up to Forgotten.

Deliverance (Forgotten Colony, Book One)

mrforbes.com/deliverance

The Pilgrim never left Earth. The Deliverance did. Want to know what happened next?

THANK YOU FOR READING
UNFORGIVEN!

THANK YOU FOR READING UNFORGIVEN!

I hope you've enjoyed this book, and all three books in the Forgotten. It's been a real joy to write and share them with you. If you loved this book, please consider leaving a review. You can do that here.

If you enjoyed the series as a whole, why not leave a short review on all of the books and help show your support for continuing installments?

A star rating and a short sentence is all it takes.

Thank you in advance.

Cheers,
Michael.

OTHER BOOKS BY M.R FORBES

Browse my backlist:
mrforbes.com/books

Starship Eternal (War Eternal)
mrforbes.com/starshipeternal

They are coming. Find the Goliath or humankind will be destroyed.
Those chilling words are the first thing Space Marine starfighter pilot Mitchell "Ares" Williams hears, waking in a hospital after an ambush nearly ends his life. He tries to ignore them, convincing himself the voice in his head is a side-effect of his injuries.

It isn't.

The warning is only the beginning. A glimpse into a struggle against an enemy older than time.

An enemy that's very real and much closer than he ever imagined.

An enemy that will do whatever it takes to keep him from finding humankind's first starship, lost during its inaugural voyage and long believed destroyed. A starship that may be the key to defeating them once and for all.

Narrowly escaping capture, Mitchell lands in the company of the Riggers: a ragtag crew of black-ops commandos who patrol the outer reaches of the galaxy. Guided by a captain with a reputation for murder, they're dangerous, immoral, and possibly insane.

They may also be humanity's last hope for survival in a war that has raged beyond eternity.

(War Eternal is also available in a box set of the first three books here: mrforbes.com/wareternalbox)

Hell's Rejects (Chaos of the Covenant)
mrforbes.com/hellsrejects

The most powerful starships ever constructed are gone. Thousands are dead. A fleet is in ruins. The attackers are unknown. The orders are clear: *Recover the ships. Bury the bastards who stole them.*

Lieutenant Abigail Cage never expected to find herself in Hell. As a Highly Specialized Operational Combatant, she was one of the most respected soldiers in the military. Now she's doing hard labor on the most miserable planet in the universe.

Not for long.

The Earth Republic is looking for the most dangerous individuals it can control. The best of the worst, and Abbey happens to be one of them. The deal is simple: *Bring back the starships, earn your freedom. Try to run, you die.* It's a suicide mission, but she has nothing to lose.

The only problem? There's a new threat in the galaxy. One with a power unlike anything anyone has ever seen. One that's been waiting for this moment for a very, very, long time. And they want Abbey, too.

Be careful what you wish for.

They say Hell hath no fury like a woman scorned. They have no idea.

Man of War (Rebellion)

mrforbes.com/manofwar

In the year 2280, an alien fleet attacked the Earth.

Their weapons were unstoppable, their defenses unbreakable.

Our technology was inferior, our militaries overwhelmed.

Only one starship escaped before civilization fell.

Earth was lost.

It was never forgotten.

Fifty-two years have passed.

A message from home has been received.

The time to fight for what is ours has come.

Welcome to the rebellion.

Or maybe something completely different?

Dead of Night (Ghosts & Magic)

mrforbes.com/deadofnight

For Conor Night, the world's only surviving necromancer, staying alive is an expensive proposition. So when the promise of a big payout for a small bit of thievery presents itself, Conor is all in. But nothing comes easy in the world of ghosts and magic, and it isn't long before Conor is caught up in the machinations of the most powerful wizards on Earth and left with only two ways out:

Finish the job, or be finished himself.

Balance (The Divine)
mrforbes.com/balance

My name is Landon Hamilton. Once upon a time I was a twenty-three year old security guard, trying to regain my life after spending a year in prison for stealing people's credit card numbers.

Now, I'm dead.

Okay, I was supposed to be dead. I got killed after all; but a funny thing happened after I had turned the mortal coil...

I met Dante Alighieri - yeah, that Dante. He told me I was special, a diuscrucis. That's what they call a perfect balance of human, demon, and angel. Apparently, I'm the only one of my kind.

I also learned that there was a war raging on Earth between Heaven and Hell, and that I was the only one who could save the human race from annihilation. He asked me to help, and I was naive enough to agree.

Sounds crazy, I know, but he wished me luck and sent me back to the mortal world. Oh yeah, he also gave me instructions on how to use my Divine "magic" to bend the universe to my will. The problem is, a sexy vampire crushed them while I was crushing on her.

Now I have to somehow find my own way to stay alive in a world of angels, vampires, werewolves, and an assortment of other enemies that all want to kill me before I can mess up their plans for humanity's future. If that isn't enough, I also have to find the queen of all demons and recover the Holy Grail.

It's not like it's the end of the world if I fail.

Wait. It is.

Tears of Blood (Books 1-3)

mrforbes.com/tearsofblood

One thousand years ago, the world was broken and reborn beneath the boot of a nameless, ageless tyrant. He erased all history of the time before, enslaving the people and hunting those with the power to unseat him.

The power of magic.

Eryn is such a girl. Born with the Curse, she fights to control and conceal it to protect those she loves. But when the truth is revealed, and his soldiers come, she is forced away from her home and into the company of Silas, a deadly fugitive tormented by a fractured past.

Silas knows only that he is a murderer who once hunted the Cursed, and that he and his brothers butchered armies and innocents alike to keep the deep, dark secrets of the time before from ever coming to light.

Secrets which could save the world.

Or destroy it completely.

ABOUT THE AUTHOR

M.R. Forbes is the creator of a growing catalog of science fiction and fantasy titles. He lives in the pacific northwest with his family, including a cat who thinks she's a dog, and a dog who thinks she's a cat. He eats too many donuts, and he's always happy to hear from readers.

To learn more about M.R. Forbes or just say hello:

Visit my website:
mrforbes.com

Send me an e-mail:
michael@mrforbes.com

Check out my Facebook page:
facebook.com/mrforbes.author

Chat with me on Facebook Messenger:
https://m.me/mrforbes.author

Printed in Great Britain
by Amazon